D0984681

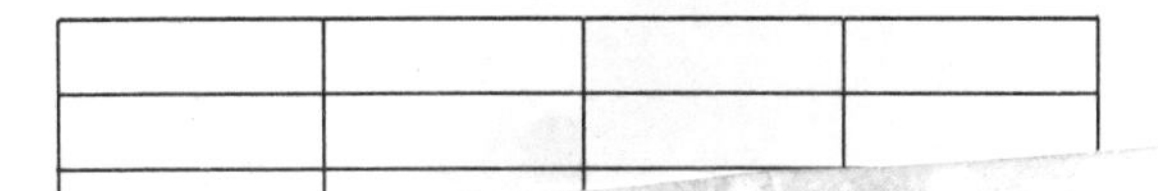

THE WARDENS

Books by Clark Howard

The Arms
A Movement Toward Eden
The Doomsday Squad
The Killings
Mark the Sparrow
The Hunters
Six Against The Rock

THE WARDENS

A NOVEL BY

CLARK HOWARD

RICHARD MAREK PUBLISHERS
NEW YORK

Library of Congress Cataloging in Publication Data

Howard, Clark
The wardens.

I. Title.
PZ4.H848War [PS3558.0877] 813'.5'4 78-13296
ISBN 0-399-90032-2

Printed in the United States of America

For My Special Son
Colin Craig Howard

THE WARDENS

CHAPTER 1

Dru Hawn knew that her mother was dying. She knew it instinctively, as one knows that autumn is over and winter has come.

In the bleak little hospital room, sitting beside her mother's bed while her father talked to the doctor in the hall, Dru wondered exactly how much time her mother had left. She's only fifty-one, Dru thought. And she's had so few years of happiness. Dru shook her head in silent frustration. It wasn't fair, goddamn it. It just wasn't fair.

But she remembered something her mother had once told her. *Nobody ever said life was fair.*

Dru tried to blink back tears but found she could not control them. She thought of all the things she knew her mother had looked forward to, things in the not-too-distant future that she had so often commented on: Dru going to college and becoming a teacher someday, Dru's marriage someday, Dru having a baby and making her a grandmother someday. So many somedays she had dreamed about. Now she was dying when Dru was only seventeen, and the somedays for her would never come.

Mother, Mother, Mother, Dru thought helplessly. Why, why, why?

More tears streaked the girl's cheeks and a brief sob shook her; she caught her breath to suppress it. She might cry but she was determined not to bawl. Biting her lip, she wanted desperately to reach out and take her mother's hand. But she was afraid of waking her. So she held her own hands, gripping them together on her breasts and closing her eyes on her tears.

In a few moments her father came into the room. Myles Hawn was a tall man, big and broad-shouldered, with a moderate limp to his right leg from the war in France twenty-five years earlier. He had a pleasant, open face which at that moment was drawn and hollow-looking. Dru dried her eyes with the backs of her hands and went over to him. She nestled against his shoulder as she had done as a child, and he automatically slipped an arm around her; but his eyes, she saw as she looked up, never left the woman on the bed.

"What did he say, Daddy?" she asked in a whisper.

"He said we could take her home," Myles answered quietly.

Dru nodded against his shoulder. Take her home, she thought. To die.

Myles squeezed his daughter's waist and removed his arm to step over to the bed. He sat on the chair Dru had left and leaned his big frame as close as he could to the sleeping woman. He took her hand, as Dru had been afraid to do, and held it to his lips. "Cassie," he said softly. "My poor, sweet Cassie—"

The woman on the bed opened her eyes. For a moment she had a frightened look in her eyes, but the instant she saw her husband it vanished. "Myles—"

"Yes, Cassie. I'm here, honey."

"I—want—to go home."

"All right, Cassie. I'll take you home first thing in the morning."

She shook her head, just once. "Now," she said. "I want to go home now."

Myles parted his lips to reply, to say no, it was nighttime, that they had to wait until morning. But the pleading in her eyes was too much for him. He patted her hand. "All right, honey," He turned to Dru. "Call the ambulance service in town and have them send out an ambulance. Then tell the floor nurse we're taking your mother back to the prison tonight. Don't let anyone give you an argument."

"Yes, Daddy."

Dru left the room. As she hurried down the corridor to the phone booth, she decided she had better also call the captain of the yard so that he could notify his guards to expect them.

* * *

Someone from the hospital must have notified the papers because there were three reporters and two photographers waiting when Cassie Hawn was wheeled out to the ambulance entrance on a gurney. Myles's expression tightened at the sight of them and his square jaw clenched like a rock. Dru's eyes flashed unconcealed anger as the men stepped forward with their open notebooks and poised pencils.

"Warden Hawn, can you give us a comment on your wife's condition?"

"I have nothing to say," he told them.

"Is it true Mrs. Hawn has inoperable stomach cancer?"

"I said I have nothing to say."

Two orderlies collapsed the gurney and slid it and the patient into the back of the ambulance. Myles leaned close to Dru's ear. "I'll ride with her. You bring the car," He got into the ambulance with his wife, and the attendant closed the door.

The reporters immediately turned to Dru. "Miss Hawn, do you know how long your mother has to live?" one of them asked.

"I hope she outlives you," Dru snapped. "Why can't you just leave my parents alone?"

"Your parents are public figures, Miss Hawn. When a fourth-generation prison warden marries the daughter of a notorious public enemy, it's news."

"That was in nineteen-twenty-seven, for God's sake!" Dru said. "Eighteen years ago!"

"They're still news," the reporter said. "And so are you." He nodded to his photographer and a flashbulb exploded in Dru's face.

"You bastard," Dru said. She stalked away from them. They followed her as far as the nurses' station, where an orderly barred their way. One of the nurses showed Dru a way out through the boiler room and she got across the parking lot to the car without being seen.

It started to rain as Dru drove off the lot. By the time she had driven two blocks, it was coming down in torrents, lashing the top of the car like hundreds of tiny pebbles. Before she could get to the state highway that led out to the prison, the street was flooded up to the car's running board.

"Damn," Dru muttered. She turned at the corner, thinking the next street over might be drier. But it was just as bad. So was the next one after that, and the next one. The downpour was flooding the gutters and washing over the curbs onto the sidewalks. Dru saw several cars stalled at intersections, and several others that had simply pulled over and stopped to wait out the deluge.

That's the smartest thing to do, Dru thought. Pull over and wait. The ambulance would have gotten through, she was sure, having had time to reach the highway, which was higher than the streets and would not be flooded. Her parents were all right.

She guided the car as close to the curb as she dared and cut the motor. She decided to leave the headlights on, for a few minutes at least, so that no one would run into her. She looked in the glove compartment and found a pack of her mother's Marvel cigarettes and a box of stick matches. She lighted a cigarette, coughing a little at the first taste of smoke. She had only tried smoking three or four times and had not decided whether she liked it or not. She wanted one now, needing something to do while she waited in the rain, and because she was a little afraid and the cigarette represented something warm and bright in the darkness.

The rain was coming down at an angle and Dru found that she could roll down the window on her side without getting wet. She looked out at the flooding street, at trees that were bent in the path of the rain, at a child's overturned tricycle with one rear wheel slowly rotating. Then she heard a screen door slamming in the wind. She looked where the noise was coming from and saw a little frame house with green shutters. She frowned, then brightened. That was the house her mother had lived in when *she* had been seventeen. Her mother had pointed it out to her one day and told her she had lived there the summer she had met Dru's father.

Dru rested her head back against the seat and took another drag on the cigarette, beginning to find it easier to smoke. She dwelled on thoughts of that day, when her mother had shown her the house and told her about her grandparents and great-grandparents.

That was the day she learned that her maternal grandfather had been Doc Baker, the notorious mail train robber and outlaw.

CHAPTER 2

In the summer of 1911, when he was nineteen, Myles Hawn came home after finishing his freshman year at Notre Dame. He was a very big young man and had played fourth-string football the previous fall. His coaches had hinted at a position on the first or second string, provided Myles returned to school in prime physical condition.

"I want to set up a place to do calisthenics, Dad," he told Nathan Hawn, warden of the prison, the first week he was home. Myles had already selected the place he wanted to use. "That piece of lawn at the end of the visitors' parking lot would be perfect."

"I don't know," Nathan said dubiously. "Your mother isn't too keen on this football business. She says it's an abuse of the human body. Couldn't you take up swimming or something?"

"Football, Dad," said Myles. "Sorry. If you want me to, I can go into town and find a place to exercise."

Nathan shook his head. "No, I don't want you sneaking off to town to do something that you should be allowed to do in your own home. Go ahead and use the place you picked. But we'll hear from your mother about it."

Myles obtained some fence posts, lumber, and tools, and laid out a small but fair calisthenics field. It consisted of a short obstacle course, some hurdles, a chinning bar, half a dozen old truck tires for razzle-dazzle running drill, and a measured stretch farther over, next to the wall, for a hundred-yard dash.

Each afternoon Myles put himself through a rigorous two-hour exercise routine. Occasionally, when he was working out, visitors entering or leaving the parking lot would pause to watch him, but usually only for a moment, until he finished a dash or a series of hurdles; then they would remember where they were and move along. No one liked to linger much around the prison. Myles paid no attention to these passing audiences; he was usually concentrating too intently on what he was doing. Until one Wednesday, when Cassie started watching him.

She had gone into the prison an hour earlier with a woman Myles assumed to be her mother. Then she had come out by herself, half an hour before their ninety-minute visiting period was over. Waiting for her mother, she had sat on the grass and watched Myles work out.

Myles tried to ignore her, but it was impossible. He *knew* she was there, he *knew* she was watching. It was natural for him to try and show off. He ran the hurdles, doing beautifully until he got to the final one. Then his toe nicked the edge of it and it went over. He stumbled the last few yards but managed to stay upright. Glancing quickly at the girl, he saw her suppress an amused smile. He felt himself turn red. Then he grinned at himself and walked over to her.

"I usually do it better than that," he said.

"What are you training for?" she asked.

"Football. I play for Notre Dame." Myles studied her. She had the softest-looking hair he had ever seen. It was the lightest of auburns and seemed to soak up the sunlight. "What's your name?" he asked.

"Cassandra Baker." She blushed suddenly and looked down at the ground. "My mother and I are here to visit my father."

"Doc Baker?" asked Myles.

"Yes." She kept her eyes down. "Do you know my father?"

"I know of him."

"Are you visiting someone?" she asked Myles, looking up.

"Not exactly. I'm home from college for the summer."

Cassie frowned. "Home?"

"Yeah. I live here. My father's the warden."

"Oh." She looked down at the ground again, turning away. "I have to go wait in the car for my mother now."

She walked away. After a moment of indecision, Myles ran after her.

"Come for a walk with me," he said. He felt a little self-conscious.

"I don't think I'd better," Cassie said.

"Why not?"

She shrugged. "I don't know. It just doesn't seem right. My daddy a convict, your daddy the warden."

"We don't have to talk about them, you know. We can talk about other things. Come on, take a walk with me."

She looked around. "Where to?"

Now he was the one to shrug. "Just around here. Over by the highway. We can look down and see Union City. Come on—"

As she looked up at him, Cassie could feel her embarassment dissolving and a warm, almost tickling feeling replacing it. Somehow she knew, either by instinct or the look on Myles's face, that he felt the same thing.

"All right, I'll come for a walk with you."

They started walking across the wide lawn. Their shoulders brushed. Then their hands. They exchanged glances, their shyness decreasing. They smiled tentatively at each other.

By the time they reached the bluff by the highway, they knew they were in love.

Cassie was seventeen that summer. She and her mother, Lannie, were living in a little house with green shutters that they had rented in Union City, near the prison. They had moved there shortly after Doc began serving his twenty-year sentence for leading the armed robbery of a Rock Island mail train.

Lannie Baker was a tall, dark-haired woman with high cheekbones from the Cherokee side of her family. She had a thin, reedlike body, flat front and back. Growing up dirt-poor and half-Indian in Oklahoma City had turned her cynical at an early age. She trusted no one in the world but Doc Baker, loved no one but Doc and Cassie.

Lannie lived by the rules her husband set down for her. She did not try to conceal who she and Cassie were. She was polite to everyone who was polite to her, and everyone else she avoided or ignored. She paid cash for everything. She dressed and acted respectably. She broke no laws. She was friendly but she did not become *close* friends with anyone.

The rules that Lannie lived by she expected Cassie to live by also. And Cassie always had, until they moved to Union City and she met Myles Hawn. Then she began to look for ways to get around her mother.

"Mamma, can I walk uptown to the drugstore for a drink of soda water?"

"I suppose. But come directly back. And don't talk to any strangers."

"Yes, Mamma."

Myles would be waiting for her at the drugstore. They would sip sodas while they held hands under the round marble table, talking in whispers, lingering as long as they felt they dared. One night they lingered too long. Lannie came uptown and caught them.

"Myles, this is my mamma," Cassie said turning fire-red. "Mamma, this is Myles."

Myles mumbled something and Lannie said, "Hello, young man." Then she turned knowing eyes on Cassie. "I thought you were coming directly home, sugar."

"It's my fault, ma'am," Myles said. "I talked her into staying and having a soda with me."

"I can't say I blame her," said Lannie. "You're a right handsome boy. But she has to go home now. Say good-night, Cassie."

The young lovers blushingly said good-night.

"Who is he?" Lannie asked on the way home.

"Just a boy, Mamma. He practices sports exercises up by the prison. It's all right to just talk to him, isn't it?"

"I reckon. But don't tell him anything. And don't get to liking him too much. We won't be staying here much longer."

"Is Daddy going to break out?" Cassie asked excitedly.

"He isn't planning to stay in prison for nineteen more years, that's for sure."

Mother and daughter slipped their arms around each other's waists as they walked home.

When Myles got home that night, he found that Lannie Baker was not the only one who had seen him with Cassie. His mother,

Doctor Reba Hawn, had seen them when she drove past the drugstore on her way home from the hospital.

"Who was the girl I saw you with down at City Drugs?" she asked casually as she updated some medical files at her desk in the parlor. Nathan was reading the paper in his nearby Morris chair.

"Just a girl," Myles said. "Her name's Cassandra."

"Pretty name. Pretty girl, in fact. Does she live in Union City?"

"Yes, ma'am."

"Of course, you know better than to get serious about a girl. Another month and you go back to school."

"Yes, ma'am."

The next night Myles and Cassie went to a secret place they had down by the river. It was under a big ancient willow with branches that fell all the way to the ground in a natural circular curtain.

"Mamma says we may be going away soon," Cassie told him.

"What about your daddy?"

"He wants us to go live in Oklahoma near Mamma's family," Cassie lied. She had no choice, she reasoned. It would not have been fair to tell him that her father was planning a jailbreak and put him in the position of having to decide whether to tell his own father.

"I don't want you to go away, Cassie," he told her. The thought of losing her made him feel ill.

"I don't want to either. But I don't see how I can get out of it."

"What if we got married?"

"We're both too young. We'd have to have permission. Mamma wouldn't give it and neither would your folks."

Myles let a moment of silence go by. Then: "What if we *had* to get married?"

"But we don't," she whispered.

"We could fix it so we did," he said. He gently pushed her back onto the thick willow moss. "If they were to think we've been sleeping with each other all summer—" He undid the top of her blouse.

"I might even get pregnant," she said. "Then they'd *have* to let us." She helped him undo her blouse a little further.

In the darkness they fumbled with each other's clothes until they were naked.

"I've never done it before," Myles admitted.

"Neither have I."

"The fellows at school talk about it a lot—"

"I watched Mamma and Daddy do it once, through a crack under the window shade—"

Myles touched her between the legs. "You're so small," he whispered. "I may be too big—"

Cassie put her hand on his erection and pulled him to her. "Try—"

They found out that she was not too small, nor he too large.

They made love twenty-six times during August, but it did no good. Cassie's period started promptly on September fourth.

"I'm sorry," she told Myles. "It must be my fault. You sure enough did your part."

"It could have been my fault as much as yours," he said. "Maybe we did it too often. Maybe a man's stuff gets diluted and weak if he does it too much. Maybe it won't make a baby. Anyway, it doesn't make any difference whose fault it is. It didn't work and we're running out of time. My mother is about ready to *drag* me into town to shop for school clothes, I've been putting her off so long. I'm supposed to leave next Wednesday."

"Do you want to just run off together?" she asked.

Myles shook his head. "First I'm going to my parents. Maybe they'll be reasonable; maybe they'll help us. If they won't then we'll run away."

That night Myles told his father.

Nathan was infuriated. "That is incredible! Have you completely lost your mind? Do you realize who Doc Baker is, for God's sake!"

"I know he's an outlaw—"

"Outlaw! That's generous! The man is a notorious criminal, the last in a long line of notorious criminals. His mother was Ma Baker, the so-called Bandit Queen. She was killed by peace officers. He had three brothers, who were also thieves, train robbers, and killers. Doc himself is suspected of at least three killings committed during bank and train robberies—"

"I know Cassie's background, Dad—"

"I'm not so sure you know *anything*! If you did, you would have avoided this situation." Nathan shook his head incredulously. "Doc Baker's daughter. My god! Why didn't you just find yourself a streetwalker?"

Myles blushed a deep red and angrily started for the door.

"Where are you going?" his father demanded.

"Into town."

"Not tonight," Nathan said. "Not in your present frame of mind. Particularly not after what you and the Baker girl have been doing for a month. You stay in tonight; we'll discuss this matter further tomorrow."

"Dad, I want to go to town—"

"And I want you to go to your room!" Nathan shouted. "Kindly remember that you are only nineteen years old and that I'm your father. Now do as I say!"

Myles stormed down the hall to his room and slammed the door behind him.

Myles was up before six the next moring, thinking he would get out early, before his father came in for breakfast. But Nathan was already in the kitchen. Bleary-eyed from lack of sleep, he sat in his bathrobe drinking coffee that he had made himself.

"Have a cup," he said to Myles. "You're going to need it."

"Am I still restricted from going to town?" Myles asked.

Nathan shook his head. "There's no need to restrict you now. You can go into town all you want. The girl won't be there anymore."

"What do you mean?"

"Doc Baker broke out just before dawn this morning. He got out of his cell when the cooks and bakers were let out to go to work. He had a smuggled gun hidden somewhere. He used it to take the South Gate guard and tower man hostage. A car was waiting for him outside. He still has the guards with him. Roadblocks have been set up all over the state, but he has a pretty fair headstart—"

"May I go into town?" Myles asked. He felt suddenly ill.

Nathan nodded. "The car keys are on the parlor mantel."

Fifteen minutes later Myles was at the little house with the green shutters. The landlady was there, sweeping the porch.

"If you're looking for the Bakers, they're gone," she said. "I guess they run off during the night. The city police was here an hour or two ago looking for them. I think the woman's husband broke jail or something—"

Myles got back into the car and drove down to the riverbank. There, in a patch of moss at the trunk of their secret meeting place, he found an envelope containing a note and a small gold locket. The note read:

Dear Myles,

I have to go away with my Mamma. By the time you read this, you'll know why.

I'm leaving you this locket, which is my very favorite of everything I own.

Maybe we'll meet again when we're grown up. And maybe we'll still be in love. I hope so.

All my love,
Cassie

Myles looked at the locket. It was heart-shaped, no larger than a dime, on a short gold chain. Staring at it, and at Cassie's note, he wanted to cry. Never in his life had he felt so empty, so completely wasted.

Cassie was gone. If he had died at that moment, he would have done so without regret.

CHAPTER 3

With one suitcase and a blanket roll, Myles left Union City on the afternoon local. He paid to ride it as far as New Madrid, Missouri; then he got off, sneaked across the tracks, and reboarded on the other side, in a boxcar instead of a coach.

The train crossed into Arkansas, and at Blytheville headed southwest toward Fort Smith. Myles sat in the open boxcar door and watched the countryside go by without really seeing it. He felt miserable beyond description, and he now had the additional burden of a guilty conscience: he had left without saying goodbye to his mother. His intentions had been good; he had gone to her office for the express purpose of telling her what he was doing. But when he got there, he found he did not have the nerve. He cared too much for his mother to hurt her on a face-to-face basis. As soon as he walked in and saw her, wearing the white smock that was so familiar to him, standing a little stoop-shouldered and smelling vaguely of antiseptic soap, he knew he could not tell her. So he just visited with her for a few minutes, and listened tolerantly while she told him that his father was only trying to do what was best for him. Then he said he had some things to do, kissed her lovingly on the forehead as if she were the child and he the parent, and left. At the corner drugstore he wrote her a note telling her the things he had been unable to tell her in person, and left it with the pharmacist to be sent over with her prescriptions that afternoon.

Myles spent his first night on the road in a hobo jungle outside Clinton. Because of his size, and the grim expression he wore, none of the older hoboes tried to take advantage of him. A couple of them were even friendly, despite his clean-cut appearance, and showed him how to cook hobo stew and gave him tips on how to avoid or outwit the railroad detectives.

Continuing his journey the next day, Myles made it into Fort Smith. He got a few days work on the Arkansas River docks, shoveling harvested corn from barges into waiting wagons. The corn had come down from the Osage reservation; the wagons were army, from the fort itself; the pay was niggardly, but it bought supper and a cot in a wharf flophouse.

From Fort Smith, Myles moved on by freight train to Ponca City, Oklahoma. He stayed there a month, working as a roustabout in the oil field north of town. For the first time in his life he did a man's work: twelve hours a day, backbreaking, incredibly dirty. For the first three days on the job he was so tired at night he could not even eat. After a week he quit.

He moved on to Enid, Burmah, Elk City. Then into the Texas Panhandle, to Amarillo, in the heart of the open-range, shortgrass cattle country. Amarillo, Spanish for yellow, with its main-street store fronts painted accordingly. It was still a hearty Western community, its Ragtown section as wide open as it had been twenty years earlier when the railroad arrived.

Myles found work in the livestock pens, work no self-respecting Texas cowboy would do: shoveling manure, filling water troughs, pitching hay. Again—long hours, hot dirty work, not much pay. But Myles liked the town and the people and the food. He stayed three months. When he left he was deeply tanned, wearing boots and a stetson, and looked as if he had been in the West all his life.

By the time he had been gone six months, Myles had worked his way down to El Paso. He had been in town a week without work the night he met Geraldo Ruiz. Myles was standing at the bar of a Mexican saloon drinking a schooner of beer. Geraldo, wearing a brilliant smile, had come in and started passing out leaflets to the patrons.

"Attention, *señors*!" he said. "We are looking for men to ride with Pancho Villa. We are going to free Mexico from the dictator Diaz."

"Would they allow an American to go?" Myles asked when Geraldo came to him.

"Anyone who pledges loyalty to Pancho Villa can go. There will be more than a few gringos."

"When do you leave?" Myles asked.

"In two days. We go by troop train to Chihuahua. There a wealthy rancher will furnish us with horses. Only I think he does not know it yet. Anyway, when we have horses, we will ride on the *Federales* at Parral. Will you join us?"

"I'm not sure," said Myles. "I'll think about it."

He spent that night and the next day alone, trying to decide what he wanted to do. In the six months since leaving home he had wandered around aimlessly. Joining the army of Pancho Villa would at least give some purpose to his life. It might also shorten it, he thought soberly. But he did not think that would matter much to him. He had not really enjoyed living since Cassie left. He went through the motions—eating, sleeping, working hard and getting paid, learning new things—but as far as actual enjoyment was concerned, it simply was not there. He did not even have sex with the women who were available. The desire was not there. The only real pleasure in his life came when he had an occasional wet dream about Cassie. Even that was followed by a deep depression.

So he made up his mind to go along with Geraldo and fight for Villa. It was, he decided, better than being a drifter.

That night he bought writing materials and wrote his first letter to his mother.

When Reba received the letter, which was delivered to her office, she read it and immediately called Nathan.

"Is he all right?" Nathan asked urgently.

"He seems to be," she said.

"Where is he?"

"The letter came from El Paso, Texas, but he says he's in Juarez, Mexico. I might as well tell you: he's getting ready to fight in the Mexican Revolution."

Nathan felt his chest thicken. "Oh my God—"

"He'll be all right, I'm sure of it," Reba lied confidently, as much to herself as to him. "He's big and he's strong. And he's smart—"

"Do you suppose there's any way he can be stopped? If I went to the governor or a senator—"

"I don't see how," his wife told him. "Mexico's a foreign country. But we can talk about it when I get home this evening."

After Reba hung up, she put her face in her hands and cried. "My baby boy," she sobbed to herself. "My poor baby boy." She held the letter to her bosom, loving it and hating it at the same time. And praying that more would follow it.

Her prayer was answered. Letters from him began to arrive more or less regularly.

Dear Mother,

We are moving south at last. With a force of five hundred men, we have captured the village of San Andrés. It will be the last small battle before Chihuahua. Our leader is General Francisco Villa, whom everyone calls Pancho. He is a *mestizo*, which is a mixture of Indian and white. Off his horse, he is bowlegged and pigeon-toed, and walks rather oddly on legs that are too short for his torso; but once in the saddle he becomes a powerful, magnificent figure that we would follow into any battle, against any odds. My closest friend, Geraldo Ruiz, and I admire him very much. Geraldo has given me a Mexican name: Milito—

Reba read each letter to Nathan. He would not read them himself because they had not been written to him, but he was not too proud to listen to them.

Dear Mother,

We have captured Torreon at last. It is an industrial town and should provide our army with much that we lack in the way of supplies. The town's judge, the head of the post office, and all Federal officers have been shot. The lower-ranked soldiers were given a choice of joining us or facing a firing squad. A few of them actually chose the firing squad. A number of Chinese were also executed. They were accused of giving poisoned food to our soldiers, but most of us know that it was really because Villa hates them so much—

Reba was acutely aware of Nathan's loneliness for Myles. Often as they sat in the parlor at night, she would catch him staring into space and know he was thinking about his only son, so far away in a strange foreign battle. The burden of guilt for Myles's leaving home lay heavily on his shoulders. Almost nightly she watched her husband age. Each letter that arrived seemed to add a year to him.

Dear Mother,
We now have Parral. General Villa sent a message to the town garrison which read: "If you are loyal to the Madero movement, come and receive me as a friend. If you are an enemy, come out and fight. I shall take the town in any case. Francisco Villa." We marched in the next day without resistance—

Dear Mother,
We are camped at a place called the Hacienda de la Loma. All the guerrilla leaders have met here to officially form the Army of the North and unanimously elect Pancho Villa its leader. Villa now has a force of eight thousand soldiers. Below the capital we hear that there is an Army of the South led by a man named Zapata—

Dear Mother,
Good news. Geraldo and I have been promoted to the *Dorados*. The word means "Golden Ones" and we wear a gold insignia on our hats. We are an elite force of 100 men. We have the best horses in the army and each of us has a rifle and two handguns. We are the ones who accompany the general on his charge when he leads the men into battle—

Dear Mother,
We have captured Ojinaga . . . we have captured Yermo . . . we have captured Camargo. . . .

The year 1912 ended. The Army of the North continued moving.

We have captured Bermejillo . . . Gomez Palacio . . . Cerro de la Pila. . . .

Then:

I am sick inside, Mother. My friend Geraldo has been killed, shot in the throat by a *Federale*. . . .

But the war went on.

We are now aboard a long caterpillar of a train. Two repair cars lead the way in case the *Federales* blow up any tracks. Twenty-two artillery cars follow. Then fifty troop carriers and five hospital cars. A second train, carrying supplies, is close behind us. In all the troop cars, the *soldados* can be heard singing "Adelita" and other songs of our Army. We have come far in two years and have much to be proud of—

We have taken Paredon . . . and Saltillo . . . and now we prepare for Zacatecas, the last obstacle between us and Mexico City. We are now 23,000 strong. . . .

And then the letters stopped.

There were no letters for three months. Reba became frantic. In desperation, Nathan took the letters they had received to a close friend of his who was a United States senator. The senator assigned an aide to work exclusively on locating Myles through the Department of State. It took them two months to learn only that Myles was not among the two dozen or so gringo soldiers of fortune captured by the *Federales* and awaiting execution by firing squad. Other than that bit of information, the Mexican government could offer no help. After all, they pointed out rather acrimoniously, the young man was fighting against their government, not for it.

An effort was made to trace him through the American liaisons of Pancho Villa in El Paso, but to no avail. The records kept by the Army of Northern Mexico were copious when it came to recording victories, horses, arms, and ammunition. But for men, they were sketchy or altogether nonexistent. Myles's enlistment papers were located, but that was all. There was no record of which commander he was assigned to, when he had last been paid, whether he had been wounded or killed, or where he might now be. An attempt was made to check on the *Dorados*, but that was Villa's own company, formed personally by him, without benefit of records.

After five months of effort, Nathan and Reba had learned nothing. It seemed hopeless.

It was a crisp, clear winter day early in 1914 when Reba stopped in at her office after her morning hospital rounds. She was on her way to the prison to have lunch with Nathan before returning to town for her afternoon office hours. While she was at her desk, an office nurse came in.

"Excuse me, Doctor, but there's a man here asking if you'll see him—"

"Office hours begin at two," Reba said.

"I told him that, but he said to ask you anyway. He has two gunshot wounds he wanted you to look at to make sure they're healing properly."

Reba frowned. "Gunshot wounds?"

"Yes, ma'am. He says he got them in a war down in Mexico. His name is Milito or something like that—"

"Oh my God—" Reba drained of color. She quickly took a small vial of smelling salts from her drawer and inhaled to assure herself that she would not faint. "Have him come in, please," she said.

She impulsively took out a mirror and examined her hair. It was awful: gray-streaked, mussed from the winter wind. And her skin was dry, beginning to sag around her eyes. She was forty-eight but was certain she looked sixty. As the door to her office opened, she quickly put the mirror away.

When he walked in, Reba scarcely recognized him. He was as brown as an Indian and wore a thick black moustache that drooped slightly over the corners of his mouth. Dressed in an inexpensive gray suit and scuffed boots, he looked very thin and not at all well. But he had the same easy smile that she had always considered his best feature, and when she saw it now, she hurried around the desk into his arms.

"Myles, Myles, Myles—" she said over and over, clinging to him, crying, touching his face, his hair, the moustache she had never seen. "Myles, my baby, my boy, my son. We thought you were dead."

"Not even close, Mother," he said, still smiling.

"But you *were* wounded?"

"Just slightly. I only told your nurse that to tease you—"

But she insisted on examining him. And the wounds she found were far from slight. "My God, Myles, don't lie to me like that," she scolded. "Forget that I'm your mother and talk to me as a doctor. This wound in the chest, did it collapse your lung?"

"Yes, but it's all right now—"

She shushed him and listened carefully with her stethoscope to all his breathing cavities.

"The wound in your side: how many ribs did it break?"

"Just three—"

"Oh, *just* three," she said in slight disgust. "Roll over on your left side."

After fifteen minutes on the examining table, Reba grudgingly but thankfully admitted that he had received adequate medical care and that there was little she could do for him.

"Put your clothes back on now," she told him, "and let's go to the prison to see your father."

"I came home to see you, Mother. Not Dad."

Reba's expression darkened. "Myles, you cannot treat your father in this manner. I simply won't allow it."

"I'm treating him no worse than he treated me," Myles said coldly. "I was very deeply in love with a girl and he wouldn't even consent to meet her, to talk to her, to judge for himself what kind of person she was. He condemned her because of what her father was, without even giving her a chance. And with complete disregard for the fact that she and I were in love. I won't be told how to treat him, Mother. Not even by you. If you want me to leave now, I will."

Reba stared at him, as if seeing for the first time that he was as different inside as he was in appearance. He was still her son, but he was very much a man now.

"Of course I don't want you to leave," she said.

She began to formulate a plan to get her husband and her son back together again.

That night, in his darkened room at the Union Hotel, Myles sat staring out the window in a mood of gloom and depression. He was thinking that he always seemed to lose everyone who meant anything to him. Cassie. Geraldo. His father.

It occurred to him that if it were not for his mother, he would literally have no one in the world to whom he could consider himself close. A pretty sad state for someone only twenty-two years old. He grunted softly. There had been a man in the hospital in Vera Cruz; a Portugee named Tuzo. He had talked often of being alone.

"Hell, that is why I go off to every war I can find," he said one time. "War helps you replace the family you do not have. It gives you comrades, leaders, followers—all the elements of a family. As soon as I am well, I think I will go to Morocco and enlist in the French Foreign Legion. That way I can have a permanent family."

The Foreign Legion, Myles thought. Perhaps that was what he should do also—

There was a knock at his door. He turned on the light and opened it. His mother was standing in the hall, her shoulders more stooped than usual, her face drawn with the strain of worry.

"Myles, your father is down in the lobby," she said. "He's come that far. I want you to come down and see him. I want you to settle this thing between you."

Myles stared at her for a moment. She looked so tired, so miserable. He thought: why drag it out indefinitely?

"All right, Mother. I'll be right down."

As Reba returned to the lobby, Myles dragged his suitcase from under the bed. Opening it, he removed a layer of clothing and looked at half a dozen pistols he had. He selected a Baumann .44 service revolver with a lanyard ring on its grip. Sticking it in his belt, he put on a coat and followed his mother down to the lobby.

Nathan and Reba were on a settee at the side of the lobby. Nathan stood as Myles approached. The handle of the gun showed under Myles's unbuttoned coat. Nathan frowned. My son? he found himself thinking. My own son?

Myles came up to him and drew the revolver from his belt. The eyes of father and son met and locked. Myles handed his father the pistol, handle first.

"I thought you might like this, Dad. As a souvenir of the Revolution."

Nathan choked back tears and looked at the gun. He hefted it once, turned it over. "It's a fine-looking gun," he said.

Reba stood up between them and put her arms around both of them. She nudged them forward.

Father and son embraced.

CHAPTER 4

Almost as soon as Myles and Dru got Cassie home, she seemed to get better—on the surface, at least. Her color returned and she began to sit up in bed; she even developed an appetite of sorts. The doctor had said that her condition would appear to improve for a few weeks before the cancer made its final inroads, and had warned Myles and Dru not to be deceived into believing that Cassie might be getting well. She *was* dying, and there was no way to change it.

Neither Myles nor Dru discussed with Cassie the hopelessness of her condition. And Cassie herself never broached the subject; she did not even permit herself to think about it. All her life she had been a fatalist, receiving equally the good and the bad that life dealt her, enjoying the good, accepting the bad. In all her life, as child and adult, she had never complained. The closest she had come was insisting that Myles move her from the hospital in the middle of the night.

"It's so good to be back in my own bed," she said the first morning she was home. She rested her head on two pillows and smiled up at her daughter. "I've lived in this prison for twenty-one years: three of them on the inside and eighteen here in the warden's quarters. And you know something? As inmate or warden's wife, I much prefer life in here to life on the outside. I don't really *like* the world out there, Dru." Cassie raised one eyebrow inquisitively. "Do you think there's something wrong with me, honey?"

Dru shook her head. "No more than there's anything wrong with Daddy. He doesn't like the outside world either. You're really well suited for each other."

"Hmmm, don't I know it," Cassie said with a secret smile. "Anyway, thank God you're not going to be like that. It's all right for us: with our backgrounds we're better off isolated from the world like this. But you're going to be different, honey. You're going to break the Hawn mold of being born and living and dying in prison. You're going to college where you can meet people who don't wear uniforms and carry tear gas clubs. You're going to study hard and become a teacher, and someday you'll marry a nice young man in a good profession, and live in a house that doesn't have a thirty-foot wall around it. And someday you'll have a baby and make me a grandmother—"

Cassie's words trailed off as she realized, as Dru had at the hospital, that for her the somedays would never come. It was the first time she really thought about her illness in terms of never seeing her dreams come true. The dreams had been with her for so long—almost since the day Dru was born—that it had never occurred to her that she might not be around to see them materialize.

Cassie suddenly had an overwhelming urge to cement her hopes and dreams into some kind of permanence, so that she would *know* that they would come true, even after she was gone. She leaned forward and gripped Dru's hand almost desperately. "Make me a promise, honey," she implored. "Promise you'll go to college and become a teacher. Promise you'll get away from this prison."

Dru smiled an uncomfortable smile. "I already promised that, Mamma. A long time ago, remember?"

"I know," Cassie said, "But promise me again, honey. Please."

"All right, Mamma. I promise."

Cassie sighed with relief, almost as if she had expected to be denied. She lay back against the pillows again and closed her eyes. Dru studied her mother in repose. Am I lying to her? she wondered. Have I been lying to her all these years, every time I promised something that I didn't really want?

Dru sighed now, as heavily as Cassie had. If she *were* lying to her mother, it would be still another of life's inequities applied to Cassie. Because her mother, Dru reminded herself, had never lied to her. During the years she was growing up, Dru was always told the simple truth about anything she wanted to know. Her mother's background, in particular, was never concealed from her or modified in any way. She was told by Cassie in plain, straightforward language that her great-grandmother had been the notorious Ma Baker, who had led her four sons into crime to escape a life of bitter poverty. Ma had ultimately been ambushed by the law and killed, along with her youngest son, Freddy. Two other sons, Lloyd and Herman, died in prison. The fourth, Arthur, who was called Doc, had been Cassie's father and Dru's grandfather.

At the same time she was learning about her mother's family, Dru was also being told by Myles about his own family, in particular the great-grandmother he had so worshiped and after whom he had named his daughter. When Dru was a little girl, Myles had told her the same bedtime stories that he himself had been told when his Great-grandmother Dru was raising him. They were stories of a hundred years of prison work, and they went back to a man named Aaron Van Hawn, who had started what ultimately became a prison dynasty.

Because of the care taken by her parents to instill in her an understanding of both sides of her family, Dru grew to adolescence with a unique perspective on crime and punishment.

"She'd make a great warden someday," Myles commented once, unaware that Dru, just inside an adjoining room, could hear him.

Cassie had become angry. "Never! I want her as far away as she can get from prisons and crime and convicts. I'd like her to get into something decent."

"Penology is decent."

"You know what I mean, Myles," Cassie said with a hint of stiffness. "Scrubbing floors for a living is decent too, but I don't want my daughter doing it."

"What *would* you want her to do?"

Cassie thought about it for a moment. "Teach, I think," she said finally. "In elementary school."

Myles knew that his daughter would never be a teacher; she

lacked the patience for it. With a dozen or so long-time, hard-line recidivists—their domestics, the library clerks, trusties—as honorary uncles while she was growing up, Dru early on became wise far beyond her years. A lady bank robber she might become, Myles often thought, but a teacher of little children—never. Myles did not, however, share that opinion with his wife.

Cassie worked on Dru for several years trying to persuade her to set as her goal the profession of teaching. Dru usually agreed with her mother simply to end the conversation. During her adolescence, she was markedly without ambition and would have consented to become a witch doctor if that had been what her mother wanted to hear.

And now I'm doing the same thing again, Dru told herself. I'm telling her whatever she wants to hear, just to get her to shut up about it. Only now it's different. Now she's dying, so I can't take lightly what I promise her. I can't agree with her just to get her to stop talking about it because soon she will stop talking forever. What I say now I must be prepared to do, because I am saying it to a dying woman. And that dying woman is my mother—

"What are you thinking about so intently, honey?" her mother asked.

Dru quickly came out of the deep thought she was in and realized that her mother's eyes were open again. "College," she said at once. "I was wondering what it would be like going away to college."

"I'm afraid I can't help you there, honey," Cassie said wryly. "When I was college age, I was on the run with your grandfather. But your dad will remember." She smiled fondly. "He was a college man when we met. He'd just finished his freshman year at Notre Dame." She sat up a little straighter. "Open that old trunk over there and hand me my photograph album. I'll show you some pictures."

Dru smiled a brief smile and went over to the trunk. She had seen the pictures many times; her mother always liked to have photographic evidence handy when she reminisced.

Opening the big album on her lap, Cassie turned without searching to the exact page she wanted. "Here's your dad in his old football uniform," she said. "You'll notice that the uniform is quite different from the ones they wear today. Football was a fairly new sport back then. Your Grandmother Reba, who was a doctor, really raised hell about Myles playing. She said the game was an abuse of the human body."

Cassie began turning the pages slowly, and Dru sat on the side of the bed and looked at the photos with her.

"This is how your dad looked when he came back from fighting in Mexico. See the moustache. That was when we found each other again—"

As she remembered it, Cassie's expression became faraway. She stopped turning the pages and just stared at the photo. Dru started to say something, but changed her mind.

Let her go back into the past all she wants, Dru thought. After all, there's no future for her.

CHAPTER 5

In the summer of 1914 the Midwest was locked in a sweltering heat wave, and Myles Hawn was tormented by a maddening dilemma.

He had been sure that he could return to his home after the revolution in Mexico and settle down to some kind of orderly existence. A man back from war, he reasoned, required very little besides peace and quiet. A simple job, some schooling, the closeness of his parents: that was all he needed. He thought.

Almost immediately he had discovered that he was deluding himself. Being around the prison, around Union City, was pure torture for him. Memories of Cassie were everywhere. He could not walk onto the visitors' parking lot, go to the drugstore in town, look at the willow trees on the riverbank without thinking of her, seeing her face, hearing her voice, remembering her touch. It was awful. Unbearable. He was seriously thinking of going out west, perhaps even going to sea.

And he might have. If a convict named Alvin Purvis had not gotten in touch with him.

Myles was working under the hood of his father's car one afternoon when the road gang was marched back in through the north gate. As the line of grimy, bone-tired convicts trudged past him, Myles suddenly felt a hand go into his back pocket and quickly out again. He stood up at once and scrutinized the moving line of men. All eyes were straight ahead; not a soul glanced at him. Myles reached into his pocket and found a folded slip of paper. On it was scribbled: *I know where Doc Baker is. I will cough tomorrow.*

The next day Myles was in the same place when the gang was brought in again. Purvis, a slight little man with close-set eyes, was the last man in line. As he walked past, he coughed.

"Mr. Nelson!" Myles shouted to the escort guard. The guard halted the line. "Mind if I borrow a man to give me a hand for a minute?" he asked.

"Go ahead, lad," said Nelson.

Myles gestured to Purvis. "You," he said, "fall out of line."

Purvis came over to the car and the rest of the formation continued on its way.

"Well?" Myles said.

"Word's got around that you'd like to find Doc Baker's daughter," Purvis said.

"That's right," said Myles. It did not surprise him that the man knew his business. Myles had grown up in the prison; he knew that the grapevine was one of the most accurate and efficient lines of communication anyone was capable of establishing. To have denied his interest to Purvis would have been tantamount to calling him a liar and losing any chance he had of gaining information.

"I know where Baker is, if you're interested," said the little convict.

"How do you know?" Myles knew he had the right under the convict code to ask for some kind of assurance.

"My brother is a member of his gang. My sister heard from him last week, and visited me day before yesterday."

Excitement surged through Myles. "What do you want in return?" he asked.

"First, your word that the law won't be told. I don't owe Baker nothing, but I don't want my brother hurt."

"You've got my word," Myles told him. "What else?"

"I'd like a better cell, a job in the library or somewheres, and an extra set of laundered clothes every week."

"I can't give you any of that," Myles said. "My father runs the prison, not me. But I can give you money. With money, maybe you can bribe somebody to get what you want."

Purvis frowned as he thought it over. "How much money?" he asked.

"A hundred dollars."

"Two hundred."

"It's a deal. I'll mail a money order to your canteen account as soon as I can get to town. Where is he?"

"I'm trusting you, you know."

"Where is he?"

Purvis took a deep breath. "In Arkansas. A little town called Hedley, just north of Little Rock. I'm trusting you to keep your word."

"I'll keep my word," Myles assured him. He was already deciding which of the guns in his collection he could sell to get the two hundred dollars.

Hedley was a burg: a courthouse in the middle of a dozen stores and twice that many vacant lots that surrounded it on four sides. Everything closed from noon until three because of the heat, which was bad, and the humidity, which was worse. Horse-drawn wagons outnumbered Model T cars two to one. Old men sat under an awning in front of the feed store and spat tobacco juice over the curb. A hound dog slept in the dust next to the courthouse, where the heat refused to let grass grow. Summer quiet and slowness prevailed.

Myles got off the early morning bus after riding all night from Memphis. He shaved, washed, and changed clothes in the restroom of a Castle gasoline filling station, ate breakfast at the Hedley Café, then stationed himself on the top courthouse step where he could see practically the whole town. There he waited.

Cassie came uptown with her mother just before eleven. Myles saw them at once, the dark-haired mother, the light-haired daughter, both so slim and youthful-looking that from a distance they might have been taken for sisters. Lannie went into the Kroger market and sent Cassie over to the drugstore. Myles crossed the little blacktop street and followed Cassie to the drugstore. She had just finished buying magazines for Lannie and cigarettes for Doc when Myles came in. He did not speak a word to her, just stood there where she could see him. When she turned and their eyes met, the color drained from her face and she dropped the magazines. Myles came over and picked them up for her.

"Come on," he said, taking her arm. He led her outside. They stood on the sidewalk in the oppressive heat. Myles devoured her with his eyes. She was no longer a girl; she was a woman now. Her face had filled out, but her chin was still pointed and pert. The hair was the same, except longer; light, auburn, it glinted in the sunlight. She stared at Myles with wide, uncertain eyes. He held her hand tightly.

"You left me a note," he reminded her. "It said maybe we'd meet again when we were grown, and maybe we'd still be in love. Well, we're grown now and we've met again. Tell me if we're still in love."

A tear ran down her cheek. She squeezed his hand. "We are," she whispered. "Yes, we are."

They looked across the street. Lannie was watching them. Myles continued to hold Cassie's hand and they walked over to her. Lannie forced a smile.

"Hello, there," she said. "You're that handsome young man from Union City, aren't you? I'll bet my little girl was glad to see you again. I wish she had longer to talk to you but we're just on our way out of town. Say goodbye now, Cassie."

"Cassie's not saying goodbye to me anymore, Mrs. Baker," Myles said quietly.

"Mrs. Baker? Why, our name is McCoy, young man—"

"Stop it, Mamma," said Cassie. "He knows who we are. His name is Myles Hawn. His daddy's the warden at the prison back in Union City."

Lannie's expression tightened. "What do you want?"

"I want to see Mr. Baker. I've come alone and nobody knows I'm here."

The woman's dark eyebrows raised. "Nobody? No laws?"

"Nobody."

She smiled again, but it was a cold smile this time. "All right. Doc might enjoy a social call from a prison warden's son. Come on along."

The three of them walked away from the square, two blocks along a dusty side street, to a frame house standing alone next to a pasture.

"Mamma, you promise me he won't get hurt," Cassie said when they got to the porch.

"I promise *I* won't hurt him, sugar," Lannie said. "But I don't run this family; your daddy does."

"I'm not going to get hurt, Cassie," Myles assured her. They entered the house and Lannie led them to the dining room. Doc was sitting at the dining room table, coatless, the sleeves of his white shirt turned up, playing solitaire. An oscillating fan blew cool air on him. On the table was a glass of iced tea and a neatly folded towel. There was a slight bulge under the towel.

"Who is he?" Doc asked. Lannie told him who Myles was and why he was there. Doc nodded and studied Myles. Pretty hot day for a man to be wearing a coat, he thought. Doc's right hand moved a fraction closer to the towel and whatever was concealed beneath it. His gaze settled on Myles's face. Doc's eyes were very light hazel, his hair auburn; Myles thought Cassie closely resembled him. "How'd you find me?" Doc asked.

"From somebody inside the walls," Myles replied. "Somebody I paid."

"You expect me to believe somebody *inside* told you?"

"Believe it or don't believe it," Myles said. "It's up to you."

"And you expect me to believe that you came here alone, without telling *nobody*?"

"Like I said, what you believe is your business."

"You'd be a fool to do that, boy—"

"I'm not exactly a boy, Mr. Baker."

"This is some kind of a trick," Doc said. His hand moved another inch. "Nobody's going to waltz in here alone like that. Not when it's me sitting here. Hell, boy, every lawman in the Middle West is looking for me. I've killed three men—"

"I've killed nine," Myles interjected.

Doc frowned "What?"

"Nine," Myles repeated. "Maybe more. In the Mexican Revolution. I rode with Villa." He hooked his thumbs over his belt buckle. "Like I told you, I'm not exactly a boy."

Doc smiled. His eyes flicked down to the younger man's hands hanging easily from his belt buckle. "You think you can pull a gun from under your coat before I can shoot you from under this towel here?"

As Doc was saying the last word, Myles was already moving his hand. In a fluid movement he drew, cocked, and leveled a Dabney revolver at Doc's face. Doc's hand instinctively moved under the towel—but there it froze. The outlaw's expression turned hard. "I knew it was a trick."

Myles uncocked the weapon and tossed it onto the table. "It's not a trick, Mr. Baker. Everything I've told you is the truth. I love Cassie and she loves me. I came here to get her."

Doc looked incredulously at the gun, then at Myles. Then at Lannie. And Cassie. "This beats any damned thing I ever saw," he said, to no one in particular. He drew his hand from under the towel and put his own pistol next to the one Myles had tossed down. "You love this here fellow?" he asked his daughter.

"Yes, Papa."

Doc looked at Myles. "Your daddy know anything about this?"

"I left home three years ago because of it," Myles said. He filled in some of the details, for Cassie and Lannie as well as Doc. "Everything is all right between my dad and me now," he told them when he finished. "I don't think the same thing will happen again. But if it does, Cassie and I will just go away. Settle someplace else. We might do that anyway."

Doc drummed his fingers on the tabletop. He glanced several times at his daughter. She was grown up now, no doubt about that. But *three years* carrying a torch for a prison warden's son—and her own daddy didn't know nothing about it. Got to have a serious talk with Lannie about *that*. Doc took a sip of tea. *Goddamn* if this didn't beat all. And there wasn't a thing in the world he could do about it, either. The boy had seen to that: getting the drop on him and then throwing in his gun. He's made me owe him one. He had me and gave it up. Now I'm beholden. Goddamn it all anyway—

But, what the hell, the outlaw decided. If I'm ever going to make it up to the girl for being such a piss-poor daddy, I reckon now's the time to start.

Doc tossed the guns onto a nearby settee and with his foot pushed a chair out from the table.

"Sit down, kid," he said. "Skip the 'mister' business. Just call me Doc."

That night, long after supper, with the heat of the day cooled only slightly by darkness, Myles and Cassie sat in the swing on the porch and talked.

"Doc's sure different from the way the newspapers say he is," Myles said.

"That's just when he's around Mamma and me," Cassie said. "Mamma says he can be awful bad when he's working."
"Working?"
"You know. Robbing a mail truck or a bank. That kind of work."
"Oh." Myles glanced in the window. Doc and Lannie were at the dining room table, discussing what to do about him and Cassie. "You got any idea what they'll decide?" he asked.
Cassie shrugged. "With daddy it's hard to tell. I know he's not going to hurt you or anything, though. Mamma said while we were doing the dishes that she thinks he likes you. Worst he'd probably do is tell you to move on, then take me and Mamma to a new hideout."
"Would you go?"
"I'd have to go, Myles. He's my daddy. I'm bound to obey him for another year, until I'm twenty-one."
"How about your mother?" he asked. "How do you think she feels about me?"
"Oh, Mamma likes you," Cassie said. She reached over and pinched his cheek. "She thinks you're good-looking."
"Does she know that we, uh—you know: back on the levee bank?"
"Lord, no! I'd have strap marks all over me if she did. Either that or Daddy would have killed me." She leaned closer to him in the swing, pressing her cheek against his neck. "Remember how good it was?" she whispered.
"Yes."
"Remember how we'd both shiver when you put it in me?"
"Yes—"
"And remember how it felt when we both got the tickle at the same time?"
Myles turned his face down and kissed her. "Why don't we go for a walk out in the pasture?"
Before Cassie could answer, the screen door opened and Doc came onto the porch. He sat in a rocker. "Still hot out, ain't it?" he said as he lighted a cigarette. He sighed quietly. "Worst heat spell anybody can remember. Burning up crops all over the country."
Lannie came out with a large glass of iced tea for Doc. "Y'all want something cold to drink?" she asked.

Myles and Cassie said no. Lannie sat on the porch steps, close to Doc. There was a long moment of silence, broken only by the night sounds of the country and the clink of chipped ice as Doc drank his tea. When he finished his cigarette, he threw the butt into the yard and immediately lighted another one. Then he looked over at Cassie.

"Your mother and me has decided to let you get married," he told her.

"Oh, Daddy!" Cassie ran to her father and hugged and kissed him, then dropped to her knees to embrace Lannie. Myles stood up by the swing and remained there awkwardly. When Doc finally looked over at him, he smiled an uncertain smile.

"Thanks, Doc," he said.

"Save your thanks," Doc told him. "You picked a rough road to travel. I just hope for my little girl's sake that you're man enough to make it."

"If I've got Cassie with me, I can do anything, Doc," Myles said confidently.

The next morning Cassie walked back uptown with Myles for him to catch a bus to Little Rock, where the train stopped. Before they left the house, Lannie kissed Myles on the cheek and Doc shook hands with him and slapped him on the back a couple of times. They seemed to genuinely like him now that they were used to who he was. Cassie was so pleased about everything that her face actually glowed; she kept hugging everyone who got close to her.

Walking to the bus station, Myles and Cassie reviewed the plans they had made the previous night. Myles was to return to the prison and tell his parents he had found Cassie again, but not say where. Meanwhile, Doc would decide on a new hideout and move his family there. From the new location, Doc and Lannie would put Cassie on a train for Kansas City. Myles would meet her there, at the Muehlebach Hotel, in two days. They had agreed that from that point on Cassie would never tell Myles where her parents were.

The couple planned to be married in Kansas City. If Nathan and Reba wanted to attend the ceremony, they were welcome; naturally, Doc and Lannie could not come: Doc was too well known. The wedding was to be simple: justice of the peace and witnesses. Afterward, the newlyweds would decide what they wanted to do with their lives.

"Maybe we could move to Indiana and you could go back to college," Cassie said.

"I'm not sure I could get a good enough job to work my way through," Myles replied. "And I don't think my dad would help me after I got married."

"*Mine* would help you," Cassie said with a hint of pride.

"Doc? You think he would?"

"I *know* he would. Course, you know what kind of money you'd be using."

Myles shrugged and they let the matter drop without resolving it. They walked with their arms around each other. Myles could feel the movement of Cassie's hip under his hand with every step she took. He bagan to remember the nights under the willows. "I wish your parents hadn't watched us so closely last night," he said.

She leaned closer to him. "So do I."

They came to the town square. Myles looked around. "I don't suppose there's anyplace we can go now."

"There's a ladies' bathroom behind the bus depot," Cassie said tentatively. "It's got a slide-bolt on the inside of the door."

They looked at each other. It was crazy, outrageous. But they had to do it.

At the depot, Myles went in and bought his ticket while Cassie went around to the ladies' room. There were only two other passengers in the station, both men. When he had his ticket, Myles went back outside. He strolled around back, hurried to the door, and tapped lightly. Cassie let him in and bolted the door behind him.

"I forgot how tiny it was in here," she said. "Can we do it standing up?"

"Looks like we'll have to."

"Wait, I've got an idea." Cassie put the toilet lid down. "You sit on that and let me straddle you—"

With her long skirt hiked up and her underwear unbuttoned and pushed aside, she half-crouched over him until they got into a workable position. Cassie did most of the moving.

"Oh, sweet Jesus," she whispered as she pumped her hips.

Myles rested his head back, mouth open, eyes closed.

"Goddamn, honey—"

Someone tried the knob from outside. Cassie and Myles ignored it.

They kept going until they finished.

Myles arrived back at the prison the next morning. His father was at the kitchen table, drinking coffee. Reba was also there, which was unusual because she should have been making her hospital rounds. The kitchen radio was playing on a shelf above the sink. When Myles walked in, they turned and looked at him. Neither smiled.

"Something's happened, Myles," said Nathan. "We've been listening to the news bulletins on the radio. The Arkansas state police raided Doc Baker's hideout late last night in Hedley."

"We were afraid you might—still be there," Reba said in a faltering voice.

Myles stared at the radio. "Cassie—?"

"She got away," said Nathan. "So did Doc, but they think he was badly wounded. The girl's mother was killed."

"Oh, Jesus." Myles sank onto the nearest chair. A putrid taste rose from his throat. "Poor Lannie." He touched his cheek where twenty-four hours earlier she had kissed him.

The radio bulletin came back on several minutes later. Myles listened to it, staring at the radio as if in a stupor. When it was over, he turned to Reba.

"Pack a bag for me, will you, Mother. I'm going to meet Cassie in Kansas City tomorrow."

Nathan came over and stood beside Myles's chair. "She won't be there, son. With her father all shot up like that—"

"Pack the bag, Mother. Please."

Myles was in Kansas City before noon the next day. He checked into the Muehlebach and left word at the desk and among the bellhops that he was expecting his fiancée and for them to let him know as soon as she arrived.

Cassie was not due until five o'clock that afternoon, but Myles loitered around the hotel for several hours anyway, thinking she might get there early, or try to call. He bought a newspaper and stared almost in disbelief at the funereal headline:

DOC BAKER'S WIFE SLAIN
BY ARKANSAS POSSE;
OUTLAW, DAUGHTER FLEE

Beneath the headline was a photograph of Lannie in her nightgown, sprawled on the floor next to a bed. Her face was not visible but the entire top of her body was blood-soaked.

Christ, I hope Cass doesn't see that, Myles thought.

Around midafternoon he walked down to the corner and had lunch in a downtown café. There was a radio playing behind the counter and he heard another report on the raid.

". . . still no sign of notorious outlaw Arthur 'Doc' Baker or his twenty-year-old daughter Cassandra after the pair fled an Arkansas state police ambush in the hamlet of Hedley, thirty miles northeast of Little Rock. Baker's wife, Lanelle, a part-Cherokee Indian, was killed in the predawn raid on a rented house at the edge of town. Her body, removed late yesterday to the Pulaski County coroner's office, was reported to have a massive shotgun wound in the upper torso, as well as several small-caliber bullet wounds in the head and body. Baker himself was thought to be seriously wounded and officers are notifying all doctors in the surrounding area to be on the lookout for him. Roadblocks have been set up around a one-hundred-mile radius. . . ."

On his way back to the hotel, Myles passed a jewelry store. He paused to look at wedding ring sets in the window. On impulse he went inside and bought one, paying cash for it out of the money he had left from selling his guns to pay Purvis. Maybe the rings will bring us luck, he thought. Maybe my buying them will help her to get here. It was insane thinking, he knew, but he could not help it. He had so little hope to cling to.

From five o'clock on, Myles was sitting in the lobby, his insides as tight as a drum. At five-twenty a young girl hurried in from the street, and for an infinitesimal glorious instant he thought it was Cassie—but he was wrong.

She's not coming, he told himself, for the first time actually letting the thought materialize in his conscious mind.

But he waited nevertheless.

Six o'clock.

Seven.

Ten.

Midnight. . .

At dawn, under the curious stares of the night help, he finally went up to his room.

He stayed in Kansas City two more days, prowling the lobby, staring at the telephone, walking the nearby streets.

Cassie never came.

Following Kansas City, Myles returned to the prison and waited. For what, he was not quite sure. A message from Cassie was almost too much to hope for. Doc's capture would be the next best thing; that would free Cassie for good. Even word that they had been seen somewhere, so he could go there and try to pick up the trail himself. Anything—a scrap of information, a rumor.

But there was nothing. Doc and Cassie disappeared completely. After a week, the roadblocks were removed and the police issued a statement that they had driven the notorious outlaw out of Arkansas. It was the best they could say.

Lannie's body was claimed by her brother, a Tulsa oil well rigger, and given a simple funeral attended mostly by curiosity seekers, newspaper reporters, and lawmen looking for Doc.

Then it was over and became yesterday's news. Nobody cared anymore except Myles. He kept waiting.

A month passed. No word.

Then, on August 4, 1914, England declared war on Germany.

The next day Myles left for Canada to enlist in the British forces.

CHAPTER 6

Myles returned to America in September of 1918, two months before the armistice. He wired Nathan and Reba from New York, saying he would be home as quickly as he could manage. Beginning two days later, they met both trains from Chicago each day, hoping he would be on one of them. He was, finally, six days later. Reba nearly fainted when she saw him.

He got off the end coach and limped down the platform toward them. His weight was down to one-seventy, making him terribly thin for his height. With the moustache gone, hair clipped short, pale from a hospital stay they did not even know about, he looked pathetic.

Reba ran to him, already crying, cursing in her mind: Goddamn wars. Goddamn them for doing what they do to a mother's son.

"Oh, Myles—Myles—my baby—"

"Hello, sweetheart," he said, hugging her. She was relieved to feel the strength in his arm, but could not help wondering just how bad his leg was. She would look at it as soon as possible.

Then Nathan was there and father and son were embracing. Nathan was crying too. "You didn't tell us you'd been hurt, son."

"You would have just worried, Dad," he said.

Nathan's tears streaked his cheeks. "We have a right to worry. How bad is it?"

Myles shrugged. "I limp, Dad. I'll always limp. But at least the leg's not attached with a strap."

Reba kept touching his face, as if to assure herself that he was real. He looks so old, she caught herself thinking. There's gray in his hair. My God, he's only twenty-six, how can he look so old?

Driving up the hill, Nathan said, "Are you ready for a good meal, son?"

"I'm ready for a stiff drink," Myles replied.

I wonder how much of that he does? Reba and Nathan thought simultaneously.

"How long ago were you wounded?" Reba asked.

"Six months. March twenty-fifth, to be exact. The fourth day of the Battle of the Somme."

"My God, Myles, all that time—" Reba began crying again. She was sitting between them in the front seat. Myles put his arm around her and pulled her to him as if she were a girl.

"Come on, now. Stop it. I'm tired of that kind of thing. Seems like all I've seen in the last four years has been women crying. All over France and half of Belgium."

Reba quickly stifled her sobs and dried her tears.

When they got to the prison, the car passed the strip of ground where Myles had once had his calisthenics field. He stared solemnly at it, remembering. Nathan and Reba noticed. They exchanged pained glances, but said nothing.

It was not until very late that night, after Reba had gone to bed, that Myles and Nathan were able to talk in private. Myles got a bottle of French brandy from his duffel bag and they had a drink in the parlor. Nathan told him all he had heard about Doc Baker.

"It seems like the man just went crazy after his wife was killed. He goes on a rampage three or four times a year, always in Arkansas. It's as if he's trying to pay the state back for that ambush. He leads a gang into Arkansas from Missouri or Tennessee or Oklahoma, and raids a town just like the outlaws did thirty years ago. The only difference is that the gang drives Model T cars instead of riding horses. But the damage they do is the same: they hold up the bank, rob half a dozen convenient stores, gun down lawmen or anybody else who tries to interfere, then drive out of town shooting up everything in sight. For three years now it's been a nightmare for people who live in small towns near the state lines."

"And Cassie?" Myles asked. "Is there ever any word about Cassie?"

"No." Nathan's voice turned sad. "Never a mention."

Myles stared at the circle of brandy in his glass. "Maybe she's dead, Dad. Maybe it was her who got badly wounded that night. She could have died and Doc could have buried her somewhere."

Nathan nodded. "Possible, I suppose. But I don't think you really feel like it happened that way. I think you feel she's still alive. Don't you, son?"

Myles nodded. "Yes." He bowed his head, putting one hand over his eyes. "I want so badly to find her."

Nathan put an arm around his son's shoulders. "Then stay here, Myles. Stay right here at the prison. That's the surest way to find her."

Myles looked at him, frowning. "I don't understand."

"Through Doc," Nathan explained. "Sooner or later he'll be caught again. He'll wind up back here or in some other prison. Or else he'll be killed by the law. Whichever way, you'll know where he is. And when you find Doc, you'll find Cassie."

Myles stared soberly at his father. Maybe he's right, he thought. Maybe it was time to stop running away from it; time to tough it out and stay put until it was resolved, one way or another. He reached down and rubbed his weak right knee. It was better to quit now anyway; if he kept running off to wars, there wouldn't be much left of him to offer a girl.

"Stay, son," Nathan urged.

Myles nodded. "All right. I'll try to."

The next day, Myles sat with his father in the warden's office.

"I don't know what kind of work I can do, Dad. I've got this game leg—"

"Forget about your leg, Myles," Nathan said firmly. "There's one job that's always been yours. Right at my side. As my deputy."

"Dad, I'm not qualified to be your deputy," Myles said.

"Officially you probably aren't," Nathan admitted. "But if you worked with me *unofficially*, without being on the payroll, for a year or so, then you *would* be qualified—and then I could appoint you." Nathan leaned forward and folded his hands on the desk. "This could work out very well all the way around. Maybe I can lighten my load a little. Your mother is constantly on me to work shorter hours, take afternoon naps, that sort of thing."

"I really wasn't looking for a high-level job, Dad," Myles said. "But if it would be a help to you, and if you think I can do it, then I'll be glad to try. God knows I've caused you and Mother enough grief over the years. Maybe I can make it up now."

Nathan shook his head. "Put that kind of thinking out of your head, son. You don't have any more to make up to us than we do to you. The day your mother and I qualify as perfect parents, that's the day we'll expect you to be a perfect son." Nathan rose and held out his hand. "Have I got a new deputy?" he asked.

Myles shook his father's hand. "You've got a new deputy, Warden."

For a year Myles understudied his father, working at his side in everything he did. He learned the warden's job from every angle: administrative, custodial, budgetary, punitive. His father piled work and responsibility on him as quickly as he could handle it. Everything he learned meshed with his upbringing, his background, and his bloodline to slowly turn him into a figure of authority in the prison. His name and his limp soon became familiar to convict and guard alike, and his word, as much as Nathan's, became law. He quickly evolved into an extraordinary deputy. Whether it was his military bearing, his ability to give orders with a sureness that precluded disobedience, the fact that he was equal to any convict in the place in terms of courage—he still had his reputation as one of Pancho Villa's fearless killers—all served to secure his place in the two communities of the prison: the officials and the inmates. In both, Myles Hawn found respect.

When the year was up, Nathan presented him with his formal appointment as deputy, and Myles went on the payroll. He proved to be an even better deputy than his father expected. He completely overhauled the prison's educational system and for the first time offered to the prisoners schooling at any level from first grade through high school. Convicts considered menaces on the outside could be seen carrying primers around with them and reading about Dick and Jane and Spot. He also established, through the legislature via his father and the governor, a schedule of wages for inmates who conscientiously did difficult prison labor. This pay was extremely modest—ten cents per day—but it nevertheless reestablished a pride of earning among those who received it and opened up healthy competition in the population for men in nonpaying jobs.

With Nathan's permission, Myles gradually abolished prison stripes, phasing out the old clothing as it became worn, and replacing it with new issues of plain blue denim. He eliminated bread-and-water punishments in solitary, and instead fed the lockups a normal meal minus meat and dessert. He initiated for the first time the opportunity for prisoners to have private talks with the deputy. Once a week, during open-cell time in the blocks, Myles sat at a desk on the flats, in full view of all inmates in the cell house, and allowed men to come to him, without a guard, and speak to him privately about any matter in which they thought he could be of help. By doing this, Myles eliminated a lot of cell house problems before they could compound, and halted many troublesome situations before they could erupt.

By the end of his third year as deputy, Myles was the man to see with a problem whether one was an official or an inmate. Everyone came to him for help. His unusual ability to go right to the nucleus of a problem was quickly recognized by everyone with whom he dealt, and utilized with almost relentless regularity.

"You're letting them impose on you," Nathan warned. "Half the things they come to you with, they could solve themselves."

"I don't mind," Myles said. "It helps me keep my finger on the pulse of the prison."

"The pulse of the prison," said Reba. "What a clever way of putting it."

"Thank you, Doctor," Myles said, giving her a fond peck on the cheek. He had become greatly affectionate and attentive toward his mother since he had been back. Even though Nathan rejected his doing penance for past grief caused, Myles still felt obliged to do so in Reba's case. She seemed so frail to him, and carried such a heavy load. Her few hundred patients took more out of her in a week than Nathan's few thousand convicts took out of him in a month.

Beyond the prison and his parents, there was little of interest to Myles. He did little or nothing for personal recreation, socialized with no one, kept company with no women. His private life was solitary, celibate. Like a monk. Or a convict. He devoted himself solely to his work and, as the years passed, all but gave up ever hearing from Cassie again.

Then, in 1924, two years after Nathan had retired and Myles had been appointed his successor, a radio bulletin brought her back into his life. Doc Baker had been shot and killed in the northern part of the state. His daughter Cassandra had been apprehended in a rented apartment in which they had been living.

Four months later, Cassie arrived at the women's section of the prison to serve a three-year sentence for harboring a fugitive—her father.

Myles had Cassie brought to his office the day she arrived at the prison. He was grimly determined that his long vigil was over. He had loved Cassandra Baker, girl and woman, for thirteen years. Twice he had found her, and twice circumstances had taken her away from him. This time it was going to be different.

"Nothing is going to keep us apart now," he told her.

"Yes, something will," Cassie said. "The bars."

Myles shook his head. "Those bars are going to keep you from leaving me," he said. "You can make parole in fourteen months. The day you get out, we'll be married."

"Myles, that's crazy. It'll ruin you. Your career would be destroyed. We've been apart so long. The best thing you can do is just try to forget me."

"I went through two wars trying to forget you," he said. "I couldn't do it when all the bad luck was keeping us apart; how do you expect me to do it when we've finally got a chance—"

"But we *don't* have a chance, Myles! I'm a *prisoner*, for Christ's sake! I'm a convicted felon! My father was just shot down a few months ago by the laws. My uncles were all criminals. Myles, my grandmother was *Ma Baker*! Even she was killed by the laws. For us to even think of getting married is stupid."

"Stupid or not, we're going to do it."

"No," she snapped. "No, we're not, Myles. I'm not going to let you upset your whole life because you fell in love with a seventeen-year-old girl back in 1911. You're so blind remembering the past that you won't look at the future. Well, I'm not blind. All my life I've had things run for me by somebody else. First by Mamma; then by Daddy. I've been on the dodge with Daddy ever since Mamma was killed. Nursing him, taking care of him, seeing that he went to the springs for his lungs. If I hadn't stayed with him, he'd have blown his brains out the first year he was alone. But I'm tired of being somebody's crutch, Myles—"

As soon as the words were out, she regretted them. She glanced at his lame leg, her face flushing red.

"I didn't mean that like it sounded."

"I know you didn't."

"I don't want to hurt you, Myles, but there's simply no sense to us thinking about marriage. Can't you arrange to have me transferred to another prison?"

"I could," he said, "but I won't." His voice became firm, flat. "You were sentenced to do your time here and this is where you'll do it."

Cassie shrugged. "Keep me here, then," she said evenly. "But we won't be getting married, Myles. Not in fourteen months—not ever."

"We'll talk about it when the time comes," he said.

She shook her head. "No, we won't talk about it at all—*Warden*."

Having Cassie in his prison was torture for Myles. She was assigned to operate a mangle in the laundry, and every time Myles inspected the women's facility, or conducted official visitors on tours, he would see her. What made it particularly difficult was the fact that he was unable to talk to her, either in private or in passing. Anything he said to her in the laundry would be overheard by half a dozen other women prisoners; and if he summoned her to his office without a legitimate reason, she would be put in the position of having to explain it to the others. So any communication on his part had, for her sake, to be avoided.

Cassie had no problem melding into the convict life. As the daughter of Doc Baker and the granddaughter of Ma Baker, her reputation for loyalty to her outlaw family preceded her. The few inmates who remembered her long-ago romance with the son of the former warden did not bother to bring up the subject in light of the Baker name and reputation carried by Cassie. So that was one burden she did not have to bear. Her work in the laundry was hot and tiring, but not more than she could handle. She did her job well, stayed out of trouble, and let it be known that she intended to do her time as easily as possible. At the end of six months, she was transferred off the mangle and given an easier assignment at the folding table.

Myles, meanwhile, had his hands full coping with a new breed of criminal that was beginning to flood his prison: the American bootlegger. In 1920 the Volstead Act had been passed by Congress. Known officially as the Prohibition Enforcement Act, it outlawed the manufacture and sale of liquor in America. Immediately it created a new category of criminal activity.

"I'm not sure how to handle these men," Myles said to his father, who still lived in the area. "They're not actually criminals in the same sense that holdup men and embezzlers are criminals."

"You're drawing imaginary lines," Nathan told him. "You're not the judge or the jury, remember. You're the keeper."

"I'm not forgetting that. It's in my position as warden that I'm worrying about the situation. Some of the ones we're getting in here on bootlegging raps are little more than kids. Eighteen and nineteen years old. They've been making moonshine for their families and friends at their daddy's whiskey still back in the hills for years. Now all of a sudden there's a market for the stuff so they start peddling it. The revenuers catch them and before they know it they're in here for five years with a lot of hard cases that can teach them how to blow a vault, steal a car, stick up a bank. That's no good, Dad. The system is supposed to help them, not teach them to be worse."

"If they've been convicted, they have to do time," Nathan said stubbornly.

"They shouldn't have to do it here, not behind *these* walls. The state needs an intermediate reformatory of some kind, a minimum security prison where kids like that can be kept away from the pros. I'm going to the capital and take it up with the legislative corrections committee. I'd like to see if I can get something constructive going on it."

Myles did go to the capital several times. But he received only opposition to his ideas. The state already had a reform school for youths under eighteen; those over eighteen who committed crimes would simply have to take their chances in the big pen. No matter how many times Myles tried to explain that such an attitude was only creating future problems, the legislators controlling the money were not impressed. Voters didn't vote for senators who built experimental reformatories, they hinted. Voters voted for men who built new roads. Then they offered Myles a drink from their private stock of bootleg whiskey.

After one of those frustrating trips to the capital, Myles always returned to the prison with a guilty conscience. He felt that he had failed every man behind the walls.

When her first year of confinement was up, Cassie routinely received an application for parole. She returned it to administration unsigned. For the first time since her arrival, Myles had a legitimate excuse to have her brought to his office. He sent for her that same day.

"I don't want a parole," she told him. "I intend to serve the full three years."

"Cassie, that's ridiculous," Myles said patiently. "You could be out of here in sixty days, a free woman."

"You're not free when you're on parole," she said.

"Don't be silly. That's con talk."

"I *am* a con, remember?"

Myles sighed quietly. He leaned forward on the desk, to get a little closer to her. "Cassie, can't we talk sensibly? Can't we try to work this thing out between us?"

"There's nothing between us to work out."

"Yes, there is. I still love you. That's between us."

"That's—" Her voice caught and she had to exert effort to control it. "That's your problem," she finally said.

"Goddamn it, Cassie!" he stormed, losing patience, slamming an open palm on the desktop. Suddenly he could control his emotions no longer. It all caught up with him: the heartbreak, the loneliness, Mexico, France, the ever-present pain in his leg—

He lowered his face so she could not see, and cried.

Cassie came around the desk. She touched the back of his head, once, very gently. "I'm sorry, Myles," she said quietly, "but I can't let you ruin your life just to get me. I'm not worth it."

She left his office to be taken back to the women's facility.

Nathan Hawn visited Cassie the next day.

"Do you know what my son is doing this very minute?" he asked. "He's writing out his resignation as warden. He loves you so much that he's willing to give up the entire rest of his career for you. He says if he disassociates himself completely from the prison and waits the other two years you have left to serve, that you might marry him then. That way, he says, you won't be wrecking anything by doing it—because he'll have already wrecked it all himself."

Cassie stared at the visiting room screen between them. She put one hand to her lips and shook her head slowly, "I don't know why I don't just kill myself," she mumbled.

"Because you know if you did, he probably would too. And you love him too much to let that happen. Don't you?"

Cassie stared at him, blinking back tears, her face ashen.

"Don't you?" Nathan insisted.

Cassie gave an anguished nod. "Yes."

"Then you'd better do something to stop him from making this mistake."

"What can I do?" There was desperation in Cassie's voice.

"Tell him to stay on as warden, that you'll marry him when you get out." Nathan shrugged. "Not that it'll matter much. If he does marry you, the governor will likely dismiss him."

"You're saying there's no hope either way."

"Not much, no."

"Then why are you doing this? Why are you trying to help?"

"Because he's my son and he's never been happy without you. I want to see him happy sometime before I die. I hope by doing this that I can make up for the mistake I made about you a long time ago." Nathan swallowed dryly and his eyes became teary. "Will you help me?" he asked. "Please."

Finally it was over for them.

Myles waited for her in his car in the bank parking lot across from the Union City bus depot. Cassie was released like every other prisoner: checked out medically; dressed in a new print dress, low-heeled oxfords, and anklets; given twelve dollars, and driven to the bus depot. Then she was on her own. The twelve dollars would buy a bus ticket to anywhere in the state.

As soon as the prison sedan dropped her off and drove away, Cassie hurried across the street and got into the car with Myles. When the car door closed, she was in his arms, burying her face in his shoulder while he held her so tightly that she could hardly breathe.

"Jesus," Myles whispered, "is it true? Is it true at last?"

"Yes, darling, it's true."

"This is really you? After all this time—"

"Really me. And really you. Really us."

He held her face between his hands and kissed her a dozen times: on the lips, cheeks, nose, eyes.

"Myles, people will see," she cautioned.

"I wish we could go someplace right now," he said.

"So do I. God, so do I."

Myles fumbled with his pocket watch. "It's nine-thirty. Our appointment with the governor is at eleven. It's an hour drive."

"We'd better go," said Cassie.

"I guess."

Myles drove over to the Riverside Highway and they headed north toward the capital.

"Do you have any idea what the governor is going to do?" Cassie asked.

"No. I wrote him a personal letter two weeks ago telling him the whole story about us. I said you were being released today and that we planned to be married as soon as possible. Just yesterday his secretary called and said he wanted to see me at eleven today. And that I was to bring you along." His expression was grim. In his inside pocket was his resignation. If the governor even hinted that his marriage to Cassie would not be acceptable, Myles would resign on the spot.

For a while as he drove, Myles put his hand down between her legs and held her. Cassie put her own hand over his and rotated it gently. "God, it's been so long," she said in a whisper, resting her head on the seat back.

After a bit, she put her hand on him for a while.

* * *

They parked in the capital parking lot at ten before eleven and went directly to the governor's reception room. The governor personally came out of his office to greet them.

"Myles, so good to see you," he said, smiling. "And this must be Cassandra."

He led them inside to chairs in front of his desk. The governor was a handsome, almost stately man just a few years older than Myles.

"Did you bring your resignation with you, Myles?" he asked from behind his desk.

Myles's mouth dropped open slightly. From the corner of his eye, he saw Cassie turn and look at him. "Why—yes, I did," he replied, surprised that the governor would ask for it so quickly. But there the governor was, his hand outstretched over the desk. Myles took the typed page from his pocket and handed it to him.

The governor did not even bother to read it. He simply tore it in half and dropped it in the wastebasket. Then he flipped on his intercom. "Send Edwards in here, please."

A stooped little man entered the office carrying some documents and a notary seal. The governor took the documents and handed them to Myles. "Applications for a marriage license," he said. "You two fill them out while I round up a couple of witnesses. I'll perform the ceremony myself. That way, if there's any political heat, it'll have to include me."

He left the office. Myles and Cassie stared at each other for a moment, then quickly set about completing the applications. As soon as they were finished, the stooped little man named Edwards notarized them and gave Myles a license already made out.

"All set?" asked the governor, returning with his secretary and a clerk. He handed Cassie a bunch of petunias. "Personally picked from the capitol garden. Which," he added, winking, "is against the law."

The governor went behind his desk and took a large, very old Bible from a drawer. He smiled at Myles and Cassie. "Ready?"

They joined hands, taking a second to look into each other's eyes. Then Myles nodded to the governor. "Ready, sir."

And so, after sixteen years of being in love, Myles Hawn, fourth-generation prison warden, and Cassandra Baker, daughter and granddaughter of notorious American outlaws, were finally married.

That night, for the first time, they made love in a bed. For eleven straight nights, both in the capital hotel and back at the prison, they made love.

And exactly nine months and four days after they were married, Cassie gave birth to a beautiful baby girl.

Myles named her Dru.

CHAPTER 7

Cassie Hawn lived for nearly six months after Myles and Dru brought her home from the hospital. For the first four of those months it was, except for her staying in bed a lot, as if she were not ill at all. Her spirits, after Dru reaffirmed her promise to go to college, were quite high; and her disposition, once merely pleasant and practical, became markedly cheerful. Each day was precious to her and she showed it.

More than anything else she seemed to enjoy her daughter. She wanted Dru with her as much as possible: sitting with her while the phonograph played, doing needlepoint with her, learning how to take care of the hosehold budget, reading to her, reminiscing and going through old suitcases full of photos, letters, and diaries handed down through the generations. In one trunk that had not been opened in years they found the journals of Druscilla Foyle, Myles's great-grandmother, after whom Dru was named.

"I never knew her, of course," Cassie said. "But your dad has told me so much about her that I almost *feel* as if I'd known her. She took care of him for the first twelve years of his life, while your Grandfather Nathan was busy planning and building the new prison, and your Grandmother Reba was becoming the best doctor, male *or* female, in Union City. Your dad worshiped the old woman, literally. That's why he named you after her. Eventually she got so old that *he* had to take care of *her*, you know. He's told me how he used to sneak smoking tobacco to her, and take her to the prison cemetery so she could visit the dead." Cassie brushed her fingertips over the buckram binding of the journal Dru had brought to the bed. "How many volumes are there?" she asked.

"Quite a few," said Dru. "The whole bottom of the trunk is filled with them. They don't really look like diaries at all; they look like account books."

"Your dad says they're ledgers issued by the state quartermaster. The prison used to get them for nothing." Cassie thumbed through the pages. "I always meant to read these journals. Maybe I will, now that I have to stay in bed anyway. Will you take them out of the trunk for me and stack them up there on the table in the right order?"

Dru arranged the books on the table and even offered to start reading them to her but Cassie said no, not just then; she would get to them later. She never did, for soon afterward her condition began to deteriorate and she lost interest in the past as well as the future; she concentrated all her attention exclusively on the present.

Myles and Dru pretended not to notice any change in her: the increased fatigue, the extreme shortness of breath, the eyes that often stared into space. Inside they were devastated by what was happening. Cassie had been the mainstay of their lives; they depended on her as they did on the air they breathed. But together they put on for her a unified show of confidence that her condition was not getting any worse. Then at night, when she was sound asleep, father and daughter often sat in each other's arms and cried like shattered children.

As she sensed her periods of lucidity becoming shorter, Cassie began to dwell on her obsession with Dru's future. She made it clear again and again that it was her dying wish that her daughter be educated as a teacher and remove herself entirely from the world of prisons and prisoners.

"Your father and I have talked it over," she said. "We've decided that it's the best thing for you."

That was not true, of course, but Myles would not have contradicted her for the world. Just as Dru would not have dreamed of denying her last wish.

"You will do that for me, won't you, baby?" Cassie asked in her weakening voice.

"Yes, Mamma," Dru answered with tears in her eyes.

* * *

The last few weeks of Cassie's agonizingly slow death saw her body deteriorate with a gradual certainty that tore at Myles's heart every time he looked at her. He had known Cassie's body with the intimacy of love since she was seventeen years old, and now as he was forced to watch her gradually wither away into a living skeleton, it was all he could do to bear it. More than once he retreated into the sanctuary of liquor to escape the helplessness he felt at being unable to relieve her suffering. When it became obvious to Dru that he was beginning to rely too frequently on alcohol, she took her first firm stand as an adult.

"Daddy, I think we should start sitting up with Mamma all night," she said. "Her time must be getting very short now and I don't think we ought to take the chance of one of us not being with her when—well, you know, in case she wakes up and knows what's happening to her. Don't you think?"

"Yes, honey, I do," Myles said. "You're absolutely right."

"We can take turns, sitting with her in shifts. Of course, that'll mean that you can't drink in the evenings."

Myles looked away, shamefaced.

"I'm sorry to embarrass you, Daddy," she said. "But I need your help. Mamma needs your help."

Myles nodded. "I know. All right. I won't drink anymore."

They began a routine of staying with Cassie around the clock in three-hour shifts. Every time the dying woman opened her eyes, one of them was there. Even in the very final stages, when her pain became so acute that she was heavily sedated with morphine, they still sat at her side. It mattered not to them whether she knew they were there, or even, toward the end, whether she knew who they were; all that mattered was that they continue to share her presence every minute that she remained alive. For the last week of her life, Cassie was little more than a vegetable: limp, totally unconscious most of the time, unable to even respond to their voices. Nevertheless, Myles and Dru maintained their vigil: they had convinced themselves that Cassie at least sensed their presence.

She finally succumbed early one morning when Dru was sitting with her. She did not wake up to die, merely expelled one final death rattle, then became still. Dru quietly cried alone for a few minutes, then got her father and they cried together. Even knowing they still had each other, both of them experienced a sudden feeling of aloneness unlike any they could remember. For Myles, the feeling was reminiscent of his early heartbreak when he had found Cassie and lost her again. For Dru it was a shattering new experience, a feeling of utter irrevocable loss. Cassie had been so much to each of them. Without her, they felt hollow.

Cassie Baker Hawn was laid to rest in a simple graveside ceremony in the prison cemetery. The prison's Protestant chaplain officiated and the services were kept as brief as possible. There were reporters at the cemetery gate, but Myles issued orders keeping them out. They were angry about it but could do nothing; the cemetery was part of the prison and Myles had absolute authority over who entered its confines.

Cassie's grave was off to the side by itself, in a place she and Myles had selected for themselves at the foot of a tall, thick oak tree. From where the mourners stood during the service, Dru could see scattered about her the headstones of many of her ancestors, dating back a hundred years. And beyond them, in the convict section, were the markers of men who had died as far back as 1828, during the construction of the state's first prison by Dru's Great-great-grandfather, Aaron Van Hawn. Looking at the many graves, Dru thought about her Great-great-grandmother Druscilla's journals, and was saddened that Cassie had not had time to read them.

When the funeral was over, Myles and Dru returned to the warden's quarters and received mourners for the rest of the day. Then they had a light supper prepared by the convict cook, after which Dru insisted her father go to bed. Myles was exhausted. The unyielding pressure of running the prison, the constant discomfort of his weak leg, and the emotional devastation of Cassie finally dying had drained from him all but the last ounces of strength. He did not present even token argument when Dru led him down to the guest room where he had been sleeping since his wife's return from the hospital.

Left to herself after her father went to bed, Dru wandered back into the master bedroom where Cassie had died and began tidying up. Most of what had to be done she had already taken care of, after the undertakers had removed her mother. Now there were just a few odds and ends.

On the table Dru found her great-great-grandmother's journals, that she herself had arranged in chronological order as her mother had asked her to do. They needed to be packed back in the old trunk, but Dru decided that she was too tired to do it right then. She suddenly had the desire to rest, to try and relax. She picked up the first volume of Druscilla Foyle's diary and half sat, half lay on her mother's settee.

Almost idly, she opened the journal to its first page. . . .

CHAPTER 8

The keelboat carrying the prisoners maneuvered close to the bank that April day in 1827, to avoid the frequent rapids in the deepest part of the river. Most of the time the boat moved smoothly and evenly on its flat keel, its progress aided by a pine hull that did not waterlog and become sluggish. It was seldom necessary to hoist the single canvas sail for windpower; the downriver flow of the current helped the boat move swiftly by water draft alone. Only when the helmsman, standing far forward with his long pole, failed to avoid a mud pocket was the journey temporarily interrupted. Then the prisoners were unchained, waded ashore under full guard, and lined up like a brace of oxen on each side of the cordelle rope, which they heaved and pulled on until the keelboat, with a great sucking noise, came free of the mud. Then the journey resumed.

Just north of Moline, where they were to pick up their second lot of prisoners, they were stuck for the first time, not in a mud pocket but on a sandbar just under the surface. Tillman, the chief guard, had come forward to where Aaron was standing.

"Permission to cordelle, Mr. Van Hawn?"

Aaron had pursed his lips briefly. Then: "I'm not a river man, Mr. Tillman. You'll have to explain what you mean."

Tillman had explained, Aaron had given permission, and the five prisoners already aboard had been taken ashore with the thick tow rope.

The journey, begun at Galena, had continued downriver past Moline, Rock Island, Burlington, Quincy, Hannibal, and Alton.

They had stopped for two days at East St. Louis to load a flatboat with supplies and lash it to the rear of the keelboat. Resuming their journey, they traveled much more slowly, with the weight of the supplies and the drag caused by the flatboat.

This was the third week of their journey. On board by now were twenty-eight convicts. Two more would be picked up in Chester, where they would also hire a stonemason. Then on to the last leg of the long trek down to Union County, north of Cape Girardeau, where they would build the prison.

Aaron, standing atop the midships cabin, watched the waters with a childlike fascination. The Mississippi was shiny with light brown mud slicks. Most of the men aboard, guards and convicts alike, thought it dirty, ugly. But even after nineteen days of living on it, Aaron still looked at the mighty river with a feeling of awe. It was a feeling unique to a person who had lived all his adult life inland, far inland, on the flat prairies that produced corn and wheat and soybeans instead of swift waters. That, Aaron thought, along with the fact that he had been born in Holland, a land of channels and canals and people of the water. Aaron was comfortable on the water, and it gave him satisfaction to think that it had something to do with his heritage. Even if he *had* only just learned what it meant to cordelle on the Mississippi.

Turning from the bow, he looked behind the parent boat at the flat vessel being towed. Seeing the supplies loaded back in East St. Louis, he had feared they would be too heavy for the keelboat to pull. But he had discovered that it was more than up to the task. Seventy feet long, with a twenty-foot beam, it could easily have carried ten tons and pulled ten more on a river like the Big Muddy Mississippi.

Aaron let his eyes move slowly over the twenty-eight shackled men who lay or sat or stood on the broad stern, their leg-irons securely locked to an iron tether bar fastened to the deck. A mixed lot, he thought, but no more so than one might come across in any levee saloon up and down the river: some old, some young, some clean, some dirty, some bearded, some not, some—well, a mixed lot, but not really that unusual. Except perhaps in one respect: they were all criminals. And they were all, under his supervision—Aaron Van Hawn's—to be punished for their crimes.

At forty, Aaron was a stocky man, solid as the hull of the boat on which he stood. Shorter than most men with whom he dealt, he made up for it with a breadth that was at once intimidating and reassuring. His eyes were direct and piercing; he seldom blinked, an oddity no one seemed to notice. His chin jutted out, arrogant and challenging in a taller man but in Aaron simply a cant of the head to compensate for the inches he lacked. As he stood on the boat now, the midday sun burned down on his high, balding forehead until he had to put on the flattopped straw sombrero hanging in the center of his back by its chin cord. He thought for perhaps the dozenth time about the log he was supposed to be keeping. There was a bound journal in his cabin, issued to him by the state treasurer, in which he was charged to enter the name, age, town or village of origin, crime, and sentence of every prisoner delivered to his keeping. He had not done so for a very simple reason: he could not write. And he was too ashamed to admit it to Mr. Tillman or anyone else in order to have it done. So he postponed it from port to port. But he knew by the way it kept coming into his thoughts that he would have to do something about it soon.

Aaron sighed quietly and turned his attention to the river again. Up ahead, on the east bank, he saw a levee and pier and some houses.

"Village of Chester, dead ahead port, Mr. Van Hawn," the chief guard called from the bow.

"Thank you, Mr. Tillman," Aaron called back. A slight smile crossed his lips. He still was not used to being addressed as "mister" all the time. Pursing his lips again, he erased the smile. You had better *get* used to it, he told himself firmly. You're a person of position now, position and responsibility. He straightened his shoulders a fraction and raised the jutted jaw an inch.

You are no longer ordinary, he told himself. You are an *appointee* of the governor.

Whether you can write or not.

A month earlier, in the midstate town of Cordelia, Aaron had been loading finished lumber on his employer's wagon, getting ready to go out and erect what he imagined would be the four- or five-hundredth barn he had put up in the ten years he had been at that trade. He was in a half-angry mood that morning; loading the lumber was not his job. It was the job of his employer's nephew.

"I've sent the boy on an important errand, Van Hawn," Able Fleece had told him when he reported for work at 6 A.M. "You'll have to load the lumber for old man Jackson's barn yourself."

"Yessir, Mr. Fleece."

He harnessed the mules and backed the wagon into the lumber yard, feeling the resentment build up in him as he worked. Able Fleece, Barn-Raising a Specialty, had fired a perfectly good free Negro and put his nephew to work in the lumber yard three months earlier. That change in personnel had reduced Aaron's status from that of senior white employee to that of junior non-relative. More and more lately he had been required to help with—or do all of—the nephew's work. This morning was another example. Loading the lumber would run him an hour late getting to the Jackson place. Which meant he would have to work an hour later that night in order to keep the barn-raising on schedule. All because Fleece had sent his nephew on an "important" errand. Several times in the past, as Aaron had started out of town with the wagonload of lumber, he had passed the nephew returning from his "important" errand: coming back from some shantytown kitchen carrying a burlap-covered plate of hot biscuits and a wooden jar of warm molasses. Aaron imagined the nephew and Fleece sitting next to the stove in Fleece's warm little office, feasting on their molasses-dipped biscuits, while he drove out to begin work an hour late.

And nothing to be done about it either, he knew. Times were not that good. There were a dozen men in Cordelia who could be hired by Fleece to replace him; men who would be happy to do his *and* the nephew's work, probably for less wages than Aaron was paid. So complaint was out of the question. Aaron had as much pride as the next man; he also had a belly that made regular and outrageous demands, and a body that liked to sleep in a bed, under a roof. So he curbed his anger, swallowed his pride, and did the nephew's work. He was doing it that morning in mid-March when his friend Grover came riding down the street in a new buggy, dressed in a new waistcoat.

Grover reined up smartly on the other side of the lumber yard fence. "I figured I'd find you doing this," he said knowingly. "I just seen young worthless heading for shantytown."

"He's on an important errand. Where'd you steal the rig?"

"Didn't steal it. Borrowed it from the governor's livery. He's got seven or eight more just like it. I can use one anytime I want to."

"He lend you the coat too?"

"No, sir," Grover said indignantly. "I bought this here waistcoat myself, at Mendel's Gentlemen's Haberdashery in St. Louie."

Aaron's mouth dropped open. He put down a plank he was loading and came over to the fence. "You been to St. Louie?"

"Sure as fish suck water. Went down there with none other than Alton T. Monroe, the new lieutenant governor of our sovereign state." Grover smiled a wide I-told-you-so smile that seemed to divide his face into two unequal sections. He was a thin, lanky man, a decade younger than Aaron and as different from him as sod from mud. Yet they had been friends for ten years and there was a genuine affection between them. Grover often left Cordelia to work in other towns for a while, but he always came back, and Aaron was always happy to see his lanky, slightly stooped, redheaded friend return. Especially today, when he himself was not in the best of dispositions and in need of something to brighten his morning. He shook his head slowly as he admiringly inspected his friend's new finery.

"Well, you always promised to be somebody someday. Looks like you've sure enough done it. That is one slick waistcoat, Massa Grover, suh."

"Got one for you, too," Grover said, pulling a bundle out of the boot of the buggy.

Aaron frowned. "You what?"

"A waistcoat. For you. Just like mine. Straight from Mendel's Gentlemen's Haberdashery in St. Louie. I didn't know what size, so I told the tailor to make it fit a fifty-gallon barrel."

He tossed the bundle to Aaron. Flabbergasted, Aaron laid it on the nearest fence post and opened it. He held the coat up in front of him, mouth agape at the sight and touch of it. "It's elegant," he said quietly.

"It's *proper* is what it is," said Grover. "Proper attire for a man who's off to collect his patronage from Alton T. Monroe, the new lieutenant governor."

"What do you mean?"

"I mean it's settlement day, my fine friend. It's time for your reward!"

"Reward for what, Grove? Make sense, will you?"

Grover twisted the reins around the buggy's whip sleeve and leaped down off his seat. He leaned both elbows on the top fence rail and smiled another of his face-dividing smiles. "Don't you remember back in September and October of last year when you nailed up handbills all over the eastern counties for me?"

"I remember. You were helping some fellow up north run for office—" Aaron's eyes widened in sudden realization. "Is that this new lieutenant governor you're running on about?"

"The same. Elected not by a great plurality of votes, as they say up at the state house, but by a narrow margin. The skin of his teeth, you might call it. A very grateful man is Lieutenant Governor Alton T. Monroe to have that high office instead of being back in Iroquois starving to death in the practice of law."

"I still don't see what all this has to do with me."

"Then I'll tell you. The four counties that carried the election for Alton Monroe were Wabash, Lawrence, Clark, and Crawford."

Aaron frowned. "Those are the four you and I put all the handbills in—"

"Exactly! Four counties that nobody else wanted to work because they're practically over in Indiana!"

Aaron nodded and smiled. "I remember down in Wabash County, when old man Fleece sent me down there to rebuild a barn that had burned, I must have put a handbill on every other tree from Lancaster to Keensburg."

"You must have," Grover eagerly agreed, "because Wabash voted ninety percent for Monroe. *Ninety* percent, Aaron! They almost didn't believe it. No other county in the state came out that strong for a candidate. Any candidate. I tell you, Aaron, you're a hero to Lieutenant Governor Alton T. Monroe and his supporters. That's why I've come to take you to the capital. Mr. Monroe has a special job to give you as a reward for your efforts."

"What kind of job?"
"I can't discuss it with you," Grover said loftily. "It's official state business."
Aaron nodded knowingly. "You don't know," he concluded quickly. "If you did, the threat of hell wouldn't stop your telling me. Here, help me on with this coat—"
Grover reached across the fence and pulled the new coat up on Aaron's barrel-stave back. It was the largest size Mendel's of St. Louis made and still it fit the Van Hawn shoulders snugly. With Aaron's rough work clothes, boots, and prairie hat, the fine new gray broadcloth coat looked grossly incongruous. But Aaron felt like a grand gentleman, one of those plantation lords such as he had seen while traveling the Virginias and the Ohio Valley many years earlier when his parents had come west from Carolina where the ship from Holland had landed them.
"How does it look?" he asked his friend almost urgently.
"Like you stole it."
"Be serious, will you, please?"
"Ah, you look like you belong on the streets of St. Louie, Aaron. Truly. Now stop preening and come along. The lieutenant governor is expecting you day after tomorrow. Are you still boarding at the Widow McGill's?"
"Yes."
"We'll just stop long enough to get your belongings. Do you want to say goodbye to old Fleece?"
"I wouldn't waste the words," Aaron said bitterly. He rolled the coat back up and handed the bundle to Grover. Climbing up on the fence, he stepped into the buggy next to his friend. Grover snapped the reins and the pair of horses moved smartly away.
Half a mile down the road, they came on Fleece's nephew, bringing the biscuits and molasses back to his uncle. Grover drew up sharply in front of him. "Hold, there! Are you the nephew of Able Fleece?"
"Why—yes, I—am—" the youth replied.
Grover drew out an official-looking document and flashed it briefly. "I am a representative of the state attorney general. I have just arrested this man for the ax murder of your uncle. I happened by just seconds after he had beheaded the poor man. I want you to run at once and remain with your aunt until the con-

stable arrives. Under no circumstances tell her of the tragedy, is that clear?"

"Yes—yes, sir—"

"What's that you're carrying?"

"B-b-biscuits and molasses, sir—"

"Give it here. It'll only slow you down when you're running to be with your aunt." Grover held out his hand. "Quickly!"

"Yes—yes, sir—" The nephew handed over the burlap parcel.

"Now be off!"

The youth dashed away toward the late Able Fleece's house. Grover snapped the reins again and the horses stepped away. He handed the parcel to Aaron.

"Dip me a biscuit, Aaron, old friend, before the molasses gets cold."

Aaron laughed and began unwrapping the parcel.

When Aaron stepped off the keelboat in Chester, he was met by Mr. Brin, the county sheriff. "Welcome, Mr. Van Hawn. You're right on schedule, sir. The lieutenant governor's dispatch said you'd be here today. Frankly, I'd have thought the Big Muddy there would have delayed you somewhere along the way."

Aaron jutted his chin out a bit and glanced back at the wide river. "I brook no delay in my duties, Mr. Brin. Not even from the Mississippi."

Brin laughed and took Aaron's hand in a hearty shake. "Good for you, sir!"

Aaron smiled, pleased with himself. He wished he had called the river "Big Muddy" like Brin had done; it made a man sound on familiar terms with it. But he would remember that next time. "These are the prisoners, I see," Aaron said, looking across the pier at two shackled men, one white, one Indian.

"That they be, sir. The white man is Darby, sentenced to twenty-one years for manslaughter. The savage is called Kee-te-ha. He's Sac-and-Fox. Five years for maiming."

"Maiming?"

Brin nodded. "Caught his squaw hunkering with a white man. Couldn't do anything to the white man without being hanged for it, so he took it out on the woman. Cut off all her toes. The white man, he turned around and said the squaw was his wife.

Claimed a circuit preacher had secretly married them. So they charged Kee-te-ha with maiming her."

Aaron nodded. He looked over at Tillman and two guards, who waited at the gangplank. "Take them aboard, Mr. Tillman." Then to Brin he said, "Where might I find Leon Triplett, the stonemason?"

"In the cemetery," said Brin.

"Pardon?"

"He died last week. Sudden. Came down with a fever one afternoon, died of it the next. Might I ask if your business with him was private?"

"No. I mean, it wasn't private. The lieutenant governor recommended him to oversee the masonry of the new prison and wall. It was a very strong recommendation. I got the impression that an arrangement had already been reached between them. I was to pick up Mr. Triplett here and continue down to the site." Aaron paced the pier a few steps, his expression a thoughtful frown. He pulled on his lower lip as he considered the situation. "Is there another stonemason in town?" he asked.

Brin shook his head. "Nearest one I've heard of is a man named Abner Foyle downriver in Bristol. Can't even say for certain that he's still there."

"Is Bristol between here and Union County?"

"It is. Near about midways, I'd say. But, mark me, I'm not saying for certain that Foyle is still there. If you want to be *certain* of finding a stonemason, you'd best turn back to East St. Louie."

Aaron shook his head. "That would take a week," he said. "My schedule won't allow for an extra week. An unscheduled stop at Bristol won't call for more than a day. I'll try Bristol." He turned to the keelboat and located his chief guard. "Mr. Tillman, stand ready to leave at once!" he ordered.

Aaron bade Mr. Brin goodbye and went back aboard. The boat, now with its full contingent of prisoners, was poled away from the Chester pier and into the downstream current again.

At the state capital, Lieutenant Governor Alton T. Monroe had greeted Aaron Van Hawn like an old comrade.

"Come in, come in, Mr. Van Hawn," he said expansively, welcoming Aaron and Grover into his newly acquired office. It was a stylish, masculine office, abundant with heavy, polished wood, ornate with brass and copper fittings, smelling faintly of leather and liquor. Monroe was a lean, handsome man near Aaron's age, but with a full head of hair and a much younger appearance. He turned to Grover with a practiced smile, saying, "So this is the friend you told me about, Grover. By god, he *is* built like a nail keg!"

Aaron, in the new waistcoat Grover had bought him, felt himself blush, and Monroe and Grover roared at his discomfort. Then the lieutenant governor came around his desk and put an arm as far around Aaron's shoulders as it would stretch, and said, "Don't take offense, Mr. Van Hawn. You'll find that we're a close-knit political family here and we only josh with those whom we respect and consider one of us. Although you and I have never met before, I am aware of the help you gave me during my campaign, and I want you to know that I consider it help of great value. Great value, indeed. I want you to consider yourself a close friend of this administration, and I hope you'll be a close friend of mine, as well."

"I will, yes, sir," Aaron stammered. "Thank you very much, sir. It's, ah—it's a privilege, sir."

"It's *my* privilege, sir," Monroe assured him. "I think brandy and cigars are in order."

Monroe poured brandy for the three of them and proffered an ornate cigar box across the desk. Aaron accepted both the brandy and the cigar. Following Grover's example, he took a sip of the brandy and lighted the cigar. It was his first experience with either.

When Aaron and Grover were seated facing his desk, Alton Monroe described the patronage he had planned for Aaron. "As I'm sure both of you are aware," he said, "our state is moving very rapidly into a period of vast population expansion. It will be the policy of this administration to encourage the continuation of that expansion. We are already drawing up plans for state-subsidized land purchases which we hope will attract families from Kentucky and Tennessee, perhaps even farther east than that. Frankly, we aren't looking for settler types. Let the scrubby people go on across the river and squat somewhere out on the plains. We want good, solid, upstanding, God-fearing farm families; people who have shown in Kentucky and Tennessee that they can make a living from good, healthy soil. And we want successful merchants and storekeepers who already have sizable stocks of wares and would be willing, for a subsidy of either dollars or land, to pack up and move their enterprises here. Just between the three of us, gentlemen, the governor is already looking at a cadre of carefully selected men who will be sent to certain areas as his personal representatives to solicit new citizens for our state. Grover, I might as well tell you that you will be one of those selected."

Grover beamed. Aaron looked at his friend in awe. This business of politics was much bigger than he had suspected. He took a puff of his fine cigar, managing to suppress a cough that rose in its wake.

Alton Monroe stood and raised his glass. "A toast, gentlemen, to the success of a great state expansion plan."

Aaron and Grover stood and drank. The brandy burned pleasantly in Aaron's throat. When he sat back down, he carefully adjusted the lapels of his fine new coat, crossed his knickered, stockinged legs, and puffed on his cigar. He felt very fine indeed.

"The problem with a major expansion effort of this scope, as I'm sure you both realize," Monroe continued, "is that it is impossible to attract *only* the types of people we all desire. With the good will come the bad. The drunkard, the lout, the petty thief, the whoremonger—that sort. Our law enforcement and judicial systems will be improved to a level of adequacy that will enable them to deal with an influx of undesirable newcomers; but we are faced with the problem of having no state penal system in which to incarcerate offenders for lengthy periods. At the present time, convicted felons are being kept in county jails throughout the state. As their number increases, this practice is becoming both too risky and too expensive. Risky because so many of them are managing to escape; expensive because the state has to pay the individual counties for their room and board following conviction. What we obviously need is a central prison in which all felons can be kept under the jurisdiction of the state. Do you agree?"

"Definitely," Grover said at once, raising his glass and drinking.

"Yes, sir," said Aaron, doing the same. The brandy still tasted good to him, but something seemed to have happened to the flavor of the cigar. He decided to puff on it only when the lieutenant governor kept his eyes on him for an extended time.

"Now then," Monroe said, "the state legislature established our first formal prison bill in its last session, but nothing was ever done about it. Of course, the governor and I were not in office at the time; if we had been, I assure you that the program would already be well advanced, instead of in its present dormant state. Since we intend to move ahead very rapidly with our expansion plan, however, we have decided that we must also give priority to the establishment of a state prison system. That's where you come in, Aaron. Your friend Grover tells me that you're an experienced building contractor."

Aaron glanced at Grover. "Ah, well, yes, sir, I have done some building. Mostly farming structures: barns, silos, and that sort."

"If you can build a barn, Aaron, you can build a prison," Monroe said confidently. He rose, came around the desk, and poured more brandy into Aaron's glass. As he did so, the smoke from his cigar trailed into Aaron's nostrils. Aaron looked at his own cigar. He felt the first inkling of nausea. "Do you know where Union County is?" Monroe asked.

Aaron swallowed, trying to force back the nausea. "Ah, down in the southern part of the state, isn't it?"

"Yes." Monroe unrolled a large canvas and hung it on a map rack mounted on the wall behind his desk. It was a colorfully painted map of the state, showing each county in bright yellow, the open woods and prairies in green, the few Indian reservations in red, and the winding, twisting Mississippi in blue. "Union County is down here," Monroe said, pointing at one of the southern river counties with his cigar. "One of this administration's most valued supporters—a northern tannery owner who is a very close friend of the governor's—has generously donated to the state a parcel of ten acres situated on a bluff about a mile in from the river in Union County. I haven't seen the land myself, but I am told that it has good water, an abundance of wood, and unlimited deposits of rock and clay. In short, it sounds like an ideal site for the building of a prison. What do you think, Aaron?"

"Yes, sir, it does sound ideal," Aaron said. He nodded his head, then immediately regretted it because it made him dizzy. Very carefully he placed his cigar on a copper ashplate on the lieutenant governor's desk. The taste of the awful thing was reeking in his mouth like swamp vapors. He took another sip of brandy in an effort to wash it away. The tactic did not work. The cigar smoke and brandy joined forces to destroy him from within. Suddenly Monroe was standing in front of him again, thrusting a paper at him.

"This is a diagram of a prison back in New England. It's operated by the Quakers. They call it a penitentiary. Its purpose, according to their philosophy, is that men sent there are to be penitent. They keep them in cells all the time, give them nothing to do, allow them no visitors, and in short force them to reflect on their individual offenses in solitude for years on end. Some of them, I'm told, lose their minds. Our philosophy of penal servitude is going to be somewhat different. We intend to work our felons. Labor cleanses the soul—at least, that's what General Andrew Jackson told the Jeffersonian Democratic party recently—and they believed him enough to nominate him for the presidency. So, as I said, Aaron, we'll use this Quaker diagram as a pattern to *build* the prison. How we run it will be something else."

As Monroe returned to the big map, Aaron set down the brandy glass and rested his head back. His eyes rolled like loose marbles. Grover, noticing for the first time that his friend was ill, looked at Aaron in alarm. He started to rise to come to his aid, but Aaron quickly waved him off and sat bolt upright just as Monroe turned back to them.

"I have been in contact with the federal government and it has agreed to provide the United States Army Corps of Engineers to construct a road from the river's edge up to the bluff where the ten acres lie. We have inquired around the state and learned that there are currently thirty felons in custody in various county jails. We are arranging to have them brought to the river towns of—" he began pointing them out on the map, "—Moline, Rock Island, Burlington, Quincy, Hannibal, Alton, and Chester. A new pine keelboat is being built right now up here, in Galena," he indicated a village in the northernmost part of the state. "The governor is assigning six men from the state militia as prisoner guards. The state quartermaster will issue them new Whitney percussion rifles, manufactured by the same man who invented the cotton gin; fine weapons—I have one myself. They will also be issued forty-one-caliber derringer pistols and other equipment and supplies from the quartermaster stores. The plan is to have the men board the keelboat in Galena and sail it all the way downriver to Union County, stopping at the towns I mentioned to take custody of prisoners. And stopping in East St. Louis to take on stores. Then, on arrival in Union County, they'll set up a work camp and use the convicts themselves to erect our first state prison." Monroe came over and stood in front of Aaron's chair. "The governor and I would like you to take charge of this project for us, Aaron. Will you do it?"

Aaron was certain he was only milliseconds away from vomiting on the lieutenant governor's highly polished boots. Out of the corner of his eye, he saw Grover watching him nervously. He managed to nod soberly in acceptance of the position.

"Splendid!" Alton Monroe beamed. He gripped Aaron's hand and began shaking it. "I'll have your appointment drawn up at once. I have a feeling that this is the beginning of a long and distinguished civil service career for you, Aaron."

Or the shortest one on record if you don't stop pumping my hand, Aaron thought. "Thank you, sir, I hope so," he managed to say.

Grover, sensing that Aaron's internal crisis was coming to a head, quickly stepped in to rescue him. "Sir, would you like me to take Aaron over to the quartermaster's office now to make arrangements for his supplies? We can do that while his appointment is being drawn up."

"Splendid idea," said Monroe. The words were like music to Aaron's ears.

Grover and Aaron bade temporary farewells to the lieutenant governor and departed his office. They hurried down the corridor of the state house.

"You damn fool," Grover said. "What was it, the cigar or the brandy?"

Aaron blanched. "Both."

"Oh, lord." They moved faster.

At the first exterior door they came to, Grover hustled Aaron outside and behind a convenient hedge. Aaron regurgitated while Grover self-consciously stood guard.

"Hold—that—" Aaron choked out the words during a pause in the process, and hastily thrust his new coat into his friend's hands.

After several long moments, a pale but obviously relieved Aaron Van Hawn emerged. "The coat," he asked anxiously. "Is it soiled?"

"I don't think so."

"Let me see." Aaron carefully examined the new waistcoat. It was unspotted. With a sigh of relief, he put it back on.

Grover patted his own perspiring brow with a handkerchief. "A damn fool," he muttered again.

"Watch your mouth, lad," Aaron said loftily. "You happen to be referring to an *appointee* of the governor. A little more respect, if you please."

"I'll give you respect," Grover said. He raised one foot to boot his friend in the rear, but Aaron anticipated his move and stepped quickly away. He moved through the hedge to the broad lawn. Grover gave chase. They began laughing.

Across the carefully manicured lawn of the capitol building, the two men ran and frolicked like two young boys.

CHAPTER 9

Bristol was a ramshackle river town that had seen better days. As Aaron walked down the single short length of dirt street that served as its main thoroughfare, he noted that the Paree Bakery Shoppe was boarded up, the McCoy Sign Works closed, and the vacant Emporium Barber Parlor stripped of its furnishings. Several other establishments still had wide window shades down and front doors closed as if they did not expect any business, even though it was nearly noon of a weekday.

A few town loafers whispered about Aaron and pointed him out as he lumbered down the dusty street, but he paid them no mind. They all knew who he was, or at least *what* he was: captain of a government keelboat the deck of which held thirty chained convicts. In a normally healthy town the arrival of such a vessel would have generated a great deal of excitement and the main street would have been alive with folks hurrying down to the riverbanks and levees to stare curiously at the prisoners. But in this strange, ill place called Bristol, the best Aaron had seen was half a dozen loiterers and a few young boys who wandered down to the dock, lingered awhile, and wandered off again. From one of the boys Aaron had learned that Abner Foyle, the stonemason, lived in a cabin at the opposite end of the town's main street. Leaving the boat to Mr. Tillman, he had jutted his chin out and strode through the lethargic little town.

The Foyle cabin occupied a weed-overgrown patch of ground

next to a six-foot-high pile of white rock dug from the ground. Standing nearby was a wagon with a reinforced frame and bed which was used to haul the rock to the stonemason's job. The cabin itself was old, weathered oak, bleached almost white by age and element; it had a pitched roof that invariably meant one or two loft sleeping rooms. That was good, Aaron thought as he approached the patch. Extra sleeping rooms probably meant a large family. The larger the family, the more apt Abner Foyle would be to take the job Aaron had to offer. Aaron was desperate to hire Foyle; it was the only way to keep from going the entire distance back to East St. Louis for a man.

The cabin door was open when Aaron stepped up on the porch. Inside, he could see a short, bent woman and a taller, straighter woman, both at a black iron cookstove handling heavy black iron pots. Aaron removed his hat and knocked on the doorframe.

"What be ye wantin'?" asked a gravelly voice behind him.

Aaron turned, startled, to see a gnomelike little man who apparently had come around the side of the cabin just as Aaron stepped on the porch. Aaron glanced in at the women. They had turned to look at him. The bent one was old, the straight one very young, a girl really. Aaron turned to the gnome.

"I'm looking for Mr. Abner Foyle, the stonemason."

"That be me," the little man said. Shorter even than Aaron, he had a slightly deformed right shoulder from years of carrying heavy stones and slabs of mortar. A white stubble of bread covered the lower part of his face, and out of each ear grew an odd tuft of white hair. Aaron stared curiously at the ear hair until Foyle again said, "What be ye wantin'?"

"I'm a representative of the state, Mr. Foyle. Name of Aaron Van Hawn. I'm an appointee of the governor, to hire a stonemason to oversee the masonry work in the building of a state prison and wall down in Union County. I'm here to ask you if you'd accept the job."

"Can't," Foyle replied. "Gettin' ready to light out of here on next week's barge. Headin' west. Manhattan, Kansas."

Aaron's bull shoulders sagged. "May I ask why you're leaving?"

"You walked through town, didn't you? Ever seen a deader

place in your life? This here town don't need a stonesmason no more. Needs a good undertaker."

Aaron shrugged. "Well, why move all the way to Kansas? Why not just move to another town back here?"

"Reckon that's my business," the old man said. He stepped past Aaron into the cabin. "Care to buy your dinner here? My old woman serves up some good eats."

Aaron nodded and followed him inside. They sat at a rough-hewn oak table that looked as if it had been made of lumber left over from the raising of the cabin. The bent old woman dished the food from pot to plate, and the straight girl served it. Aaron paid little attention to either.

"Mr. Foyle, I don't aim to meddle in your business," Aaron said, as the girl put a plate of repulsive-looking stew before him, "but I can tell you for truth that this state and this area are going to be growing to beat all pretty soon. The governor has plans to make it—"

"Governor, shit!" said Foyle. "I don't live according to no goddamn governor and his plans. Christ almighty, if I did that, I'd starve and waste away! Eat your stew."

Aaron looked distastefully at the dark brown mess that seemed to be curdling in front of his eyes. "This job down in Union County would guarantee you work for six months, Mr. Foyle," he argued.

"I'll have guaranteed work for two years in Manhattan, Kansas," the old man countered. "Army's going to build a cavalry post there." He jabbed his spoon at Aaron. "Eat your stew."

Aaron glanced up. The woman and the girl were watching him intently. He looked at Abner Foyle, wolfing down the muddy-looking mixture with its peculiar, unidentifiable lumps. It would be an insult not to eat it, he knew. And if there was even a remote chance that he could talk Foyle into taking the prison-building job, he did not want to destroy that chance with a personal slight. Steeling himself, he shoveled a heaping spoonful of the slop into his mouth.

As the taste of the stew reached his buds, Aaron's eyes widened in surprise. It was good. He swallowed and quickly took another bite. It was really *very* good. The surprise he felt was obvious. He looked at the two women watching him and smiled sheepishly. Not a word was spoken, but for a moment everyone

in the room seemed to know what everyone else was thinking.
Old Abner Foyle studied Aaron thoughtfully, craftily. Not once did he pause in his perpetual-motion eating, but throughout it all his eyes were narrowed and he was concentrating almost intently on his guest across the table. The two of them ate in silence, cleaning their plates as best they could with the crude frontier spoons, then resorting to biscuit halves to sop up what remained.

When the last bite was in his mouth, Foyle rose from the table and fetched a whiskey jug from a nearby shelf. On his way back to the table, he tossed a barely perceptible nod to the bent old woman. She immediately took the girl by the arm and led her out of the cabin. Foyle sat down and poured a double finger of whiskey into the copper cups out of which he and Aaron had drunk their coffee. Aaron winced slightly at the smell of the liquor; the lieutenant governor's brandy was still fresh in his mind. But again, he refrained from speaking lest he inadvertently offend the old man.

"That was good food," he said to Foyle. "Your missus and your daughter are good cooks."

"The girl ain't my daughter," said Foyle. "She's my niece. Orphaned eight years ago, thanks to the goddamned Sac-and-Fox savages. Her paw was my brother. I took her in."

"That was right generous."

Foyle shrugged. "She's kin." He took a sip of his whiskey. "Glad you liked the dinner. Though I'd venture a man as healthy appearing as you must be well-fed by your own wife."

"I don't have a wife," said Aaron.

"Don't you now." Foyle's eyes narrowed just a fraction again. A slight bulge appeared in one cheek where he was rolling his tongue around inside his mouth. "You know, Mr. Van Hawn, I'd admire to help you with that job of building you've got to do, if only I hadn't already promised a friend of mine out in Kansas. He's offered me a right smart wage to take some of the work off his hands, and I'm not ashamed to admit that I need the money. What with my wife and this orphaned niece of mine. 'Course I have my boy Vester, who's a stonemason like myself—"

"You have a son who's a stonemason?" Aaron asked with unconcealed interest.

"That I do. Fine craftsman, too. As good as me; 'course, it was me taught him. And strong: shoulders like you yourself, and another foot of height. He's a great help to me now that I'm in my declining years and still have my orphaned niece to support. Why, if it wasn't for my obligation to her, I'd be willing to go on out to Kansas alone and let my boy Vester stay behind for as long as it took to build your prison. But I'm just afraid that with my health failing a little every day, why, I just wouldn't make it." He paused for another sip of whiskey, then added, "Not with the girl."

Before Aaron could comment, a big, thick young man tromped through the door in heavy boots. "I got the wood cut to make them moving boxes, Paw," he said amiably. He stopped when he saw Aaron.

"This here's Mr. Van Hawn," the old man said. "My boy Vester." He jerked his head toward the stove. "Get yourself a plate of mush. And tell me how much wood you cut and in what lengths."

"Well, I done two dozen four-foot poles—"

As the youth ladled out his stew and talked to his father, Aaron turned slightly where he sat and looked out the unshuttered window. The two women were at a cast-iron tub of water set up on bricks in the yard. The older woman was putting soiled clothes into the tub and submerging them with a stick. The girl was down on her knees, bent far forward, working a flint-rock to start a fire between the bricks. As she leaned forward, her hips and buttocks spread out tautly under the long cotton dress she wore.

Aaron studied the girl as she got the fire going and stood up again, brushing herself off. She was quite tall, he noted; probably taller than he was. Her eyes were large and round, open wide as if she were in a constant state of surprise. She seemed to have mismatched lips, the lower one so much fuller than the upper that it protruded. Had it not been for the openness of her expression, the bottom lip would have made her look as if she were pouting. Her face was surrounded by auburn hair, long and tangled, as yet unbrushed that day. She was not pretty. And yet—Aaron frowned—and yet, she was not quite homely either.

Aaron turned back to the table, not quickly enough to catch Abner Foyle watching him closely. Vester had joined them now and was wolfing down a plate of his mother's stew. Aaron thoughtfully took a sip of whiskey. After a moment, he said to Abner, "How old is the girl?"

"Eighteen this past January," Foyle told him. "She was a winter baby. Them be the healthiest, you know."

"I've heard that."

"Vester here was a winter baby and look at the size of him." The old man shook his head. "Jesus, it's shameful there ain't no way for him to help you on that prison wall. Big as he is, and the way he works with stone, why, you'd have her built in no time at all."

Vester looked up from his feeding. "What prison wall is that, Paw?"

"Shut up," Abner told him.

"Yes, Paw." Vester resumed eating.

Aaron glanced out the window again. The fire under the tub was burning freely now and steam was rising from the water it held. While the bent old woman used a sheath-knife to shave chips from a cake of soap, the girl used the stick to agitate the clothes in the water. Her expression was wide-eyed and intent as she worked. A lock of hair had fallen over her forehead. As Aaron was watching, she used one sleeve to blot perspiration from her upper lip.

Aaron turned back to Foyle. "What's the girl's name?"

"Druscilla. Named after my own maw. That's one of the reasons she's so precious to me."

"I'm surprised you haven't given her in marriage already. She looks to be ready enough for it."

"The girl's a comfort to me in my declining years. Never had no daughters of my own. Just four boys. Vester here's the last one of them. I couldn't let the girl go to just anybody. My poor dead sister-in-law would haunt me from her grave if I did. A few lads from the village have come to call now and again, but they mostly backed off when they found out she didn't have no dowry—"

"No dowry?" said Aaron.

Foyle shook his head. "I told you she was an orphan girl. It's shameful, but that's the way it be. The man that gets her will have to take her with just the clothes on her back and what she can carry." The old man sighed a dramatic sigh. "I expect she'll end up an old maid. Ain't many men will set still for a woman without a dowry. Fellow like yourself, now, a man of position, responsibility, an *appointee* of the governor; why, sir, when you take a wife, I'd venture you'd certainly require something of value along with her." He looked over at his son. "Time for you to get back to work now, boy." Vester nodded, gulped down his remaining food, and strode obediently from the cabin. Foyle watched him go, then said to Aaron, "Strong as an ox, that boy. Works sixteen hours a day before he even *starts* getting tired. Real valuable worker, my Vester."

Aaron drummed his fingers on the bleached oak tabletop. He cleared his throat uncomfortably. "I, ah—I've thought from time to time about marriage myself, but somehow never did get around to it."

"The press of your official duties, I'd warrant," said Foyle. "It's been my experience that a lot of successful men don't get around to taking a wife until later in life. I reckon your position with the state has kept you well occupied over the years."

"I've kept busy, yes," Aaron said, glancing away with the lie. He pursed his lips for a moment, thinking about the past, the barns he'd raised, old man Fleece and his shiftless nephew, the labor he'd put forth and the little he had to show for it. He *had* to do well on this assignment that Alton Monroe had given him. He *had* to succeed.

And to succeed, he had to have a stonemason.

Aaron cleared his throat again. "My own thinking on the matter has always been that a woman's dowry was secondary to other considerations."

"Is that a fact?" said Abner Foyle with great interest. "What other considerations?"

"Well, ah—let me see—ah—"

"Good health?"

"Why yes—"

"Good cook and seamstress?"

"Yes, that's it—"

"Nice even disposition?"

"Yes."

"Virginity?"

"Yes. Certainly."

"The girl has all that, Mr. Van Hawn."

Aaron sat staring at the old man, his mouth agape, wondering if he had indirectly committed to anything. Contracts were made curiously on the middle frontier, and he had little experience with riverbank people. He decided he had best let the old man make the next move. He sat back and folded his hands in his lap. Foyle eyed him craftily, the slightest trace of a smile showing in the white stubble.

"By your leave, Mr. Van Hawn," he said, "I'll be blunt. You're the type of man I'd rest easy knowing my niece was wed to. You're mature and responsible, and your future appears to be secure. If you was willing to take the girl without a dowry, why, to make it up to you, I'd be willing to let Vester stay here and work on your prison and wall for, say, six months—"

"A year," said Aaron, leaning forward, calculating rapidly.

"Eight months," the old man countered.

"Ten."

"Done!" Abner Foyle slammed his palm down on the table like an auctioneer hammering the block. Aaron sat back, slightly surprised that the bargaining had started and ended so quickly. Foyle was already turning his head and shouting out the door. "Wella! 'Scilla! Get yourselves in here!"

The women hurried in, the old bent one first, then the girl. They stood side by side, respectfully, at the old man's chair.

"This is my old woman, name of Wella," said Foyle, "and this here is my niece, Druscilla." Aaron rose and bowed slightly to each, as he had seen men do at the capital, and as his friend Grover had practiced to do in their room one night. "This here gentleman is Mr. Aaron Van Hawn of the state government," Foyle completed the introductions. He rose also and clasped his hands behind his back, looking a touch off balance due to the slight deformity of his shoulder. "Mr. Van Hawn has asked for 'Scilla in marriage and I have agreed," he announced.

The girl bowed her head slightly and looked at the floor, saying nothing, but the old woman put one hand over a nearly toothless mouth and began to whimper. The whimpering turned to loud sobs; the sobs to agonized moans, the sound of which immediately filled the cabin. Aaron winced and backed off a step. He wondered if the old woman's mind had snapped. He glanced anxiously at the door, thinking of flight, but old man Foyle was at his side in an instant.

"Pay her no mind," he whispered. "She gets like this when the family makes changes. I'll just give her a minute." He stepped over to a mantel and turned over an hourglass. Fine sand began to run out of the top into the bottom.

Aaron stood uneasily across the table from Wella Foyle as she moaned and groaned and shrieked as if her husband had just sold her into bondage. She made little clutching, groping motions at Druscilla's sleeve. The girl remained very still, eyes downcast, hands clasped in front of her. After several moments, the old woman's loud agonizing began to subside. Tears streaked each of her cheeks and she began crying in a more normal manner.

"My pore little orphan girl," she lamented. "My pore, pore little motherless baby! Getting turned out into the world again with naught but a stranger to care for her! Oh, my pore, pore little angel child—"

Aaron was certain that the girl would break into tears and begin her own lament at any moment, but to his surprise she remained outwardly calm and collected. He immediately admired her for it. As she stood there with head bent, he noticed that she had unusually wide, square shoulders for a woman. Her tall, angular frame was fragile looking, but Aaron optimistically thought that she was probably much stronger than she appeared. He fervently hoped that her health, as Foyle had boasted, was good. He had far too much responsibility facing him to have to worry about a sickly woman.

When Abner Foyle decided that his wife had been allowed enough crying time, he turned the hourglass back over and said, "All right, woman, that'll do." To Aaron's astonishment, the old woman sniffed back her crying and immediately began to dry her eyes. Abner Foyle sat back down at the table. "Come here, girl," he said to Druscilla. She came to him at once and stood before him in her same stance: eyes downcast, hands clasped. Except that now she was looking directly at the old man because he was seated. He reached out and put his hand on hers. "You're my own brother's child," he said quietly, "and no matter what else I do, I'd never see you married no less than good. I ain't the smartest man in the world, nor the most honest, but one thing I can do and that's judge men. This here man I'm giving you to is a good man if ever I seed one. He'll make you a proper husband and treat you well. That's all I have to say. Now you and your Aunt Wella use the rest of the day to make ready. You'll be married come seven o'clock this evening."

"Yes, Uncle Ab," she said. She glanced up at Aaron; he smiled the barest of smiles and she looked quickly away. Turning, she took the old woman's arm and they quickly climbed the stair-ladder to the sleeping loft.

Foyle turned to Aaron. "Seven o'clock tonight, Mr. Van Hawn. Bring one witness from your boat. I'll have the preacher here."

Aaron and the old man shook hands.

Just before seven that evening Aaron was on his way back to the cabin, walking with Mr. Tillman through the depressing little town of Bristol. He was wearing the new waistcoat Grover had given him, and wishing that his friend could be there with him on his wedding night. Even though it was a contract marriage, Aaron could not help feeling that it had some meaning, some significance. He was forty years old and up until recently his life had been an almost unbroken sequence of days and months and years filled with much labor and little reward. Now, in the space of scarcely a month, his entire existence had changed. He had met the lieutenant governor, received an appointment from the governor, was in charge of six guards, thirty convicts, and a keelboat—and now was about to take a wife. Plus which, people called him mister.

Walking next to him, Tillman cleared his throat. "If you'd like me to, sir," he suggested, "I can move the prisoners ashore tonight and have them sleep up the landing a ways."

Aaron frowned. "Why would you do that, Mr. Tillman?"

"I was thinking maybe you and your missus would be using the boat cabin tonight. Your missus might feel more at ease if the aft deck didn't have thirty men lying there listening."

Aaron felt himself blush slightly. "I see. Yes, you're right. But I wouldn't want to chance losing any of the prisoners."

"I'll put 'em on a tether chain and lock it to a piling. And keep a double guard on watch."

Aaron pursed his lips and considered it. Finally he agreed.

"Very good, Mr. Tillman. A good suggestion. My thanks."
Aaron glanced several times at his chief guard as they continued through town. He was just beginning to appreciate Tillman. Not only was the man orderly and efficient in his duties, but he seemed genuinely eager to help in other ways. He had taught Aaron the practice of cordelling without being smug or lofty about it, and now he was thinking about making Aaron and his bride more comfortable on their wedding night. Aaron was starting to like the man. He was glad Tillman was going to be with him throughout the building of the prison.
"You married, Mr. Tillman?" he asked.
"No, sir. Not 'less you count this uniform as being married."
Aaron nodded. It did not surprise him that Tillman was unmarried. Militia men usually did not stay in one place long enough to court a fiancée. Plus which Tillman, at thirty, was not a handsome man; far from it. He had unnaturally prominent front teeth that pushed his lip out almost to the point of disfigurement; and a broad, flat forehead that made him look Mongoloid. He could probably have found a wife if he had been a storekeeper or farmer and stayed in one place long enough for a woman to get used to him. But moving around in the state militia, his chances were greatly reduced.
"How long have you been a militiaman?" Aaron asked.
"Since I was fifteen. I went in as a cook's boy."
"You must like it then, to have stayed in as long as you have."
"Yes, sir, I do."
"Well, you do a good job, Tillman," Aaron said. "I'm glad to have you with me."
"Thank you, Mr. Van Hawn," the chief guard said, swelling a bit. "Thank you very much."
They reached the cabin and were met by Abner Foyle, his son Vester, and a black-coated man introduced to them as the Reverend Lamper. He was a tall man, almost equal to Vester's height, but much thinner. His teeth were stained yellow and Aaron detected whiskey on his breath.
"I'm obliged to request that we get on with the ceremony," the preacher announced as soon as Aaron and Tillman were inside. "I have to pray over a funeral in the morning in Portertown. Have to ride all night to get there. Very little rest for a man of

God in this raw country. If you'll call the women out, Brother Abner—"

Druscilla and her aunt were summoned from the loft. As Druscilla backed down the stair-ladder, Aaron noticed Reverend Lamper's eyes fixed steadily on her backside. As soon as she was down, the preacher stepped quickly over to her and took one of her hands. He kissed the back of it. "You're a lovely bride, my dear. Lovely. Step over here, please—"

Druscilla drew back from him slightly, and turned her face away when his whiskey breath reached her, but she allowed him to guide her to a place in front of the hearth, and stood where he told her to. Her glance met Aaron's in passing, but she quickly lowered her eyes. Aaron, however, did not look away. Since everyone else was also looking at the bride, he took the opportunity to study her again. She was dressed now in an obviously old but nevertheless becoming off-white dress that had once been gray and had been bleached and rebleached until it was as close to white as it would ever be. The dress was too short for her by four inches, and it stretched snugly across her wide shoulders and angular hips. It also fit rather closely in front, and for the first time Aaron saw that his bride-to-be had a bosom of sorts. And he was not the only one who saw it; the good reverend was flicking his glance to Druscilla's breasts every chance he got. Aaron suddenly had a picture of the preacher lying in chains on the deck of the keelboat.

"Now the groom," the preacher said. He smiled a yellow smile at Druscilla. "The very fortunate groom—"

Druscilla blushed a deep red and her oddly mismatched lips seemed to tighten a bit. Aaron stepped up beside her, looking straight ahead. He tried to stretch his spine an inch to make himself taller. He became aware at once how rich his new waistcoat looked next to the poor, substitute white of Druscilla's dress. Perhaps, he thought, he should not have worn it. But he could not deny being glad that he had. It was his *wedding*, by God, and he *liked* being the finest-dressed man in the room. Besides, he was reasonably certain that Druscilla would want it that way too. Women, he understood, liked for their men to look fine.

"Gather 'round now, folks," the preacher urged. "It's a long ride to Portertown. Gather 'round." When everyone was in place, he began the ceremony. "We are congregated here this evening to join in holy wedlock this man Aaron and this woman Druscilla. Be there anyone here who objects to this union?" A great hollow sigh escaped from the breast of Wella Foyle. Abner Foyle threw her a warning look and she quickly lowered her eyes and was quiet. The preacher continued. "Aaron Van Fawn," he said, mispronouncing Aaron's surname, "do you take this woman Druscilla as your wedded wife, to protect and keep, now and always? Answer, 'I do so take.'"

"I do so take," Aaron replied.

"Druscilla Foyle," he said, looking at her breasts, "do you take this man Aaron as your wedded husband, to honor and obey, now and always? Answer, 'I do so take.'"

"I do so take," the bride said, eyes downcast. For an instant, she felt Aaron's elbow brush her own. She trembled. A tear welled up in each eye but she managed to hold them back. Suddenly she felt awful inside. There was something terribly wrong with all this. It did not match her dreams at all. She had an almost overpowering urge to flee. Then she became aware that the preacher was speaking again.

"By the authority vested in me by the Church of Jehovah, I say that you, Aaron, and you, Druscilla, are now husband and wife, and decree that so you shall stay until our lord god Jehovah does part you. Amen. Brother Vester, will you saddle my horse, please. Young woman," he took Druscilla's hand and kissed it again, "my congratulations." Leaning close to her, his whiskey breath assaulting her again, he whispered, "Hold nothing back from your husband on your wedding night, girl. Give him all. All!" His leer changed to a sober smile as he turned to Aaron and shook his hand. "Happiness, brother. Health and happiness. Many children." From his coat pocket he removed a tattered, leather-covered book the size of a man's billfold. "Write your names in here while I bid Mr. Foyle goodbye," he instructed, giving the book to Druscilla so that he could touch her hand again.

The preacher walked away, leaving them alone together for the first time. Druscilla lowered his eyes and stepped over to a shelf where there was an ink reservoir with a quill-tip. Aaron followed her. She took the quill, dipped it in the well, and deftly wrote her name on an open page of the preacher's book. Aaron stared at her in wonder. *She could write!*

Druscilla, meeting his eyes directly for the first time, held out the quill and book to Aaron. He took the book but ignored the quill. Studying her signature, he nodded in approval. "You have a fine hand," he said.

"Thank you." She felt herself blush again, but only slightly this time. He had spoken so *quietly* to her, not sharply as some men addressed their wives in public.

Aaron gave the book back to her. "Do my name too," he said, "so they'll both be in your fine hand."

Now she blushed her mortified blush. "I'm sorry, sir, but I—I don't remember your name. Please forgive me."

Aaron saw that she was embarrassed almost to tears. He quickly took out his governor's commission and unfolded it for her. "Here, this is my name here. This is what it looks like, see here. You can copy it from this."

She gave him a grateful half-smile and took the commission. Aaron watched as she carefully copied his name in her own practiced script. He thought of the log back in his cabin on the boat. Wouldn't it look *splendid* done in her fine hand. Standing next to her, he felt a slight rush of affection for this girl-woman whom he hardly knew. His wife, he thought. She was now his *wife*. He could scarcely believe it.

In a moment she turned to him with the book. He stared at her at first, not understanding what she wanted. Then he realized that she was showing him what she had written, for his approval. He took the book and studied it thoughtfully. Then he smiled.

"Very nice, very nice indeed. I may just let you do all the writing for us."

Druscilla Foyle Van Hawn smiled her first full, personal smile for him. In spite of her larger bottom lip, it was to Aaron a delightful smile, and he returned it in kind.

As they stood there smiling at each other, Druscilla's expression suddenly changed to one of apprehension. Aaron frowned, then glanced over his shoulder where she was looking. He saw the Reverend Lamper coming back over to them, yellow teeth exposed in a lecherous smile. His jaw tightened slightly and he patted Druscilla's arm.

"That's done with, my girl," he said reassuringly. "You've a husband to look after you now."

Squaring his tree-trunk shoulders, Aaron stepped in front of his new wife to protect her from the approaching offender. As he did so, he became the tallest man in the cabin.

Later that night—after the Reverend Lamper had departed; after everyone else had partaken of Wella Foyle's wedding supper for her niece; after Mr. Tillman had excused himself early to move the prisoners ashore; and after Druscilla had bade a tearful goodbye to her aunt—Aaron and his bride left the cabin and walked through town toward the river. Druscilla had two bundles to take with her: one of clothes, wrapped in a threadbare greatcoat; the other of a few meager personal possessions saved from the massacre of her family and burning of their home eight years earlier. The latter were wrapped in a fur pelt Vester had made from the hides of all the rabbits the Foyle family had eaten the previous winter. He had given it to Druscilla as a wedding present.

Aaron had noticed a genuine affection between Dru and her big, good-natured cousin. It did not surprise him, since they had practically been raised as brother and sister. At one point during the evening, Vester had caught Aaron alone and said, "I'm sure glad 'Scilla married a fine man like you, Mr. Van Hawn. She's a right good girl and she deserves a good husband. I sure do hope y'all will be happy."

Aaron had been genuinely touched. He sighed now as he and Dru walked along Bristol's main street, Aaron carrying the larger of her bundles. It was an uncommonly bright night, with a brilliant silver moon dominating a cloudless sky of absolute black. There was no one about on the street. A light breeze rustled some nearby beech branches. A dog whined somewhere in the darkness. As Aaron and Druscilla walked along, their shoulders occasionally brushed. When it happened, they parted quickly. Halfway to the river, Aaron decided to try and make conversation. He cleared his throat.

"I noticed that your uncle and Vester call you 'Scilla. Is that how everyone calls you?"

"Mostly," she answered quietly. "A long time ago, my daddy called me Dru. But he was the only one ever did."

"Did you like being called Dru?"

"Kind of."

They walked along in silence for a few paces, then Aaron asked, "Would you take offense to my calling you Dru?"

"Not if you'd like to," she replied quietly.

"Dru it will be then." He glanced sideways at her in the moonlight, wishing all their problems were as easily solved. Ahead of them, down the riverbank incline, the silhouette of the keelboat loomed. Aaron swallowed dryly.

"Do you have anything you like to be called?" Dru asked.

"Me? No. Just Aaron is fine. I've never been called anything else."

"Aaron it will be then," she said, in the manner of his own speech.

They started down the incline. Aaron cleared his throat again. "I'm, ah—I'm sorry that you found the preacher so offensive."

"It wasn't your fault. Uncle Ab got him."

"I meant I'm sorry that everything wasn't more to your liking, it being your wedding and all. It should have been something that would give you a pleasant recollection."

"It's past," she told him. "I don't mind."

They reached the dock and crossed it to the pier where the keelboat and its flatboat of supplies were made fast. A guard walked a lonely patrol around the perimeter of the flatboat. Down the dock, Aaron could make out the still forms of the prisoners, and of two guards watching over them. At the gangplank of the keelboat, Tillman waited for them.

"Ma'am," he said, bowing slightly to Dru. Then he addressed Aaron. "The boat is unoccupied, Mr. Van Hawn," he reported. "I took the liberty of having fresh water put on board for you. And I secured some good winter apples and cheese from our stores, in case you'd like a bite to eat."

Aaron nodded, pleased even more with the chief guard. He decided to start thinking about what was proper in the way of a reward. For the present, he merely said, "Very good, Mr. Tillman. Very good indeed."

He escorted Dru aboard and across the deck to the solitary cabin. Opening the door, he saw that Tillman had been good enough to light the kerosene lamp for him. Its light made the plain little cabin seem cozy and inviting. The apples and cheese were in a small Indian basket on Aaron's trunk next to the bed. Dru picked up the basket and examined it.

"How pretty," she said. "It's a Winnebago. I can tell by the markings."

Aaron looked at it and nodded. "Yes, you're right." Actually, he did not know Winnebago markings from any other. Such things had never held an interest for him.

Dru put her pelt-wrapped bundle in a corner and stood looking around the cabin. Besides the trunk, it contained only a washstand holding a milk-glass bowl and pitcher, a large water keg, and a bed—a very narrow bed.

"There's not much furniture," Aaron said self-consciously. "I'll have some built."

Dru said nothing. She removed her cape and hung it on a convenient peg. Aaron, avoiding her eyes, picked up an apple and bit a piece out of it. They were standing on opposite sides of the cabin, with the bed between them. Each of them kept looking away from it, then finding that their eyes were drawn back to it as if by magnetism. After several long moments of silence, Dru finally reached down with self-conscious awkwardness and drew back the goose-down quilt. Then she marshaled her courage and looked directly at her new husband.

"The longer we wait, the worse it'll be," she said.

Aaron nodded. "Yes." His mouth was suddenly dry again, despite the bite of apple he had just chewed up. He looked at the apple, with a bite missing from its smooth roundness. He did not want any more of it, but did not know what to do with it. He could not put it back in the basket, and there was no place else to put it. He thought briefly of throwing it on the floor, but dismissed that idea as slovenly. Finally he grew tired of holding it and worrying about it; he opened the door, stepped out on deck, and threw it into the river.

When he closed the door behind him in the cabin again, Dru said, "Do you think the lamp is too bright?"

"I don't know. Do you?"

"I think so."

Aaron moved over to where the lamp swung from the cabin roof. He carefully turned the wheel and lowered the burning wick until its flame was barely a flicker.

"Thank you," Dru said. She began undressing.

Aaron removed his waistcoat and hung it on a peg. When he looked around, Dru had her back to him and was naked to the waist. Aaron's lips parted. He watched as she slipped a flannel gown over her wide, bony shoulders, then started removing her other garments under it.

Nervously, Aaron stripped off his shirt and the gray long-underwear top he wore. He sat down on the water keg to pull off his boots. When his boots were off, he looked over at Dru again. She was facing him in her gown and bare feet. Her great round eyes looked with fascination at his massive shoulders and thick chest and upper arms. Putting his boots aside, he stood and faced her with a helpless expression.

"Druscilla, I—I'm not a wordly man—" he said, embarrassed, avoiding her eyes again.

Dru frowned. "Surely you—I mean, as old as you are—you must have—"

"A few times," he admitted. "Mostly when I'd had too much ale. And mostly with—well, paid women who knew what to do." His face grew very red.

Dru studied him for a moment, though not so long as to make his discomfort increase. Then she shrugged. "We must try," she said matter-of-factly.

Aaron nodded.

Dru climbed into bed, allowing Aaron a flash of long, white leg as she lifted her gown. Aaron quickly finished undressing, leaving on only his long-underwear bottoms. Extinguishing the lamp, he climbed into bed with her.

In the dark, so close in the narrow bed, they explored each other. Tentatively at first—

"Your arms are like logs," she said.

"I can count your ribs under your gown," he told her.

"I've never touched a man's bareness before. Not even when I used to wrestle with Cousin Vester—"

"You're very soft up here—"

And then with more familiarity. And more eagerness—

"Let me open your gown at the top—"

"You're so warm. And you smell so—strong—"

"I've seen babies do this often enough—"

"Let me feel you there—oh, god!"

"Pull your gown up—"

"Please be careful—please be easy—"
"I'm not sure where—"
"Here—here—now—oh, Jesus—"
"Oh—oh—goddamn—Jesus—oh—oh—"
In the darkness, as his great chest heaved with each thrust, Aaron buried his face in the crook of her shoulder and clutched at her breasts. Through the tissue and muscle of her throat, low moans of lust and pain sounded against his face. A line of saliva ran from the corner of his mouth onto her neck. He closed his eyes. As his body reached the threshold of spending itself, he tried to concentrate on her soft, pliable breasts. But when the moment came, he found himself thinking of the logbook, and how splendid the prisoners' names were going to look in her fine, stylish hand.
By the time he forced himself to think of her breasts again, it was too late.

CHAPTER 10

The keelboat was already moving the next morning when Dru awakened. Even before she opened her eyes, she could feel the slap of the undercurrent against the floor under the bed. And hear the creak of the beams as they resisted the surface pressure of the water. She sat upright in bed and looked frantically around, as if seeking a route of escape. Then she realized where she was. She glanced down at the empty place next to her. Eyes wide with the wonder of what she remembered, she touched the tenderness between her legs, feeling and probing to see if she was all right. She concluded that she must be, except for a tiny bit of soreness. Aaron really had not penetrated her that far. He was much, much smaller than she had imagined men to be. Briefly she wondered if all men enlarged to the same size.

She got out of bed and made it up at once, as her dead mother had taught her to do. Then she threw off her gown and, standing naked, washed herself with cold water from the pitcher. When she was finished, she dressed quickly and went to the cabin door. She opened it an inch and peeked out. Directly across the deck, past the rail, she saw the shore, perhaps sixty feet away, passing quickly by. She opened the door still further. Back toward the rear of the boat she saw the threescore men Aaron had told her about. Convicts they were. Chained at the foot like wild animals. Turning her head, she looked toward the front of the ship. She saw her cousin Vester sitting on the deck with hammer and stone chisel, breaking head-size rock into fist-size rock. He glanced up and she waved to him. It gave her a comfortable feeling to know that he was aboard. She and Vester had always been the best of friends; she hoped now that he would become friends with her husband also. She smiled a slight little smile. Her husband. How odd that sounded.

She stepped out on deck and walked forward past a small cookstove lashed to a mast by its lion's-paw legs, spewing smoke as a fat, moustached man in leg-irons cooked gravy on it. Up the rail stood Aaron and Mr. Tillman. When Tillman saw her coming, he excused himself. Aaron came down the rail to meet her. For a second each instinctively avoided the other's glance. Then they both realized how foolish that was, and they looked at each other and smiled.

"Hello," Aaron said.

"Hello." Dru glanced out at the shore.

"Are, ah—are you all right?" Aaron asked.

She blushed a little. "I seem to be."

He nodded and jutted his chin out an inch. "Good."

The boat was passing a long stand of closely grown pine trees that lined the beautiful, uninhabited shore. Dru's eyes sparkled at the sight of it. "The country is so pretty down here," she said.

"Yes. Good trees. Good healthy wood. I hope it's like that where we're going. We'll need a lot of good healthy wood."

Behind them, the fat man at the cookstove yelled, "Gravy's brown here, Mr. Tillman!"

Aaron and Dru turned to see Tillman walk back to the afterdeck. He removed a key from his vest pocket and unlocked the tether bar. Lifting the free end out of its cradle, he let it drop to the deck. "Line up for grub!" he said loudly to the convicts.

The prisoners got to their feet on each side of the bar and moved slowly toward the free end. As each in turn reached the end, the shackle around the bar was slipped off. A guard kneeling on each side then unlocked the shackle and clamped it on the prisoner's free leg. The prisoner then had both legs shackled, with a fourteen-inch chain connecting his ankles. So hobbled, they were allowed to hop-walk up to the cookstove where a wooden plate of biscuits and gravy was dished out to each of them.

The Indian Kee-te-ha, who had maimed his squaw, came hop-walking by as Aaron and Dru watched. Dru noticed that his right ankle had been rubbed raw by the shackle. It was seeping blood and pus.

"That Indian," she said. "He seems to be injured."

Aaron gave Kee-te-ha a cursory glance. "The shackle must have done it before we picked him up."

"Can't he be treated?"

"I don't know." Aaron studied her. "He's a Sac, you know. Didn't the Sacs kill your folks?"

"Yes, they did. Do you have medicines in the flatboat supplies?"

"I suppose," Aaron said.

"He could be treated then. Don't you think he should? A one-legged man wouldn't be much help building the prison."

Aaron looked thoughtfully at the Indian for a long time. Then he summoned a guard and sent him back to the flatboat to search for medical supplies. The guard returned a while later with a packet labeled PHYSICIAN'S KIT. Dru examined its contents. She found a tin of healing salve. "This should do."

The prisoners were now back on the afterdeck, squatting against the rail, eating. "Bring the Indian forward," Aaron told the guard.

Kee-te-ha was brought to the forward deck. Aaron had the shackle removed from his right ankle. The guard opened the tin of salve and handed it to Dru.

"Do you have to do that yourself?" Aaron asked.

"It's all right," Dru said. "I know how."

That had not been Aaron's point, but he let it go. The guard sat Kee-te-ha on a keg and Dru reached for his foot with the salve. The Indian made a sudden animal sound and jerked away. The guard raised his rifle threateningly. Aaron pulled Dru back.

"Wait, it's all right," she said. "He just doesn't know what it is. Let me try again."

She approached Kee-te-ha again, this time taking a bit of the salve and rubbing it on the back of her hand. The Indian watched her suspiciously, his eyes black and hard like musket balls.

"It doesn't hurt," Dru said in a soft, reassuring voice. "See, I'm putting it on myself."

Frowning, fearful, Kee-ta-ha let the white woman first touch his abused ankle very gently, then slowly spread a layer of thick yellow salve over the wound. As she worked, his eyes flicked constantly from her to Aaron to the rifle-holding guard. Gradually, reluctantly, he seemed to realize that what she was doing was not a trick to harm him.

When Dru finished, she said, "It should have a bandage."

Aaron and the guard exchanged glances. The guard had nothing to offer, but Aaron was wearing a red bandanna around his neck. Dru looked pointedly at it. Aaron glanced distastefully at Kee-ta-ha, sighed resignedly, and pulled off the bandanna. Dru folded it and tied it carefully around the Indian's ankle. Then the guard returned him to the afterdeck.

"These men are criminals, you know," Aaron said when he and Dru were alone again.

"Does that mean they aren't to be treated like human beings?" she asked. It was not a snide question; it was innocent and sincere.

"No, it doesn't mean that at all," Aaron replied. He felt slightly embarrassed. "But I think you ought to keep in mind that they aren't like other people. They're different."

"How?" Again, it was asked as a child would ask about babies.

"They do things that decent people wouldn't do."

"Commit crimes, you mean?"

"Yes."

"Besides that, though, they're just like other men. Aren't they?"

"I'm not sure," Aaron said. "I haven't been around them enough to find that out yet. But I think you should use care around them."

"All right." She closed the tin of salve and put it back in the physician's kit. Then she looked around the forward deck. The fat man in the leg-irons was still working at the cookstove. "Aaron, I'm hungry," Dru said.

Aaron took her over to the stove. The fat man removed his hat and bowed. "Pete French, at your service, *madame, capitan,*" he said in a Gallic-accented voice. A thin moustache curled up at each end when he smiled.

"Tell him what you want," said Aaron.

"Whatever he has," said Dru. "Biscuits and gravy is fine."

Aaron nodded to Pete French. "Some side-meat too. and coffee."

"*Oui,* at once."

Aaron and Dru went forward on the rail to wait for Dru's breakfast. Dru looked back at Pete French as he cooked. He worked with a certain flourish. "Is he a good cook?" she asked.

Aaron nodded. "He and his wife ran a dining hall up in Alton, near where the Mississippi forks with the Missouri. Mr. Tillman told me about it; he ate there a lot when he was stationed in Alton with the militia. It was a big tent dining hall that could feed fifty people at a time. French did all the cooking and his wife did the serving. Tillman says they got most of the flatboat trade from both rivers."

"How did he get here?"

"He raped a thirteen-year-old girl," Aaron replied conversationally. "Her family was heading out-river to Kansas City. They stopped overnight near French's place. He caught the girl in the woods."

Dru looked over at the fat little man again. He was humming a cheerful tune as he went contentedly about his work. A picture came to her mind of him tearing the clothes off a young girl, a child helpless in his grip, and violating her while she begged unheeded for mercy. Dru shuddered.

Perhaps these men *weren't* like other men, after all.

Later in the journey, the keelboat began to pass northbound river traffic. Near Cairo there were half a dozen woodboats plying the shallow waters near shore to pick up freshly cut timber. A woodboat was nothing more than an ordinary flatboat, except that it had a woven rope fence stretched along its sides to keep the timber from rolling off into the water. The boats would fill up with as much as they could safely carry, then pole back downriver to cut and sell the wood to merchants and townspeople, or to the lumber mill, or to one of the larger boats coming off the Ohio River at Cairo, or coming up the Big Muddy all the way from New Orleans.

Most of the woodboats were worked by young rivermen in their early twenties. When Aaron and Dru would watch them from the rail, they would often smile at Dru and wave and yell. "Mighty pretty daughter you got there, sir!" Or, "Throw us a kiss, miss, when yore paw ain't watching!" Aaron would frown darkly at them and cease waving immediately; but Dru would return their smiles and waves, and then take Aaron's arm reassuringly. She would squeeze his muscle and whisper in his ear, and presently he would be smiling and waving at the young louts again.

Now and then a mackinaw would come by, carrying a family, or two or three, heading for the new west. The mackinaw was another version of the flatboat, except that its hull was built higher to carry its deck farther up out of the water. It usually had a lean-to erected somewhere amidships to provide shelter during sudden rain squalls. Some of these sturdy river travelers had actually been hewn on the upper Allegheny or the lower Monongahela, then poled to Pittsburgh and down into the Ohio, on to the Mississippi, then the Missouri, and finally into the Kansas River itself. The mackinaw was to the rivers what the big Conestoga was to the overland trail.

In the afternoon, south of Cairo, they encountered their first New Orleans side-wheeler. It was a huge, four-decked vessel that completely dwarfed the keelboat. Its two smokestacks, standing side by side on the bow like a pair of great raised cannons, spewed trails of black smoke in its wake. The two lower decks were packed tightly with burlap-wrapped bales of cotton that had been stored in New Orleans warehouses since the previous August when it had been picked. The cotton was now on its way up north to be sold at higher winter prices. On the upper decks, well-tailored men and expensively dressed women with parasols—travelers from New Orleans to St. Louis—gathered at the rail to stare down at the keelboat and its chained human cargo. The sight of white men in shackles was unusual to the predominantly southern passengers.

The two vessels passed very close to each other, and as they did, Dru, at the rail with Aaron and Vester, looked up directly into the faces of the women. They stared down at her with unconcealed curiosity, opening lacy fans in front of their lips when they wanted to comment on the sight. With the women examining her so openly, Dru suddenly felt very drab and threadbare in her plain old frontier frock. There was no telling, she thought, what those women, in their afternoon yellows and greens and orchids, took her for; the only female on a convict ship. Before the side-wheeler was half past them, Dru turned from the rail and hurried into the cabin. Aaron, smiling and waving beside her, watched with a puzzled frown as she left. Later, when the big boat was well upriver of them, he went to the cabin and found her sitting in the corner, holding her bundle of meager belongings on her lap, crying. Hoping the men outside could not hear her sobs, Aaron sat on the water keg facing her.

"What is it?" he asked awkwardly.

She shook her head. "Nothing."

"I'm your husband now. I have a right to know."

She looked up at him with great wide eyes, her large bottom lip out now in a genuine pout. "I feel so homely," she said. "Those women on the paddle-boat—they looked so fine and beautiful."

"None of them looked any better than you," Aaron said. "Except for the dresses, of course."

Dru blinked rapidly, spilling more tears down her cheeks. "You couldn't mean that."

He knelt beside her. "But I do," he said. He was frowning now. He had meant it for a lie when he said it; but suddenly, looking closely at her, he realized that he was sincere. Truly. She *was* a pretty woman—to him anyway; and if she had been dressed in satin and crinoline instead of faded cotton, she *would* have been the equal of those women on the big wheeler. Aaron took her hands. "I do mean it, Dru. I give you my word."

She wiped her cheeks on the sleeve of her dress and sniffed back the tears that had been on the verge of coming. "I don't believe you. But I thank you for saying it."

"Listen. Do you know what the shebang boat is?"

Dru nodded. "It's the merchant boat that visits the river settlements that haven't a general store."

"Right. Mr. Tillman told me about it. We'll be trading with it between supply runs up to East St. Louie. And the first time it comes, you can buy yourself a dress."

Her eyes widened even more. "You mean a *new* dress? A store-bought dress?"

"I do indeed. Of course, it probably won't be as fancy as them women had on today—"

"It won't have to be!" she said excitedly. "Just so it's brand new! And from the store! Oh, Aaron, thank you! Uncle Ab was right: you *are* a good man!"

She flew into his arms, knocking him and the keg backwards. The keg split a stave. Within seconds, both of them were sprawled on the cabin floor with water spreading out under them. They looked at each other and burst out laughing.

The next morning, Aaron had some boxes moved on board from the flatboat and arranged them as a makeshift desk and chair for Dru. He sat her there with the government logbook that had been assigned to him, and a quill-point and ink. Stationing himself beside her, he had Tillman bring one prisoner at a time forward. He questioned them, while Dru recorded their vital statistics.

"Name?" said Aaron.

"Caldwell."

"Say 'sir' when you address Mr. Van Hawn," Tillman said sharply.

"Caldwell, sir."

"Age?" said Aaron.

"Fifty-three, sir."

"What town or village are you from?"

"Town of Ripton, sir."

"Crime?"

"Disposal of mortgaged property, sir. A horse."

"Sentence?"

"Two years."

Another was brought up.

"Name?"

"Kelsey, sir."

"Age?"

"Twenty-seven, sir."

"Town or village?"

"Newburg, sir."

"Crime?"

"Arson,sir."

"Sentence?"

"Ten years, sir."

One by one, they all came forward.

"MacPherson, sir. Thirty-one, sir. LaGrange, sir. Cheat and defraud, sir. Five years, sir."

"Casey, sir. Sixty-three. Lawton Township. Receiving stolen goods. Three years."

Hop Sing. Forty-seven. St. Charles. Sodomy. Ten years.

Lewt. Thirty-one. Pitt County. Murder. Life.

Jingo. Thirty-four. Cleavertown. Robbery. Fifteen years.

Willis. Thirty-one. Titusville. Concubinage. Two years.

DuLange. Thirty-six. Lockport. Mayhem. Six years.

Darby. Twenty-eight. Village of Chester. Manslaughter. Twenty-one years.

It was while Darby was on deck that the helmsman shouted back to Tillman, "Live sandbar, Mr. Tillman!"

Tillman hurried to the bow for a look, then reported back to Aaron. "Signs of wild fowl, sir. And a few egg holes."

Aaron glanced at Dru and his jaw jutted out. He liked giving orders in front of her. "Drag anchor, Mr. Tillman. Cordelle to the bar. Unlock Pete French and have him lay to with a sack. Send two men along with hunting loads."

The keelboat's anchor was heaved over the stern and began dragging in the mud of the river bottom; on the bow, the helmsman poled backwards. The keelboat quickly slowed to a stop, the flatboat behind it floating up to bump lightly into the aft hull. Four convicts were sent over the side with the cordelle rope. They waded onto the sandbar and planted themselves firmly and held the boat in place against the draft of water around it. Pete French and two hunting guards quickly jumped onto the bar.

Aaron and Dru went over to the rail where Vester stood and watched as the small sandbar was plundered. Rising to about three feet out of the water, it was perhaps a hundred fifty feet long, fifty wide. Some scrub brush grew in a cluster along its center rise, and river tides had dug a few channels and pits; but otherwise it was level, easy to plunder. Pete French went at once to the sand pits, scooping with both hands. After a moment he leaped up and gave a loud yell. "Yee—oh! Duck eggs aplenty!" Dropping to his knees, he began cheerfully to put the eggs into his burlap sack.

The two guards had gone to the cluster of scrub and were poking in it with their rifle barrels. The weapons were loaded with wadded shot instead of mini-balls, the amount of gunpowder under the percussion cap decreased by half. The result was a makeshift but effective shotgun. The two hunters prodded the scrub from each end toward the middle. They had gone only a few feet when a pair of wild turkeys bolted from their hiding places and leaped squawking into the air. The distance was short and the shots easy; both birds were brought down from less than a dozen feet in the air. A cheer from guard and convict alike went up from the boat.

Aaron and Vester were looking down the rail, smiling, listening to the men cheer, when the convict Darby came up behind Dru and held an ax blade to her throat. "If you or any of your men move, Van Hawn, I'll cut her throat," he said in an awful voice close to Dru's ear.

Aaron froze, his eyes widening, lips parting in sudden cold fear. Vester stared at the convict in horror. Two guards started to rush forward but Tillman stopped them. The convicts on the afterdeck formed a group and stirred nervously. Down on the sandbar, French and the hunters moved over and stood uneasily by the men on the cordelle rope.

Dru was terrified. Her face drained of color; her large bottom lip began to tremble. One of Darby's hands held the blade firmly against her neck; the other clutched at her left breast to hold her still. Darby was breathing heavily; his breath was putrid in Dru's nostrils.

"What do you want?" Aaron asked in a hollow voice.

"What do you think I want, you damned fool?" Darby snapped. "I want to spend the next twenty-one years somewheres else, not in the stinking prison you're going to build. Tell all your men to lay down them rifles."

Aaron nodded once and all weapons were laid down.

"Now give me the key to that tether bar—"

Tillman came over and gave him the key. Darby put it between his teeth, clutched Dru's breast again, and backed along the rail with her. When he got to the edge of the afterdeck, he yelled over his shoulder at the two dozen convicts still chained to the tether bar. "I'm going to open the bar for y'all! Soon's you're loose, pick up them rifles! We'll throw everybody but the woman off and sail this tub down to the gulf!"

Aaron, infuriated by Darby's manhandling of Dru, and now his threat to take her with him, closed his hamlike fists and stalked toward him.

"Stay back!" Darby snarled. He pressed the blade harder against Dru's flesh. Tillman threw both arms around Aaron and held him back.

"No, Mr. Van Hawn!" Tillman said urgently. "He'll kill her, sir!"

Aaron could have broken Tillman in two, but he allowed the chief guard to corral him, because he saw Dru's neck turn very red and he knew Tillman was right: Darby *would* kill her. Without hesitation.

When everyone was under control again, Darby tossed the tether-bar key to Kelsey, the arsonist. "Unlock that bar!" he shouted.

Kelsey dragged his tether chain to the end of the bar, where the big padlock was located. He fumbled with the heavy key, but finally got it into the lock. Then he heard Dru scream.

As Darby held her at the edge of the afterdeck, Dru had seen the Indian Kee-te-ha move away from the group of prisoners and come toward her. Darby, who was turned partway around watching Aaron and Tillman, did not see him. Kee-te-ha came up to Dru with hands outstretched, face scowling, the very image of what every red man was supposed to look like to every white woman on the frontier. Instinctively, Dru screamed in terror.

Darby's head jerked around at the sound. His own instincts surfacing, he exerted more pressure on the axe blade. But a half second before, Kee-te-ha's hand shot forward and gripped Darby's wrist, turning the razor-sharp edge away from Dru's throat. Viciously twisting the blade down, Darby opened the back of Kee-te-ha's hand in a neat slice along the top knuckles. As the two men struggled, the Indian's blood ran down Dru's bosom like rivulets of sweat. She sucked in her breath, but before she could scream, she felt the pressure released from her neck and her breast: Kee-te-ha was slowly pulling Darby's hands away, at the same time twisting the bloody ax blade from his grip. An instant later, her body free, Dru jumped away from the struggling men. Aaron ran toward her. She looked back at Kee-te-ha just as he wrenched the blade from Darby's hand and, using his powerful arm as an ax handle, laid open the white man's head with it.

The keelboat was back under control in an instant. At the tether-bar lock, two guards with retrieved rifles backed Kelsey up against the rail and took the padlock key away from him. Below, on the bar, the four cordelle men and Pete French were hurried back aboard. Tillman and the other guards dispersed the rest of the convicts back along the tether bar. Dru was in Aaron's arms, sobbing and panting for breath.

"All right," he whispered in her ear. "All right now. You're all right now—"

Two guards moved in on Kee-te-ha with raised rifles. The Indian was still holding the ax blade. At his feet, Darby was clutching at his open skull, moaning and jerking spastically. The guards pointed their weapons at Kee-te-ha.

"Wait!" Aaron commanded. With his arm around Dru, he walked her forward to where the Indian stood. "Back off," he said to the guards. He got a leg-iron key and knelt in front of Kee-te-ha. Removing his shackles, he tossed the irons across the deck. Standing, he looked steadily into the Indian's eyes while saying to Dru, "Try to get that ax head away from him, will you?"

Dru stepped over and took Kee-te-ha's hand. He relinquished the blade without resistance. "I'll tend to his hand," she said. Aaron nodded and Dru led the Indian forward. Then Aaron turned to the prisoners. His face was ashen, grim.

"The punishment for laying hands on my wife is death," he announced evenly. He took a rifle from a nearby guard, pointed it at Darby, and fired into the wound opened by Kee-te-ha. Darby pitched once on the deck, then lay still. "Now then," Aaron said to Tillman, "remove convict Kelsey's shirt and lash him to the mastpole."

Kelsey pulled his chain forward, pained and innocent. "Mr. Van Hawn, sir. I didn't do nothing, sir," he whined.

"You tried," said Aaron.

As Kelsey was being bound to the pole, Aaron removed his waistcoat and rolled up his sleeves. Convicts and guards alike looked in awe at his powerful, muscle-corded arms. Unstrapping his thick leather belt, Aaron held it by the buckle and stepped up behind Kelsey. "The punishment for attempting escape is thirty lashes."

Squaring his shoulders, Aaron laid on the first blow. Kelsey screamed. His scream was punctuated by the second blow. And before he could get his breath, the third landed. Aaron whipped him methodically, using a rhythm developed through years of hammering and sawing. The fourteenth blow opened Kelsey's flesh. On the twentieth, he fainted. By the thirtieth, his back was a mass of swollen, purple tissue with shreds of skin either hanging from it or beaten down into it. Three convicts and one guard got sick to their stomachs looking at it.

When he stopped the whipping, Aaron, drenched with sweat, turned to Tillman. "Take four prisoners and bury Darby on the sandbar."

Aaron went forward. Dru and Kee-te-ha were standing at the cabin door. The Indian had a fresh bandage on his cut hand. Aaron went into the cabin and fetched a blanket. He gave it to Kee-te-ha and pointed to a place by the cabin door. The Indian looked at Dru. she touched his arm and smiled. He nodded brusquely, wrapped the blanket around his shoulders, and sat in the place Aaron had indicated.

When Aaron and Dru went into the cabin, Aaron said, "I wonder if he'll be there in the morning."

"I think he will," Dru said.

"We'll see," said Aaron.

The next morning Kee-te-ha was gone.

CHAPTER 11

When Aaron, Vester, and Tillman went ashore in Union County, they found the army corps of engineers camped a quarter-mile in from shore. The commanding officer was a weary, disgruntled captain named Vorhees.

"Well, we've got your goddamned road built for you, Mr. Van Hawn," he said disgustedly. "And let me tell you it was a miserable job. Whoever picked this godforsaken ground to build anything on ought to have his senses checked."

Aaron frowned and glanced at Vester and Tillman. "What's wrong with it?" he inquired.

"Ground's too sloped, for one thing. Every time it rains, the high ground floods and floats everything right down to the riverbank. And the wood's no good, for another thing. It's mostly scrub or rotted with termites. And there isn't any decent drinking water higher than thirty, thirty-five feet down, and you have to sink your well through clay and rock to get to *that*." He shook his head in disgust. "I sure hope the state didn't pay much an acre for this disaster."

"I'm sure it didn't, sir," Aaron said quietly.

He led Vester and Tillman up the road to the top of the bluff where the donated ten-acre parcel lay. A rough, uneven plot of land, it had a desolate, threatening look to it, as if daring anyone to try and cultivate it. Singly, the men split up and walked around, inspecting, examining, speculating. After a time, they gravitated back to each other.

"What do you think, Vester?" Aaron asked.

The big-shouldered youth shrugged. "There's plenty of good native stone here, that's for certain. And the ground's got good clay content for making bricks. I just ain't sure about the timber. Like that army feller said, it's mostly scrub—"

"We'll go downriver for timber if need be. Use the keelboat. Mr. Tillman? What do you think?"

"Bringing in the wood by boat will take a lot of time," Tillman said thoughtfully. "I'd worry if we didn't have some kind of good shelter by first frost."

"That's at least six months off; we've the whole summer." Aaron paced a few steps, then faced them with his jaw jutted out as far as it would go. "I think we can do," he decided. He nodded vigorously. "I think we *will* do it."

He stalked back down the hill, Vester and Tillman following.

Aaron bought two dray horses from Captain Vorhees, giving the officer a state draft redeemable for cash at the capital. Because he was not supposed to sell the animals, the captain made out an army report saying that they had been injured and put out of their misery. Aaron witnessed the report, taking it to the boat for Dru to sign his name. "I've sprained my hand," was the excuse he gave her for not signing it himself.

Part of the flatboat deck was removed and assembled as a sled on shore. Supplies were loaded on it and lashed down, the dray horses dragging them up the hill. It took two days to get all their supplies inside a large pyramidal tent on the bluff. One corner of the tent was set aside for Kelsey the arsonist, unable to move since his whipping by Aaron. The supply tent sentry watched over him, saw that he did not go thirsty, and supervised his feeding by another convict.

Tillman made exploratory trips into the woods to evaluate the timber situation. His report was not encouraging. "There's some pine, some elm, but mostly it's scrub white oak, brittle as thin ice or soft as moss. Within a mile radius, which is as far as we'd want to drag timber, I'd estimate we have only enough to do us two months. Then we'll have to use the river."

"Use it we will then," Aaron vowed.

The convicts were unshackled and marched up to the bluff. Only twenty-seven were left now, and Aaron cursed the foul luck that caused him to lose ten percent of his work force before the task had even begun. He stood on a keg and faced the surly group of men. "You're going to build a prison right here where you stand," he told them. "It will be a place for you to live and serve out your sentences. A place for you to eat your meals and to sleep. I've been told it will take a year to build. I don't believe it will, because until it is built you will all be living outside, and I don't think any of you want to live outside all winter." A low mutter of disapproval rippled through the men. Aaron ignored it. "For the rest of the day, you can dig ground beds and fill them with leaves to sleep on, and dig privies for yourselves. Tomorrow at daybreak you begin work."

While the prisoners set about making their bivouac as livable as possible, Aaron and Vester ran a rough survey of the ten acres to decide where the stone pit would be dug, the kiln built, and the main well sunk.

"The best rock will be in the back corner of the acreage," Vester told Aaron. "The farther from the river, the less mud we'll get when we set to digging."

"Where do you want to burn your bricks?" Aaron asked.

"Close to the building site as I can get. You know, after the kiln's built, 'Scilla can use it to cook, if she's a mind,"

"Dru won't be coming up the hill," Aaron said, "I don't want her around the prisoners. We'll live on the boat."

Vester nodded. He did not think it was necessary to keep his cousin quite so sheltered, but he did not say so. It was her husband's decision to make. "How's she been since what happened the other day?" he asked, referring to the escape attempt.

"Better than I expected," Aaron said. "I thought she'd be leery of everything for a while."

"Not 'Scilla," the big youth said. "She don't let too much get her down. Paw always said she was the smartest one on either side of the family. The quietest one, but the smartest."

"Your paw may have been right," Aaron said thoughtfully. He too had noticed Dru's apparent capacity for learning. Anything new that came along was immediately grasped by her; she rarely had to study it. Her understanding of a situation or a problem was quick, perceptive, thoroughly logical. She was easily the most practical, sensible woman Aaron had ever known.

After he and Vester decided on the best place to sink the compound's main water well, Aaron picked out the least rocky area of the bluff and paced off four hundred feet in one direction, three hundred in another. He marked the two lengths of ground.

"That will be the wall," he announced. "Twenty feet high. It will be erected first, before the cell house."

After he said it, he stood in the middle of the bluff, picked up a handful of dirt, and looked around. He had just made his first major decision and he felt both good and bad about it. There where he stood would be built the state's first penitentiary. It would be his doing: he would oversee it. That made him feel good. Then, when it was finished—what? What future lay in store for him once he had turned the prison over to the state? Was he then to revert to his former status of barn-raiser?

Aaron shook the thought from his head. He must not let himself dwell on such depressing matters. He would take care of the future when it came. Right now he had a prison to build.

He tossed the dirt back to the ground and stalked off to find Tillman.

While the prisoners lived outside, and Tillman and his men lived in tents on the bluff, Aaron and Dru remained in the cabin on the beached keelboat. For several days after their arrival, Dru was moody and out of sorts.

"Is it that Indian?" Aaron asked.

She nodded. "I was so sure he wouldn't run away."

"I was, too."

Dru sighed. "I guess we can't expect to understand an Indian."

"Or a convict," Aaron added.

Dru did not argue.

The newlyweds had already fallen into a comfortable familiarity with each other. They had few, and only minor, differences. Neither would have dreamed of arguing. Each of them gave something of value to the other: Aaron a combined strength and gentleness that Dru considered herself fortunate to get; and Dru a youthful, feminine vibrancy Aaron had never experienced in a woman. The twenty-two-years' difference in their ages was never in their thoughts; the two of them fit well together, and that was all that mattered.

Their relationship in bed was much as it had been their first night together. Aaron went at once for Dru's breasts. "I love these—love them—love to do this to them—ah, how I wish I could suck something out—" Dru patiently satisfied his suckling desire until he was finished and ready to enter her. Then it would be all over in a moment or two. Afterwards, Dru would be left with a vague sense of unrest, as if there was something more that she should be doing, or that Aaron should be doing, or that should be happening and was not. Without having any formal knowledge of the physical act, she wondered if Aaron was not penetrating her as deeply as it was possible for her to be penetrated. If he wasn't, she supposed it was because he was not long enough to do so; perhaps because he was short in stature. She guessed that size had a lot to do with it. This thing of sex apparently was going to take a while to learn.

Meanwhile, she was left with an indistinct feeling of absence. But she did not find fault with Aaron because of it. She was sure he was doing the best he could. She would never attempt to reprove him in any way, because she had developed a genuine affection for this thick-bodied little husband of hers, and thanked her good graces every day that she hadn't been given to some heavy-drinking riverman, or foul smelling trapper, or lecherous old preacher like Reverend Lamper. She had to admit that old Uncle Abner Foyle had done all right by her as far as marriage was concerned.

Even if the old bastard had kept her forty dollars dowry money and made her promise never to tell Aaron.

The work on the bluff began very slowly. Jobs were assigned on the basis of size, strength, and experience. The strongest convicts were set to work digging Vester's pit. It was begun in a two-acre corner of the parcel selected by Vester as probably having the greatest shale deposits. The men approached the job reluctantly, chipping at the ground with picks and spades as if they were afraid to injure it. After ten full days, they had barely opened the surface and had only a skimpy pile of stone with which to begin the wall.

While the pit men were stalling, other convicts were supposed to be leveling the ground for the compound, using heavy logs dragged back and forth by the dray horses. This should have produced a smooth, flat surface. Instead, it was pocked and rooted where the logs had not been dragged across enough, or unevenly trenched where they had been dragged too much. With each try at correction, it got worse.

The kiln being built to make bricks did not progress any better. Three times Vester worked the clay walls of the oven into shape, wet them down good with water brought up from the river, and braced them with wooden supports he had cut and assembled himself. And three times he returned from other duties to find a support out of place and a wall collapsed before the clay could harden.

There were other problems. The well was not being sunk fast enough and the drinking water supply on the flatboat was dangerously low. The timber crew was felling trees on top of other felled trees, which delayed the measuring and sawing until they could be dragged apart. The men were constantly breaking ax handles and saw blades.

Aaron knew the men were deliberately resisting the work, purposely misusing their tools; he had expected this, but he did not know how serious it was until Vester and Tillman came to him at the end of their first month.

"Unless something is done to make the men work harder," Tillman said, "the job will never get done. We'll run out of supplies long before we're due to get more."

"And I'm bound to stay only ten months," Vester reminded Aaron, "then my paw's expecting me out in Kansas."

Aaron discussed it with Dru that night in their cabin. "The trouble is, the prisoners have nothing to gain by working diligently," he said. "They can't be paid because it's against the law. We don't have enough rations to give them extra helpings. The only thing they have to look forward to by working hard is their own shelter next winter. It seems that they'd rather resist the work than look to their own comfort." He shook his head. "They're an odd lot, these convicts."

"But they're still men, just like any other men," Dru said thoughtfully. "Other men work; there must be a way to make these work also."

"I don't see how," Aaron said. He sat heavily on the bed, his big shoulders drooping. Just a month earlier he had found it so easy to decide things, like where the cell house was to be built, where the well would be sunk, what hours the prisoners would work. Easy things. Now, when something went wrong, he was at a loss how to deal with it. "They've nothing to gain by working," He said. "Nothing except a better place to sleep, and that doesn't seem too important to them."

"What *is* important to them, do you suppose?"

Aaron shrugged. "Probably nothing except their freedom."

He stared at her, letting his last words hang in the air. She stared back, obviously thinking the same thing he was thinking. His expression, which had been tightly knit and troubled, now became thoughtful, contemplative. Their freedom—

"You could, you know," Dru said.

"I'm not sure I have the authority."

"You do." She got his commission from the trunk. "It says you are to 'proceed with dispatch in the construction and founding of a penitentiary, using any and all means which you consider proper in effecting completion of that task.'"

"Is that what it says?"

"Yes. Haven't you read your own commission?"

"No need to," Aaron replied, jutting his jaw. "The lieutenant governor personally told me what to do." He cleared his throat. "As long as you have it out, read the whole of it to me."

Dru read, and Aaron learned for the first time exactly what his commission authorized. He had far more power than he had imagined.

That night, after Dru was asleep, Aaron went out on deck and stood by the rail listening to the night sounds of the river. He thought about the commission and the authority it gave him, and wondered just how far he dared go in the exercise of that authority. He wished Grover were there to advise him. Thinking of his lanky friend, living the life of a gentleman in the state capital, made him smile. What would *he* do? Aaron wondered. Let prisoners free early for working hard, or not?

Aaron sighed. This business of making decisions was not so very easy. Particularly for someone with no experience at it. All his life, working as a barn-raiser, he'd had decisions made for him. Usually by sour-faced people like old man Able Fleece. Aaron made up his mind then and there that whether he ever learned to make decisions or not, he would *never* allow himself to become like Able Fleece.

Perhaps, though, he could learn something from Fleece, he thought, frowning in the moonlight. Fleece made decisions and he got things done, got barns built; but no one who worked for him liked him very much. Aaron was the only person who had ever stayed with him more than a year or two. Probably because I was a bigger dullard than most, he told himself. But how, he wondered, could old Fleece have been a better man? What would have made the people who worked for him like him?

Fair treatment, Aaron decided. Fleece was never fair to his workers. He always managed to get more out of them than he paid for, and they knew it and resented it. Which was why most of them, the smart ones, ultimately moved on. Even he, after all his years with the old man, had moved on, with not a thought of loyalty. Fair treatment. That was the whole of it.

And wouldn't it be the same with any man, free or not? Wouldn't a convict respond as quickly to fair treatment as anyone else? Aaron could not see why not. Give him something of value—*fair* value—for his labor, and he would work for it.

But dare he do it? he asked himself. Dare he free convicts early without specific approval?

As he was pondering the question, he felt a hand on his arm. He turned in surprise to find Dru there.

"Are you troubled?" she asked.

"Yes."

"About freeing the men early in return for work?"

"Yes."

"Have you asked yourself which is more important?"

"What do you mean?"

"Which is more important: the few men you would turn loose early, or getting the prison built?"

"Why, the prison, of course. The prison will be there long after the men are dead."

"Well, then."

Aaron pursed his lips in thought. Perhaps that was the formula. Fair treatment combined with doing what was most important. Perhaps being able to decide that was what made a man a good leader of other men. He jutted his jaw and nodded curtly at the night. If it was, he would find out.

"You're right," he said, patting Dru's hand, "the prison is the important thing. I'll talk to the convicts tomorrow."

The next morning, Aaron had the prisoners assembled.

"The work is not going well," he announced. "You all know it.

You also know why it is not going well, and so do I. So today we are beginning something new. No man has to work unless he wants to."

A murmur of surprise and suspicion surfaced in the convict lines. Several of the men openly jeered the news. One man spat, it was so ridiculous to him.

"It's true," Aaron affirmed. "Any man who doesn't want to work can spend the day shackled and sitting in the middle of the compound. But any man who does work can have his sentence reduced by half."

The men grew quiet and stared at their keeper. Their faces instantly became a mixture of incredulity and doubt. But with a glimmer of hope. "How's that again, sir?" called Casey, the receiver of stolen goods.

"Half," Aaron repeated. "For every day of honest labor you give me, I'll take a day off your sentence. Your three years would be reduced to eighteen months, Casey."

"And mine to thirty months?" asked Finley, the embezzler.

"Yours to thirty months," Aaron assured him. "That's my offer. You can work your way out early or you can sit idly and serve it all. Makes no difference to me. The prison will get built, one way or another, if it takes five years. Those who want to work, report to Mr. Tillman. Those who don't, come sit on this box—" With his heel, Aaron dug a ten-foot-square mark in the dirt. "Make your choice!"

The lines of standing men dissolved as they hop-walked over to Tillman for work assignments. Only two came out to the dirt square: Lewt, the murderer with the life sentence, and Jingo, the robber who was serving fifteen years.

"Half of fifteen is still too long to serve, Mr. Van Hawn," said Jingo with a smile. "I expect I'll have to escape."

"Your privilege to try, Jingo," Aaron replied.

Lewt and Jingo sat down on the ground and watched as the rest of the men were directed off to work.

During their second month on the bluff, Aaron was surprised to observe a settlement of sorts being started by strangers down by the river's edge. One day a mackinaw beached a hundred yards upriver from Aaron's keelboat and a woman and her two adolescent sons came ashore. They pitched two small tents, set out traps for game to eat, and began building a clay-and-timber cabin. No one knew who they were until the woman approached Aaron and told him she was the wife of a prisoner named Rudd, who was serving six years for assault with a gun.

"I come here to be near my husband," she said. "I'd be obliged if me and my boys could visit him now and again."

Aaron had Rudd brought in from the rock pit. "I'm letting you have three hours with your wife and sons today," he told the prisoner. "And you can have three hours every Sunday afternoon as long as you stay out of trouble."

That was the start of it. Word spread; by the end of the month there were two other convict wives there. Then three more, with families. One woman hung a laundry sign on her tent and started taking in wash. Another offered her services as a seamstress, while still another baked and sold pies to Tillman and the other guards.

Soon afterward, two brothers named Pullman poled a flatboat up from Cape Girardeau and carted ashore enough supplies to start a small store in a pyramidal tent. Their sign read GEN'L. MDSE. and they stocked sugar, salt, molasses, coal oil, bolt cloth, and gunpowder. They also bought for resale fresh-skinned deer, rabbits, and other edible game from hunters and trappers who passed through. One brother remained in the store for a fortnight while the other poled back downriver for fresh supplies.

With the creation of the settlement, Aaron realized that there were now two separate and very different communities which would have to exist in close proximity. The community up on the bluff was a closed and guarded one, seen only from a distance by the others except for maybe three hours on Sunday. This bluff compound came to be known familiarly as Prison Hill. Its sister community down by the river was congenial and open; by comparison, hospitable to anyone who came to it, whether from up on the Hill or from elsewhere. It offered a home to prison families and a sanctuary to guards from the bluff when they were off duty. That community came to be called Prisontown.

For some reason he could not explain, Aaron was troubled by the prospect of having a free community so close to his prison. He knew there was nothing he could do about it; knew as well that it was not really *his* prison, that whatever problems arose because of the close proximity of Prisontown would eventually be someone else's problems. Even so, he could not help worrying over it. Some instinct told him that the two communities being so close together was unhealthy.

Unhealthy to whom, he had not decided.

One day during their third month, a lone horseman walked his mount slowly up the road leading a bound prisoner by a rope. The rider was Mr. Brin, the county sheriff from the village of Chester, whom Aaron had met when he picked up prisoners there. The prisoner was Kee-te-ha.

"Thought I'd give you this Indian again," Brin said. "Caught him prowling around town one night. I knew his five years wasn't up, so I guessed he'd run out."

Aaron nodded. "He escaped from the boat just before we got here."

Brin dismounted and looked around. "Looks like you're making right smart progress," he observed.

"Progress has been good," Aaron allowed. "Come, and let me show you about."

Aaron took the sheriff on a tour of the bluff. He showed him the rock pit, now nearly an acre wide and thirty feet deep; the double-kiln where Vester baked hard, oversized bricks; the lumber compound where four convicts cut, trimmed, and planed the timber now being hauled from upriver on the flatboat; and the beginning of the prison wall, which was staked and ready for its first rock. "Four months we've been at it," Aaron said. "We'll finish it in twelve. Sooner if we get some more hands. Mr. Tillman takes the boat back north in September to start another run down the river to pick up new prisoners." Aaron walked with Brin back down the hill. "Will you take your noon meal with us?"

Brin accepted the invitation. He ate with Aaron and Dru on the afterdeck of the boat, which Dru had converted to an outdoor kitchen and summer eating area. During the meal, the sheriff told them the latest news as he had heard it from travelers passing through Chester. Dru, normally eager to hear what was happening in the outside world, was unusually subdued during this particular visit. It was not until later, after Brin had ridden off, that Aaron realized why. Dru stopped him as he was preparing to return to the hill.

"Are you going to lash him?" she asked.

"The Indian? Yes. I have to."

"Aaron, he saved my life."

"I know. I don't like lashing him. But I must have firm rules with respect to prisoners escaping. If I don't whip that Sac, half a dozen men will cut and run the first chance that turns up."

Dru's eyes showed anguish. "Is there no other way? No other punishment?"

"No. I made the rule; I must keep it."

Aaron walked back up to the bluff. Dru remained on the afterdeck. Twenty minutes later, she heard Kee-te-ha scream as Aaron laid the first blow on him.

By the beginning of September, when Tillman took the keelboat back upriver, a two-room cabin was ready for Dru and Aaron to move into. It was at the top of the road leading up from Prisontown, and just outside one corner of the now nearly complete wall. A bed and some other rough-hewn furniture was put together by the men in the lumber yard, and the couple spent their first married night ever on dry land.

"Feels odd not to hear the water beneath us," Aaron whispered to her in the dark as he found her breasts.

"Yes." Perhaps, she thought, it would make a difference. Perhaps the slight movement of that boat had somehow reduced Aaron's movement so that he could not—well, *perform* as he otherwise might have.

But it was not so. The act was still over all too quickly, and Dru was left feeling as hollow on land as she had been on the river.

Now that they lived on Prison Hill, Dru had much closer contact with the prisoners than before. During her share of their downriver journey, she had observed them only from a distance—except for the horror of Darby's aborted escape—and while she and Aaron had lived on the beached boat, Aaron had not permitted her to go up the hill. The men, he explained, were living outside and often went around in a state of partial undress. Plus which, the two privies did not have doors on them.

Now it was different. Aaron had seen to it that construction of the wall was concurrent with construction of their cabin. When the wall was sufficiently complete, Aaron ordered the men to move their bivouac inside. New privies were dug, and the convict kitchen, under Pete French, was also moved inside. The men now came out only to work. Even so, because many of them worked right there on the bluff, as opposed to the pit or the woods, it was impossible for Dru not to come into contact with them. Aaron did not like it, but there was little he could do except caution her now and again that convicts, as they had both learned, were not to be trusted.

One prisoner Dru could not help trusting—and tried to help—was Kee-te-ha. After his whipping, he had taken Kelsey's place in the corner of the supply tent. Kelsey had long since recovered and been sent to the rock pit. When Kee, as Dru had taken to calling him, regained enough strength to work, Dru had nagged Aaron into giving him an easy job. Aaron made him water boy for the entire compound. Kee spent the day leading around one of the dray horses with two water kegs slung across its back, a dipper tied to each one, to allow the men to drink. Later, after they moved up the hill, Dru would smile and speak to the Indian whenever she got the chance. On a few occasions she slipped extra food to him when no one else was around. At first he had refused to take it, apparently fearing that Aaron might whip him for it; but eventually his appetite overcame his fears and he took whatever she gave him.

Vester was also kind to Kee whenever he had the chance. Knowing the Indian had saved Dru's life, and because she was kin, he felt himself under an unwritten bond to follow Dru's example in his treatment of Kee. He was aware that Aaron probably would not have approved, but he favored Kee nevertheless—with extra food, fur skins from trapping, a drink of whiskey now and then—and his doing it was a secret between him and Dru. Vester rather enjoyed it, too; it reminded him of how he and Dru had often conspired to fool his parents when they were growing up. He winked at her now whenever Kee was around, and she knew what he was doing, but they never discussed it.

Before summer was over, work finally began on the cell house. Following the design of the Quaker penitentiary, it was to measure eleven rods by two rods, and be two stories high. The upper floor would consist of fifty back-to-back cells, twenty-five facing north, twenty-five south. The cells would be ten feet deep and six feet wide, with stone walls one foot thick on all sides. The doors, which were being made by a state blacksmith in Kearney, some thirty miles away, were to be of solid iron with a small peephole which could be closed from the outside. The first floor of the structure would be divided into several large rooms: guard barracks, mess hall, supply shed, armory, and an office for the warden.

Because of the time-consuming necessity of going upriver for healthy timber, then having to drag it up the hill by dray horse, it had now become obvious that the cell house would not be finished until at least after the first of the following year. As the evenings grew cool, both Aaron and the convicts began to get restless and edgy. They all hoped fervently for a mild winter.

Dru was not able to buy her new dress on the shebang boat because the merchant ship never called at the little prison settlement. But one afternoon, on a day that the elder Pullman brother came back with a boatload of new merchandise, Aaron came home and announced that they were going down the hill to visit the store. When they got there, Tad Pullman, the younger and smarter of the brothers, brought out a dress that Aaron had ordered especially for Dru. It was brown, with globe sleeves, and a bodice decorated by a flower-crocheted sash. Without qualification, it was the ugliest dress Dru had ever seen.

"Aaron, it's very pretty," she said. "It's a fine dress."

Aaron swelled with pride as he paid Pullman for it. That night, Dru modeled it for him and Aaron thought she looked beautiful. Later, in bed, Dru was extra responsive to him, actually feeding her breasts into his hungry mouth. He was such a good man, her Aaron, and he tried so hard.

In October, Tillman returned with the new prisoners. There were only nineteen this time, and of that number, four of them refused to work: two murderers doing life and two highway robbers, partners, sentenced to fifteen years each. They all joined Lewt and Jingo in the "idle box," which was now a corner area inside the wall. In spite of the four idle newcomers, Aaron's work force was increased by fifty percent, and with the new manpower he foresaw completing the cell house before year's end. He had not reckoned with the weather.

The first snowfall came early in November. It was a heavy snow, but not a permanent one; it came at night, surprising everyone except the sentries, and lasted only two days before it melted away. The first morning snow lay on the ground there was a carnival atmosphere among the men. Lining up for breakfast, they engaged in the horseplay of young boys, throwing snowballs, sliding on a trail of ice where water had seeped from the well and frozen, and modeling a short, barrel-like snowman which everyone knew was an effigy of Aaron, but which no one admitted.

By midafternoon, all the joy had gone out of the snowfall when it began melting and softening the ground; when its chill finally seeped through to the bones of the men in the pit; when they all realized that their nights of sleeping outdoors had suddenly changed from cool to cold. The next morning, when the last of the snow melted and left in its wake a sea of mud, the convicts unanimously cursed it for the scourge it was to them.

While they were still cursing the mud, the temperatures plunged to zero and froze the ground solid. The wind began to blow, howling up through the forest like a wail of death. Aaron and Tillman stood on the bluff and looked down at the river. Great chunks of dirty brown ice floated along in the rapids.

"It's a blizzard," Tillman said ominously. "Sure as we're standing here, one's coming." He swallowed dryly, stretching his upper lip tautly over the big front teeth it did not quite cover.

"I think you're right," Aaron replied. "That sky reminds me of the way it looked just before the big blizzard of seventeen. Let's hope to God it's not as bad as that one." He took a deep breath and rubbed his hands together. "We'd best see if we can prepare ourselves for it. You take some men and double-secure the two boats against ice floes. I'll see what I can do up here."

The frigid wind whipped at Aaron as he crossed to the lumber yard. The convicts there began to complain at once. "The wood's frozen, Mr. Van Hawn. We can't cut it."

"Leave it," said Aaron. "Follow me."

He took them to the supply tent and selected a variety of staple foods to be moved inside the walls. "Take all the rolled oats, all the noodles, turnips, lima beans, and coffee. Pitch a number two tent where the idle box is. Store everything there." In a corner, Kee was chopping ice from the frozen water kegs. Aaron gestured and the Indian followed him over to the cabin. Dru was already stuffing rags in the window cracks, "That's good," said

Aaron, "but we'll need a lot more protection than that. Have Kee bring in those spare planks out back and show him how to nail them over the window. I'll be back later."

In the middle of the compound, he found the crew from the rock pit straggling in against the wind. "Ground's froze!" Vester yelled. "I never seen it so hard!"

Aaron led the men inside the walls. There was instant relief from the wind as soon as the big, solid gate was closed behind them. But the incessant howling was replaced by a silent, threatening cold that was ominously frightening. The convicts looked up at the sky with fearful eyes. Aaron went over and inspected the partially built cell house. The framing was up, and some of the interior walls, but it was far from being anything but a skeleton yet. Still, it was better than no shelter at all.

"You men move into the cell house structure," Aaron said. "That will give you some protection, at least. Everybody get your blanket and other possessions and find the best place you can."

The men broke ranks and hurried away. Aaron sent a guard out to have the timber crew brought in. Then he found Pete French in the cook tent. "Move your kitchen inside the walls. Set up in a corner so you'll have shelter to cook. I'll send some men over to help you move the firewood supply."

When Tillman came back up the hill, he reported that Prisontown was closed up tight, "Everybody's nailing shutters on," he said. "They're expecting a bad one."

"They're expecting right," said Aaron. "Look there." He pointed toward the northern sky. Two hours earlier it had been clear and blue. Now a huge black cloud mass hung uncommonly low to the land.

"My god," said Tillman. Instinctively, he pulled his cap lower over his broad, flat forehead, as if it might protect him from the gathering threat.

"Have the guard tents struck and moved inside the walls. Make sure the stoves are lashed down and the stovepipes well secured. Then take a count to see that everyone's safely inside. Do it quickly; that cloud won't hold there long."

Aaron hurried back to the cabin. Working together, Dru and Kee had boarded all the windows and hung wagon canvas over the front door. Aaron took Kee with him and got a supply of drinking water and coal oil for the cabin. Then they made several trips to lay in extra food rations. By the time they had finished, the wind was blowing so hard and so cold it hurt to breathe.

"Aaron, please let Kee stay here with us," Dru asked.

"Don't be silly," Aaron replied shortly. "The man's a convict."

"But he might freeze out there—"

"So might the others."

Aaron took the Indian inside the walls. "What's the count, Mr. Tillman?" he asked.

"Everyone's accounted for except convict Rudd!" Tillman yelled above the wind. "He may have gone down the hill to help his family! Shall I go after him?"

"No, forget him! Get everything settled in here as best you can! Keep two guards on the gate at all times! Where's Vester?"

"Putting some braces on the kiln to keep it steady in the wind!"

"Make sure he gets back in safely!"

"Yes, sir!"

As Aaron started back for his cabin, the black cloud opened and the snow began. It came down in an almost solid white sheet, slanted in its descent by the velocity of the wind. More sleet than snow, it attacked everything in its path with millions of icy needles. In a matter of seconds, Aaron's face was throbbing with pain, and his ears were so cold that they began to grow numb. When he finally burst through the door of the cabin, he was panting for breath, his great chest heaving.

"Here," Dru said, putting a steaming copper cup in his mittened hands. He nodded and leaned up against the wall. The cup contained a soup of beans and green onions. He sipped at it gratefully, its steam rising to his eyes and making them water.

"I swear, never have I seen cold like this," he said, gasping. "It's not fit for man or beast—" His words broke off and he stared at Dru. His eyes grew wide.

"What is it?" Dru asked urgently. He looked stunned, as if he'd been slapped.

"The horses. I forgot about the horses."

"Perhaps someone else took care of them"

"No. Everyone only did what I told them to do. The horses still have to be tended to."

"You can't go back out in this, Aaron."

"If I don't, the horses will freeze. They're standing in their stalls; they can't move around to keep warm. They have no blankets on them. No hay."

Dru gripped his arm. "Aaron, you cannot risk your life to save two horses."

Aaron frowned. "It's not to save the horses. It's to save the prison. We need those horses to drag sleds of brick. To drag the iron doors up from the river when they get here. To drag rock from the pit." He looked around. "Give me that muffler."

He tied a heavy woolen scarf around his lower face, then another over his hat and under his chin. Around his waist he looped a sturdy hemp rope. "I'll tie one end of this to the porch post," he said. "That way I'll be sure to find my way back."

Dru pulled back the wagon canvas to let him out. In just the seconds she had the door open, the wind raged into the little cabin, rattling Dru's cooking pots and whipping at everything else that was hanging on the walls. The canvas snapped back and lashed her cheek, reddening it. She had to put her whole body against the door to close it.

When Aaron had the guide rope tied fast, he went around the corner of the wall toward the stable. He was at once blinded by the snow. He bent his head and forced himself forward. The wind whipped a relentless tattoo on his trouser legs, flapping them like naval flags in a gale. It burned his lungs to breathe. The air was so cold, it hurt his teeth when he sucked in a breath. For every two steps he took, the wind drove him back one of them.

It took Aaron fifteen minutes to negotiate a hundred yards. His knees and calves felt oddly like warm water when he finally reached the stable. He forced open the door and fell to the ground inside. The horses, already frightened by the howling wind, bolted noisily at his sudden appearance. Aaron lay panting on the hay-strewn ground until he caught his breath. He was sorely tempted to lie there longer—the hay next to his face felt warm, even *smelled* warm—and he would have stayed right there and waited out the storm with the horses had Dru not been alone in the cabin.

After a moment, he got to his feet, untied the guide rope from around his waist, and went about tending the horses. He pitched enough hay into each feeding bin to fill them both up, and broke the top off the water keg so the horses could get at the ice to lick it for water. Then he threw a heavy United States Army horse blanket over each of the animals and buckled it under the neck. Last, he propped open both stall gates so that the horses could move around for warmth. Before he left, he rubbed both of them on the ears.

"Good luck," he said quietly to each.

With the guide rope tied securely to his waist again, Aaron pushed back outside and dropped the crossbar to lock the stable door. Turning, he bent his head to the brutal wind and pulled himself along by the rope. Because of the rope, going back should have been easier than coming over, but it was not. The velocity of the wind had increased, and now it was hitting him dead-on, holding him back, forcing the breath down into his lungs until he had to turn his head to exhale. The wind was relentless.

After ten full minutes, Aaron had gone only thirty yards, not even a third of the way back. But he did not know that. The blowing snow was so thick that he could not see five feet in front of him. All he knew was that the bitter, bitter cold was drawing away all of his strength and he had to rest. He dropped to his knees.

Must be halfway there, he thought. God, it's cold, so cold. He thought of Dru and the warm cabin and the bean-and-onion soup. Clutching the rope with both hands, he rose and plodded forward.

Soon Aaron's eyelashes and eyelids were frozen with frost. His face, under the woolen scarf, was fixed in an agonized squint. His great back was hunched, the bull shoulders thrown forward as his hands pulled him along the rope scant inches at a time. It was taking him so long. . . .

He dropped to his knees again. It was nice to rest. It actually felt warmer when he stopped. He had an odd desire to tuck his head in his arms and go to sleep. Only the thought of Dru kept him from doing it. He rose and resumed the instinctive hand-over-hand pulling. But he did not take a dozen steps before he went down again.

Too far and too cold, he told himself. Just cannot make it.

But Dru and the cabin and the soup continued to beckon. On

his knees, he slid himself forward. It was fairly easy, because the ground now had a sheet of icy snow on it. In fact, thought Aaron, this was easier than walking. Less wind resistance, he imagined. Considering himself very crafty, he moved forward smartly.

After a while his breath gave out again and he had to stop. His eyes were almost closed now from the heavy ice on his lids. From the knees down, he was soaked in frigid wetness. The rest of him was glazed like a frosted window. All alone in the blizzard, he had become an icy specter.

He tried to go forward on his knees again. He could not. He fell down, burying his face in drifting snow. It had been thirty-five minutes since he left the stable, but he had no concept of time. An hour or a minute, there was no difference now. The moment was suspended for him. He closed his eyes all the way. He began to feel very warm.

Lying with his face in the snow, Aaron wanted to go to sleep. But the clutching, pulling hands would not let him. They were insistent hands, demanding hands. And there was a voice that accompanied them.

"Aaron! Aaron, get up! You must get up or you'll freeze!"

The hands became fists and began pounding on his hunched shoulders. The yelling voice was close to his face. It was Dru. His wife had come for him. He reached out for her. "I can't see!" he yelled.

Dru took his hand and helped him to his knees, then to his feet. She found his other hand and put both of them on her shoulders. "Hold onto me, Aaron!" she yelled above the wind howl. She walked slowly forward, holding to the guide rope. Aaron followed.

Once Dru was there to help him, it seemed like no time at all before they reached the cabin and stumbled inside. As he had done in the stable, Aaron dropped heavily to the floor. Dru collapsed beside him. They were exhausted. Neither of them moved, except to reach for the other. As soon as their hands touched, they knew they would be all right.

Outside, the storm roared, as if angry at losing them.

The blizzard lasted sixteen days. At one point, the cabin in which Aaron and Dru lived was completely covered by snow except for a two-foot circle where it melted around the stovepipe.

The drifts were so deep that Aaron left the cabin only three times to check on Tillman and the men.

Down in Prisontown, an old man and a boy were caught outside in the raging wind and froze to death. Ice floes sixty feet long were carried down the river at frightening speeds, crushing all boats in their path. The prison flatboat was torn from its mooring and broken in half like a dry stick. The men inside the new prison wall managed to survive by keeping constant small fires going and allowing no one to sleep long enough to freeze. The skeleton of the cell house structure was just sufficient to break the bitter wind and protect the convicts from deadly snowdrifts. Pete French kept hot food ready around the clock, and half a dozen men at a time were allowed in the cook tent to eat and get warm. The guards had oil stoves in their two tents and survived without casualty. Aaron and Dru, after the first night, waited out the storm in relative comfort.

The convict Rudd was never seen again. Nor were his wife and two sons, those very first settlers in Prisontown. Somehow they had escaped in the storm.

Vester Foyle never made it back from the kilns. Lost in the raging storm, he wandered in the wrong direction, away from the compound. When Tillman and a search party finally found him, he was huddled up against a tree trunk, frozen to death.

And sometime during the blizzard, the Indian Kee managed to escape again.

CHAPTER 12

In the late spring of 1828, Lieutenant Governor Alton Monroe arrived at Prison Hill to inspect the new state prison. He was accompanied by Grover, who had become his chief aide, and by a small group of lesser dignitaries who were also members of the state government or its judicial system. The facility was inspected at noon. All prisoners were dressed in freshly laundered clothes and lined up along an open section of the wall. Aaron walked with the lieutenant governor and Grover as they toured the upstairs cells, the downstairs mess hall, armory, and guard quarters.

"This is splendid, Aaron, splendid," Alton Monroe said a number of times. "You have done an exemplary job. Don't you think so, Grover?"

"I do, indeed, sir," Grover answered each time, winking at Aaron. "Surprising, too. A man with a new bride as pretty as Druscilla, you wouldn't think he'd devote so much time to his duties."

Monroe and Grover laughed loudly as Aaron turned red. Then they slapped him on the shoulders and he laughed with them, proud to have them treat him as an equal. His chest swelled as they continued to compliment him on his achievement of building the prison.

Monroe and his party had arrived an hour earlier. Aaron had met them in front of his cabin.

"Hello, old friend!" Grover had said, leaping down from the coach before it even stopped and striding over to him. They shook hands heartily and clasped each other by the shoulders. For a split instant, Aaron felt as if tears were coming to his eyes, he was so glad to see Grover agian.

"By God, Grove," he said in a low voice, "you look like a big city gentleman from hat to boot!"

"I am, you country lout." He patted Aaron's expanding midsection. "You haven't been starving yourself, I see."

Aaron looked sheepish. "Grove, there's somebody I want you to meet." He hurried into the cabin and brought Dru out. "This is my wife, Grove. Druscilla."

Grover's mouth dropped open. "Well, I'll be damned." He swept his hat off. "Pardon my language, ma'am." He bowed and took her hand. "Druscilla. What a delightful surprise. Are you really married to this old barn-raiser?"

"Yes, I am. And I'm so happy to meet you at last. As my husband's oldest and dearest friend, please consider our home your home."

"Why, thank you, Druscilla," said Grover, raising his eyebrows, impressed. "What a pretty speech."

"She rehearsed it," Aaron said proudly.

Dru looked at him in mortification. "Aaron!"

Grover laughed and put his arms around both of them. "I am delighted, Aaron. Really delighted. She's an absolute dear. Now wait here, both of you. I want to bring the lieutenant governor over." He hurried to where the coach was parked. A moment later he returned with Alton Monroe.

The reunion between Aaron and the lieutenant governor was less exuberant than with Grover, but just as sincere and friendly. Alton Monroe genuinely liked Aaron, and was most impressed with Dru. "I hope you'll be eating with us after the inspection tour, Mrs. Van Hawn."

"Thank you, sir, I will," she replied with a curtsey that made Aaron swell with pride.

Now the group was moving across the prison yard after leaving the cell house.

"How many convicts do you have now, Aaron?" the lieutenant governor asked.

"Fifty-two, sir. Some of the counties have started delivering men here as soon as they're sentenced, instead of holding them for the keelboat."

"Good. That's the way it should be. We're getting some decent roads built down this way now; shouldn't have to use the boat at all." He looked around, pleased. "Yes, Aaron, you've done quite a commendable job here."

"Thank you, sir." Aaron looked around too, and as he did he felt a great emptiness come over him. This was *his* prison; *he* had built it. Now it was to be given to someone else. Turned over to a stranger. Relinquished like a favorite daughter given in marriage.

With the exception of Dru, it was all he had. What was he to do when it was gone? Go back to raising barns?

"Well," said Alton Monroe, "I for one have worked up an appetite. How about the rest of you?"

That was Grover's signal that the tour was over. He sent the rest of the escort party down the hill to Prisontown, while the lieutenant governor, Aaron, and he went back to the cabin to join Dru for the noon meal. Dru had made the cabin an uncommonly pleasant place for Aaron and her to live, and Monroe complimented her on it as if it were a mansion.

"Elegant," he said. "Absolutely elegant. You've done as good a job with your quarters, Mrs. Van Hawn, as your husband has done with the prison. You're both to be congratulated."

"Thank you, sir," said Dru, with another proper curtsey. "It should be comfortable for whoever moves in next."

Alton Monroe smiled as they sat down to eat. "Suppose we talk about that," he said slyly. "Aaron, how would you like to become the new prison's first warden?"

Aaron and Dru stared at their visitor. Grover grinned and winked at his friend again. Aaron was not prepared for such an offer. He wished Grover had warned him. Inside his chest, his heart began to pound.

"I—I'm not sure I'm qualified—"

"Who is?" said Monroe. "No one, really, unless we get some Quaker from New England, or import someone from Britain. The governor doesn't care for either alternative, and neither do I. We want someone from our own state. We think you're the man for the job, Aaron."

Grover leaned forward and touched Aaron's arm. "You're an intelligent man, Aaron, and a fair one. This job is perfect for you, believe me."

"He's right," said Monroe. "I'm going to offer Tillman and his men the opportunity to transfer from the state militia to the new prison service as guards. If they accept, Tillman can be your guard captain. He can run things while you supervise the building of your new house."

"New house?" said Aaron.

"Yes. Charming as this cabin is, it's no place for the warden to live. I'm going to get an appropriation for a small mansion—say ten or twelve rooms—to be constructed nearby as a permanent warden's residence."

Aaron and Dru exchanged quick glances. Dru's eyes were wider than usual. A mansion. Ten or twelve rooms. She had never even *been* in a house that large.

"I want to ask your advice on something too, Aaron, aside from your accepting the wardenship or not," said Monroe. "Now that the prison is built, what are your thoughts as to how the prisoners should pass their time? Tell you why I'm asking: a friend of the governor—the same man who donated this land, actually—has another parcel nearby where he's considering building a knitting mill. If there are no other immediate work projects for the prisoners, why, the governor thought we might put them to work in the mill. On a lease-labor basis, to help offset the cost of the state supporting them. What do you think?"

"I suppose that would be fine," Aaron said, frowning uncertainly. "They should be kept busy, I suppose."

"My sentiments exactly. Why, they could even help build the place. The landowner could bring in the same stonemason you hired in Paducah after you lost the first one in that terrible blizzard." Monroe glanced at Dru. "Oh, I am sorry, Mrs. Van Hawn. That gentleman was a relative of yours, wasn't he?"

"My wife's cousin," Aaron answered for her. He glanced at Dru. She seemed outwardly unaffected by the comment, but he knew that inside she must have felt a clutch of sadness. Dru had been quite shaken by Vester's death, as had Aaron himself, who had grown quite fond of the big, gentle youth.

"I'm sorry for you," he had told his wife, feeling a hit of guilt. "If I had known something like this would happen, I never would have bargained to bring him here."

"I don't fault you, Aaron; it's God's will," she had said through her tears. "But you didn't get your ten months' labor from Vester. I'm sorry the worst of the bargain had to be yours."

Aaron took her in his arms. "The *best* of the bargain is mine," he told her, in the softest voice he had ever used. "Without a day of Vester's labor."

His words, which meant so much to her, had lessened considerably the shock of her loss. They were closer at that moment than they had ever been.

Aaron reassuringly touched Dru's hand now as the lieutenant governor apologized for the oversight.

"My sympathies," said Monroe, "and my pardon for mentioning it." He resumed with Aaron. "Now then, if this arrangement can be formalized, Aaron, would you have any objection to my sending down a man to keep books on the whole thing? He would work for me but be under you. We can call him a deputy warden or some such thing just for the record." Monroe stopped suddenly and smiled widely. "Listen to me. I'm talking as if Aaron had already accepted this job."

"Aaron's a reliable man, sir," Grover said solemnly. "He'll want to serve our state where he's best suited. Won't you, my friend?"

Aaron slowly nodded his head. "Yes. Of course."

"You'll accept the post then?" asked Monroe.

Aaron and Dru exchanged glances. Each saw relief in the face of the other. They *did* have a future, after all.

"Yes. I will accept," Aaron said. "I will be the warden."

That summer, work began on both the knitting mill and the new warden's residence. The mill was back on the bluff, half a mile from the rock pit, which was the prison's rear boundary. The road built by the army engineers was extended back to the mill property. Each morning, thirty-four of the prisoners would have the shackle taken off their right ankles, and with a cord of rawhide would tie the leg-iron up around their calves so that they could march down the road to work. When the men had their irons tied up like that, they were referred to as "corded." With both ankles shackled, they were "hobbled." Walking to work corded, their loose shackles clinked loudly in unison with each step of their left feet.

Aaron and Dru's new house was being constructed on a knoll some forty feet above where the cabin stood. It was to be a colonial home with a four-columned portico and a spacious front lawn. One view from the porch would look directly at the prison and surrounding compound; the other would look down at Prisontown and the river. Eight men worked on the mansion; two of them were carpenters by trade, one a murderer who had chosen work instead of the Idle Box, and the other a man working to halve his five-year sentence for cheating and defrauding a mill out of a wagonload of lumber.

One afternoon in midsummer, when the house and the mill were both half finished, Aaron and Dru were sitting on the porch of the cabin sharing an apple and watching a line of eight chained men being led up the hill. The men, in the custody of three upstate constables, were delivered to Tillman, who waited for them at the top of the road. After Tillman had properly signed for them, he had his own guards march them over to line up in front of Aaron.

"New men, sir," Tillman said, saluting casually.

"Thank you, Mr. Tillman." Aaron rose, jutting his jaw, clasping his hands behind him. He still enjoyed performing for Dru. "My name is Van Hawn," he said to the new arrivals. "I am the warden of this prison. Before you are taken inside the walls for the first time, let me say a few things to you that might make your sentence easier to serve."

As Aaron spoke, Dru worked at a small basket of mending on her lap. The basket was the same one that had held the fruit Tillman had given them on their wedding night. As she worked, her eyes on the mending, she sensed someone staring at her. She glanced up and met the eyes of one of the convicts. He was a tall, rangy man with dirty blond hair that curled all over his head. He had an aquiline nose and thin lips. His eyes were brilliant blue. The convict's name was Theron Verne. Dru had not seen him for more than two years, but she remembered him from the old schoolhouse in Bristol. They had gone to school together as adolescents.

Dru looked away from Theron Verne's eyes. She did not quite know what to do. On an ordinary occasion, she would have bowed her head slightly in acknowledgment. But this was not an ordinary occasion: the man was a convict, being brought into her husband's prison in chains. He should not even be looking at her; Aaron had *killed* a man for touching her; he might very well have Theron lashed for staring that way. She decided to keep her eyes down and look at him no more.

"If you want to work," Aaron was saying, "you can earn your way out of here in half the time of your sentence. And if any of you have particular skills, such as carpentry or masonry or blacksmithing, and you apply those skills diligently, you might work out sooner—"

Theron Verne tentatively raised his hand. Aaron frowned slightly; convicts did not usually interrupt his welcoming speech with questions. "Yes?" he said gruffly.

"Sir," Theron said, "would those special skills include lawn gardening?"

"Lawn gardening?"

"Yessir. Putting in grass and flowers. One of the constables said a fine new house being built on the knoll was for the warden. I was thinking how much finer it would be with a nice green lawn and some rows of flowers."

"Are you a lawn gardener?" Aaron asked.

"I have been, yessir."

"What's your crime?"

"Burglary, sir."

"Any violence?"

"None, sir. I robbed houses only when no one was home."

"Your sentence?"

"Twelve years, sir."

Aaron stroked his jutted jaw and nodded thoughtfully. "I'll consider it. Stay on your best behavior until the building's done, then we'll see."

"Yessir," Theron said, grinning. "Thank you very much, sir. Very much indeed."

The men were led away without Theron and Dru exchanging any more looks. Dru had kept her eyes down throughout the conversation. But she knew without looking that it was Theron who had spoken with her husband. For a passing moment, Dru had considered telling Aaron about him. She knew inside her that it was the right thing to do.

But she did not tell him.

In the fall, just before the knitting mill was finished, Clement Niles arrived at Prison Hill. He was Alton Monroe's bookkeeper, the man who would keep records on the convict labor to be leased to the mill. His arrival coincided with the Van Hawns' move into the new residence; they were vacating the cabin in which Niles was to reside.

"I hope you'll like the cabin," Dru said as she and Aaron showed him around. "My husband and I found it comfortable."

"Is it well heated?" Niles asked. "I chill very easily."

"Oh, it's quite warm," Dru assured him.

Aaron studied the newcomer while Dru talked to him. He was an unusually thin man of about thirty, and had about him a hint of pallor which made him appear ill. Though the weather was still very warm, with not even a hint of winter in the air, he coughed from time to time as if his lungs were cold. His eyes looked bad too; they were much too white, the pupils very light and weak. He's sick, Aaron decided. He won't last long.

After Dru excused herself and returned to her own work at the new house, Aaròn and Niles sat down and settled things between them. "The lieutenant governor said you were to be called a deputy warden," Aaron said.

"For lack of a more appropriate title. I'm to assure you, however, that the running of the prison will continue to be solely your responsibility. My function will primarily be to keep books on the leased labor and collect the money for the state—"

"And for the lieutenant governor," Aaron said quietly, his tone neutral, nonaccusatory.

Clement Niles narrowed his eyes and studied Aaron for a silent moment. "Successful politics is an expensive occupation," he replied. "Alton Monroe would like to become governor someday."

"So he's preparing early."

"Exactly."

Aaron thought it over and finally shrugged. "It means nothing to me. I'll not question your books."

"I, ah—I could arrange a small share for, ah—"

"No need," Aaron said, quickly stopping him before the offer could be fully made. "I'm paid well enough. So long as there's no interference with my running of the prison."

"There won't be," Niles assured him. "Incidentally, I *am* a good bookkeeper, and this business with the mill will only occupy a portion of my time. I'll be happy to keep your supply books and convict records if you want me to."

"That's good of you. My wife has been doing the books up to now."

"Say no more. I'll consider it a privilege to relieve her of that nuisance."

When Aaron told Dru that Niles would be keeping the books in the future, she was a bit disappointed. "I thought you liked for me to do that," she said. "I thought you wanted all the books to be in my fine, stylish hand, as you call it."

"I didn't feel I should insult the man by refusing his offer," Aaron explained. "Anyway, I don't think it'll be for long. The man's not well. You heard him say he chills easily. When winter comes, he'll go back to the capital quick enough."

"I'll give him the books tomorrow," Dru said.

Aaron nodded. He filled a new pipe he had bought at the Pullman Brothers store and lighted it at the cookstove. He had been smoking for several months now. Dru did not like the smell of the pipe, but she said nothing about it.

"I should think," Aaron said, "that you'd be glad to have Niles take those books off your hands. What with the new house, this will give you time to do all the things you want to do. You'll have to be in charge of the men I set to building the furniture, you know. And the house help, soon as I pick out who it'll be. And I guess we might as well get that lawn gardener to work on the grounds too. You'll have to show him how you want things done, you know."

Dru thought of Theron Verne. She had wondered where he was working. Since he was never around the compound, she guessed he was either in the rock pit or building the mill. There was no way she could ask Aaron, now that she had concealed from him that she knew the young convict.

Feeling guilty because she was thinking about Theron, Dru went over to where Aaron sat smoking his pipe. She curled up on the floor next to his chair and laid her cheek against his knee.

"There *is* a lot to do," she said. "I suppose it will be easier if Mr. Niles does the books."

"Of course it will," Aaron said. He stroked her hair with his free hand.

Dru sighed quietly. It was an odd little sigh; a sigh of vague, remote discontent. Dru had no notion at all what it meant.

The new house was beautiful. It far surpassed anything that either Aaron or Dru had ever dreamed they would live in. The portico stretched across the front of the new house, which faced southeast to get the most winter sun. An entry foyer led in to a large dining room on one side, an equally large parlor on the other. Beyond the stairway was a drawing room. Behind the dining room was a huge kitchen and pantry, and to the side of that was a downstairs bedroom. Upstairs was a master bedroom and sitting room, and three other rooms which Dru decided would be a sewing room, a guest room, and possibly a nursery. Although on the latter she was not at all certain. It seemed to her, from all the loose information she had acquired, that she surely should have been pregnant by now. Yet her monthly time came promptly every month. She still had the vague feeling that something was not being done quite right.

She had no time to worry about that, however; there were too many things to do around the *huge* new house. The sheer size of the place frightened her at first. How would she *ever* keep it clean? And get enough furniture to fill it? Aaron solved the first problem for her when he assigned two convicts to work as domestics. One, who was to be a kitchen helper, was a black man named Tea Leaf who was serving five years for stealing a bale of cotton. The other was a rather dull-witted farm lad named Arlo, who had taken his employer's horse without permission and was caught with the animal before he could return it. His sentence was ten years. While Tea Leaf worked in the kitchen, Arlo was to be a general handyman, chopping firewood, drawing water from the well several times a day, keeping the big house spotlessly whitewashed on a continuing basis, and in general doing whatever Dru needed doing.

The furniture problem was solved by Dru herself. Aaron had already assigned three carpenters to build furniture for her, but she discovered early on that they were limited to beds, bureaus, and basin-stands, all constructed solidly but with absolutely no imagination at all. She finally went down the hill and discussed her problem with the younger Pullman, Tad. His solution was to simply order ten rooms of furniture from St. Louis. Because of the cost, that was out of the question. But it did give Dru an idea. She would order *one* room of furniture and have her prison carpenters duplicate it. She could order one fine dining room chair, one fine settee, one armchair, and anything else that she needed. Upholstering material could be obtained through Pullman's. This excellent idea pleased Dru, who was delighted with herself for thinking of it.

On the day that Dru's first pieces of furniture arrived, the same keelboat delivered the first looms for the new knitting mill. A dozen prisoners, with their shackles corded, were taken downhill under guard and set to work loading the looms onto the same sled that had been used eighteen months earlier to haul Prison Hill's first supplies up to the summit. That sled, made of part of the deck of the flatboat destroyed in the blizzard, had served out the winter as the floor of the prison supply tent. Now a large room next to the guards' barracks held all the supplies, and the sled had been unused since the previous spring. A wagon now brought supplies up the hill, so they had no use for the sled until the looms arrived for the mill.

A Scot from the company that manufactured the looms accompanied them to Prison Hill and supervised their installation. His name was MacCune; he was an individual who classified convicts somewhere between donkeys and oxen. On the second day of the installation, one of the prisoners assigned to him accidentally let a corner of a loom slip off its brace onto the floor. The corner was chipped. MacCune was infuriated. He grabbed a loom wire and lashed the man across the face. The guard on duty at the time of the incident reported it to Tillman, who reported it to Aaron.

Aaron stalked out to the mill. The prisoner, with a bloody rag binding his open cheek, was still at work. Aaron examined his wound. "Mr. Tillman, this man is excused from work," he said. "Have him taken back and his face tended to."

MacCune came forward. "I'll need another man to replace him," he said in an authoritative tone.

"Replace him yourself," said Aaron.

"What was that?"

"You heard me, mister. You injured the man, now you do his

work. That's the rule in my prison." He stepped very close to the Scot. "And you're not to strike any of these men again, is that clear?"

MacCune's back stiffened. "I was assured by the owner of this mill that I would have your full cooperation in the installation of these looms. He told me the lieutenant governor had guaranteed it."

"Cooperation doesn't give you license to punish prisoners. These men are in *my* charge. I'm the one who directs punishment—and no one else."

MacCune's mouth turned into a thin line. He tossed down his mounting tool. "You're a bit too uppity for me. I think I'll leave the job half done and report the matter to the mill owner."

"I don't think you will," said Aaron. He gestured to a pair of guards. They blocked MacCune's way as he started to leave. The Scot whirled around, red with anger.

"You can't keep me here against my will!"

"Can't I?" Aaron said. He looked at the group of prisoners and picked out one of them: Casey, the old man who was serving three years for receiving stolen goods. "How much time do you have left, Casey?" he asked.

"A month and two days, sir."

Aaron turned to a guard. "Unshackle him."

The guard removed Casey's leg-iron.

"Put it on him," Aaron said, indicating the Scot.

MacCune tried to run. The guards stopped him quickly and expertly snapped the shackles above his ankles.

"You bloody bastard!" MacCune yelled.

Aaron stepped up close to him again. "You'll wear that iron until the last of these looms is installed. And if you lay a hand on one of my prisoners again, I'll put the lash to your back." He pointed a stiff finger in the Scot's face. "Mind you, do a first-rate job on the looms. And be on your best behavior. I'll be watching you like a hawk."

As Aaron walked away, the group of prisoners cheered him.

That night, back inside the walls, they told the story over and over again to the men who had not been there. And they gave Aaron a nickname that was to remain part of his identity for the rest of his life.

First it was Van Hawn the Hawk.

Then it was Van Hawk.
Then simply the Hawk.

Because of the many other things that had to be done around the new house, and because another winter was coming on, the lawn gardening was put off until the following spring. The winter that year was mild and short, perhaps to make up for the previous winter's blizzard. By the first week in April warm breezes had replaced chill air, the ground had softened, and early buds colored the gaunt trees. When the weather had held for ten days, Aaron finally had Tillman reassign Theron Verne to lawn gardening work.

Theron, hobbled, reported to the back door of the Van Hawn mansion and was met by Tea Leaf, the black kitchen helper. "What you want, white boy?" the big cotton thief asked.

"I'm to report to the mistress," Theron said. "To start work on the grounds."

Tea Leaf let him in and had him sit on a stool in the corner. "Ah'll get Miz Dru," he said importantly.

As soon as Tea Leaf was gone, Theron spread his feet wide to keep the leg-irons quiet and left the stool. He looked around the kitchen. He located the meat knives and cleavers; briefly inspected the well-stocked pantry; and ate some of the leftover bacon that Tea Leaf had on the huge iron cookstove. When he heard footsteps coming through the dining room, he widestepped back to the stool again.

When Dru entered, Theron got quickly to his feet and stood with hat in hand. "Come with me, please," Dru said. She led him out back and around to the front of the house. A broad flat of raw earth faced the big mansion from the edge of the knoll up to the wide front portico. "Mr. Van Hawn would like this plot to have a formal look to it," she said. "What would you recommend doing to it?"

Theron studied the area, knelt down to snatch a handful of dirt, and checked the sky for sun direction. He had changed some in the ten months since he arrived, Dru thought. His tallness was less rangy now, more muscular. Probably from working in the pit, she decided; men seemed to solid-up quickly when they handled heavy rock twelve hours a day. A brief, sad thought of her cousin Vester flashed through her mind. She had written her Uncle Abner and Aunt Wella out in Manhattan, Kansas, to tell them that their youngest son had frozen to death in the big blizzard, but she had never received a reply. It was possible, she supposed, that they were now dead also.

"Would you want flowers, ma'am?" Theron asked. "Or just lawn turf?"

"Flowers would be nice. What kind?"

"Well, in this soil here, I could probably get you some petunias, verbenas, marigolds, maybe nasturtiums. I'll have to irrigate everything, and they'll take a lot of care," he smiled easily, "but I gues I'll have plenty of time for it. Eleven more years to go."

"Five and a half, actually, if Mr. Van Hawn reduces your sentence to half."

"Do you think he might do that, ma'am?"

"If you do a good job, yes." She looked into his brilliant blue eyes. "Theron, how in the world did you end up here?"

Theron shook his head and gazed into space. "I was just plain stupid, 'Scilla—I mean ma'am, excuse me. After Daddy and Mamma died, why, I—"

"Mr. and Mrs. Verne are dead?" Dru said, surprised.

Theron nodded. "Three years ago in that pox up in Chelsea County. That's where we moved when we left Bristol. They both died the same week."

"How awful," Dru said.

Theron nodded and looked away from her. "I didn't have nobody after that; no family or nothing. Like you would have been, I guess, if your Uncle Ab hadn't taken you in. 'Course, that wasn't no excuse for starting to steal. I'm not trying to blame it on that, 'Scilla—I mean ma'am, excuse me, I called you by name again—"

"It's just a habit, you can't help it," Dru said.

Theron smiled. "You're right. If I was to do it in front of Mr. Van Hawn, I reckon he'd understand."

"I'm not so sure," Dru said, glancing around as if afraid that Aaron might be near.

"Why is that?" Theron asked. "You told him we knowed each other, didn't you?"

"No."

"Why not?"

"I don't know why not. I just didn't."

Theron started work the next day. Under guard, he searched the woods until he found an area that had enough forest grass to cover the lawn area Dru had shown him. With spade and ax, he carefully cut and lifted squares of the grass, along with its roots and the soil it was growing in, and carried them to a wagon on the nearby road. When he had enough, he tilled the ground in front of the mansion, raked a patchwork of small trenches for irrigation, ran water through them, and laid the squares of grass neatly in place. It took him ten days to do it, and it looked splendid when he was finished. As he was wetting it down, Dru came out and admired it.

"It's beautiful, Theron. Mr. Van Hawn will be pleased."

"Thank you, ma'am." He smiled at her. "Working with it reminded me of when we was in school. On days when it was too hot to stay inside, old Mrs. Meecham used to let us do our studies on the lawn out back. Remember?"

"Yes." Dru returned his smile. "I remember one little boy who didn't get much studying done, too. He was alway busy throwing burrs in my hair."

"You had the prettiest hair in the class." He looked frankly at her hair, which was in a bun. "Is it still long like it used to be?"

Dru felt herself blush. She looked down at the ground. "I guess it is. I've never cut it."

When she raised her eyes, Theron was still looking at her.

"I've got to go now," she said, and left.

After the turf had rooted and showed no signs of turning yellow, Theron went to work on the flowers. He dug deep beds along the front of the mansion and down each side of the lawn, and filled them with the blackest, richest humus he could find in the forest. The seed he needed was obtained by Dru through the Pullman Brothers. She recognized all the seed names except one.

"Theron, what kind of flower is a bodenia?" she asked, when she gave him the seed packets.

"Can't tell you," he said.

"Why not?"

His blue eyes sparkled mischievously. "It's a surprise."

"Surprise? For who?"

"For you, who do you think?"

She blushed, pleased. "What do they look like?"

"You'll see."

Teasingly, he made her wait. She came out several times a day to see if the bodenias had broken soil, and later, when they were podded, to see if they had opened.

"Oh, Theron, I'm dying to see them," she said. He only laughed.

When the day finally came that the bodenia pods opened and the pale brown petals unfolded, Dru thought they were the most beautiful flowers in the world.

"I picked them because their color always reminded me of your hair," Theron told her. "All the other flowers are to make the lawn look nice, but the bodenias are just for you."

"Thank you, Theron," she said quietly. She felt a warm glow inside, unlike anything she had ever felt before.

In the extreme heat of the day, Theron often worked with his shirt off. He had a perfectly proportioned physique: broad shoulders, a smooth, hairless chest, flat belly, lean waist, all deeply tanned from first the pit, then his gardening. He was always careful to put his shirt on whenever he saw Dru coming, but she nevertheless had ample opportunity to see him naked to the waist. And although she was filled with revulsion at herself for doing it, she could not help comparing Theron's youthful, attractive body to the shorter, paler figure of Aaron.

One day, when she walked to the edge of the woods to snip vines for her indoor plants, she came on Theron collecting moss from an oak trunk. Instinctively, she looked around for the perimeter guard, but he was nowhere to be seen. Theron smiled at her.

"The guard's around in front," he told her. "He lets me come back here a lot by myself. He knows I ain't going to hang 'em on a limb."

"Hang them on a limb?"

"The chain. Hang 'em on a limb means to get out of the legiron, hang it on a tree, and run off."

"And you wouldn't do that?"

"I might," Theron said, "if you weren't here."

Dru reached up and touched her throat. "You mustn't say things like that."

"Why? Because you're the warden's wife and I'm one of his convicts? Does that mean I ain't allowed to have feelings?" His expression became strained, almost angry.

"It doesn't mean you can't *have* feelings, Theron," she said quietly. "It just means you have to keep them to yourself." She swallowed dryly and added, "Like I do."

Theron locked eyes with her. He dropped a handful of moss he was holding and wiped his hand on the shirt he had hung nearby. Taking her hand, he gently pulled her to him, held her against his bare chest, and kissed her softly on the lips.

She let his mouth linger on hers for as long as she dared, let her body quiver in the warmth that coursed through her, closed her eyes to the indescribable tickle in her stomach; then she pushed away from him and hurried back to the house.

She stayed away from him for three days, and then she could fight her feelings no longer. It was midmorning, hot and humid, and he was pulling weeds from the marigold beds. Her shadow fell across him and he stopped and looked up. Her breasts looked very large from down there.

"Theron, promise me you won't try to escape," she said.

He shook his head. "I'd never make you a promise I mightn't be able to keep. You don't know what it's like inside those walls at night, 'Scilla. You can't imagine how lonely I get."

"Suppose I can—help you not to be so lonely?"

Theron stood up. His eyes narrowed slightly. He noticed that Dru had a faint line of perspiration across her upper lip. "If you're warm, we could go back to the kitchen for some cool water," he said.

She nodded. "All right."

They walked back alongside the house. Dru paced her steps to accommodate his leg-irons.

"Who all's in the house?" Theron asked.

"Just, ah—Tea Leaf. My handyman Arlo is out chopping firewood."

They went into the kitchen. "Get your mistress a dipper of water," Theron said to Tea Leaf. The big black threw him a hostile look; he did not like taking orders from Theron, but he nevertheless hurried to the burlap-covered oaken cask and ladled out a dipper of cool water.

After she had drunk, Dru said, "Tea, go over to the supply shed and get me a sack of sugar, please. I want to bake this afternoon and there's not enough on hand."

"Yes'am," said Tea Leaf. He glanced at Theron. "Is I to go right now, ma'am?"

"Yes," said Dru. "It'll be all right."

Tea Leaf took off his white bib apron, tightened the corded chain around his calf, and went out the back door. Theron and Dru remained very still, listening to the *clink*-pause-*clink*-pause of the big man's corded shackle as it rattled with every step of his left foot. In seconds it faded to silence.

Theron faced Dru. She was standing by the smooth bread table where Tea Leaf rolled out the day's dough every morning. The table still had a light trace of fine white flour on it. Dru put one hand down and left a print in the flour. She kept her eyes riveted on Theron. He came over and stood very close to her. He bent his head to kiss her. She saw him wet his lips with his tongue just before their mouths met.

The kiss was long and soft, hungry on both their parts, but not desperate. When it was over, Theron reached down and whipped Dru's skirts up around her waist. She drew in her breath and it caught in her throat. She tried to speak but could not. Theron's hands, rock-pit strong, opened the front of her pantalettes with a quick, clean tear. Her feet left the floor and he sat her on the edge of the table. Balancing herself, she felt flour under both hands now. Theron's lips were eating at her neck. With her head tilted far to one side, she looked down and saw his trousers fall around his ankles, covering up the leg-irons.

She closed her eyes and waited for the first thrust.

CHAPTER 13

Early in 1830 Aaron and Dru were visited again by their friend Grover. He came to lay the groundwork for Alton Monroe's campaign for a second term as lieutenant governor.

"This is the important one," Grover told Aaron and Clement Niles as they sat in the drawing room after dinner. "This is the one that will tell us whether Alton will ever be governor. If we were in one of our neighboring states, we'd have nothing to worry about. Alton could ride back into office on the coattails of the governor, who is extremely popular and bound to be reelected. But unfortunately our legislature saw fit to designate the offices of governor and lieutenent governor as separate entities, so Alton will have to campaign on his own again, just like he did in twenty-six."

Aaron studied Grover as he talked. His friend had changed a great deal in the past three years. The old Grover he remembered had not used words like "designate" and "entities." Nor had he drunk so much brandy or smoked so many of the rolled black cheroots he now carried. Grover *looked* good; he now dressed in expensive tailored waistcoats, had a gold watch from England, and wore boots made of the finest leather. But he did not smile as much anymore. And the mischievous twinkle had gone out of his eyes. If that was what the capital did to people, Aaron thought, then he was grateful to be far downstate at the prison.

"I'm sure it isn't necessary for me to remind either of you that your jobs are patronage positions," Grover continued. "If Alton is defeated in the fall elections, your jobs will terminate as soon as his successor is sworn in. So will mine, for that matter." He paused to pour more brandy and suck in on his cigar. He was the only one smoking *and* drinking. Clement Niles, who was nagged by a persistent cough, but who *had*, to Aaron's surprise, survived the winter, never smoked. He only sipped moderately at a glass of brandy. Aaron avoided the brandy and sat smoking his pipe.

"Our job, then, is to get Mr. Alton Monroe reelected," Grover said. "If we do that, it's very likely that we can all work for the state for another dozen years, because once Alton has been lieutenant governor for two terms, he's a cinch to be governor for two more. So," he unrolled a map on Aaron's desk, "I'm going to depend on you two to handle the eight southern counties for me."

"You mean post handbills again?" Aaron asked.

Grover stared at him for a moment, as if not certain he had heard right. "Hardly that, Aaron," he said quietly. "It wouldn't do for the warden of the state penitentiary and an assistant state auditor to go around the countryside posting handbills. That sort of work will be done by hired hands or volunteers. What you and Clement will do is travel around; stop in all towns as if you're passing through on business; visit with a few merchants, with the local minister, with the mayor, the saloonkeeper, the people passing on the sidewalks. You'll spread the word. Talk up Alton Monroe and what a fine job he's done. Remind them how low their taxes are; Alton doesn't have anything to do with that, but they don't know it. Mention the new roads being built around the state, and the faster mail service they've been getting; that's all federal doing but it doesn't matter. Anything that's good, connect Alton's name with it. Anything that's bad—"

"Blame it on Washington," Aaron put in.

Grover's eyebrows raised. He and Niles stared in surprise at their colleague. "That's the ticket, Aaron," Grover said, quite pleased. "That's what I like to hear."

Grover clamped the cigar between his teeth and smiled. Only at that moment did he definitely make up his mind to let Aaron represent the lieutenant governor downstate. Clement Niles he was already sure about; Niles was near his own age, and was careful and clever. Aaron, on the other hand, had not matured as much as Grover had hoped he would. His view of things, confined as it was to the prison, was too narrow. Even though

Grover was planning to let Aaron *start* working the southern counties, he had thought to keep a close eye on him through reports from Niles. If Aaron did not work out, if it appeared that he was not impressing people, then Grover planned to send him back to the prison and put someone else in his place. He had been considering Tillman as a substitute.

But Grover saw now that his contingency plan was not necessary. Once again Aaron had proved that he had the one asset Grover had found so essential in the business of politics: with his one simple statement Aaron had shown Grover that he had resourcefulness.

"You'll be just fine, Aaron," Grover said confidently. "Just fine indeed."

Grover had been right to send Aaron out to cover the countryside for Alton Monroe, because Aaron was still enough like the people in the southern counties to be able to talk to them on an almost neighborly basis. The counties he worked in the campaign went as strongly for Monroe in the election of 1830 as they had in 1826, with the incumbent lieutenant governor winning no less than eighty-five percent of the votes in any single county. Clement Niles, on the other hand, lost one of his assigned counties and barely carried the other three. Townspeople did not take to the thin, sickly man with the peculiar cough the way they took to robust, straightforward Aaron.

Nevertheless, Alton Monroe was overwhelmingly elected to a second term, and the following January, Aaron, Dru, and Clement Niles boarded one of the big nine-passenger, six-horse coaches that now stopped in Prisontown, and journeyed to the capital for the inauguration. For the occasion, Dru purchased two new dresses from the Pullman store, after accidentally on purpose spilling lye on the brown monstrosity Aaron had bought her and ruining it.

On the day they left for the capital, while riding down to Prisontown in the wagon, Dru saw Theron in a work party felling trees for firewood. She and Theron had been apart for four months, since cold weather had come and Aaron had assigned him back inside the walls. The previous summer, while Theron had been turning the mansion's front lawn into a rainbow of colors, they had been intimate whenever they had the chance: in the kitchen, the root cellar, the nearby woods out back, and once, when the house was deserted, even in Aaron's study, an act for which Dru later felt deep shame. Aaron was so good to her, and she cared so much for him, that she literally despised herself for what she was doing. But contemptuous as she was of herself, she could not resist the smell and touch and thrust of Theron Verne. He had opened her up wide, gone far inside her as Aaron had never done, and made her feel that at last she had done it right. Her thrill with Theron inside her had convinced her that it was poor Aaron's smallness that had left her feeling so unsatisfied and unused. Theron was so much larger, and it was so much better when she did it with him. Size, she decided, must be the answer.

Theron, Theron, Theron—he was on her mind constantly. And when they were together in their stolen moments, she abandoned all the world but him and what he did for her. When the feeling of him surged through her like a warm inner caress, she did not care whether they were caught or not. Death would have been a fair price to pay for such ecstasy.

During the long winter she accepted what Aaron could do for her, but she ached for her convict lover. Spring was a long time coming that year.

In April, Kee was brought back again. Three bounty hunters brought him in, slung face-down over the back of a mule that they led behind their horses. They reined up in the middle of the compound and Aaron was summoned.

"Name's Harry Frameman," said the leader. He was a bearded man with an eyepatch. "I seen a notice on a Injin down in Cape Girardeau. This be the man?"

"That's him," Aaron said quietly. He looked up at the knoll to see if Dru was watching from the house. He did not see her. He sighed very quietly. God, how he dreaded whipping that Sac again.

"There's a twenty-dollar bounty on him," said Frameman. "Are you the one pays it?"

"No," said Aaron. "You have to collect at the state treasurer's office in the capital." He turned to Clement Niles, who stood nearby in a small group of curious guards and prisoners. "Mr. Niles, get this man a warrant for twenty dollars, please." Niles nodded and crossed the compound to the cabin, which was his combination home-office. "Where'd you find him?" Aaron asked Frameman.

"A mile or so south of New Castle. He might have been traveling with a band of Iroquois that went through New Castle the day before. Can't say for sure, though." Frameman glanced back at the still form on the mule. "He's a right frisky one, I'll say that for him. Ran off from us twice. We whipped him the first time we brought him back, but it didn't do no good."

"What did you do the second time?" Aaron asked.

Before Frameman could answer, Niles returned with the warrant. "That makes it legal, I reckon," Frameman said. He nodded to one of his men. "Cut him loose."

The second man guided his mount to the mule, bent over, and with a sheath knife cut the rawhide connecting Kee's bound hands. The Indian was looking up now, starring at Aaron and Niles with wide, terrified eyes. Aaron looked at him and gestured irritably with one hand. "Come on, get off that mule."

Kee swallowed and pushed himself back off the animal. When his bare feet touched the ground, he groaned in pain and fell helplessly alongside the mule.

"What's the matter with him?" Aaron asked.

"Right leg's broke," Frameman replied matter-of-factly. "That's what we done to him after he run off the second time. He didn't run off no more." Tugging his hat down over his forehead, Frameman reined his horse toward the road. "Let's go," he said to his men. The three bounty hunters rode off.

Aaron had Kee carried inside the walls. A cot was set up for him in a small grain-storage room next to the pantry, and a guard was sent down to Prisontown for the doctor.

There had been a doctor in the settlement since early January. A winter paddleboat heading downriver to New Orleans had gotten iced in making a stop to deliver some goods to the Pullmans. Half a dozen of the male passengers, a young doctor included, had come ashore to explore the river town. They spent most of the night drinking in a tent saloon run by a man named Kellerman. The next morning, when water had been heated in huge iron drums and poured along the edge of the pier to dethaw the stuck vessel, the hung-over drinkers staggered back aboard. All except the doctor, who had fallen asleep behind one of Kellerman's drinking tables. He was still there at midday when the paddleboat slipped free of the ice and continued its journey south.

The doctor's name was Gilbert Robin and he was running away from a young married woman he had made pregnant in Chicago. His socially prominent lover had refused to leave her husband to marry Robin, and he could not bear to remain there and see his child raised by another man. He was only twenty-six, barely out of medical school, and he drank a great deal. It did not seem to bother him that he was stranded in Prisontown, with the next boat not due for a month. It bothered him even less when the boat finally arrived, for by that time he had taken up with Cordelia Walls, a comely young woman who lived there with her mother and sisters while they waited for her father, Lewis Walls, to serve out a ten-year sentence for arson. Walls had built a house for a man in Junction City, and when the man refused to pay for it, had burned it down. Unfortunately, the fire he set burned down two other houses as well.

By the time the spring thaw came and with it busy river traffic, Doc Robin, as he was by now fairly commonly known, was sharing a comfortable cabin with Cordelia and treating half the town's inhabitants. He continued to drink a great deal, especially after treating little children, but no one, not even Cordelia, knew why. He had been drinking the afternoon he was summoned up to the prison to set Kee's leg.

"How did he break it, Warden?" he asked Aaron.

"He didn't," Aaron replied. "It was broken for him." He told Robin about the bounty hunters.

"Did one of them have an eyepatch?" the doctor asked. Aaron said he did. "They're down at Kellerman's drinking." said Robin. "I saw them there just before your guard came for me." He sighed heavily. "Well, we might as well see if we can undo what they've done. Get me two box slats and three leather belts."

With four convicts holding Kee down, Doc Robin snapped the broken bone back in place and set it firmly to mend.

When Doc went back down the hill, he saw the horses of the bounty hunters still tied in front of Kellerman's. He went to his cabin and found the strongest and fastest-acting cathartic that he had. It was a fine yellow powder that he kept for dosing horses and oxen when he had an occasional veterinary call. He had never used it on a human before.

He went over to the saloon tent. Lamp Kellerman, the owner, was behind the raw wood bar cleaning his hunting rifle. The three bounty hunters were at a table next to the dry heating stove. Doc noticed that the bottle in front of them was nearly empty.

"Back so soon, Doc?" said Kellerman. He was a peg-legged man with wooden false teeth. He often bragged to customers that his leg and teeth had been carved from the same timber.

"Let me have a bottle, please, Lamp," said Doc. The bounty hunters gave Doc a cursory glance, then resumed their own low conversation. Doc uncorked his bottle and poured a drink. When Kellerman went back to cleaning his rifle, Doc held his hat in front of the bottle and poured a heavy dose of the cathartic into it. It settled at once. The color of the whiskey, Doc thought, was even somewhat improved by the yellow powder; it became more golden.

Doc sipped at his drink until he saw the bounty hunter with the eyepatch pour the last of the whiskey from their bottle. Then Doc rose to leave, just as the bounty hunter called to Kellerman.

"Another bottle, bartender."

Kellerman started to put aside his rifle again, but Doc quickly raised a hand. "Keep your seat, Lamp. I'll give the gentlemen this bottle; I'm leaving." Kellerman stayed where he was and Doc put the bottle of spiked whiskey on the bounty hunter's table as he walked out of the tent. Eyepatch nodded his thanks as he reached for the bottle to finish filling his glass.

Doc crossed the flat dirt street and sat down on a bench in front of Pullman's. He sat there for two hours, watching the traffic in and out of Kellerman's. Between the three of them, the bounty hunters made eleven trips around the tent to Kellerman's privy. Twice there were fights over the single available seat. One of them eventually got so weak that he could not make it back into the saloon, and collapsed outside. Frameman became so violently ill inside that Kellerman came running across the street where Doc sat.

"Doc, come quick!" he said. "There's a man in my place lying on the floor holdin' his gut like he's dying!"

Doc got up and looked at an ornate watch that his father had given him. "Can't help him right now, Lamp," he said. "Time to go check on a patient of mine who has a broken leg."

Doc walked away and never did tend to the three men. They stayed in Kellerman's, too ill to move, for four days, then dragged out of town like three ghosts. Doc never told anyone what he had done.

Within six weeks after the bounty hunters had left, Kee's leg had mended well enough for him to limp around the compound. After he had been up and about for a week, Aaron assembled the prisoners and had him stripped to the waist and bound to the whipping post. Dutifully, Aaron laid thirty lashes on the Indian's back, then had him sent to the grain room to recuperate again.

After the whipping, Dru refused to speak to Aaron for a week.

As soon as the ground had thawed, Theron was assigned as lawn gardner again. On his first day back at the house, Dru sent Tea Leaf into the woods to look for blackberries, and Arlo down to the river to catch catfish. Then she took off everything under her dress and called Theron into her upstairs sewing room. It was an insane thing to do; if Aaron had come home unexpectedly, there would have been no acceptable excuse for the convict being upstairs. Or anywhere else in the house, for that matter, except the kitchen. But Dru was so starved for him that she ignored caution and pulled Theron up the stairs. "Hurry," she said when they were inside. She pulled up her skirts. Even her feet were bare. Theron opened his shirt and trousers, and guided her down to the floor. They were in the sunlight from the window, and the floorboards were warm on Dru's buttocks and Theron's knees. His leg-iron rattled as he maneuvered to enter her. She bent her head forward and pressed her mouth against a round, red birthmark he had just over the ridge of his left shoulder. It was shaped like a quarter-moon. Suddenly, she caught her breath at the size and hardness of him, then gasped as if he might burst her open.

"Oh, God—Christ—"

"Oh, goddamn—" Theron whispered. "Oh, goddamn—"

It was over very quickly and then they were up and straightening their clothes, both aware of the danger of where they were.

Later, when they were outside inspecting the winter damage to the flower gardens, they had their first opportunity to talk.

"In January when we went to the capital for the inauguration, I almost waved when the wagon went by where you were working."

"I remember that day," Theron said. His brilliant blue eyes seemed to have lost some of their luster. "It was cold as hell working in the woods that afternoon. Then when I got back to my cell, I couldn't get no sleep for thinking about you in some nice warm featherbed somewhere with your husband."

"Is it bad for you in the wintertime?"

He grunted softly. "Bad ain't the word for it, 'Scilla it's god-awful. I ain't sure I can make another winter."

"But you've got to, Theron," Dru said. "You've got to do *all* your time." She thought of Kee. "I couldn't bear to have you run off and then get brought back."

Theron saw the fear in her eyes. "Don't want to see the Hawk lay his lash on me, is that it?"

"The Hawk?"

"Van Hawk. Your husband, Madame Warden. Don't you know we all call him the Hawk?"

"No, I didn't know." Dru wondered if even Aaron knew.

"If there was only some way I could work for you all winter too," Theron said thoughtfully. "Do you think Van Hawn might let me take Arlo's place if something happened to him?"

"What could happen to him?"

"How do I know? He's so dumb and stupid, he might fall over the railing of the cell house and break his neck."

"Don't do anything to hurt him, Theron," Dru pleaded. "I don't want him to get hurt."

"Well, maybe you can think of something then. But I've got to get off those winter work parties. I can't stand them anymore, I tell you."

Dru pressed her teeth into her lower lip. She blinked her eyes rapidly as she often did when she had to think fast. "In the fall," she said with a slight nervousness, "I could tell Aaron that Arlo wasn't doing his chores well, that he was loafing about when he should be working. Aaron would send him to the pit and you wouldn't have to hurt him."

"Do you think I could get his job then?"

"I don't see why not," Dru said. It was a lie. She knew that Aaron would never put Theron inside the house on a permanent basis. Aaron was too good a judge of convicts; he would never trust Theron. And he would be immediately suspicious if she were to recommend anyone except Kee for the job.

"It sure would be nice if we could do it during the winter too, wouldn't it?" Theron said.

Dru wet her lips. "Yes."

Theron looked back at the house. It was quiet, still, inviting. "Let's go do it again right now."

"All right."

As they walked back, Theron said, "Can you give me some money now and again? One of the guards sneaks stuff up from the settlement store and sells it to the cons. Tobacco, soap, crackers, things like that. Charges double for it, but it's worth it. Sure make life a little easier for me."

"How much money, Theron? I don't have very much."

"Just a dollar every now and then."

Dru bit her lip again. Most of what they bought at Pullman's was paid for by state draft. She had a little money for other expenses, but very little. Still, if it would make things better for Theron, she supposed she could do something. "I guess I can manage that," she told him.

When they got to the back door, Dru went on in and Theron waited on the porch. When she was ready, with her skirt pulled up, on a burlap sack of beans in the pantry, she called to him.

"Hurry, Theron—"

In the summer of 1831 there were sixty-six convicts on Prison Hill. Seven of them remained in the Idle Box all day. This was now a barred cage in the middle of the prison yard, large enough to accommodate a dozen men sitting or lying about on the ground. It was fashioned entirely of bars: roof, sides, door. The men inside were exposed to whatever weather nature decreed: wind, sun, rain, snow, cold. Each morning these men were asked by Mr. Tillman if they would rather work than spend the day in the Box. Each morning Tillman was answered by a strong silence. No convict who chose the Box had ever asked to leave it. It seemed to be a point of pride with them.

Of the other fifty-nine prisoners, fourteen were assigned either to the kitchen, to the cell house as cleaning men, as domestics to the warden, or in some other service-type work. The remaining forty-five men worked in the knitting mill. Each morning after breakfast they were assembled in the yard and one by one their right shackle was unlocked. Each man took the rawhide lace from his belt and corded his chain just below his left knee. Then they were marched under mounted guard out the gate and down the road to the mill. It was dusty road in the summer and rock-hard road in the winter. The men walked in two single files, one on each side of the road. Talking was not allowed. Occasionally a man would break and run, trying to get into the nearby thicket before a guard on horseback could overtake him. None of them ever succeeded. For their effort, they would be whipped and, when they had recovered, taken to the pit and made to dig and break rock from dawn to dusk for a month. The pit was no longer in operation on a regular basis, because the prison had no immediate need for stone, but it served as a good place for punishment. After a lashing and a month on the rocks, a prisoner was usually grateful to be back in the mill.

There was a civilian foreman in the mill who maintained the looms and sent repair reports to the owners in Chicago, but it was generally understood by all that Clement Niles was the man in charge of the operation. Niles kept figures on the manpower leased to the mill by the state, and the production achieved by that manpower. He made daily inspections to see that there were enough men in the proper jobs to keep production at a peak. If the cotton spreaders—the men who opened the big bales and spread out the cotton for feeding into the looms—were not keeping up with the weavers, then Niles would close down some of the looms and send the men back to help with the spreading. The same with the cutters and trimmers and loopers and rollers. Wherever he saw the work process bogging down, Niles would shift the labor force. By balancing it, on an almost daily basis, he kept the mill operating at near maximum efficiency and kept the lieutenant governor in the capital and the mill owners in Chicago happy with his performance.

Niles and the Van Hawns had become close friends. A cautious preliminary association during the bookkeeper's first few months had developed into a casual, easy acquaintanceship and finally into a comfortable friendship. It was Dru who initiated it.

Once Niles moved into the cabin, and winter set in, she would take him an occasional plate of fried chicken or pot of stew. She knew he was a poor eater, he had been up to the mansion several times for supper: token invitations, usually given once a month to Tillman, Doc Robin, and the Pullman brothers. At such gatherings, Niles would always graciously compliment Dru on the quality of her cooking, and then eat only a few bites of each dish. He seemed to be chronically ill: stomach discomfort, shortness of breath, persistent head and chest colds, and a perpetual body chill which he claimed lasted from the first day of September until the last day of May. Doc Robin diagnosed him as having stomach ulcerations, asthmatic breathing passages, and bronchial lungs; his recommendation was that Niles embezzle all the mill receipts and relocate in New Orleans, taking himself along as private physician. After the banter, Doc seriously advised him to consider a warmer climate.

"I've lived in a warmer climate," Niles replied. "I lived in Charleston for a time, and also in Atlanta. I was in no better health in either place than I am now. But thank you for your advice."

Doc said no more. It was obvious that Niles had little respect or use for doctors.

It was when he had a particularly bad attack of influenza that the Van Hawns became closer to him than mere business acquaintances. Dru visited him when he was sick, saw how bad he really was, and sent for four trusties to move him up to the mansion.

"Mrs. Van Hawn, I prefer to remain in my own quarters, if you don't mind," he objected.

"I do mind," she snapped. "You aren't able to take care of yourself. At the house, I can look after you."

Niles sat up in bed, looking pale and weak, but very determined. "Madam, I insist on being let stay here."

"Clement," she replied firmly, calling him by his given name for the first time, "you are *going* to the house. Now please be quiet."

Four convicts moved him, feather mattress and all, into the spare bedroom on the first floor of the mansion. There, for a week, Dru dosed him with beef broth, onion soup, and a potato-stock stew with a variety of unidentified contents floating in it. She also rubbed him down with Selmer's Salve and kept warm cloths on his chest and throat. In the evenings, she and Aaron sat and talked with him to keep him company. It was during those informal conversations that both Dru and Aaron discovered that they liked Clement Niles, and he them. It was a pleasant realization for all of them.

After he had recovered and returned to his cabin, Niles took to spending two or three evenings a week at the mansion. His appetite did not improve, but his stomach condition did; Dru had secretely obtained a list of bland foods from Doc Robin and was discreetly including them in the bookkeeper's dinners, as well as taking them to his cabin two or three times a week.

To repay Dru for her nursing care, Niles selected an elegant blue dress for her from the Drew and Miller catalog the Pullman Brothers had, and ordered it sent down from St. Louis. For Aaron's hospitality, he ordered a fine set of playing cards and a cribbage board. Aaron was a touch jealous about the dress, but Dru assured him in bedroom privacy that it was not nearly as nice as the brown one he had bought her, and which she was still heartbroken over ruining. Aaron got over his pique quickly enough, after one of Dru's perfected sessions of physical responsiveness, and asked Niles to teach him the game of cribbage. Niles did, and for months afterwards the two men had a cribbage contest every evening after supper. During the summer, they played by the light of a dozen kerosene lanterns placed strategically around the huge front porch, enjoying their after-dinner cold tea, Aaron smoking his pipe. It was a quiet, peaceful time for both men.

While for Dru, in the darkness behind the house, her bare buttocks on the cool rock wall around the well, legs raised and spread, it was a few minutes of lustful enjoyment with Theron.

Theron had been saving the money Dru gave him. Since early spring, when she slipped him the first dollar, throughout the summer, when she gave him whatever coins she was able to salvage from her household money; into the early fall, when several times he asked for and received a dollar for "something special" he wanted to buy. Actually, he bought nothing, then or earlier. There *was* a guard dealing in contraband goods inside the walls, but Theron never patronized him. Theron saved his money for something else.

One day in early October, he left the work he was doing—turning the bottom soil and putting down turf to keep the flower beds healthy during the approaching winter—and walked around to the kitchen of the mansion. Tea Leaf eyed him suspiciously as he came in the back door. "Mistress ain't here," he said. "What you want?"

"I need some more turf seed," Theron said. "It's in the pantry."

"Ah'll get it," Tea Leaf said quickly. "Ain't no ones but me and Mistress 'posed to go in the pantry."

While Tea Leaf filled a gourd with tiny black turf seeds, Theron stepped over to the meat board and stole a six-inch butcher knife. He slipped it under his belt out of sight.

"Here's yo' seeds," Tea said, handing him the gourd.

Theron left the house. He went back out front, walked past the half-turned flower beds, and headed down the knoll toward the walls. The gate guard stopped him and examined the gourd. "Them's the last of the seeds for the warden's lawn," Theron explained. "Miz Van Hawn said when I got low to ask Mr. Tillman to send a man down to the settlement for some more."

The guard passed him through and watched as he crossed the yard to the main level of the cell house. Tillman's office was second from the end, between Aaron's office on the corner and the guard barracks in the middle. Theron knocked and entered. Tillman looked up from his desk. Theron threw the seeds stingingly in his face and rushed around the desk. Quickly he put the knife to Tillman's neck and relieved him of his sidearm.

"Get out the key and take off this here goddamn chain," Theron ordered.

Tillman unshackled him.

"Now let's walk outside and over to the Idle Box, Mr. Guard Boss. And you'd best look like ever'thing's all right, too. Any shootin' starts, you'll be the first to die. Get moving."

They left the office, Tillman in the lead, and walked to the barred Idle Box. Lewt, the murderer, and Jingo, the highwayman, both members of the original contingency of prisoners, were in the box along with six other long-termers who chose not to work. Theron had Tillman open the door.

"I'm hanging my irons on a tree limb, boys," Theron said with a smile. "Anybody wants to join me, just step up and let Mr. Guard Boss unlock you."

They joined him. When they were unshackled and out, Theron had Tillman lead them to the gate. They captured the gate guard and marched right out of the prison and down the road toward Prisontown.

Halfway down to the settlement, Tillman and the gate guard were shackled in some leg-irons Theron had brought along for just that purpose. They were left in a ditch, unharmed.

"I think we better split up now," Theron told them. "There's nine of us. Three go south, three go east, three go north."

Theron and two others headed north. They ran all day and part of the night, until they came to a village. The two others did not know Theron had any money, and he did not tell them. He was supposed to keep watch while they broke into a general store and stole some clothes. Instead, he ran off and left them, and they were caught in the act. Theron then changed directions and headed east. The next day he came on a fairly isolated farm and with Dru's money purchased clothes and something to eat. The farm family asked no questions and Theron went on his way without incident. He headed north again, toward a part of the state where he had never been.

Jingo, Lewt, and another convict were shot and killed by a downstate posse before nightfall of their first day out. The three prisoners who had gone east wandered onto two off-duty guards fishing in a creek a mile behind the mill. The guards were armed; the convicts were captured.

Of nine escapees, three were killed and five retaken. Theron Verne made good his getaway.

One week after Theron's escape, Dru learned she was pregnant.

"I'd guess you were about two months along," Doc Robin told her. "This is going to make Aaron a mighty happy man."

"Yes," she replied quietly, "it will." She was convinced that the child was not Aaron's; he barely penetrated her the four or five times a month they now made love. It had to be Theron's child; Theron, with his huge member that seemed to send a gush of semen up inside her, while with Aaron, it seemed to be only a dribble. It never occurred to Dru that she was exaggerating in her own mind the differences between her husband and her lover. Aaron had never completely satisfied her, and Aaron was small and ejaculated less than Theron; and Theron was large and ejaculated more and never failed to satisfy her; therefore it had to be the difference in their size. The matter of age never occurred to her, or physical condition, or even technique. Size she had thought it was in the beginning, and size she still thought it was. And now, with Theron gone from her, his stature and prowess grew even more in her mind.

Dru had been stunned by the news of his escape. For the previous month, ever since the leaves had started turning red, she had been racking her brain to think of a way to get Aaron to transfer Theron to the house as a domestic. Winter was coming, and she knew that Theron would be getting desperate about the long cold months ahead. But strain as she did, she could think of no way to approach the subject with Aaron without being so ridiculously obvious that it was foolish to even try.

Her dilemma, which had gone unresolved, was now over. Theron had meant it when he said he could not stand another winter on the labor crew. With no thought at all to how Dru would feel about it, with not even a goodbye to her, he had escaped. And, although he did not know it, left her pregnant.

Aaron was furious that a man he had trusted would so blatantly betray him. The knife that Tillman later described was quickly traced to one missing from the kitchen meat board. Tea Leaf and Arlo were questioned closely. There was no evidence to implicate them in the escape, but Aaron transferred them back inside the walls anyway. Aaron's inquiry into the break brought to light that two guards had observed the nine convicts without their shackles on, but had thought nothing of it since they were in the company of the guard boss, Mr. Tillman. Aaron at once issued a new order to all guards that anytime a convict was observed without a leg-iron on, he was to be shot without warning.

The five men who were captured were brought back to Prison Hill and put in the Idle Box again. Each morning for five days one of them was taken out and given his thirty lashes by Aaron in view of the assembled inmate population. Aaron administered the punishment on five consecutive days so that his arm would be fresh for each man, and none of them would take a worse beating than any other. Even with the lash in his hand, the Hawk could never be accused of being unfair.

The three dead convicts were also returned to the Hill. Their bodies were put on display in the prison yard for a day and all prisoners were required to march by and view the remains. Then they were taken to a plot of ground beyond the rear wall, on a knoll facing the warden's house, and there buried. They were the first convicts to be buried on the Hill. One of the prisoners on punishment work in the rock pit stood looking up at the knoll as the three raw wooden coffins were lowered into the ground.

"Poor dumb peckerwoods," he said aloud. Two other cons heard him and that night talked to others about the "peckerwoods" now buried up on the knoll. Before long, the place where the graves lay came to be called Peckerwood Acres.

A month after the break, a man named Cleon arrived at Prison Hill aboard a wagon carrying two wire cages. In the cages were two gray bloodhounds. "There you are, sir," he said to Aaron, "just as you ordered."

"Are they trained?" Aaron asked. "Will they track men?"

"These here dogs," Cleon vowed, "are trained by a man in Louie-ville, Kentucky, who's been a'training dogs to chase runaway blacks. Slave owners say his dogs is the best there is."

"Chasing slaves is one thing," Aaron said dubiously. "Those blacks have a powerful scent. Dog don't have to be real good to run down a black. But the men I've got here, they're mostly white. Except for one Sac I've got who's run off a couple of times. What I need is dogs that can track a white man."

"These here hounds can track any man living, I don't care what color he be," Cleon assured Aaron. "If any dog I sell you don't live up to my words, you shoot him, send one of his ears back to me, and I'll return every dollar you paid for him."

Aaron took the dogs. He never had to shoot one and Cleon never got an ear sent back to him. The dogs were splendid mantrackers. Every convict in the prison came to hate them with a passion.

* * *

As Doc Robin had predicted, Aaron was delighted with the news of Dru's pregnancy. But Dru had a miserable time. She seemed to suffer every discomfort there was: nausea, water retention, excruciating backaches, chronic depression, and a dozen more. "I can't understand it," Doc Robin said. "You're twenty-three years old and you've got a long torso and good square hips. You're perfect for carrying a child. Why is everything wrong with you?"

"You're supposed to tell me that," Dru replied in a peevish voice. "You're the doctor, not me."

"I know who the doctor is," Doc snapped. He was not about to take any rudeness from a patient, not even Dru. "What I'm trying to determine is why the doctor's patient is acting like she is. Are you and Aaron happy together?"

"Aaron and I are very happy. Why do you ask that?"

"Pregnancy is a peculiar condition, Dru. It's physical *and* mental. A perfectly normal, healthy woman can completely ruin herself physically if she has a mental problem—"

"Are you saying I'm crazy?" she demanded.

"If I was, you wouldn't have to ask to be sure. A mental problem doesn't necessarily mean being crazy. It can mean being worried about something, being unhappy, having a guilty conscience—"

"I do *not* have a guilty conscience," Dru interrupted defensively.

This time Doc did not snap back. Instead, he studied her thoughtfully. So that was it. The very proper Mrs. Druscilla Van Hawn had done something wrong. And apparently could not forgive herself for it. So her mental distress was upsetting her physical balance and initiating or aggravating a series of pregnancy discomforts.

"Whatever it is that's bothering you, Dru," he told her, "I'd advise you to put it aside somehow and stop dwelling on it. If you don't, it's going to affect your baby."

"How?" she asked urgently. "How will it affect my baby?"

Doc shrugged. "I can't say exactly. The baby might be unusually nervous, or a chronic crier, or an asthmatic. The point is, your mental and physical condition might cause your baby any number of mental or physical problems throughout its entire life. That's why you must control yourself."

Dru bit her lower lip and nodded. "All right, I'll try. I'll try very hard. Thank you, Gilbert."

Doc smiled. She was the only one who called him by his given name. Cordelia called him Rob, short for his surname. Everyone else simply called him Doc or Doc Robin.

On his way out, he paused and gave her a final thought. "Remember, Dru, whenever we do something that we shouldn't, it isn't the doing of it that's important. What matters is whether anyone is hurt by it. If no one has been hurt, then the act itself is insignificant."

Doc's parting words made sense to Dru. She sat down and took inventory of herself. What she had done with Theron was wrong, but who had it hurt? Certainly not Aaron; he did not know about it. Not Theron; he had enjoyed himself with her body and talked her out of enough money to help him escape. Herself, then? Yes, she had to admit that she had been hurt. Hurt by Theron simply leaving her as he had; hurt by his lying and lack of trust; and hurt, also, by his absence when she needed him, needed *it.*

But she would get by it, she determined. It was her baby she had to consider now. She could not let her thoughts hurt the baby. Not her guilty thoughts about what she had done, or her angry thoughts over Theron leaving her as he had, or even her yearning thoughts when she desperately wanted him back. None of that must be allowed to affect her baby. But in order to protect her baby, she had to protect herself. She had to keep those same thoughts from affecting her.

Dru mustered all her willpower and self-control and forced herself out of the daily spells that thoughts of Theron were casting upon her. She ruled him out of her mind, banished him from her thoughts whenever he manifested there. She was firm, merciless, cruel. She plunged into a schedule of activity designed to occupy all her time, all her attention, and to leave her weary enough at the end of the day to permit prompt, dreamless sleep.

Almost immediately she began to feel better. The nausea disappeared and the toxemia gradually reduced. Her backaches subsided. The daily depressions were cast off entirely, replaced by a consuming interest in a new wall coloring throughout the mansion, new nursery furniture being made by the prison carpenters, and an inordinate amount of attention being lavished on Aaron in his new role of father-to-be. All of it worked, and worked very well. Doc Robin was especially pleased. A month later, he said, "Now you're the kind of mother you should have been all along. You send for me quickly when you start having labor pains; with those wide hips of yours, you'll have this baby like a cow drops her calf."

The baby was born an hour after daybreak on a morning in June. Doc was there to deliver it, and Cordelia came along to help. Aaron was not sure it was proper for the daughter of a prisoner to be in his house, helping to bring his first child into the world, but Clement Niles and Mr. Tillman both assured him that it was nothing to worry about.

The birth was very easy, as Doc had said it would be. The baby was a boy, nearly ten pounds in size. Aaron named him Monroe, after his patron, the lieutenant governor of the state.

When Dru held the child in her arms for the first time, she was relieved to see it looked a great deal like her, but in no way resembled Theron Verne. She silently thanked God for that.

CHAPTER 14

In 1834, Alton Monroe campaigned for election to the governor's office for the first time and won. A young lawyer named Palmer Curran was elected to Monroe's old office as lieutenant governor. On the weekend following the election, the retiring governor hosted a gala victory ball for his successor, whom he had endorsed, and for his successor's successor, whom they had both endorsed. The celebration was held in the governor's mansion and invited guests traveled the length and breath of the state to attend.

Aaron and Dru made their second journey to the capital, this time traveling alone because Clement Niles was in bed with influenza again. Dru did not particularly want to make the trip; one visit to that noisy, crowded city filled with loud, rude people had been more than enough for her. She had not enjoyed the inauguration trip four years earlier, and she did not expect to enjoy this one.

"I really shouldn't be going," she told Aaron, searching for a way out. "Clement is very sick and needs someone to look after him."

"Clement is always sick," Aaron reminded her. "Doc and Cordelia can see to him."

"He doesn't like Doc seeing to him, you know that. Nor Cordelia either. He doesn't like anyone taking care of him but me."

"And I don't like traveling to the capital alone," Aaron said firmly. "The matter is closed."

In a pique, Dru went off to the nursery to check on the children. She had two now; another boy had been born the previous August, when little Monroe was fourteen months old. Aaron had named him Grover, after his old friend. This second child was Aaron's.

Dru had been responsible for her own pregnancy the second time. She knew exactly how and when she had done it. On Thanksgiving the previous year, they had entertained Niles, Tillman, Doc, Cordelia—who at Dru's insistence was now welcome in their home at any time—and the Pullman brothers and their wives. Dru had drunk some wine while cleaning up at the end of the evening. She had overindulged and later, in bed with Aaron, she had shown it. With her long legs wrapped around his hips, she had pumped herself up to him like a bitch in heat and extended him to a virtuoso performance that left him wide-eyed and panting, and left her as near to satisfaction as she had been since Theron Verne escaped.

Theron had been gone for more than three years now. There was still a notice out on him, and for a long time, whenever the marshals or bounty hunters arrived at the Hill, Dru had peered anxiously down from the portico windows to see if he was among the chained men being brought in. He never was, and she felt both relief and disappointment. Half the time her sane self hoped he would stay away forever and never be brought back to complicate her life again; and the other half of the time her vindictive self hoped that the bastard would be caught so that she could have the pleasure of seeing Aaron lay the lash to him. After awhile, after she became pregnant with little Grover, she had stopped looking altogether, and had all but stopped even thinking about Theron now except at rare, remote moments.

Dru's best friend now was Cordelia Walls, this despite Aaron's uneasy feeling about the woman's father being one of his prisoners. Cordelia was twenty-five, the same age as Dru, and the women found in each other a mutuality of understanding that made each totally comfortable with the other. They saw each other almost daily, either at the mansion or down in Prisontown in a new house Doc had had built. Cordelia had assisted Doc at the birth of both of Dru's babies. In the absence of any blood kin on either parent's side, she acted as a self-appointed surrogate aunt to them. Now, with Dru reluctantly preparing for the journey north, it had been decided between the two women that little Monroe and Grover would be left with Cordelia instead of being bundled up and taken in the big coach with their parents.

"I'm not sure I like the idea of them being left down in the settlement," Aaron grumbled.

"What would you have us do?" Dru asked tartly. "Leave them here in the house alone? Let the trusties take care of them?"

"We could take them with us. They wouldn't be too much trouble."

"Not for *you* they wouldn't. No, they definitely are not going with us. If you don't want them left down the hill with Cordelia, then let me stay here. I don't care to make the trip anyway."

"You're going," Aaron said. "That's final."

After Aaron considered the matter privately, he had to admit to himself that there really was no reason *not* to leave the children with Cordelia, other than her father's status as a prisoner. Little Monroe and Grover were both crazy about Cordelia, and there was no doubt that she felt the same about them and would give them the best of care. Doc had a very nice house now—Aaron himself had helped select the lumber for it—so the children would be warm and sheltered. And it wasn't as if Prisontown was still the raw, backward settlement it once had been. Although a sizable portion of it was still made up of convict families, it was developing into a thriving, respectable community.

With the building of the east riverbank road and the coming of the overland coach line, Prisontown had evolved from a semitransient shantytown into a fairly stable little village. From a nucleus formed by the Pullman brothers, Kellerman the saloonkeeper, and a woman named Carrie Carmichael, who had opened a bake shop, a small cluster of businesses had begun to sprout up. The Pullmans had sold their fresh meat concession to a butcher named Swann and he had opened a small meat market next door to them. A shoemaker had come to town one day and decided to stay. His name was Harry Fogel and he soon sent for his cousin, Harry Berg, who had a dry goods stock. The two Harrys set up a combined clothing and dressmaking business with a boot and shoe shop. It was not long after that, with two coaches a week passing through on the Cape Girardeau-Chester run, that the town acquired a blacksmith, a barber, and a printer with a small hand press. Pete French's wife Etta also moved to town, coming down from Alton to open a restaurant while she waited for her husband to finish his sentence. Whether or not she had forgiven Pete for his crime, the rape of the thirteen-year-old girl, she visited him every Sunday for conferences about the running of the new business.

Etta French was not the only prisoner's wife to start a business in the settlement. Carrie Carmichael's bakeshop was started on money gained from the sale of the Carmichael farm in the corn belt, after Carrie decided to move to Prisontown where her husband John Carmichael had been sent for manslaughter. Cordelia Walls's mother and sisters all took in washing and ironing. Jessica Vintner, whose husband Saul was serving five years for embezzlement, supported herself with a small mending and sewing business. Those who did not engage in businesses of their own often worked for the town's merchants. Elouise Starwell, wife of long-term bank robber Luke Starwell, cut cloth and made shirts and dresses for Harry Berg. Several other women cooked and waited tables for Etta French on days when a paddleboat docked and its passengers and crew came ashore, and on Sundays when people came to town to visit men at the prison. Nearly everyone worked at something, and it mattered not to anyone whether this person or that had convict kin or not. All people were the same in Prisontown; everyone accepted everyone else. That was how the community had started, and it had not occurred to anyone that it should be different. Anyone except Aaron, that is.

Aaron had been bothered for some time about the gradual integration of the two communities. "Somehow it just doesn't seem right," he said to Tillman. "There's too much coming and going between prisoners and outsiders. When I started this visiting business, I didn't realize so many people would take advantage of it."

"It's the riverbank road," Tillman said. "We aren't as isolated as we once were."

"That's true," Aaron said. "Things were a lot less complicated in the old days. We didn't have all these women and children trudging up the hill every Sunday. Didn't have guards going to town and associating with wives and daughters of convicts." He thought of his own situation. "Didn't have a convict's daughter visiting the warden's house like she was a relative."

"Well, times change, sir."

"Yes, I suppose," Aaron had replied, nodding thoughtfully. He had tried not to let it trouble him, tried not to give it any conscious thought. But it was always there, like a slight itch in his mind, and it remained with him for years. When he and Dru went to the capital for the victory ball, he spoke to Grover about it. "It's an unnatural community," he said, for lack of a better way to describe it. "Everybody is friends with everybody else."

"What's wrong with that, for God's sake?" Grover asked. "I wish it was that way around the statehouse!"

"I can't tell you what's wrong with it," Aaron admitted. "But I have a very strong feeling that it's not the way things should be. There should be *lines* of some kind to separate us from them—"

"Us?" Grover said, frowning.

"Yes. The keepers. The state."

"Don't forget they're the state too, Aaron. Those wives and children of the convicts. They haven't done anything, and they mustn't be punished for anything their husbands or fathers did. You must remember that."

"I understand that, Grover," Aaron assured him. "I wish I could explain it better. I wish I *understood* it better."

"Ah, well, it's still fairly new, this prison business. Eight years isn't really that long to get to know a thing. Give it some more time. It'll probably work itself out."

"I'm sure you're right," Aaron said.

Actually, he had not been sure, and in the end he would learn that Grover had not been right.

By 1837 Prison Hill held a hundred-forty-one men and had doubled in size to twenty acres. Nearly half of the original fifty single-man cells now contained two prisoners. The rock quarry was reopened on a full-time basis to provide stone necessary to construct a second cell house. A new generation of trees had to be ravaged to provide lumber for its frame. And because there was no room inside the prison yard, the end wall had to be blown down with gunpowder and rebuilt after the two side walls had been extended fifty yards. Aaron wanted to extend them a hundred yards and double the size of the cell house, but his request was refused. It would cost too much.

"I don't understand it," he complained to Dru at the breakfast table. "Surely those people at the capital are able to predict approximately how many prisoners the state will sentence in a year's time, or two years' time. Don't they realize that five years from now we'll have to tear down *this* wall and do the same thing all over again?"

"Don't ask me, Aaron," was Dru's cursory reply. "Ask your friend the governor." She glanced across the table. "Finish your oatmeal, boys, and we'll take a buggy ride into town."

The two Van Hawn boys immediately began to eat faster. Monroe was now five, and his brother Grover four. Monroe—Dru thanked God—looked very much like her; only his brilliant blue eyes seemed like Theron's. Grover was a miniature duplicate of Aaron. Their father worshiped them, and they him. Although Aaron was now fifty, he seemed not to have aged a day since his firstborn was able to crawl around and play. He was constantly involved in one game or another with them. Dru, on the other hand, only twenty-eight, usually looked her age and often felt older.

After breakfast, Aaron would romp with the boys for a while and then get ready to go down to the prison. Before he left the house, he liked to get Dru alone in the bedroom, pull her dress down off her shoulders, and nuzzle at her breasts for a moment or two. "I like my morning sugar-titty," he would say.

"I know you do." She usually held her breasts up and out for him.

"What are you going down the hill for today?" he asked this morning.

"The school committee is meeting to decide on a teacher. We want to get one here before September."

"Find a good one and have him commit a crime. We'll get him here soon enough."

"Would you mind coming over to the other one? It would like a turn too."

"I'd be happy to." Aaron changed to the other breast.

"When is Clement due back?" she asked.

"In another week. After he and the owners get everything settled about building the new tannery, he's going up to Clinton to visit his sister for a day or two." He gave each breast a final little suck and straightened up. "I'm going now."

After he left, Dru usually sat in her rocker for a while, dreamily fondling her breasts herself; occasionally having her own private thoughts about Theron.

Aaron inspected the prison every day except Sunday. Mr. Tillman accompanied him. The first leg of the inspection was a walking tour of the compound: the lumber mill, brickyard, stables, and storage areas; and inside the walls: the kitchen, pantry, barracks, armory, the upstairs cells, and the Idle Box.

At the gate, a pair of saddle horses would be waiting to take the two men on the second leg of the inspection. That was the part Aaron liked best: riding out to the pit every morning. He had used the inspection as an excuse for buying the two mounts, and he thoroughly enjoyed having them. He had tried to get Dru to go riding with him on occasion, but she did not like horses. Aaron could hardly wait until Monroe was a little older; he wanted to teach him to ride as soon as possible.

Riding out to the pit, the two men cut in and out of the woods where work parties were felling and splitting trees. At each stop, the guard in charge of the party would salute their approach and Aaron would rein up and chat with him for a moment. Then he and Tillman would continue on their way.

At the quarry, the two riders dismounted. "Good morning, Mr. Tyree," Aaron greeted the prison's current stonemason.

"Morning, Warden, Mr. Tillman." He was an older man who often reminded Aaron of Dru's Uncle Abner Foyle. Tyree knew rock and stone like a preacher knew the good book. The new cell house he was building was a masterpiece of stone work.

"How is this crew doing?" Aaron asked, looking down at the men laboring in the pit. It was still early, but already their bodies were covered with a layer of sweaty grime.

"They're getting the rock up, right enough, Warden," said Tyree. One corner of his mouth was brown from years of tobacco juice.

"You let me or Mr. Tillman know if they slack off any," Aaron told him. "I want the new cell house up before winter."

"She'll be up, Warden," the old stonemason assured him.

Aaron and Tillman rode on, toward the mill. Normally their inspection would have been over; Clement Niles usually inspected the mill and spent most of the morning out there checking on production. But with Niles up at the capital, Aaron had added the mill to his itinerary. They were met by Danforth, the loom maintenance man, as they dismounted at the rear dock.

"Everything running smoothly, Mr. Danforth?" asked Aaron.

"Yessir, Warden, it appears to be."

"Well, let's have a quick look." Aaron strode through swinging doors into the bolting room where the knitted cloth was rolled for shipping. The room was hot and oppressive, its air too heavy for comfortable breathing. The convicts worked with their shirts off and rags tied around their foreheads to keep the sweat out of their eyes. A guard with a rifle stood on a raised platform at each end of the room.

Followed by Tillman and Danforth, Aaron proceeded through the stretching and cutting rooms into the weaving room where the looms were located. In there, the air was even worse; it was sweltering hot and thick with floating particles of cotton dust. The men at the looms had their mouths and noses covered with crudely fashioned cloth masks to filter what they breathed. Every few minutes, one of them would pull the mask off and hold his breath while he quickly dipped the cloth in a bucket of water at his side. Then he would tie it around his face wet and resume working the loom until it dried out again. Two guards patrolled the room on a catwalk up near high, open windows where masks were not necessary.

"There must be some way to get more air in here," Aaron said above the noise of the looms.

"I don't know how, Warden, unless we tear down a wall," Danforth said.

"Are these men allowed rest periods to go outside?"

"No, sir."

Aaron's jaw jutted. "I'm going to speak to Mr. Niles about that when he returns."

Aaron walked up an aisle, followed by Danforth. Tillman brought up the rear. As Tillman passed one of the looms, a convict looped a braided rope around his neck and jerked him violently out of the aisle. Neither catwalk guard saw it happen. The convict threw Tillman to the floor, put a heavy shoe on his chin, and viciously put all his weight on the foot. Tillman, eyes wide in surprise and fear, felt the heavy shoe slowly split his upper lip and push his big buckteeth out of their gums and back into his mouth. Unable to cry out, he clutched at the convict's leg and began to choke on his own blood. Then the convict suddenly shoved down harder and broke Tillman's neck.

Taking the chief guard's pistol, the convict crawled under the noisily operating looms to a point near the catwalk. Then he calmly raised up, took careful aim, and shot both guards.

The looms suddenly stopped. The armed convict ripped off his mask. "This goddamned hole ain't fit for humans to work in!" he screamed. "Tear it down! Kill the fucks who keep us here!"

Aaron and Danforth, both unarmed, stood in the middle of the aisle, stunned to disbelief by what was happening. All around them, convicts rose and tore off their wet masks to reveal faces contorted in long pent-up rage. Before either of them could muster a defensive thought, they were engulfed by a rushing tide of prisoners.

Danforth tried to break and run, and was kicked solidly in his testicles by the nearest convict. He fell to the floor and six of them pounced on him.

Aaron had just turned to look in the other direction when a mightily swung wooden bucket split open the back of his skull. He felt himself falling forward, saw the lint-covered floor rising up in front of him, and felt a vicious shoe toe smash into his face and push his left eye back into his head. His last earthly thought was that he would never taste Dru's warm nipples in his mouth again. Then a permanent blackness took his mind.

As Aaron lay dead in the aisle, the maddened convicts went wild around him.

CHAPTER 15

In the fall of 1946, less than a year after her mother died, Dru Hawn dutifully went away to college to keep her promise to become a teacher.

From the very beginning she loathed college: college life, college people, college attitudes. After being raised in one of the largest state prisons in the country, growing up around convicts and guards whose daily existence revolved around the real-life conflicts of captivity and freedom, intrigue and conspiracy, authority and nonconformity, sometimes life and death, Dru found the college environment almost intolerably bland. She wrote to Myles saying, "I hate this place. I feel like a high school student made to go to kindergarten."

Myles wrote back: "Give it a chance, honey. Remember, you promised."

Dru lived in one of the dorms, sharing a room with, as she wrote Myles, "a ninny from Toledo who *lives* for football players and victory dances."

For the first two months she was on campus Dru declined to date. She found the young men who approached her so utterly lacking in everything she admired in a man—maturity, strength, character, confidence—that she could not bear to socialize with them. She did not realize it at the time, but because of her very limited exposure to and experience with the opposite sex, she was subconsciously comparing them all to her father. In such a contest, against a man who had ridden with Villa, fought in

France, and faced the country's most feared desperado in order to win his wife, the college youths were pale indeed.

Although she would have liked to live out her college days as a recluse, eventually Dru had to capitulate to social pressures. The ninny from Toledo, whom Dru grudingly began to like, told her that there had been several comments made about her lack of desire for male companionship. Some of the Toledo girl's boyfriends even kidded her about having a "peculiar" roommate. Dru was furious. She wanted to be her own woman, to get through the stupid school as easily as possible in order to satisfy the commitment she had made to her dying mother. But she soon learned that being herself and getting through school easily were not compatible goals. Being herself would not make life easy for her. There would be talk, speculation, innuendos, curiosity. The only way to get through college with a minimum of worry and irritation was at least to appear to be like everyone else. It grated on Dru's pride to do so, but eventually she decided that a little pretense was worth a lot of peace of mind. She started dating and was amused to learn later that her original attitude was retrospectively attributed by the gossips to shyness.

The first semester dragged by with maddening slowness. Dru's time was taken up first by her studies, which she found ridiculously easy, never receiving less than an A in any class; by writing her father a short, chatty note every other night, which, unlike her earlier letters, contained no complaints to worry him or make him think she would not keep her promise to Cassie; and by dating once a week, on Friday nights, to provide a token appearance of conformity to keep her name out of the campus gossip. In all, it was a very laming existence, mentally, emotionally, even physically. Dru did not see how she could possibly survive four years of it.

In her moments of deepest depression, she would turn to the volumes of diaries written by her great-great-grandmother. The words of the original Dru, put down so long ago, somehow filled her with a calmness that she could get from few other sources. It was a feeling she had first experienced shortly after Cassie died, when she began with that first volume Cassie had intended to read. From then on, whenever she felt out of sorts, Dru would return to the big, ancient trunk, take out whichever volume she had been reading last, and for an hour or two return to the past in the company of the woman after whom she had been named. When it had finally come time for her to go away to school, Dru got permission from Myles to take several of the volumes with her. Little had she known at the time how important they would be in helping her maintain her sanity in the alien environment of college.

At Christmastime Dru thankfully went home, and she and Myles spent their first melancholy holiday without Cassie. It was a sad-happy time for both of them: sad because it brought back so many memories of Christmases past; happy because they were together again for a while. In spite of the void left by her mother's absence, Dru was deliriously happy to be home again. She found the big prison as comforting and welcoming as if she had returned to some isolated country village where she had grown up. For the prison *was* her village, and as much as Cassie would have resisted the notion, that was where her roots and heritage lay.

"I know Mamma would have a fit," she told Myles on Christmas Eve, "but I just love this place. I can't imagine living anywhere else. When I finish school, I think I'll get a job teaching at the Union City elementary school, so I can live here with you and come home every night."

"You're presupposing that I'll be here forever," Myles said. "Don't forget that I'm a political appointee, and there's a new governor taking office in January; a man I don't even know. After his inauguration, I may have to come to the university and move in with you and the Toledo ninny."

"Oh, Daddy, that's silly and you know it. You've been warden for more than twenty years. And Granddad Nathan was warden for *thirty* years before that. Why, he designed this prison, he *built* it."

"Yes, and right in the middle of it he was replaced as warden, too."

Dru was surprised. "I didn't know that."

"Well it was only for a short time."

"I'll probably read about it in Great-great-grandmother Dru's diaries," she said.

"No, it was after the Mistress died that it happened."

"The Mistress?"

"Yes. That's what everyone eventually came to call Great-grandmother. The Mistress of Prison Hill. Back in the old days, because it was situated on a hill overlooking Union City, the institution was called Prison Hill. And Great-grandmother had been here so long, she was the Mistress. I think the cons started it."

"How long was Granddad Nathan not warden?" Dru asked.

Myles suppressed a smile. "Nineteen days. The man appointed to replace him was the head of the state police. The prisoners hated him. Not only had he been responsible for many of them getting caught, but there was a rumor that he had deliberately called some of his troopers out of a little town up north in order to let the Ku Klux Klan lynch a couple of prisoners in jail there. Anyway, the day he arrived to take over as warden, the prisoners went on a work strike. Every industry in the prison shut down. Well, the new warden, being force-oriented, laid down a no-work no-food rule: he refused to feed the population." Myles smiled at his daughter. "You and I both know what kind of results a rule like *that* will get. The men became more determined than ever. After a week, some of them got word to the outside and a lawyer of one of the cons obtained a court order forcing the warden to start feeding them again. After that he was helpless. The men were eating again but they still refused to go back to work. For every day there was no prison production to offset the cost of running the place, money had to be taken out of the general tax fund. After two weeks, it began to present a potentially serious financial problem. The new governor, who had appointed the new warden, found himself faced with a crisis his first month in office. He finally made a personal visit to the prison and had a long talk with his new appointee. When he left, he took the man with him. They stopped in Union City to see your Grandfather Nathan. An hour later Dad was back in the warden's office. The prisoners returned to work the next day."

"If the new governor we're getting next month decided to replace you," said Dru, "do you think the prisoners would strike?"

"I'm afraid not," Myles replied clinically. "Too much has changed over the years. Being warden isn't the personal job it used to be. There are too many cons now, too much paperwork, too many duties delegated to deputy wardens; why, I doubt if I know ten percent of the men doing time here, whereas your grandfather probably knew half of them. By name *and* number. No, if today's population strikes, it won't be because the men are unhappy with the warden; it'll be for more privileges, better food, something like that."

"But you don't really think he'll replace you, do you, Daddy?" she asked.

Myles could see the concern in her face. "I don't imagine so," he said, and leaned over to kiss her on the cheek.

There was assurance in Myles Hawn's voice, but there was doubt in his eyes.

Dru read about it in the paper one morning several weeks after her return to school. The story made the bottom of the front page:

HAWN REPLACED AS WARDEN OF PRISON

The item reported that the new governor, in one of his first appointments, had named one Manfred Lehr to replace Myles Hawn as warden of the state's maximum security penitentiary at Union City. Lehr was a well-known young professor of criminology and penology who was expected to apply many new ideas and techniques to the running of the prison. He was replacing Myles Hawn, who had been warden for more than two decades. The governor commended Hawn for his long service to the state, but said it was "time for a change, time for a younger man with a younger outlook." Hawn, the article reminded readers, had first attracted public attention eighteen years earlier when he had married Cassandra Baker, daughter of the notorious public enemy Arthur "Doc" Baker, and herself a former inmate of Women's Prison.

Dru called her father at once. "How long have you known?" she asked.

"A couple of weeks," Myles admitted.

"What are you going to do?" she asked.

"I've already moved into Union City for the time being," he said. "I'd hoped you wouldn't find out about it this soon."

"Well, I did. And I'm coming home."

"No, you are not," Myles said firmly. "There is absolutely nothing you can do here. Please just stay in school."

"I'm not going to let you go through all this alone, Daddy. I'm coming home."

"No, you are *not,*" her father repeated. "You are going to do as I tell you to do, young lady—and I am *telling* you to stay in school. Is that clear?"

"Yes, Daddy, it is. Very clear. But I am coming home anyway."

She hung up the phone and went directly to pack her bag. Eight hours later she was getting off the bus in Union City. Myles was there to meet her. He put his arms around her and held her close.

"How did you know which bus I'd be on?" she asked.

"I didn't. I met two others before this one."

"Where are you staying?"

"At the hotel. I reserved a room for you too."

"Can I get you to take a girl to dinner?" she asked.

"Only if you'll pay the check. I'm unemployed, remember?"

They laughed and walked arm in arm out of the bus station. Not once did either of them mention their earlier conversation on the phone.

CHAPTER 16

Myles was awakened the next morning by Dru knocking insistently on his door. He got into his robe and let her in.

"Daddy, there's been a break up on the hill," she said urgently, shoving a morning paper at him.

Myles frowned and started reading, while Dru continued to bombard him with facts about what had happened.

"Seven long-termers went out over the north wall sometime during the night—"

"That's impossible," Myles muttered to himself. "There's a roving guard inside the north wall."

"The night shift didn't know any of them were gone until the four A.M. cell count."

"They must have gone out between two and four then."

"The paper says midnight."

Myles shook his head. "If they had gone out at midnight, the two A.M. count would have shown them missing. Does it say how they got out of their cells?"

"I don't think so."

Myles found the names of the escapees. "Charles Capehart, Roger Tooley, Neil Connor—" He grunted. "They didn't have to get out of their cells, they were already out: they're night workers. Capehart's a baker, Tooley cleans and oils heavy machinery in the industries building, Connors is a night clerk in Admin. The others probably all work nights too." Myles shook his head.

"I can't see how they got past the roving guard; he can see the entire length of the north wall from any point on his post. Plus there's a gun tower at each corner of the wall."

"What are you going to do about it?" Dru asked.

"Me? Nothing, honey. It isn't up to me to do anything."

"You could go up there and demand to know how it happened," Dru said testily. "After all, it was your prison for twenty years. You've got a right to be told how a thing like this—"

"I don't have any rights at all, Dru," her father interrupted. "You'd best remember that. And as for it being *my* prison—well, that's just not so, honey. It may have *seemed* like that to you at times, but the prison has always been the state's; I was just the keeper."

"But you've got to do *something,*" Dru insisted.

Myles patted her cheek. "I am. I'm going to have breakfast."

Dru was beside herself because Myles would not immediately plunge into the controversy surrounding the escape. She felt that the break was an insult to his prison administration in particular and his career in general. Throughout the day she pestered him mercilessly. "If Mamma was alive, I'll bet you'd do something," she hinted darkly.

"I would indeed," he said from the club chair by the window, where he sat reading. "I'd go on a nice long vacation. Might do that anyway. How'd you like me to take you to Mexico? I could show you all the old battle grounds. Of course, you'd have to skip a semester of school."

For a moment Dru grasped hungrily at that thought. Just the suggestion of not having to go back to school was delicious. But she would not allow her conviction to be swayed.

"Daddy, this is no time to be thinking about vacations. You've got your *reputation* to defend! This escape is a direct reflection on *you*!"

"Be thankful it didn't happen a week ago," he reminded her. "While I was still on the job. Now *that* would have hurt my reputation."

"Honest to God, Daddy, you're impossible," she exclaimed. She returned to her own room to pout.

On their way in to dinner that evening, Myles was stopped by a group of reporters. "Mr. Hawn, can you give us your views on how the break took place this morning?"

"All I know about it is what I read in the morning editions and heard on the radio, gentlemen."

"Do you think it was a break that had been in the planning stages for a long time, Mr. Hawn? And if so, do you feel any of the responsibility for it?"

"To answer the second question first: no, I feel no responsibility for the break. During my tenure as warden there was never an instance of successful escape involving the north wall, because it was always very secure. If there was a breakdown in security, it had to have happened after I left office. As for the break being in the planning stages for a long time or not, there's no way of telling at this point. It may have been a well-laid-out plan or a spur of the moment thing. The only way to find out for sure is to catch the escapees."

"Sir," one of the younger reporters asked, "do you feel, as some sociologists do, that the job of warden should come under the jurisdiction of civil service instead of being appointive?"

"No, I can't say that I do," Myles replied frankly. "I am the fourth generation in my family to serve as a prison warden in this state. As a matter of fact, my great-grandfather, Aaron Van Hawn, supervised the construction of the state's very first penitentiary. All of us in my family were appointed and reappointed by governors of the state. I really can't argue with the system after four generations."

There was some agreeable laughter among the reporters. Dru studied her father closely. He had never really got along very well with the press; he had always felt that the papers had been unfair to Cassie for remaining loyal to her father. But now, as Dru watched, he was being extremely polite and patient in dealing with the members of the fourth estate. Almost, she thought, as if he were using them.

"Do you have any plans for the immediate future, Mr. Hawn?" he was asked.

Myles smiled briefly. "As a matter of fact, my daughter and I are making tentative plans right now for an extended vacation in Mexico. Now, gentlemen, if you'll excuse us, we have a table waiting in the dining room."

As they walked into the hotel dining room, Dru pinched his arm and whispered, "You think you're smart, don't you?"

Myles winked at her and did not reply.

By the next morning, four of the seven escapees had been captured. Capehart, Tooley, and Connor were still at large. And sometime during the night, Connor had invaded a farmhouse, shot down the farmer in cold blood, and stolen the victim's pickup truck. When the news of that tragedy was reported in the press, the public became incensed. Vigilante posses were formed all over the state, the National Guard was mobilized, all time off, leaves, and vacations were canceled for every law enforcement group in the state, and a massive manhunt commenced.

By the third day, widespread protests to the state capital had begun. The newly inaugurated governor was deluged with requests for audiences from half the civic, social, and religious organizations in the state. Telephone calls were so heavy that twice the switchboard shorted out from overloads. The normal volume of complaint mail quadrupled. Opinion was runniing as high as nine-to-one against the governor's appointment of the new warden.

At the Union City Hotel, Myles was on the phone talking privately with John Ragan, the prison's captain of the yard. They had known each other since Myles was a boy.

"John, I've got to know the straight story about that north wall," Myles said. "How did it happen?"

"The new warden," Ragan said. "He's budget-minded. Said he was going to show us how to trim costs and stay within the budget sent down by the state treasurer. He removed from duty and reassigned four roster guards, two night electricians, a standby Admin clerk, two armory officers—and one roving night guard."

Myles sighed quietly. "The north wall roving guard."

"The same," Ragan verified.

After he finished talking with Ragan, Myles walked to the window and stood staring out while he contemplated the situation.

"You're maneuvering to get the job back, aren't you?" Dru asked.

Myles nodded absently. "Yes." Then he looked directly at her. "I don't know anything else, honey. Besides running a prison for twenty-odd years, the only other things I've done were go to Notre Dame for one year and fight in two wars. I've lost your mother already. Someday I'll lose you."

"I won't leave you, Daddy," she promised.

Myles smiled sadly. "Yes, you will, honey. You'll fall in love and want a husband and children, just like most girls your age. I wouldn't want it any other way. But when that happens, I'll be left pretty much alone. That's why I've got to have my job. I've got to have the prison."

"How do you plan to get it back?" Dru asked.

"Just by being here," he answered. "By letting the governor, and the public, know that I'm still around, still available. The new warden, this young fellow Lehr, has already made the worst mistake possible: he moved a guard that didn't appear necessary. That left a flaw in the prison's security. Capehart and the others immediately saw that weakness and took advantage of it. Now some innocent farmer is dead because of it. I don't think there's any question that the governor will have to make amends by removing Lehr. It might be embarrassing because he'll be admitting that he made a mistake putting him there in the first place. But politically it will be better than compounding the mistake by letting him remain where he can possibly do more damage in the future. So Lehr will be out very soon. What I have to work on is making the governor realize that he should put *me* back on the job, instead of perhaps giving it to someone else."

"How are you going to do that?" Dru asked.

"I don't know," Myles said. "I've been laying the groundwork by being nice to the press, but it'll take more than that. As I said before, the main thing is to be here, to be visible. And hope that an opportunity comes along to make the governor realize that there's really only one person who should be warden of that prison—and that person is me."

Myles got his first opportunity to emphasize his presence that very evening when he was invited to be interviewed on a local radio show. It was to be an open forum participated in by several reporters who were in town to cover the prison break. Myles knew that the broadcast would be heard in the capital; he consented to it at once.

Dru went with him to the studio and was given a chair in the control room. She was tense and nervous. Driving over, Myles had said, "This thing could go either way, you know. These fellows might cut me to ribbons tonight. Or I might come off looking like the only solution to a very ugly problem. It's a gamble, pure and simple." Dru made up her mind then and there that if he *did* get cut to ribbons, and if he *didn't* get his job back, she would definitely quit school and stay with him, wherever he ended up. And, she promised herself, she would not marry, ever. Not for as long as he needed her. Sitting in a corner of the booth, watching her father casually lower himself into a chair and knowing how much his leg hurt every time he bent it to sit down, she was certain that she had never loved him more than she did at that moment. She thought of her mother, and wondered if perhaps she was now loving her father for both of them.

"Good evening, ladies and gentlemen," the program host said as the broadcast began. "This is 'Interview on the Air,' a weekly broadcast featuring a prominent figure from our state in a completely unrehearsed question-and-answer session. Our guest this evening is Mr. Myles Hawn, who for more than twenty years served as warden of the state prison at Union City. In addition to Mr. Hawn, we are also pleased to welcome news reporters from several of the finest newspapers in the state. We'll introduce them to you in a moment, and let them begin asking questions of our guest on 'Interview on the Air.' Please stay tuned."

During the commericial, Myles looked over and waved at Dru. She waved back, forcing a smile. When her father looked away, she crossed her fingers and said to herself, "Oh God, let these men be good to him." She felt a pang of conscience both at saying a prayer and appealing to a group of men whose occupation she had always despised.

Suddenly the program had started and the first question was being asked. "Mr. Hawn, in all honesty, do you think the recent prison break would have occurred if you had not been replaced as warden?"

It was a loaded question, a truthful answer to which would be a direct criticism of the governor. But Myles was prepared for it.

"I don't think it would have occurred in the exact manner that it did," he replied. "But given the prisoners involved—all of whom were long-term convicts who probably constantly plot escape—I have to conclude that the attempt was inevitable."

"Then you don't hold the governor responsible?"

"Of course not. No more than I would hold responsible the police officers who arrested the men or the judge who sentenced them."

"Mr. Hawn, your successor, Warden Lehr, is known to be a strong advocate of rehabilitation as opposed to punishment. Do your own views correspond with his?"

"Not entirely," said Myles. "I believe in rehabilitation, certainly. And I am opposed to unnecessary, or unusual punishments. But I don't consider either of those, rehabilitation *or* punishment, the primary function of a prison. First and foremost the purpose of a prison is to incarcerate: to hold and keep felons out of the mainstream of society. Our first responsibility is to protect the public. Of course, *if* while keeping these men locked up we can also rehabilitate them in some way, fine. But that should be a secondary goal."

Dru, listening, felt a wave of relief rush over her. He was doing *magnificently.* Totally at ease, totally in command, totally confident. Her breath came more easily and she uncrossed her fingers.

The broadcast continued. Myles fielded questions about virtually every facet of penology.

"Mr. Hawn, how do you feel about practical experience versus formal education with regard to running a prison?"

"I think experience must prevail," he said. "Textbook logic would be fine if you could get the cons to read the textbooks."

"Sir, what's your opinion of the state's civil service system?"

"It's always worked very well for me. Every officer I have—rather, had—at the prison, came to me through the civil service process. With very few exceptions they have all become dedicated and loyal custodians."

"Are you in favor of a legislative review board to approve the governor's appointments?"

"Absolutely not. The governor is elected by the people to a difficult and trying office. I believe he must retain the right to put in positions of trust those men in whom he has confidence, and who will cause him the least concern possible in whatever area of responsibility he puts them."

So it went for thirty minutes. The newsmen, Myles found, were very fair and made only mild attempts to snare him in controversy. His politeness of the past few days, he felt, had paid off.

When the program was over and Myles went back to where Dru was waiting, he said, "How did I do, honey?"

Dru slapped him fondly on the arm. "You *know* you don't have to ask. You just want praise." For a second her eyes became watery. "Oh, Daddy, Mamma would have been so proud of you tonight."

Myles put an arm around his daughter's shoulders and they walked out of the studio.

CHAPTER 17

Outside the radio station, as Myles held the car door for Dru, he heard a voice whisper from the nearby shadows. "Warden!" it hissed.

Myles felt Dru tense beside him. He quickly took her elbow and guided her into the car. She got in and let him shut the door, but she immediately rolled the window down so that she could hear.

"Who is it?" Myles asked into the darkness, even though he was sure he already knew.

"It's Capehart, Warden. Charley Capehart."

"What do you want, Capehart?"

"Me and Tooley want to give up, Warden. Only we're scared of what we heard Connor done to that farmer. Tooley and me didn't have nothing to do with that, Warden. We haven't seen Connor since we separated late last night in the railroad yard south of town."

"Is Tooley with you now?" Myles asked.

"No, sir. He's hiding in a grain elevator with a busted ankle. He broke it dropping off the wall."

Myles thought briefly of Nathan Hawn, his father. He remembered how, when Nathan was supervising the construction of the new prison, his father had pondered the proper height of the wall. He had fluctuated between twenty-eight feet, thirty feet, and thirty-two feet. "I want it to be secure without being ridiculous," he had said. But he finally chose the highest height, and

Myles remembered that in doing so he had commented, "The higher it is, the more likely a prisoner is to break an ankle dropping from it." So, Myles thought, his choice had proved right.

"Can you help us, Warden?" Capehart asked.

"I'm not warden anymore," Myles said. "If you want to surrender, why don't you just go on back to the prison?"

"We might not make it, Warden—Mr. Hawn. Tooley can't move very fast on that ankle; that's the reason Connor left us behind. We're scared if we try to make it to the prison, we'll run into one of those posses with the dogs. If it wasn't for Connor, we wouldn't even be givin' up. But we don't want to be hunted for no killing rap that we didn't have nothing to do with."

Myles put a hand on the roof of the car and drummed his fingers, half in indecision, half in annoyance. He had been looking for an opportunity to make the governor notice him, but he did not particularly like the situation that had just presented itself to him. To personally take two of the remaining three escapees and turn them over to the proper authorities was going to look like a scene from a Saturday serial. A real grandstand play; melodrama's finest hour.

Yet, Myles knew, he really had no choice. Because Capehart was right about the posses: they *would* cut the two men down, without provocation.

He opened the rear door of the car. "Get in the back seat," he told Capehart. "Keep low."

The convict got in and slumped far down in the seat.

"Are you armed?" Myles asked.

"No, sir. Tooley either."

"All right. Tell me how to get to Tooley."

Capehart gave him directions and Myles drove toward the grain elevator. On the way Capehart said, "You wouldn't have a cigarette, would you, Warden?"

"I don't smoke," Myles said.

"I have some," Dru said withoug thinking. Myles looked at her in surprise. Dru felt her color rising and was very glad that it was dark. "I, uh—just happened to, uh—" She felt like a ninny for stammering.

"Give him one," Myles said. He shook his head. "Just like your mother," he muttered.

They got to the grain elevator and Capehart went in and got Tooley. He returned half carrying the injured man. "Hiya, Warden," Tooley said, smiling a tight-lipped smile that reflected the pain he was in.

"Hello, Tooley," said Myles. Then to Capehart, "Put him down on the seat. You sit on the floorboard."

Myles drove back toward town. Dru got out her cigarettes again and passed them back to Capehart. Myles threw her an annoyed look but said nothing.

"Thanks, miss," said Capehart. He lighted a cigarette for Tooley and one for himself. Both Myles and Dru heard him whisper, "She's Doc Baker's grandkid."

Dru could not help but feel a rush of pride, for Cassie's sake, but Myles could only shake his head in resignation. No matter what happened tonight, the story in the prison tomorrow would not be about how Myles Hawn, son, grandson, and great-grandson of prison builders and keepers, had kept two escaped convicts from falling into the hands of a civilian posse; rather, it would be about how the granddaughter of Doc Baker, great-granddaughter of Ma Baker, had shared her cigarettes with them. Such were the ways in which prison legends were born.

Myles drove to state police headquarters, which was the command post for the manhunt. He parked as close to the front door as he could get, "All right, let's go," he said. Capehart helped Tooley out of the car. "Stay close to me," Myles instructed.

He led the two convicts inside, measuring his pace so that they could keep up with him. In the foyer, several troopers started forward but Myles gestured them back; and since they were still used to his being warden of the state prison, they instinctively obeyed. Myles continued into the lobby. The two escapees, looking more apprehensive every step, stayed right behind him. Across the lobby, a dozen loitering reporters and photographers glanced at the trio. Their mouths dropped open almost simultaneously.

"Jesus God," one of them muttered.

Myles and the convicts stopped at the reception counter. "Is Colonel Baer in?" Myles asked the trooper on duty.

"Yessir, Warden. I'll ring him, sir."

The reporters hurried over to Myles, whipping out their notebooks. At once the lobby was filled with shouted questions and punctuated with flashbulbs.

It was midnight when Myles and Dru finally got back to the hotel. When they stopped at the desk to pick up their keys, Myles was given a telephone message. "A Mr. Ladd, sir," the clerk said. "He's called long distance three times. He asks that you return his call no matter what the hour."

In their rooms, Myles contacted the operator and returned the call. It only rang once before a man's voice answered.

"This is Myles Hawn speaking," said Myles.

"Yes, Mr. Hawn. The governor wishes to speak with you, sir. One moment, please."

Presently another voice came on the line. "Good evening, Mr. Hawn."

"Good evening, Governor."

"I heard your interview earlier," the governor said. "I want to compliment you on your demeanor and discretion. You had several excellent opportunites to really damage me, but you didn't. I appreciate that. I take it you want your job back."

"Yes, sir, I do."

"All right, you've got it. I'll remove Lehr and make the announcement sometime tomorrow. Do you think you'll have any problem undoing the damage he's done?"

"I don't think so, no."

The governor sighed wearily. "For the life of me I can't understand how a man as brilliant as Lehr could have pulled such a colossal blunder. During my recent campaign he organized the education votes from kindergarten teachers up to university department heads and got me the greatest depth of support from the education sector of any candidate in the state's history. Then I reward him by giving him the job he wanted, and in a matter of days he turns it into a shambles. What did he do wrong, Hawn?"

"Probably just moved too fast," said Myles. "Reorganizing a prison isn't like reorganizing a department store. Changes have to be made very slowly, and only after a great deal of thought. And one thing that can never be done is to reduce the security standards. Cons know the prison routine as well as the guards do. They watch for flaws, weaknesses, carelessness. If a regular guard is sick, they look for his substitute to make a mistake. If a guard has just gotten married or become a father, they watch him closely because they know his mind may be on something besides his job. There are many factors involved, Governor; many unwritten rules that have to be followed on a day-to-day basis."

"What you're saying is that it takes practice to successfully run a penitentiary."

"Yes, sir, I suppose I am."

The governor grunted. "I guess it takes practice to run a state too. I've got some learning to do."

"You'll do all right, Governor," Myles told him.

"Yes, I will," the governor said confidently. "Incidentally, a reporter friend of mine called me earlier and told me all about what happened at state police headquarters tonight. I don't know how you arranged that, Warden, but it was a beautiful move."

"I didn't really *arrange* it, sir."

The governor laughed. "You'll never convince me of *that.* Well, goodnight, Warden. And thank you again."

Myles hung up and turned to Dru. "Tomorrow we'll go back home," he said simply.

A week later, Myles put a reluctant Dru on the train to return to school.

"I really shouldn't be going back," she protested. "You need someone to look after you."

"I'll struggle along until summer vacation," he assured her.

""Daddy, I really don't see why I have to—"

Myles touched her lips with one finger. "Yes, you do, honey. You see why."

Dru sighed quietly. "All right, Daddy. You're right. I see why."

She got aboard the train and stood on the platform.

"See you at Easter, honey," Myles said.

"Yes. Easter." She smiled a sad smile. Under one arm she carried two more of her Great-great-grandmother Dru's journals. As the train began to move, she held on to them almost desperately. She waved to her father and he waved back.

"Easter," she said again, to herself this time.

The train moved down the track, leaving the depot behind. Dru entered the coach and went to her seat. She sat looking out the window, holding the two journals to her bosom.

Holding them like that, she felt less alone. As if someone was with her.

CHAPTER 18

The first thing Monroe Van Hawn did when he woke up that June morning was smile. It was going to be the most important day of his life. It was his twenty-first birthday, and the day he was to become a guard at Prison Hill. And, although no one knew about it but him, it was also the day he planned to become engaged to Beth Colson, daughter of Captain of the Yard Sam Colson. His mother, he knew, would throw a fit about that. She wanted him to wait until he was twenty-five to marry. Not that she was an example of any such precedent; she had given birth twice by the time *she* was twenty-five. But she would still have her fit, he thought. He smiled again. For all the good it would do her. He and his stepfather would bring her around eventually.

Monroe tossed back the sheet and got out of bed. His was the downstairs bedroom, under the stairs. Through the wall, he could hear the kitchen help already at work. He smelled side meat cooking and it instantly made him hungry. He went to his bureau, poured water into the bowl, and washed and shaved. He could have had hot water from the kitchen, but he did not want to take the time. He wanted to get out of the house before his mother came down. Beth was being fitted for a dress that morning down at Jessica Vintner's shop in Prisontown, and she had promised to slip away and meet him on the levee afterward.

As he shaved, Monroe studied his face. It was his mother's face, really, for he resembled her almost identically. They had the same mismatched lips, the same large eyes, even the same lean, square shoulders and hips. Only the color of their eyes was different, his mother's being brown while his were a brilliant blue. He thought of his brother, who looked nothing like either him or their mother. Grover had been the image of their father. Monore sighed quietly. How he wished his brother could be there that day.

When he finished shaving, he quickly dressed and went out to the kitchen. Claude Lemoyne, their cook, was at the stove, and Paris Murad, his helper, was churning butter. Both men were lifers, both murderers.

"Morning," said Monroe, taking a plate from the cupboard. "I'll eat in here."

"Who is it you don't want to see this morning, your mother or your stepfather?" Lemoyne asked knowingly.

"Mother," said Monroe. "I have something to do in town and I don't want her finding anything for me to do around here."

Lemoyne broke four eggs into a skillet and teased them to fry sunny side up. "Paris," he said to Murad, "watch the stairs for the Mistress." Murad left the churn and went to a point near the foot of the stairs where he could see the feet of anyone coming down from the second floor. When Murad was out of hearing, Lemoyne turned back to Monroe. "Will you bring me something from town today?"

"What do you want?"

"Something for this bad tooth of mine."

Monroe looked askance at him and suppressed a smile. "You ever going to get that tooth pulled?"

Lemoyne shrugged. "Maybe. Someday." He lifted the skillet off the flame the instant Monroe's eggs were perfect. Taking the plate from Monroe's hand, he filled it with eggs, side meat, and sliced tomatoes. Monroe sat at the help's table to eat. Lemoyne poured him a cup of coffee.

"I'll be a guard after today," Monroe told him. "I won't be able to get you things from town anymore."

"Other guards do it," Lemoyne said.

"I don't care. I won't. Once I put on that uniform, I break no rules."

Lemoyne sat down with him and poured coffee for himself. "Good thing I don't feel so strongly about breaking rules. There's a rule against trusties gossiping, you know. If I stuck to that one, I wouldn't be able to tell you what Cap'n Colson and his wife said last night about you marrying Miss Beth."

Monroe's eyes narrowed. "Are you trying to bribe me, Claude?"

"No, sir, Mr. Monroe, you know better than that. I'm just trying to do my time as easy as I can."

Monroe ate in silence for several minutes. He and Lemoyne exchanged glances but neither spoke. The game of convict trading had begun. It was an intricate game played strictly by convict rules. A convict made it known that he knew something of interest to an officer. He did not offer to tell him what it was; just let him know that he *could.* The officer had to determine what the convict wanted in return for the information, and decide if it was worth it. Then he had to *ask* the convict to tell him what he knew. By asking, he was agreeing to give the con whatever it was he wanted in return. In this case. Monroe already knew what Claude Lemoyne wanted. If he asked Lemoyne for the information, he would be striking a silent bargain to get it for him.

Monroe finished eating and pushed his empty plate away. "All right, what did they say?" he asked.

"They said they expected you to ask for Miss Beth's hand any day. They said your mother was going to raise holy hell when you did. But they agreed that it would be a good match for Beth and they said if your mother tried to get them to disapprove of it, they'd refuse her."

"Who told you all that?"

"Tom Hoke. He's a forger who works in their kitchen. They was talking about it after dinner."

Monroe nodded. It was really not surprising or unusual news. Beth probably would have told him pretty much the same thing sooner or later. But it was nice to be reassured as to where Beth's parents stood.

"Okay," Monroe said. "What kind do you want?"

"That White Lightning you got last time was pretty good. Or else that Texas Plains Whiskey."

Murad hurried in from the hall. "The mistress is coming down!" he whispered urgently.

Monroe stepped quickly to the back door, and slipped out of the kitchen. He ran across the lawn and down the knoll toward the compound stable where his horse was kept. On the way he passed the gate leading to Peckerwood Acres. There were a dozen convicts buried there now, each with a simple white cross bearing the man's last name and the year of his death.

Off in a corner, removed from the white crosses, were three other graves. One of them had a large headstone which had been cut and chiseled sixteen years earlier by old Mr. Tyree. The stone read:

AARON VAN HAWN
B. 1787 D. 1837
FIRST WARDEN

Late in the afternoon following Aaron's funeral, Governor Alton Monroe, Grover, and Clement Niles returned to Niles's cabin to decide two things: who was to be the new warden of Prison Hill, and how many prisoners should be hanged for the killing of Aaron, Tillman, and Danforth.

"I suggest we get right to the most important issue," the governor said. "The future of the prison. As far as I'm concerned, there's only one man to run it. That man is you, Clement."

"I agree," Grover said quickly.

"No," Clement Niles said. "I'm afraid not."

"May I ask why?" Monroe said shortly. He was not in the best of moods. The destruction of the mill was going to cost him considerable money. The riot would no doubt be used by his opponents to try and hurt him politically. And the vision of Aaron Van Hawn's two little sons at the graveside was the kind of unpleasant scene that always caused him sleepless nights.

"My health," was Clement Niles's reason. "I'm not up to running this place."

"Nonsense!" snorted the governor. He stalked across the room and silently lighted a cigar. That was the sign for Grover to enter the argument.

"Look, Clement," the lanky aide said, "you don't have to run the prison like Aaron did, you know. It can be run administratively. You can delegate the responsibility for inspections and punishments and the like. Just because Aaron did everything himself—"

"Grover, I am *not* a well man," Niles interrupted firmly. "If I were, I'd take the job in a minute, if only to be able to allow Druscilla and the boys to remain in their home."

Grover and the governor exchanged glances. "I hadn't thought about that," Grover said. "Dru *doesn't* have anyplace to go, does she?"

"I'm afraid not."

The two men fell silent for a moment. Alton Monroe stepped back over to join them. "Clement, I'm going to say something to you and I hope you won't take it the wrong way. It occurs to me that your becoming warden here might very well resolve your health problem *and* Druscilla's future."

"I don't see how."

"Think about it for a moment. Hasn't it been Druscilla who's cared for you all these years whenever you've been ill?"

"Yes."

"And if you were warden and living in the mansion, wouldn't she still be able to care for you?"

Niles coughed slightly. "What are you getting at?"

"You tell him, Grover," said Monroe.

"Marry Druscilla," said Grover.

Niles had spoken to Dru two nights later. He had gone up to the mansion with Doc and Cordelia to have supper with her. They had eaten late; the boys were already in bed. Later, they had all gone out onto the proch and enjoyed the pleasant evening. The prison was quiet; below the knoll they could see the troopers of the state militia as they patrolled the walls and compound.

"How long will they keep the prisoners locked up?" Doc had asked.

"Until after the executions," Niles said.

"Have they decided how many men to hang?"

Niles nodded. "Ten."

When the night air began to grow cool, Doc and Cordelia got in their buggy and left. Niles and Dru went into the drawing room. That was when Niles broached the subject of her future.

"Dru, I realize this is a most inappropriate time to say what I'm going to say, but it is necessary for me to speak to you about something before you make any definite plans for the future. I'd like to know if you would consider marrying me."

Dru looked surprised, so Niles quickly added, "I don't mean immediately, of course. There would have to be a waiting period. I should think six months would be proper."

Dru floundered slightly in her surprise. "Six months?"

"Yes. That's a respectable length of time. And it would give little Monroe and Grover time to adjust to the idea. Mind you, I don't intend to try and take their father's place. I'm quite different from Aaron, as you know. I'm not in the best of health and couldn't romp with them the way he did. I'm afraid the best I have to offer as a father is that I'd be a good provider. The governor has assured me a permanent wardenship for as long as our party is in the statehouse."

Dru's surprise had given way to concern. "Clement, being warden of Prison Hill is a difficult job. Are you certain you want to take on something that arduous, considering your health?"

"I've discussed that with Alton. He's going to have Grover find me a man to replace Tillman, except that he'll have more authority than Tillman had. He'll be in charge of the prisoners and will relieve me of all but administrative duties. We're going to call his job captain of the yard." Niles coughed again: a rough, scratchy cough that groped at his throat. Dru poured him a glass of water. "Thank you. Druscilla, I want you to know that it means a great deal to me for you to think about my well-being when you've just lost your husband."

Dru sat next to him on the settee and took his hand. "Clement, you have been Aaron's and my dearest friend for a long time. Of course I'm concerned about your well-being."

"I want you to know that it would not be my intent to—ah, exercise any marital prerogatives. It would be perfectly satisfactory to me if you would simply run the mansion and take care of me when I'm ill. The raising of your sons I would also leave strictly to you. I think you'd find that you could have everything pretty much your own way."

"That's a very generous offer, Clement."

"Prison Hill has become home to both of us. This way, neither of us would be uprooted. Nor your boys, either. Will you consider it?"

Dru thought briefly of Theron Verne, wondering where he was and how she would ever go about finding him. Then she quickly put him out of her mind and thought of poor, dead Aaron. She sighed. What a good man he had been. She thanked God he had never known of or even suspected her infidelity. She smiled slightly to herself. Of course, she had been very good at keeping things from him. She had known for several years that he could not read or write. She had found out purely by accident. Aaron had been copying Monroe's and Grover's names, practicing in secret so that he would not have to go through life unable to write the names of his sons. Dru had found some of his practice sheets and had known at once. But she had never let on, never even hinted to him that she knew. He went to his grave thinking he had successfully fooled her.

She sighed again, very quietly, and considered the two sons he had left her to raise. There was some money, of course—Aaron had been a thrifty man—but it would not last until they boys were grown. And her prospects for earning more were scant. She would need help, there was no denying it.

She looked at Clement Niles, sitting next to her—pale, thin, his eyes watery most of the time, his cough persistent. But, like Aaron, he was a good man, and she was certain he would take proper care of her and the boys. It would be foolish of her to reject Clement's offer, particularly in the silly hope of finding Theron Verne. . . .

She squeezed Clement's hand and smiled at him. "I'll accept your offer, Clement," she said. "Gratefully."

Two months later, the new captain of the yard arrived. His name was Jack Ironwood and he had been found by Grover in the Missouri river town of Eastlin, where, as town constable hired by a group of merchants, he had found it necessary to kill six men in order to restore the community to peace and tranquility. Three of the men had been dispatched by pistol shot, two by long knife, and one with his bare hands. Those hands were huge, larger even than Aaron Van Hawn's had been. The day Ironwood rode up to the house, Dru thought that she had never seen such hands.

"Good day, ma'am," he said, smiling from the saddle of a wild-eyed strawberry roan. Dru stared at him from the porch. He was a big man, as tall as lanky Grover but thirty pounds heavier. He wore a thick black moustache. Part of his left earlobe was missing. Around his waist he wore a cartridge belt and a brace of

Welton pistols. He removed a black, flat-crowned sombrero when he spoke to Dru. "Might I trouble you to tell me where I can find Mr. Clement Niles?"

"I'll fetch him," Dru said. As she went into the house, she knew instinctively that the man's eyes were watching the way she walked. Clement was at the desk in the drawing room, working on plans for the new mill and a tannery to be built nearby. Dru accompanied him back to the porch. They found little Monroe and Grover looking up at the rider with wide eyes and open mouths.

"I'm Jack Ironwood, sir," he introduced himself. "I have a letter from Governor Monroe."

"Please step down, sir," said Clement Niles. "This is Mrs. Van Hawn, my betrothed. And her sons."

Ironwood bowed deeply to Dru and gravely shook hands with the boys. Then Clement took him into the drawing room and shut the door.

An hour later, when Clement accompanied him back to his horse, Monroe looked up at Ironwood's mutilated earlobe. "Mister?" he said.

Ironwood looked down at him from a tremendous height. "Yes, boy?"

"What happened to your ear?"

"Monroe!" said Dru. "Leave Mr. Ironwood alone!"

"I don't mind telling him, ma'am, if you don't mind him knowing," said Ironwood.

"All right," said Dru, who wanted to know almost as badly as her son.

"A Mohawk Indian bit it off, boy."

Monroe's eyes bulged. "Actual?"

"Actual. 'Bout fifteen years ago."

Smiling again, Ironwood swung into the saddle and rode down to the compound, leaving his amazed new acquaintances watching from the portico. He never did tell any of them that the Mohawk had been a squaw.

At dawn the next morning, Ironwood had the prisoners lined up inside the walls. He stood with his great hands on his hips, next to the barred cage in the center of the yard.

"They tell me this contraption is called an Idle Box. Who are the men who spend their days in it?" Five lifers, all killers, stepped forward. Ironwood waved them toward the door. "Go ahead and get in it then," he said.

As the nearest man started to get into the Box, Ironwood smashed a brass-knuckled fist into his face, breaking his nose and cheek and reducing his upper lip to bloody pulp. Two militiamen dragged him away.

"Next man," said Ironwood.

No one moved. Ironwood's dark eyes swept the faces. He waited a full minute. Still no one moved.

"So much for the Idle Box," he said. "From now on, every man in here works." He pulled a sheaf of papers from his hip pocket and consulted it. "George Copp, step forward!" he ordered. A square-faced man with one squinting eye stepped out of line. Ironwood walked over to him. "Your commitment papers say that you're serving twenty-one years for manslaughter. You killed Elmo Hicks in a knife fight in Moline, is that right?"

"That's right, Captain," said Copp.

Ironwood's brass-knuckled fist flew again. Copp pitched onto his back, jaw broken.

"Elmo Hicks was a friend of mine," Ironwood said. He looked at the papers again. "Wiley and Moxon, step forward!" Two prisoners moved fearfully out of formation. One of them began to tremble. Ironwood motioned them over in front of him. "You two were sentenced to ten years apiece for acts against nature with other men." The two convicts looked down at the ground. Ironwood folded the papers and put them back in his pocket. Then he suddenly grabbed each man by an ear and smashed their faces together. They crumpled to the ground, moaning and bleeding. "I can't abide peculiar men," Ironwood announced.

He paced back and forth in front of the prisoners. The yard was silent except for the clink-clink of his silver spurs and the faint squeak of the black leather holsters as his legs moved. The men watched him with a mixture of fear and hatred. Finally he halted and faced them again.

"Listen close," he said. "These are my rules. From now on, you work from dawn to dusk. You will stand at all times when you are out of your cells; that means *all* times, even when you eat. And one side of your heads will be shaved every fortnight so that you can easily be identified if you decide to run off. For violation of rules, you will be flogged. Stealing will be twelve lashes, fighting eighteen, and general disobedience and misconduct twenty. Those will be with the strap. For weakening your chains in any way, you'll get thirty lashes, for indulging in disgusting acts, either alone or with another prisoner, also thirty, and for escape, fifty. Those will be with the cat-o'-nine. All punishment will be carried out by me."

Ironwood started to walk away. Then he thought of Dru and turned back.

"One other thing. The punishment for laying hands on any member of the warden's household will be hanging."

With that, the new captain of the yard strode away.

A week after Ironwood's arrival, one of Dru's garden trusties came running into the kitchen. "Miz Van Hawn! That Injin's come back again!"

Dru's face drained of color. Kee had run away for the third time on the day of the knitting mill riot. Dru had not learned about it until after Aaron's funeral. Because of the confusion of the riot, the deaths, and the state militia taking over, no reward notice went out on him. As far as Dru knew, his absence had not been noticed, at least not officially; Dru was certain that Clement was aware of it, although he had never mentioned it to her.

"Did bounty hunters bring him back?" she asked the trusty.

"No, ma'am! He come back by hisself. And he brung a squaw with him!"

Dru hurried down the knoll to the gate. Kee was being held at gunpoint by the gate guard. He sat bareback on a large pinto horse. Behind it, on a travois, lay an Indian woman, holding her hands over her face. Just as Dru got to the gate, Ironwood rode up on his roan.

"This here Sac is a runaway, Captain," the guard said. "He's hung his irons on a limb three times."

Dru stepped forward. "Captain Ironwood, may I have a word with you, please?"

Ironwood dismounted and followed Dru off a short distance.

"Captain Ironwood—"

"Please call me Jack, ma'am."

"We've only just met. That would hardly be proper."

"My apologies. I wouldn't think of suggesting anything improper with you, ma'am." There was a twinkle in his eye as he said it.

"Captain Ironwood, I'd like to tell you about Kee, this Indian—"

Ironwood listened attentively as she related the incident a decade earlier on the keelboat and told of Kee's subsequent escapes and whippings by Aaron.

"It sounds like Mr. Van Hawn was a stern man," Ironwood commented.

"He was a man of high principle," Dru countered. "He believed in dispensing equal justice to every prisoner."

Ironwood smiled roguishly. "Well, fortunately for you and the Sac, ma'am, I myself am not burdened with any such principles." He looked over at Kee. "Come here," he said in fluent Sac-and-Fox dialect.

Kee threw one leg over his mount's neck and slid to the ground. He was halfway to Ironwood before the gate guard realized he had dismounted. When he was in front of Ironwood, the big white man questioned him at length in his own language. Several times Kee gestured back toward the travois as he answered Ironwood's questions. Finally, Ironwood turned back to Dru.

"He says he wasn't running away to try and escape serving his sentence. He was running away to try and find his squaw. The woman on the travois is the one he maimed; she's got no toes and can only limp around. He says that regardless of what she did with the white man, he still covets her and wants to protect her. He finally found her this time out; that's why he come back of his own accord."

Dru shook her head sadly at Kee. "He could have served his sentence twice by now. He was only given five years."

"Yes, but a man who escapes must start his term all over again. That's the law."

Dru bit her lower lip; tears almost came to her eyes. "Captain Ironwood, I'll be in your debt if you could see your way clear to reduce his punishment. He's been whipped twice and had his leg broken—" She left her sentence hanging. "God, I feel so awful about this."

"Then put it out of your mind," Ironwood said. He turned to Kee and spoke rapidly but firmly in dialect. Kee nodded, knelt quickly and touched Ironwood's boot toes with his fingertips, and hurried back to his horse. Ironwood waved to the gate guard to let him pass into the compound. "It's over now," Ironwood said to Dru.

"What did you tell him?" she asked.

"I told him to go to my cabin and make a camp behind it. I said I'd let his woman cook for me while he served his sentence. I said my generosity was a gift from you. And I told him that if he made a fool of me by running off again, that I'd track him down and kill him."

"No whipping?" Dru asked.

Ironwood shook his head. "No whipping."

Dru smiled. She touched Ironwood's arm. "Thank you—Jack."

The big man did not return her smile. His expression remained solemn. "I have to ask you something," he said. "I have to ask if you are committed to marrying Mr. Niles."

Dru swallowed her feelings and forced herself to answer. "Yes, I am. Clement has been a great comfort to me and I owe him a great deal. He's not a well man and he needs me. I'll marry him on the first day of the new year."

Ironwood nodded resignedly. "My poor luck."

"I hope you'll stay on anyway," Dru said.

"Yes, I will."

Dru and Clement Niles were married four months later in a ceremony at the mansion attended by Dru's two sons, Doc Robin as best man, Corelia Walls as maid of honor, the Pullman brothers and their wives, and a number of other merchants and businessmen from Prisontown. Jack Ironwood was also a guest. It was a far different wedding from her marriage to Aaron ten years earlier. Instead of a drab, bleached dress made by her Aunt Wella, this time Dru wore a blue satin gown all the way from Chicago. And instead of a simple sit-down frontier supper, the trusty cooks and bakers had prepared a buffet banquet as lavish as any of the guests, except Doc, had ever seen. Finally, instead of a yellow-toothed, whiskey-breath circuit preacher like the lecherous Reverend Lamper, a very proper Baptist minister came up from Paducah at Clement's request.

The wedding party was a splendid affair: warm cordial, everyone friendly. For Dru it would have been perfect except for two things: Clement had been feeling poorly and coughing sporadically most of the day; and throughout the evening her eyes seemed forever to be meeting the dark stare of Jack Ironwood. They spoke directly only once during the evening, when they met by chance at the punchbowl. Ironwood raised his glass to her.

"My very best wishes, Dru," he said.

"Thank you, Jack. I hope you mean it."

"I do," he assured her. "I want you to be happy, whatever it takes."

Dru looked down at the gleaming crystal cup she held. "I've grown very—fond of you these past months, Jack—"

"And I you."

"If Clement didn't need me so much—"

"There's no need to put it into words," he said quietly.

"Thank you. I treasure your friendship, Jack."

She squeezed his hand and left him at the table.

After their guests had left, Clement followed Dru to the master bedroom. It was the first time he had seen the room. During their engagement he had been respectably correct in his conduct toward her. He had worked in the mansion, and dined there with her and the boys, but promptly at eight o'clock, in full view of all trusties and guards, he had returned to his cabin.

Now they were alone. The boys had gone home with Cordelia. All the trusties had been sent back behind the walls. Dru began to undress.

"I really think you'd be more comfortable if we slept separately," Clement said. "My coughing will only keep you awake."

"You're my husband, Clement. I think we should sleep together. If you cough, you cough."

He sat wearily on the side of the bed. "Dru, I—I tire so easily. I'm exhausted just from the party tonight. I'm afraid I'll disappoint you."

She came to him in just her chemise. "You won't disappoint

me, Clement. And I will try not to disappoint you." She pushed him gently back onto the bed and got on her knees beside him. "You don't have to do anything. Just lie there. Let me do everything for you."

Clement Niles closed his eyes and Dru began removing his clothes.

CHAPTER 19

After Monroe slipped out of the kitchen and ran down to the stable, he saddled the fine Appaloosa his stepfather had given him for his eighteenth birthday and rode across the compound to see Sam Colson, his future father-in-law. The gate guard passed him inside the walls with a friendly wave and he walked the horse over to Big Sam's office. Colson occupied the office that had once been the warden's and had belonged to Aaron. When Clement Niles took over as warden, he had decided there was no need for him to have an office inside the walls, so he had given it to Jack Ironwood. Big Sam Colson had inherited it when he took Ironwood's place.

Colson was at his desk when Monroe entered. "Morning, sir," said Monroe.

The captain of the yard smiled and rose, extending his hand. "Good morning. And happy birthday to you, lad. Since you're twenty-one today, I think it's time you dropped the 'sir' and started calling me Sam."

"Thanks, Sam!" Monroe said, pumping the captain's hand. He smiled widely, already beginning to enjoy his new manhood.

"So today's the day your stepdad's going to make you a guard, eh?" said Colson. "And tomorrow you go to work for me."

"Yes, sir! I'll get my uniform tonight at my birthday dinner."

Colson grunted. "Beth and her mother are probably *already* dressing for that." He returned to his chair and sat back, lighting a cigar. He was a thick-set man, shorter than average, who vaguely reminded Monroe of his dead father, the little he could remember of him. Except that Big Sam had a belly that overhung his belt, something Aaron, by virtue of his constant activity, had avoided. Colson had been captain of the yard for seven years. He was an easy-going man who, unlike Jack Ironwood, did not go out of his way to make life harder for the convicts. But then, he had taken over the job after Ironwood had run the yard for nine years. There was little call for him to be a harsh captain; Jack Ironwood had long since broken the spirit of the convict population. By the time Colson had arrived, the prisoners were a thoroughly intimidated lot, reduced by Ironwood's brass knuckles and cat-o'-nine to a body of zombies.

Big Sam and Monroe walked over to the mess hall and had a cup of coffee, then Monroe accompanied the captain on his morning inspection rounds. Monroe was as well known inside the walls as most of the guards. He had virtually grown up among the convicts and knew the nooks and corners of the yard and cell house as well as he knew the big mansion on the knoll. Unlike his brother Grover, who had shown no interest whatever in the prison, Monroe seemed to have been born to be a guard. Their mother was constantly amazed by them as they were growing up. Monroe, probably the natural son of a convict, who looked nothing like Aaron Van Hawn, loved the prison Aaron had built almost as much as Aaron himself had loved it. While Grover, who was a physical duplicate of Aaron, had a wild, adventurous spirit that could have been more easily matched to Theron Verne. Dru often wondered if when Monroe was born, a little of Theron had not been left inside her to mix with the genes Aaron put there to produce Grover. She wished she could ask Doc Robin if such a medical oddity were possible, but of course she could not.

When the inspection tour was over, Monroe and Big Sam returned to the captain's office and Monroe mounted his horse again. "Tell Beth I'll see her tonight up at the house," he said. "Tell her I'll have a surprise for her."

"I expect it won't be all that much of a surprise," said Colson. "Except to your mother, maybe."

"Well, at least I've got you and Mrs. Colson on my side."

"And your stepdad too, I'd imagine."

"Him most of all," Monroe said gratefully.

As Monroe was walking his horse toward the gate, he passed

the old mess hall in the original cell house. It had been converted to a dormitory and work area for female prisoners. It would accommodate twenty women, although there had never been more than six there at any one time, and presently there were only four. They lived in one end of the long room, cooked their meals and ate in the middle of the room, and worked at stitching and mending tables at the opposite end. Outside the dormitory were big iron tubs in which they did the guards' laundry. In their free time, they were allowed to make dresses and other articles and send them down to Pullman Brothers to be sold.

When Monroe was passing the dormitory, a woman his mother's age came out on the stoop and spoke to him. "Happy birthday, Monroe," she said.

Monroe stopped. "Thank you, Miz Herraday."

Letitia Herraday squinted up at him, shielding her eyes from the sun. "Lord, lord," she said wistfully. "You was only eight years old when I first come here. Following your stepdaddy around like a little pup. Now here you are all grown up and fixing to get yourself married."

"Yes, ma'am, I guess I am." Monroe shook his head slightly. He had long ago stopped being surprised by the fact that prisoners knew everything that went on in the personal lives of the warden, his guards, and their families.

"Today is Nell's birthday too, you know," the woman said.

"Yes, ma'am, I know," Monroe said quietly.

"She's twelve today," Letitia said wistfully. "She was born on your ninth birthday. Your mother said she was the prettiest little girl baby she had ever seen."

"Yes, ma'am."

Monroe felt awkward with the woman, as he always did, but he was careful to be as polite to her as he would have been to a woman in town. His mother was godmother to Letitia Herraday's daughter, and Letitia, who had been the first female prisoner at Prison Hill and who had given birth to the child there, occupied a unique position within the walls. She received no better treatment than any other female prisoner, but because she was the first, and because of what Dru had done for her with the baby, she was accorded a respect by guards and male prisoners that the other women prisoners, as they came and went, seldom enjoyed. She never abused her position or tried to take advantage of it, because she was serving life for murder and was smart enough to want to make it as easy as possible on herself. But sometimes, as with Monroe, she was uncomfortable to be around. All he could do when he happened to meet her inside the walls was be patient. He knew from experience that she would not detain him long.

"If you and Beth Colson go to St. Louis on your honeymoon, will you stop in and see my little Nell?"

"Sure will, Miz Herraday," Monroe promised.

Letitia thanked him, wished him a happy birthday again, and finally went back inside. Monroe, relieved, rode on to the gate.

The arrival of Letitia Herraday at Prison Hill in March of 1841, was both preceded and followed by a great deal of controversy. Grover, then in his fifteenth year as Alton Monroe's chief aide, had been the one to bring the news that she was coming.

"The governor has no choice in the matter," he tried to explain to Clement and Dru. "The woman has been convicted of willful and deliberate murder. She must be sent to prison."

"The woman is expecting a child, Grover!" said Dru. "You can't send an expectant mother to prison."

"We have no choice, Druscilla."

"In the past, expectant mothers have always been pardoned by the governor," said Clement.

"For lesser crimes. Theft and such. But this is murder, Clem."

Clement Niles rose and stood by the fireplace to warm his back. He coughed a spot of blood into a handkerchief. It was an unusually cold February and he was having a difficult time with his health. "I still don't see how Alton can do this," he said. "It's unprecedented."

"He knows that. But there's no alternative. If it were any other crime but murder, he'd either pardon her or let her serve her sentence in a county jail the way women have always been allowed to do. Or if she had killed someone besides her own husband, or killed him in a different way, perhaps then some adjustment could be made in carrying out her sentence. But the woman intentionally poisoned her own husband, with chemicals she stole from his own chemist's shop. It was an outrageous crime and the jury decided she should spend her life in prison for it."

"But she's *expecting*!" Dru said again, desperately, as if she were finding the men too stupid to understand it.

"The men of the jury knew that, Dru."

"Oh, yes," she snapped. "The *men* of the jury."

Clement returned to his chair. Dru immediately spread a shawl over his legs. "I hate to see you open the door to female prisoners," Clement said.

Grover shrugged. "It's inevitable, Clem. As long as they commit the crimes, they have to serve the punishment. Besides, I don't think it'll work that much of an imposition on the prison. The state rarely has more than half a dozen women in jail at any one time. You can find a place for them somewhere. Away from the men, of course."

"What about the baby?" Dru asked stiffly. "Shall we have her give birth in a cell?"

"That's up to the warden," Grover said, passing the decision to Clement.

"I'm sure we can make arrangements other than a cell," he said. "Dru can help."

That was how it came about that the old mess hall was converted into a female dormitory, and one small end of the yard fenced off from the rest of the prison area. It was all ready a month later when a state marshal and his wife escorted Letitia Herraday up the hill to begin her term. Dru was there with Jack Ironwood to meet her. She was a tall, nervous woman with a pinched expression devoid of friendliness or trust. Dru had an immediate impression that she had silently suffered a great deal of abuse. She decided to be as nice to her as possible under the circumstances.

"It should be comfortable enough for you here," Dru said, when they got to the new dormitory. "At least it's better than a cell."

"What about my baby?" Letitia asked. "What will become of it?"

"We'll see that it gets to your relatives," Dru said.

"I have no relatives. At least none I'd want to give my baby to." She looked around the dormitory. "Does my baby have to be born here?"

Dru looked at Ironwood for an answer. "I'm afraid so, Mrs. Herraday," he said. "But we've got an understanding doctor down in town. I'm sure he'll be willing to put in the birth record that the child was born in town."

The woman shook her head. "That won't make much difference. Prison Hill or Prisontown; the name Herraday will tell who its mother was."

After Letitia was locked in, Ironwood walked partway back to the mansion with Dru. "Don't worry too much about her," Ironwood said. "I'll see that it's made as easy on her as I can."

"Thank you Jack." She smiled tentatively at him. "It seems you're always doing nice things for me."

"I'm happy to help when I can."

"And you never ask anything in return."

"There's nothing I can ask for," he replied frankly. "You're a respectable, married woman. I wouldn't dishonor you by asking you to be otherwise. Anyway," he smiled, "I like your husband. He's a good man and he's treated me fairly. And I like your sons, both of them. I wouldn't taint your family in any way. No matter how much I cared for you."

Dru stopped and faced him. "I care too," she said simply. "And someday—" She could not find the words to finish her sentence.

But Ironwood understood. He nodded. "Someday," he said quietly.

Dru walked on to the mansion alone.

Clement Niles and Dru had settled into a comfortable, content marriage that imposed on neither of them. Clement, as had been his lifelong habit, maintained his introverted ways and seemed at times almost like a boarder instead of the master of the house. As long as his needs were attended to and the mansion kept immaculate, he never complained or criticized. When he was ill, he expected to be cared for, but that was the extent of his demands. Sexually, he accepted whatever Dru gave him, and always left it up to her to make the overtures. If she did, fine—he enjoyed it; if she did not—well, he needed his rest anyway. His health, while never improving, did not seem to measurably worsen either. For the most part it remained the same: poor. He was constantly at odds with Doc Robin, who, at Dru's persistent urging, was forever attempting to treat him. On more than one occasion he threatened to bar Doc from the mansion. But he never did. Doc was the only person who was his intellectual equal, and with whom he enjoyed prolonged conversation.

Clement's daily routine remained much the same as it had been before he was appointed warden. Each morning he rode in his buggy to inspect first the rebuilt knitting mill, then the new leather tannery. Ironwood and six guards always accompanied him on his inspections; no chances were taken on a recurrence of the 1837 riot which had claimed the life of his predecessor. Under Ironwood's firm rule, any convict approaching within ten feet of the warden was to be shot. Clement never at any time spoke to a prisoner, never entered the walls, never became personally involved in any way with the custodial or punitive aspects of the prison's operation. All of that was left strictly up to his captain of the yard, Jack Ironwood.

Black Jack, as the convicts called Ironwood, directed a brutal, merciless regime that permitted no laxity of regulation on the part of prisoner or guard. Floggings were held daily after supper. Deaths from overwork were not infrequent. Visting privileges had been reduced to once a month instead of each week. Guards were strictly forbidden to fraternize with convict relatives living in Prisontown. In reviewing the causes of the 1837 riot, Ironwood had firmly established to his own satisfaction that the casual relationship between the inhabitants of the prison and the town had indeed contributed to the unrest and subsequent revolt of the prisoners. Therefore, he made many new rules with respect to that relationship, and by doing so severely restricted it.

There were occasional complaints in the state capital about inhumane treatment at Prison Hill, but for the most part they were unsubstantiated and quick to pass. There were nearly three hundred criminals at the prison by then, and most legislators felt that if they could be contained and kept away from lawful communities, the warden and his captain and guards were entitled to use whatever methods they saw fit.

In 1842 Governor Alton Monroe stepped down after two terms in the statehouse and was elected to the United States Senate. Palmer Curran, his lieutenant governor for eight years, was elected to succeed him as governor. Curran's first official act after being sworn in was to reappoint Clement Niles warden of Prison Hill.

Clement had talked of what he would do if he were not renamed warden, and his talk invariably mentioned places like St. Louis and Memphis and New Orleans, and both he and Dru told each other that it might be nice to move away and start a new life somewhere else. But they were both secretly relieved when Clement was reappointed, for it meant they could remain in the mansion for at least another four years, probably eight. The mansion had been Dru's home since she was little more than a girl. She was not really sure she would feel comfortable anyplace else. On the evening after she learned of Clement's reappointment, she wrote in her journal that she was happy she would not have to leave the place that had been her home for fifteen years.

Dru had been keeping a journal since the day after she married Clement Niles. She made it a point to make an entry every day. She put down her experiences, her thoughts, things the boys did, discussions with her husband at the supper table, and interesting occurrences at the prison or in town. On dull days when she had nothing to write about, she added to a continuing reminiscence about her early days with Aaron and what it had been like when the prison first started. Although she was not consciously aware of it, she was writing a history of penology in the state along with her own family history. Her memory was superb, so much so that she was able to accurately recall and include in her pages actual conversations until then long forgotten. She included everything in her journal except the affair with Theron. That remained her dark, shameful secret.

It was the shame she felt at having been unfaithful to Aaron that now prevented Dru from doing the same thing to Clement. Her love for Jack Ironwood had been growing constantly almost from the first day she met him. Had he been an ardent suitor and concentrated on breaking down her will, she was sure she would long since have surrendered. But because of his strict code of honor, and her own deep self-recriminations about Theron Verne, her desire was kept carefully under control.

Ironwood was a great comfort to have around, with his confidence and strength and authority. He was like a much larger, more self-assured Aaron, except, thankfully, he was much more flexible. Although he was unrelenting about everyone else abiding by the strict rules he laid down, he nevertheless did not hesitate to break them himself where she was concerned. Because of her he had practically made Kee and his squaw members of his household. He now lived in the cabin that first she and Aaron, then Clement, had occupied. A separate hogan-type hut had been constructed behind it to accommodate the two Indians. And he had taught Kee to speak broken English so that the Indian could halfway converse with her. That had made her very happy.

It had been Ironwood who had come for her during Monroe's ninth birthday party when Letitia Herraday went into labor. "I sent for Doc but he's not home," Ironwood said. "I've got two men looking for him. Meantime, the woman needs somebody right now."

Dru returned to the walls with him. When they reached the dormitory, Letitia was on her side on the floor, screaming for help. Her left knee was raised up grotesquely. "It's coming!" she yelled. "The baby's coming! Somebody help me!"

Dru's experience in childbearing was limited to her own two labors, but she seemed instinctively to know what to do. She had Ironwood take the mattress off the cot and put it on the floor. Together they got Letitia on it. With Ironwood's knife, Dru slit off the woman's lower clothing and covered her with a sheet. By the time that was accomplished, the infant's head was out.

"It's killing me!" Letitia screamed. "I can't stand it!"

"Hush, it's not killing you," Dru said. "Hold her wrists, Jack."

One at a time the infant's shoulders escaped the vagina and then suddenly it was slipping out onto the mattress as if no effort at all had gone into its arrival. It was red and choking; Dru wormed one finger into its mouth, pulled the tongue into place, and turned it face-down, umbilical cord still attached, across its mother's thigh. She slapped it smartly across the buttocks and it screamed as loudly as its mother had. Bundling its bloody little form in part of the sheet, Dru placed it carefully between Letitia's legs. "You hold still now," she said. Ironwood could not tell if she was talking to the woman or the baby. All he knew was that she was pale and trembling. "I'm not going to do anything more until the doctor gets here," she said.

Doc Robin arrived a few minutes later and finished the delivery. The baby was a girl.

"You did a good job, Dru," he complimented. "If Cordelia ever leaves me, I think I'll steal you away from Clement."

"You'll have to fight me for her, Doc," said Ironwood.

Doc Robin started to laugh, but then he saw something in the big captain's expression that made him change his mind. Well, I'll be damned, he thought. The man means it.

Dru said nothing. Ironwood brought her a basin of water so she could clean up, and gave her his own bandanna to dry her hands. Then he escorted her back to her son's birthday party.

A month later, Dru and Clement Niles journeyed to St. Louis, taking the Herraday infant with them. Letitia had named the child Nell, the same name that she had given to a previous baby that had died in infancy.

"I hope whoever gets her will let her keep the name," she had told Dru that morning.

"I'll insist on it," Dru replied. She bit her lower lip. "Are you absolutely sure there isn't some relative—"

"No," Letitia said firmly. "There's no one. I want *you* to find her a home. I trust you. I don't trust anybody else."

At first Dru had considered keeping the baby herself. Clement had advised against it. "It wouldn't be right," he said. "The child would be too close to its natural mother. It would drive the Herraday woman crazy."

So they had taken the baby to St. Louis. Through friends he had there, Clement learned of a middle-aged couple who had never had children of their own, and who, now that they were well off financially, were looking for one to adopt. Dru went to see them. She told them the circumstances of the child's background and birth. The woman broke down and cried. "The poor little orphan," she said tearfully. It reminded Dru of how her Aunt Wella had wailed for her the day she had been given to Aaron Van Hawn. This woman seemed to be the same kind of good person her Aunt Wella had been. Based on that judgment, Dru gave them Letitia Herraday's baby.

"I hope I've done right," she worried on their way back to Prison Hill.

"I'm sure you have, dear," said Clement. He patted her hand

in the fond way he had of doing. Dru leaned her head on his shoulder.

"You're a very kind and understanding man, Clement," she said. "I am a fortunate woman to have you for a husband."

Clement smiled, pleased at her words. He cared for her very much; as much, really, as he was capable of caring for anyone. Coughing slightly, trying to hold it back as much as possible because her head was on his shoulder, he hoped fervently that she would find someone worthy of her after he was gone.

CHAPTER 20

On his way down the hill to town, Monroe met a young couple heading up toward the prison. They were driving an inexpensive buggy being pulled by a slightly overweight mare. The man stood up and hailed Monroe as he was about to ride past. Monroe reined up.

"Morning," the man said. "You from the prison?"

Monroe glanced at the woman. She was Beth's age, not nearly as pretty, but with a soft look about her that was attractive. He looked back at the man. "Yes, I'm from the prison. I'm a guard there." He was only stretching the truth by a few hours, he reasoned. The couple was obviously impressed.

"My name's Owen Landis," the man said, stretching an arm out to shake hands. "This here's my wife Clara. Do you think I could get a job at the prison as a guard?"

Monroe looked him up and down. He was one of those rail-thin young men who was also rail-*hard.* His upper lip had the faint shadow of a beginning moustache on it. "I'm not sure they need any more guards," Monroe said.

Owen Landis's face fell a little. "I was sure hoping I could get on. Me and Clara run off and got married, and now I got to find some way to support us. Don't know how to do much besides shoot. I'm a real good shot. That's why I thought maybe I could get on at the prison."

"Just married, you say?"

"Day before yesterday," Landis said. He grinned at his bride and stuck his chest out a little.

Monroe looked at Clara Landis again. She had strawberry hair that fell in great rolls to her shoulders. Her bosom, as far as he could see down the front of her dress, was a field of freckles. When her eyes met Monroe's, she blushed and looked down. They were both thinking the same thing. Married two days. She just started doing it.

"You might be able to get on," Monroe said. "Won't hurt to ask anyway. Ride on up to the main gate yonder. Tell the guard there you want to see Captain Sam Colson. He's captain of the yard. He'd be the one to take you on."

"Say, thanks!" Owen beamed. "Thanks a heap!"

Monroe nodded curtly, as he had seen Jack Ironwood do when thanked by a subordinate, and rode off down the hill.

At the bottom of the hill, Union Street began. It ran straight down to the levee where it intersected River Street, part of the Riverbank Road running the length of the state all the way up to St. Louis. It was from River Street that the big Concord coaches rolled into town for their meal stops, reining up in front of Pete and Etta French's restaurant on Union to discharge passengers for the ninety-minute rest. Pete French had been out of prison for fourteen years now, and a lot of people in Prisontown had forgotten he had ever been a convict. Certainly none of the Concord passengers knew it, just as they did not know, as they strolled down Union Street, that half the people with whom they came into contact were somehow connected with the big prison that loomed over the town. Carrie Carmichael still had her bakery, and now her husband John, who had finished his manslaughter sentence, helped her run it. Jessica Vintner had expanded her sewing and mending shop into a dressmaking business; Saul Vintner, who had completed his embezzlement term a decade earlier, now kept books for the two Harrys—Fogel and Berg, Dry Goods and Footwear. Elouise Starwell, wife of bank robber Luke Starwell, still worked for Harry Berg; her husband had taken part in an escape attempt after seven years on Prison Hill and had had to begin his sentence over again.

The town, in its twenty-fifth year, had grown considerably since Aaron Van Hawn's day. There was now a barber shop, a blacksmith barn and livery stable, a printer with a hand press who published a one-sheet newspaper every Saturday, a billiard hall, a meat market, a harness shop, and a farm implement store to serve the dozen or so small farmers who had started soybean, wheat, and corn crops nearby. There was also a large apple orchard just outside town, and a hog farm, and a cattle and dairy produce ranch, all of which employed former convicts or members of convict families. Lamp Kellerman still had his saloon, much larger and fancier now that it had moved out of the tent into a permanent building. And the Pullman brothers had the equivalent of a frontier department store, having expanded three times in the years since they opened. There were also some town idlers who came and went: itinerant handymen, drifters, an occasional professional gambler, a few whores. Backed up to the rear of the Union Street businesses on both sides were the homes of the permanent residents. They ranged from rather elaborate two-story colonials, equal in size and style to the warden's mansion, to one-room boxlike affairs with stovepipe chimney, one door, and no windows. Some of the houses had been built from native wood by local carpenters; others had been ordered prefabricated from Lyman Bridges, Ready Made Houses, in Chicago, and nailed together when they arrived by freight barge.

Some of Prison Hill's guards now lived down in the town; some of them had families and houses of their own, others boarded with nonprison townspeople. As Monroe rode along Union Street he waved to some of the off-duty men and their wives passing on the plank sidewalks. Monroe was popular with the men, disliked by no one. He had an easy way about him and a ready smile that offered instant friendship. And even though he was stepson to the warden, he neither asked for nor expected preferential treatment. He was much better liked by the guards as a group than was his stepfather or his soon-to-be father-in-law.

As he rode past Jessica Vintner's shop, he glanced in to see if Beth was anywhere in sight. She was not. He spurred his mount down to River Street and cut south toward the lower levees. The levels rose six feet from the highest spring water level anyone could remember. They had been built by leased labor from the prison, paid for by the association of riverboat owners who were required by the state to prevent their big paddle wheels from flooding the banks.

Monroe walked his horse to the end of the Prisontown levee and guided it around several tons of stacked steer hides waiting to be hauled up to the tannery. Where the levee ended, he dismounted and led his horse onto the riverbank and over to a stand of willows. He dropped the reins to the ground and left the animal to munch grass. Walking out to the edge of the bank, he sat under one of the larger trees where he always waited for Beth. He jerked up a blade of grass and hung it between his lips. Before him, on the broad, muddy river, a big stern-wheeler churned water and glided along on its way north. Monroe's expression saddened. He could never look at a riverboat without thinking of his brother Grover.

In 1844 the boys had been eleven and twelve. Monroe was still tall and big-eyed like his mother. Grover, the youngest, was a duplicate of his father; he had the Van Hawn chest and shoulders, and the strength of an ox. On a morning in August, after Clement Niles had left on his morning inspection tour, and Dru had gone down the hill to shop and visit Cordelia Walls, Grover went to his room and dragged from under the bed a blanket roll he had prepared that morning. He dropped it out an upstairs window into the backyard, then strolled casually through the kitchen picking up fruit, biscuits, and other foodstuff as he went. He put the food in a flour sack, tied it to his blanket roll, and was about to leave when his older brother came around the house.

"What are you doing?" Monroe asked.

"Going to Independence," said Grover.

"You're crazy," Monroe said. "If Ma catches you, she'll kill you."

"She ain't going to catch me. When I get to Independence, I'm going to join up with a wagon train and head for California."

"Wagon trains don't go as far as California," Monroe said.

"They do so. Abe Flowers who runs the telegraph for Captain Jack told me. There's been wagon trains going clear out to California for better'n a *year*!" He slung the roll across his back. "Well, I got to be going. Tell ever'body I said goodbye." He stalked off toward the woods, where they had a secret trail that led down to the river.

Monroe thought about the situation for a moment. There had been a state telegraph line at the prison for a month now and it was true that they were receiving a wealth of news of the type which had only filtered down, or completely missed them, in the past. Grover had attached himself to Abe Flowers the day the telegrapher reported for duty, and from then on was the prison compound's unofficial but highly reliable source of news. So if Grover said there were wagon trains trekking all the way to California, it was probably so.

Monroe ran and caught up with his brother. "How come you didn't ask me to go with you?" he demanded.

"I didn't think you'd want to. Besides, one of us ought to stay here with Ma."

"Ma can take care of herself," the twelve-year-old said gravely. "But I ain't so sure about you. If I let you go off by yourself, I'll probably get blistered good. I better go with you."

Monroe had sneaked into the house, fixed a blanket roll of his own, and sneaked back out again. He had left a note telling his mother that he and Grover were going to California.

The two boys made their way down to the riverbank and followed it to the levee, then to the dock. They hid under the dock until the regular Tuesday morning side-wheeler edged in to take on and discharge passengers. While the boat was docked, they climbed along a blade of the big wheel and slipped below decks. They hid in the cargo hold. When the boat slipped its mooring and started northward again, the two brothers gravely shook hands.

Dru missed them at noon and found the note a short time later. She almost fainted; her heart felt as if it were rising up to her throat. Becoming instantly desperate for help, she thought at once of Ironwood. Clement Niles was at that moment but one room away, but Dru did not even consider him. She rushed directly to Jack Ironwood.

"They probably stowed away on the morning packet," the big yard captain said. He took Dru into the next room where the telegraph key was located. "Is there a telegraph line in Chester?" he asked Abe Flowers.

"No, sir. Nearest one is St. Genevieve."

"The Tuesday packet doesn't dock at St. Genevieve. What about Crystal City?"

"Yes, sir. There's one in the constable's office there."

"Telegraph him to search the packet boat and hold two runaway boys. Tell him I'm coming after them."

Ironwood took the two best horses in the prison stable and started north. At Chester, thirty-five miles away, he learned that the packet was four hours ahead of him. He pressed on to St. Genevieve. There he found that the boat had passed by three hours ahead of him. He left one of the horses and rode on. It was nighttime when he got to Crystal City. The boat was gone, two hours past, and the boys were not there; the marshal's telegraph key was not working.

Ironwood bartered for two fresh horses and rode all night, but he was not able to make up the distance between him and the boat. He rode into East St. Louis at dawn and found the docked packet but not the boys. On foot he searched the docks; there was no sign of them. Then he learned that a boat bound for Kansas City had an hour earlier wheeled north to the fork of the Missouri. On still another fresh mount, he ferried across the Mississippi, cut around St. Louis, and rode north to the river shantytown of Machens. He beat the riverboat there by twenty minutes. Standing in the center of a hired flatboat anchored in the side-wheeler's path, he drew his pistols, fired into the air several times, and stopped the big boat in the middle of the river. Boarding, he forced an outraged captain to help him search the vessel. Monroe and Grover were in the forward hold.

The boys were terrified. After Ironwood took them ashore on the flatboat, he did not utter a word to them except in the form of orders. All the way back to East St. Louis by horse, and all the way back down the Mississippi by paddleboat—this time as paying passengers—not once did he speak to them. His face remained a constant scowl, his eyes dark and piercing, his manner a silent threat. When they landed at Prisontown, he took them each by the arm and led them into one of the empty freight rooms. He locked the door behind him and removed the great black gunbelt he wore. Taking the holsters and cartridges off the belt, he dangled it before them.

"This belt is made of caribou hide from the Yukon territory," he said. "It'll tear the flesh right off your bones. If you ever again do anything to hurt your mother, I'll use it on you. I care for your mother a great deal and I won't permit the likes of you two to break her heart. Do you understand me?"

"Yes, sir, Captain Ironwood," they said quickly in unison.

"Remember my words then, and mind them well. Never hurt your mother again!"

"Yes, sir!"

Ironwood reassembled his gunbelt and put it back on. Then he escorted the two boys back up the hill to their mother.

On the night after Ironwood returned her sons, Dru went to his cabin. It was a dark, stormy night, more windy than rainy, full of noises and shadows, and easy for Dru to slip past the compound guards. The door to the cabin was unlocked and she entered without a sound—she thought. Then she heard the faint click of a pistol being cocked.

"It's me, Jack," she whispered.

He came to her in the darkness. The scent of his warm body reached her nostrils as he stood before her. She touched his hard, bare chest. "Take my cape," she said.

His hands found her shoulders in the dark and lifted away the cloak. He knew instinctively that she was naked under it. He touched her breasts and waist and hips, and gathered her into his arms. They kissed, and as they did, she reached down and touched him. She was surprised to find that he was very small, as Aaron had been. From the build on him, she had expected him to be more like Theron Verne. She was a little disappointed, because now she did not expect to enjoy him. But then, she reminded herself, that had not been her purpose in coming. She was doing it to reward Ironwood for returning her sons. Or so she told herself.

"Is this because I brought the boys back?" Ironwood asked in the dark.

"It's because of everything," she said.

"I don't want it to be this way. It's not right—"

She held him as she wanted him and raised one leg and hooked it around his hip.

"I don't want you until you're mine," he insisted.

"I am yours," she said hoarsely. "Right now—" She slipped over him and when she did he clutched her buttocks with both hands and lifted her other foot off the floor. They drew in their breaths together, moaned softly together, worked their bodies as if one mind were directing them. When it happened to them, it happened to both at once, and for each it was the summit of their physical being.

Dru, head thrown back, lips parted in wonder, had never felt such sensations before. Her body became a surging harmony of intense pleasure. For the first time in her life, she was aware of every inch of herself. And when it was over, she stared wide-eyed in the dark and thought: *It isn't size after all!*

Afterward, they lay naked, side by side, on the rough wooden floor, and Dru remembered that it was in that same cabin that she and Aaron first went to bed on land. She smiled fondly at the memory. Reaching out, she touched Ironwood's hand. "It has never been that good for me, Jack."

"Nor me," he said. "But I wish we hadn't."

"Why?"

"Because I'll want you all the more now. And I won't let myself have you. I won't let myself become a disloyal son of a bitch to the man I work for."

"I hadn't intended this as the start of anything," Dru said. "It was just for tonight."

"It'll be much worse for me in the days to come," he said.

"And for me," she told him.

There in the darkness, they turned together and held each other very close.

Monroe and Grover never ran away again. From the day of their return, they lived in the shadow of Jack Ironwood. He became the surrogate father that Clement Niles, because of his health, had never been. In the summer he taught them to fish and forage and track. In the winter he taught them to shoot, hunt, stalk, and trap. They learned horsemanship in his big saddle, learned to tell direction day or night by shadows and stars, learned to wrestle, to run the woods, to tell Chickasaw signs from Choctaw. And once, when Dru let him take them downriver to Paducah, he bought them each an Indian squaw-teacher for the night and let them learn about women. He also gave them their first taste of whiskey and tobacco, and let the resultant sickness wear off in the woods before he took them home.

The boys came to idolize Captain Jack, as they called him, and although Clement Niles was well aware of the relationship, to his credit he never resented it.

"I'm grateful for the interest you take in my stepsons, Jack," he said when Ironwood, Doc, and Cordelia were dinner guests one evening. "They need someone like you who can do all the things with them that Aaron would have done if he had lived."

"I enjoy them, Clem," the big yard captain replied. "Not having a family of my own, they help me pass the time. Besides, when I'm with them, I feel very, very smart."

Clement laughed. "That aspect of it never occurred to me. Perhaps I should try teaching them bookkeeping."

"You should find a wife, Jack, and have children of your own," Cordelia said.

"I'll find one someday, I expect," Ironwood said quietly.

Ironwood remained at Prison Hill without complaint for two years after his trip to retrieve the runaway boys. Then he came to Dru one day and told her he was leaving.

"We're going to war with Mexico," he said. "The news just came over the telegraph. President Polk is sending General Zack Taylor and his army down to take Texas."

Dru felt sick. "Jack, please don't," she pleaded. "Prison Hill needs you here. *I* need you."

"I'll come back," he promised. "You know I won't be able to stay away from you permanently. But right now I need to do something different, like fighting a war."

He rode off to join Taylor's army at the Mexican border. Monroe and Grover were desolated by his leaving. Dru had never felt emptier. Even Clement was distressed to see his captain of the yard go. He did not appoint anyone to take Ironwood's place; instead, he assigned three guard lieutenants to share the responsibility. "Your place here will be waiting when you return," he told Ironwood. "Godspeed."

Six months later, they heard that Taylor's army had defeated the Mexicans at Buena Vista, and that Winfield Scott and twelve thousand troops were moving on Vera Cruz.

"If they take Vera Cruz, it's practically over," Clement told his family. "That'll cut off Mexico's supplies from Europe."

"I knew Captain Jack could lick them Mexes," said Monroe, who was then fourteen.

"Captain Jack can lick *anybody*," Grover put in.

"Let's just pray that he isn't wounded or killed," Dru told the boys. To Clement she said, "Sometimes I feel like he's one of the family."

"Yes, I do too," said Clement Niles. Clement began to cough and excused himself from the table. In the privacy of his study he coughed up a rope of spume dotted with dark, almost black traces of blood. He spat it into a piece of writing paper and burned it in the fireplace.

Sitting at his desk, Niles thought about Dru. For some time now he had suspected that she was in love with Ironwood, and Ironwood with her. He knew that they were not bedding together, because Dru always seemed to be exactly where she was supposed to be. Ironwood too, for that matter. So they were restraining intimacy, probably out of respect for him, and he much admired both of them for it. In reality he would not have objected to their bedding together as long as they did it discreetly and no one knew about it. He himself had never been a physical person, and he often thought that a woman like Dru, who *was* so physical, must need much more sexual relationship than she got with him. The limited activity in which they engaged was always at Dru's initiation; he, because of his health and fatigue, was the passive one. He had thought several times of frankly telling her that he would not object to her seeking solace elsewhere as long as she was discriminate; but each time he found himself unable to summon the courage to do it. He was afraid of insulting her, and of reducing himself in her image. So he never spoke of it.

In the spring of 1847, Jack Ironwood returned to Prison Hill. He had been wounded in the left thigh at Vera Cruz and walked with a slight limp, and his thick black hair now had avenues of gray coursing through it. He came back ragged, weak, and hollow-eyed, but to Dru and her family he was a glorious hero home at last. The Van Hawn boys stood in awe of him all over again. They were fifteen and fourteen now, rapidly adding inches to their height.

"You boys have growed some," Ironwood said when he saw them. "Don't expect I'll be whipping you at wrestling much longer." The boys beamed in delight.

"Welcome home, Jack," said Clement Niles with a weak handshake. Ironwood managed to conceal his surpirse at Clement's appearance. The warden was four years younger than Ironwood but looked ten years older. His flesh had an almost transparent look to it and his throat drew in on each side from labored breathing. His frame was stooped and brittle-looking. "I'm happy to have you back, Jack," he said. "The prison needs you."

"I doubt I'll be much use for a while, Clem," Ironwood said.

"Nonsense. Dru will have you nursed back to health in no time. Good food and rest, that's all you need."

Dru and the boys went with Ironwood down to his cabin, which had been made ready for him by Kee and the squaw. Kee was finally serving the last year of his sentence and Dru had made arrangements for him to work at Polk's Livery down in Prisontown when he was released. "He should work out just fine," she said.

Ironwood agreed. "He knows horseflesh well enough, that's for certain."

Monroe and Grover unsaddled Ironwood's mount and carried his belongings inside. "Can we see where the bullet hit you, Captain Jack?" Grover asked.

"Not in front of your mother, lad. The wound's a bit high."

Dru sent the boys down the hill to fetch Doc Robin to come and examine Ironwood. When they were gone, she said, "When do *I* get to see where the bullet hit you, Captain Ironwood?"

"When you're a free woman, Mrs. Niles," he replied. "Just as it's always been."

"You forgot that once," she reminded him.

"I'm not likely to do it again, though. Not with your husband as close as he is to death's door."

"Is it that plain?" Dru asked. "Being around him all the time, we tend not to notice."

"It's that plain," Ironwood assured her. "It'll surprise me if he lasts another winter."

"Aaron said that once," Dru recalled. "More than eighteen years ago."

Doc came and gave Ironwood a thorough examination. "Good food and a lot of rest," he prescribed, exactly as Clement Niles had said earlier. "Call that cook of yours in here."

Kee's squaw was summoned and Doc spoke to her through Monroe, who had learned the Sac dialect from Ironwood. "Tell her he's to have lots of meat," Doc said. "Barely cooked. Lots of blood still in it. And plenty of milk. Also lots of those red beans that grow in that black ground back of the quarry. I'm not sure just what those beans are getting out of that dirt, but whatever it is is certainly good for a body's blood." Doc glanced at Dru. "I wish Clement would eat more of them."

"Clement eats only what he wants to eat, Gilbert, you know that."

Doc grunted. "I hope this one won't be as hardheaded. I'd like to see you keep one of them alive."

"Don't worry about me staying alive, Doc," Ironwood said as solemnly as if giving his word. For a brief moment his eyes locked with Dru's. "I intend to live to a ripe old age."

Doc, who noticed the look that passed between his patient and Dru, nodded knowingly. "I hope you do, Jack," he said quietly. And he thought: God knows you've waited long enough for her.

CHAPTER 21

As Monroe sat on the riverbank on the morning of his twenty-first birthday, watching a big stern-wheeler pass and reminiscing about his brother Grover, a comely young woman named Beth Colson hid behind a nearby tree and silently removed her slippers. In stockinged feet, she slipped quietly up behind Monroe and put her hands over his eyes.

"Guess who?"

Monroe felt her ample breasts flatten softly against his back. "Ramona Davenport," he said, naming Prisontown's most well-known whore. He felt Beth's hands being removed from his eyes. Instinctively he ducked his head just as one of them flew past where it had been. He laughed and turned, in time to grab her around the waist as she tried a second blow.

"I'll give you Ramona Davenport!" she scolded.

"Oh? When?" Monroe pinned her arms behind her back and held them there.

Beth's eyes widened as she feigned anger. "Maybe you'd like to marry *her* instead of me!"

"Mother would never approve." He pressed his mouth to her neck just below the ear. She caught her breath and went limp against him. He let go of her hands and she put her arms around his neck. As he ate at her neck, she kissed his hair and ran her fingers through it.

"Have you ever bedded with Ramona Davenport?" she asked.

"No," he lied.

"Have you ever bedded with *any* woman?"

"A few Indians," he admitted.

The thought excited Beth. "What was it like, with Indians?"

"It was fun. They were very young girls: thirteen and fourteen. They like to touch with their tongues a lot. They lick a man all over."

"That's disgusting," she said, feeling very warm. "Did you do the same thing to them? Lick them all over?"

"No. But I will with you. If you want me to." His lips had moved down to her bodice and were pressing the upper mound of one breast. He was rigid now and he knew, because she had told him once, that Beth would be getting moist between her legs.

"How long do you think we'll have to wait after we become engaged?" she asked.

"We don't have to wait at all," Monroe told her. "We can go back in the willows and do it right now."

"I mean wait to get married."

"Oh. I don't know. A year, I imagine."

Beth sighed impatiently. "I wish it wasn't so long. Sometimes I feel like I'm going to burn up."

Monroe swept her into his arms and started for the willows. The great trees stood back forty yards from the levee, in a stand so thick and close that their tumbling, moss-covered branches merged together like waterfalls to form a thick curtain around them. Within the shroud of willows, the ground was cool and the daylight muted.

"We can't do this, Monroe," Beth said as he laid her on a bed of white moss between two trunks. "I might have a baby too soon."

"You won't have a baby from kissing," he told her. He reached under her skirts and pulled gently at her pantalettes.

"Where on earth are you going to kiss me?" she asked, trembling.

"You'll see."

Monroe bared her legs and parted them. Beth let her head go back on the moss, feeling faint. Monroe quickly removed his shirt and undid his breeches to release himself. Then he leaned his face down into the softest moss of all.

* * *

Monroe had been fifteen the first time he saw Beth Colson. She had arrived in Prisontown with her parents on the Wednesday coach from East St. Louis. At thirteen she had been a younger version of what she would be at nineteen: well-formed, well-developed, flawless of complexion, pert and pretty. Monroe and Grover had been straddling the hitch rail at the coach station when the family arrived. Jack Ironwood had been there with a buggy to meet them. "Sam, I'm glad you could come," the big yard captain said. "I'm going to need you."

"Has it happened yet?" Colson asked.

"No. But it's not far off. Come along. I'm moving you right into my cabin. I'll stay in the guard barracks temporarily."

After they had all gone off in the buggy, Monroe and Grover ran down to the livery and found Kee. The Indian had been free for several months and was living with his squaw in a shanty behind the stables. Somehow, he seemed to know everything that went on up at the prison. The boys often came to him to find out things that they were not supposed to know.

"Kee, who's the new white man Captain Jack just met?" Monroe asked.

"Secret," Kee said.

"How big a secret?" Monroe asked.

"Maybe three-lemon-drop secret," the Indian said.

Monroe gave Grover a penny and sent him hurrying up to the Pullman Brothers to buy three lemon drops. When Grover returned, the candy was given to Kee.

"White man new yard captain," he told the boys.

Monroe and Grover looked at each other with mouths agape. New yard captain! Did that mean Captain Jack was leaving? As if reading their minds, Kee answered the question.

"Iron Fist not leave," he said, referring to the captain by the name his brass knuckles had earned him among the other Indian convicts. "Iron Fist soon be warden."

Again the boys stared incredulously at each other. Did that mean that *they* were leaving? Was their stepfather taking them and their mother away from Prison Hill?

"If that's so, I'll run away again," Grover threatened, jutting his jaw out and looking exactly like Aaron.

"You won't neither," the older, more composed Monroe said. "We promised Cap'n Jack."

They ran home and asked their mother about it. "No," Dru said, "we aren't leaving Prison Hill, so stop worrying about it."

"How come there's a new captain of the yard then?" Monroe asked.

"Yeah," said Grover, "who *is* leaving?"

"I can't explain it right now," Dru said evasively. "Stop worrying me about it. You'll know soon enough."

The boys resorted to their ultimate final source of information: a wife-murderer named Lem Skoog who was the mansion gardener. It was never necessary to bribe Lem. He got as much good food from the mansion kitchen as he wanted; with apples, raisins, potato peelings, and sugar, he fermented his own private stock of liquor in two jugs buried in the flower beds; and he had a young homosexual, called a sissy by the cons, who took care of his physical needs in exchange for smuggled cakes and pies. Lem always knew exactly what was going on, and the boys had never known him to be wrong.

"Nobody's going nowheres," Lem told them when they brought their problem to him. "Except yore step-paw. He's going to his grave. Cap'n Ironwood is going to be the new warden. Yore maw's going to marry him."

The boys walked away stunned. Clement Niles *dying*? It did not seem possible. He had been around all their lives, first as an honorary uncle, then a stepfather. He had always been sick; their mother was forever nursing him back to health from something. But it had never occurred to them that he would actually *die*.

The boys began to feel guilty. In the ten years that Clement Niles had been their stepfather, they had done little more than tolerate him. All their affection had gone to their mother; all their admiration to Jack Ironwood, General Zack Taylor, and various riverboat captains. Clement had been a very bland part of their lives; he had been in the background; he had blended in. Now he was dying.

Monroe and Grover set out to make amends. They had once built a fan rack to go on Dru's desk to hold her collection of fans; and they had constructed a shallow box for Captain Jack to keep his cigars fresh; but they had never made anything for Clement Niles. Now they decided they would. Further, they would make him *two* presents. After much thought, they decided on an ink-well stand and a book holder.

The boys begged enough wood from the lumber yard and again cajoled Pete Newagon, the town carpenter, to let them use his old tools. They set up shop in a corner of his shed and went to work. Sawing and planing and sanding, working on them every moment they could steal away from their chores, they managed to finish both objects in less than a week.

But by that time Clement Niles was dead.

Druscilla Foyle Van Hawn Niles was married to Captain Jack Ironwood sixty-one days after the death of her husband. She had wanted to wait longer, for the sake of appearances, but Ironwood refused to hear of it.

"I've waited ten goddamned years for you," he said. "I'll not wait another."

"I'm not suggesting we wait a year. Just six months."

"No. We'll wait sixty days, as required by law. No longer."

"Be reasonable, Jack. Think of what people will say. Think of how it will look to the boys."

"The boys don't give a damn what we do, and I don't give a damn what people say. Sixty days. That's final."

Ironwood was right about Monroe and Grover: it did not bother them how soon their mother married him. The quicker the better, as far as they were concerned. They had spent several days feeling badly about Clement's passing—particularly since they had not been able to give him their presents; then, after the funeral, it had suddenly dawned on them that soon *Jack Ironwood* would be their stepfather. For some reason, they had failed to connect their mother's new marriage with the fact that Captain Jack would then replace Clement Niles as *their stepfather.* He would be living in the mansion with them, eating meals with them—why, they would see him all the time! The thought both thrilled and delighted them. As the weeks passed after Clement's funeral, they became as impatient as Ironwood.

For the first time that summer, the boys began to go separate ways. Monroe, who was fifteen, started paying a great deal of attention to Beth Colson. Her father had become captain of the yard, as Kee had said, and Ironwood had been appointed warden. Palmer Curran, who had recently been inaugurated for his second term in the state house, made the appointment, in counsel with United States Senator Alton Monroe and his aide Grover, who were now spending most of their time in Washington.

With his older brother occupied for the first time with a girl, Grover Van Hawn found himself left pretty much to his own designs. There were other boys his own age in town, but some of them were prisoners' sons, with whom he was not allowed to associate, and others, sons of guards, seemed to naturally shy away from him because he lived up in the big mansion. It was easier, Grover found, to go his own way alone, without having to consult anyone.

Grover took to sitting on the levees for hours on end, watching the riverboat traffic. He was as fascinated by the big Mississippi as his father had been. Soon he was loitering on the docks, making friends with pilots and helmsmen when they docked, running errands for them, or directing them to Ramona Davenport's shanty. Although he was still bound to his promise not to run away, Grover felt no restrictions on him when it came to making short trips on the river. By learning all the schedules, he found that he could travel thirty miles up and down the river on alternate boats and still be home in time for supper.

No one knew of Grover's wanderings on the river, not even Monroe, who was preoccupied with Beth, and least of all Dru, who was preparing for her marriage to Ironwood. There was now considerable talk about the wedding. In town the discussion ran to the short mourning time between husbands, and the fact that Clement Niles was being cared for by Dru when he died.

"Who in hell else *would* be caring for him?" Doc Robin usually stormed when the topic came up in his presence. "She was the man's *wife*, for God's sake! She nursed him for ten long years! He finally died of congestive lung failure complicated by pneumonia. I was there and I can assure you that nothing sinister took place. As for Mrs. Niles and Captain Ironwood only waiting the length of time required by law for her to remarry, I think that's their business. Anybody who wants to comment on it should do it to Ironwood's face."

That usually ended it. No one in his right mind wanted to

challenge Ironwood in any way. His prowess as a fistfighter, knife-fighter, and gunfighter was legendary.

Only among the convicts was there open conversation about the wedding. Down in the pits, on the yard, on the chain walking to and from the mill or the tannery, the men found stolen moments to talk when they could not be overheard or observed.

"So old Black Jack is taking over the mansion, eh?"

"Ah, and the woman too, I hear. I suppose she comes with the house by now."

"She probably thinks his cock is as hard as his fist. Maybe it is, at that."

"Pity it wasn't him that died instead of old Niles."

"I just wish they was some way I could get some saltpeter into his food on the day of the wedding. Something to keep his cock soft. I hate to think of him rutting it in her when I've been without a woman for six years."

"Try the new sissy that came in last week. Got an ass as smooth as a baby's, not a hair on it."

"It ain't the same as it is with a woman. That mistress of the mansion, now there's a fine piece of woman. Long legs and a nice wide ass. I can just imagine old Iron Fist ramming it to her—"

The actual wedding night of Dru and Ironwood lived up to even the wildest fantasy imagined by any of the convicts. Ironwood had hungered for Dru so long that he came to her virtually insatiable. Nothing was enough for him, nothing could stop him—not even ejaculation. He just went on and on, doing things to her, having her do things to him, until he was ready again. For Dru, after the frustration of Aaron, the dread of exposure with Theron, and the monotony of Clement, being with Ironwood, openly, wantonly, greedily, was like a release from sexual purgatory. When their bedroom door closed behind them, when they knew they were alone at last, with no restrictions, with the boys at Cordelia's, the house help back inside the walls for the night, nothing to interfere with what each wanted, they went into a near frenzy with passion.

"Let me see it," Dru virtually demanded, groping at her new husband's clothes.

"You'll do more than see it." He peeled her naked, then began manipulating her body as if she were weightless, lifting and turning and bending her, holding her up so that her breasts hung in his face, spreading her upside down to love-suck her, and showing her what he wanted her to do to him, things he had learned on the frontier from squaws tutored by the French.

"I don't know how to do that," she protested once.

Ironwood placed her head where he wanted it. "Learn," he said.

"I can't." She looked away, unable to face him, and spoke her terrible desire. "You'll have to tie me and force me."

Ironwood took the rawhide laces from his holsters and hog-tied her on the bed, ankles to wrists. Then he did everything to her that he knew how to do, and she wallowed in it.

After the frenzy was over and the surface lusts taken away by the wild passions they worked on each other, after the contortions and rawhide and forbidden whispers were done with, after the room and the night grew quiet around them, Ironwood put himself over her and gently entered her for the last time. They made slow, delicious, orthodox love for an hour, drifting in and out of sleep like two opium smokers, their minds always coming back to the juncture of their connection as if it were the center of their universe. Which, for a while, it was.

When she finally closed her eyes that night, Dru Ironwood felt that she was a complete woman and a complete wife. For the first time in her thirty-eight years.

For two years after her wedding night, Dru could not have imagined any woman being happier than she was. Married at last to a man whose love and passion matched her own, she settled back in total contentment to approach her forties and watch her sons grow to manhood. With her full range of emotions released for the first time in her life, she became a doting wife and mother such as her friends had never seen. Without realizing it, she centered her very existence on the three males who now constantly gravitated around her. Nothing they did went unnoticed.

"You grimaced getting off your horse today, Jack," she would say. "Have you hurt yourself?"

"A little stiffness in my back, is all."

"Take off your shirt and I'll rub some salve on it."

"Oh, don't bother, Dru. It's nothing."

"Take off your shirt, please."

"Yes, Dru." It did no good to argue.

With the boys she was equally persuasive.

"Monroe, is Beth Colson the only girl you see?"

"Yes, she is, Mother." Except for Ramona Davenport, whom he saw whenever he managed to save enough money.

"Don't you think it would be nice to see other young ladies? Seventeen is a bit young to see only one girl."

"I don't really like anyone but Beth, Mother."

"Mr. Swann, the butcher, has a very pretty daughter. So does that Mrs. Dixon who works at Berg's Dry Goods."

"Mrs. Dixon's husband is a convict, Mother. I couldn't see her daughter. Captain Jack's rules."

"Hmmm," said Dru. "Sometimes I wonder what good a rule like that does. Your Aunt Cordelia's father was a convict, you know. And a sweeter woman never lived. I may just speak to *Warden* Ironwood about that rule."

"Good idea, Mother," Monroe would say. He knew she never would. And she never did.

With Grover it was always the riverboats. "I can't understand what you get out of sailing up and down that awful river every chance you get," she nagged. "There are so many other things you could be doing."

"Mother, you don't understand it because you never travel by water. Everywhere you go, you take a coach. If you'd ever try a boat—"

"I *have* tried a boat. I didn't like it."

"Mother, I'm not talking about that keelboat you and Pa came here on. That was over twenty years ago. Riverboats have changed since then. Why, they've got side-wheelers now that just ease down that Old Muddy like they was sliding on ice. I rode one down to Cairo last week that—"

"Cairo! You went as far as Cairo! Alone!"

Grover bit his tongue, but it was too late. There was nothing to do now but admit all. "It was on the *White Cloud*, Mother. She's the swellest, fastest steamboat on the river. Mr. Payson, the pilot, is a friend of mine. I run errands and—well, help him find his way around when he's in Prisontown. He lets me ride with him any time I want to. In the pilothouse, too. When I get to Cairo, I always come right back on the packet."

"I've heard there are men on the docks at Cairo who keep nigra slave women to let out to sailing men for—well, bad things. Is that so?"

"I never saw any, Mother," the boy lied. "Honest."

"I'm not sure that riverboat travel is completely safe," Dru said, directing the subject away from Cairo's waterfront whores.

"It is, Mother," her youngest assured her. "It's as safe as coach travel. Honest."

Dru was not convinced, so Grover conspired with his stepfather to prove it to her. Ironwood recognized in Grover a yearning to travel the river that would probably be satisfied only if he became a pilot. He agreed to help the boy show Dru how safe the big wheelers were to pave Grover's way if he decided in the future to sign on as a pilot's helper. The time they chose for it was Dru's second wedding anniversary.

"How would you like to go to St. Louie for your anniversary?" Ironwood asked at supper one evening. "You can do some shopping and visit little Nell."

"I think that would be nice." Dru rarely passed up an opportunity to visit her godchild. Letitia Herraday's daughter was eight that summer, a lovely, long-haired child loved dearly by her foster parents.

"I thought we'd take the boys along too," Ironwood said. "Let them run loose for a day or two. They won't be any bother."

Dru's eyes had narrowed just a fraction. Jack rarely suggested taking the boys on any of their trips together. Usually he wanted to get her away alone so that they could indulge themselves in some of the more exotic offerings of St. Louis—such as warm milk baths and steamed herb treatments. But perhaps, she reasoned, he was including them for her sake, since they were growing up so quickly.

Dru gave it no more thought until the day the trip was to begin. The family drove down the hill in their buggy and did not stop at the coach station. They proceeded instead toward the river where the *White Cloud* was docked.

"Exactly where are we going?" Dru asked in her coolest voice.

"St. Louie, my dear," said Ironwood with a smile.

"You know what I mean," Dru said, fixing him in a frigid glare.

From that point on, the deceit was abandoned and the pleading began.

"Just try it," Ironwood urged. "It'll be something new for you. An adventure."

"I don't need any adventures, thank you."

"It's really very safe, Mother," said Monroe.

"Oh? Did you learn that from your brother?"

"Mother, please!" Grover begged. "My friend Mr. Payson said I could show you the pilothouse."

"I prefer to see the inside of a coach."

She remained resolutely in the buggy while the three of them paced around her and took turns imploring her to reconsider. Nearby, the *White Cloud* sounded its boarding whistle. They made a final, concerted effort by appealing to her sympathies. They all stood in a row and looked as contrite as possible.

"We shouldn't have tried to fool you," Ironwood admitted. "We thought it would be a surprise."

Dru grunted quietly.

"We're sorry, Mother," said Monroe.

"It was my fault," Grover told her. "I wanted you to see why I feel the way I do about riverboats."

Dru's eyes flicked from one to the other. The three men in her life. All looking like whipped puppies. She glanced over at the *White Cloud* as it lay formidably at the dock, its twin stacks spewing two trails of smoke as it prepared to get under way. Her glance went back to the three of them. At that moment she could not have loved them any more dearly.

"All right," she said. "Just this once."

Grinning happily, they hurried her aboard.

"I hope I don't get sick," she added, to give them something to worry about.

Dru did not get sick on the trip; in fact, she rather enjoyed it. Making love with Ironwood in their cabin brought back memories of Aaron and reminded her what a good man he had been. She was glad too that she had relented and agreed to come on the boat trip, because it made Grover so happy, and Grover was so much like Aaron in every way.

In St. Louis the *White Cloud* docked at the steamboat levee that stretched along the edge of the city. It was May 17, 1849, and there were twenty-three other steamboats anchored at the St. Louis levee that day.

"Ain't that a sight, Ma!" Grover said excitedly. "Look at 'em! Lined up almost as far as you can see!"

Dru smiled and put an arm around her youngest son, sharing his happiness.

Ironwood and Dru left the boat and took rooms at the Grace Hotel. They spent the day shopping: Dru for dress material and a gift for her godchild; Ironwood for cigars and some cuts of belting leather. Monroe and Grover, who were staying on board the *White Cloud*, wandered about seeing the sights of the city most of the day; then they joined their mother and stepfather for supper at the Grace. When supper was over, they all retired, weary after a busy day.

The fire aboard the *White Cloud* broke out an hour after Monroe and Grover had returned to their cabin and gone to sleep. Grover awakened first, to the sound of voices yelling and footsteps running on the open deck above the ceiling. The cabin was filling with rolls of smoke coming under the door. Grover grabbed his brother and shook him awake.

"Monroe! The boat's on fire!"

Together they ran to the door and flung it open. A blanket of smoke rushed in on them. They saw no flames, but an immense heat engulfed them. They tried to go down the corridor to the deck stairs. The heat grew more intense; then the smoke parted and they were faced with live flames: bright, licking, hot. The stairs were burning all the way up.

"The cabin!" Grover yelled. "There's a porthole!"

They rushed back to the cabin. Grover tore down the curtains and flung open the porthole cap.

"It's too small!" Monroe yelled.

"It's bigger than it looks! Try it!"

Monroe, lean and supple, stuck his head and one shoulder through the opening. By grasping the outside trim and wiggling and twisting his body, he got through to the hips. Then he stuck. Inside, Grover grabbed him by the thighs and roughly manipulated him back and forth like a posthole digger. In a moment Monroe's hips were through and Grover was helping him scramble the rest of the way out.

Monroe held onto the hull trim, clinging to the outside of the boat like a spider. "Come on!" he yelled to Grover. "Hurry!"

The flames had spread through the cabin door now and were creeping along both front bulkheads. Grover put his head and one shoulder through the porthole as Monroe had done, but he could not maneuver his other shoulder through. He was Aaron Van Hawn's son, and the Van Hawn chest and shoulders were too thick and hard and unyielding to pass through an opening that the much leaner Monroe had barely negotiated.

Desperate, Grover pulled back inside and stripped off his shirt. The flames had reached the side walls now and their heat at once reddened his bare skin. He reached up and caught an open ceiling beam and, grasping it, swung his legs through the porthole. Outside, Monroe grabbed them with one arm and held tightly. Grover moved his hips like a cork, slowly working them past the restricted circle of the opening. He got through up to his chest, where he stuck.

"Pull!" he yelled at Monroe. "Jesus, pull, pull!"

Monroe pulled, tugging as best he could with his free arm while balancing himself and holding on to the hull trim with the other. But the more he pulled, the more Grover became stuck, his thick chest constricting to slip through another inch, and then expanding to seal itself in place. Grover's ribs felt as if someone were standing on them. Instinctively, he knew the instant he was trapped.

"Stop pulling!" he screamed. "Push me back! Push!"

Monroe tried to push him but it was hopeless. His brother was wedged in the porthole like a railroad spike driven into a crosstie. He was half in and half out of the burning ship, and could not move in either direction.

Grover began to cry as the crawling flames burned around the cabin from each side wall and came toward him in both directions. Then, when they reached him, he started screaming.

On the outside of the hull, Monroe listened in sick horror as his brother's screams turned to gurgles, his frantically kicking legs stiffened, straightened, and grew rigidly still. By then the outside of the hull was becoming too hot for Monroe to remain where he was. There was a sheet of fire above his head where the upper decks were burning, and he knew that at any second the flames inside would burn their way through the hull.

Monroe cast a fleeting glance around him. Everything was fire. All twenty-three steamboats at the long dock were burning. The dock itself was in flames. And in from the water, fifteen city blocks of St. Louis had become a conflagration.

Tears streaking his face, Monroe bent and hugged his brother's legs, then turned and dove into the Mississippi.

More than four years after Grover's death, Dru still had not gotten over it. That was why, on the day of his twenty-first birthday, Monroe was apprehensive about speaking to her of an engagement between himself and Beth Colson. He had talked it over with Ironwood, but his stepfather had not been encouraging.

"You're all she's got left of her own flesh," Ironwood said. "She doesn't want to lose you so soon after losing Grover."

"She wouldn't be losing me," Monroe reasoned. "I'll be a guard, working right here on the hill, and we'd be living in the compound."

Ironwood shook his head. "Doesn't matter. There'd be another woman in your life, and to your mother it would mean she'd lost you."

"What should I do then, Captain Jack? I *want* Beth—but I don't want to hurt Mother."

"There's not much you can do, son. Things will have to be the way your mother wants them, at least for now. Speak to her about Beth on your birthday and see how she takes it. If she's firmly against it, then let the matter rest for a while. I'll work on getting her to change her mind. At most, it'll mean waiting six months or a year."

Monroe agreed to follow his stepfather's advice, but he did not relish the idea of waiting an extra year for Beth; so, using the information Ironwood had given him about his mother being afraid of losing him, Monroe devised his own scheme for getting Dru's blessing.

"I'm going to appeal to her sense of loss over my brother," he told Beth in the privacy and shelter of the levee willows. "I don't like doing it, but there's no other way."

Beth, her undergarments and clothing now back in place, shook her head irritably. "I think your mother is being very unreasonable if she opposes our engagement. You'd think she'd be happy that you weren't running off to Oregon or somewhere."

"It's just that she's lost so many people that she loved," Monroe explained. "First my father was killed, then Mother's second husband died, then Grover went. I suppose she feels better with me right in the same house with her."

"Mamma's little boy," Beth teased.

"Don't be too hard on her, Beth," Monroe said, with a peculiar edge to his voice.

"I'm sorry, sugar," Beth cooed, reversing herself at once. Apparently it did not do to be too critical of the Mistress of Prison Hill to her son. "It's just that I want to marry you so badly, Monroe."

"I know," he said, forgiving her at once. He took her in his arms. "I want to marry you just as much. Maybe what I have in mind will work with Mother."

They went together to see Dru that afternoon. She gave them a few moments in the parlor, amidst preparations for Monroe's birthday party that night. "What is it that can't wait until tomorrow when I'm this busy?" she asked, although she already knew what they wanted.

"Mother, Beth and I would like to announce our engagement tonight. We'd like to have your permission."

Dru flicked her glance at Beth. The girl was a bit too pretty, a bit too smug, for Dru's taste. It was as if she thought *her* father was the warden and Monroe's the captain of the yard, instead of the other way around. "Why the haste?" she asked in a decidedly cool voice.

"It's not haste, really. Beth and I have been in love almost since she came here. We'd just like to get started with our life together. We'd like to start having our children." Monroe looked down at the thick hooked rug that covered the floor. "I've never spoken of it before, but I miss my brother very badly. I'd like to see if I can have a little boy like him. Somebody to raise and romp with and enjoy like I remember Papa doing with Grove and me."

Glancing up, Monroe saw that his mother's eyes had become teary.

"I'm sure that no little boy could ever replace Grove in your own feelings, Mother, but I think you'd enjoy having a grandson all the same."

Dru's lips had compressed a fraction. Monroe frowned as she rose and shifted her glance from him to Beth and back.

"You have my permission," she said in an even, neutral tone.

Then she turned and walked out of the room.

Monroe, jaw slightly agape, stared after her. He did not know if she had given her blessing because she was genuinely touched by what he had said; or whether she knew that his words were only a ploy to get a favorable answer. If the former, then she had left the room because she was moved; if the latter, because she was disgusted. One way, she would have been wishing Beth and him happiness; the other, she would have been telling them that they deserved each other.

Monroe did not find out, either before or after his marriage to Beth, what his mother had really felt that day. But it puzzled him for only a short time, and Beth not at all. They were allowed to become engaged, and subsequently to marry, and that was all that mattered to them.

As for Dru, she suddenly stopped being possessive of her surviving son and left him to his new wife. Some said it was because she was such a good mother and knew to do the proper thing. Others said it was because she did not care as much for Monroe anymore.

However she felt, Dru spoke of it to no one. Her true feelings were confided only to her diary.

CHAPTER 22

By mid-1853, Prison Hill had been enlarged to accommodate five hundred convicts, and a second new cell house was slowly being built which would hold five hundred more. The prison compound now comprised eighty acres, of which fifteen were enclosed behind a new wall eight hundred feet square and twenty-five feet high. The cells were still cramped and oppressive, cold in the wintertime, sweltering in the summer, but at least now the interminable darkness had been eliminated by a small gaslight spigot in the back wall of each cell. The flame was not large enough for much more than lighting a prison-made corncob pipe or warming one's hands of a winter eve, but to the four-hundred-odd prisoners who had previously lived in darkness from sundown to daylight, it was like a beacon from heaven. Warden Ironwood had not approved of the innovation—he did not believe in coddling convicts—but the state legislature had included it in the plans of the engineers sent down to oversee the construction, so there was nothing he could do about it.

A measure which Ironwood did approve was the state's new hanging law which had been passed a year earlier. The measure banned hangings by individual counties and set up a procedure by which all condemned men would be transported to the state prison and there be put to death by a legally appointed executioner. The hangings were to be presided over by the warden of Prison Hill, or his appointee. The new statute incensed the warden's wife.

"I think it's disgusting," Dru said. "Hanging men right in our front yard. Who is this new governor anyway? Why did he sign such a bill?"

"The new governor is a gentleman named Carter Lehman," said Ironwood. "He likes to do things like they're done in the East. States like New York, New Jersey, and Pennsylvania have been hanging at the state pens for years."

"I don't care what the *eastern* states have been doing. I say it's a disgrace. A gallows practically on our doorstep."

"It won't be quite that bad, Dru," he said patiently. "Everything will be done inside the walls. Only the prisoners and witnesses will see it."

"Yes, but we'll *know* it's happening."

Ironwood sighed. He had no answer for that.

The man hired by the state as its official executioner was an Englishman named Hubert Griffid. He was a rotund, cherubic-looking little man with a totally chilling personality. The Ironwoods, along with newlyweds Monroe and Beth, and yard captain Sam Colson and his wife, entertained Griffid at dinner on the evening before his first execution at Prison Hill.

"I learned my trade at Newgate Prison under Sir Norman Sand," Griffid told them conversationally. "He was one of the first hangmen to use the submental knot. That's a knot designed to snap the cervical vertebra. It can be used in a much shorter drop than the old occipital knot. *That* bloody knot required a fifteen-foot drop to even divide the tissues of the neck—and half the time you had to have a man or two hidden under the trap to grab the bloke's legs and swing a bit. 'Course, a lot depends on the rope employed too. I favor three-quarter-inch Eye-talian hemp meself. Sir Norman, he used to use inch-and-a-quarter five-strand, tested to a ton of dead weight. To my mind, that's a waste. Half-ton test will do the job every time, long as it's stretched ahead of time."

Stretching the rope was Griffid's reason for arriving at Prison Hill a day before the execution. A heavy bag of stone from the quarry was hung at the end of the rope for twenty-four hours, to insure that it would not pull all the way to the ground when the condemned man plunged through the trap. Stretching, he explained, was a necessary part of his preparation.

"Necessary or not," Dru stormed after his first visit, "I'll not have that man at my table again. Mildred Colson almost blanched when that little ghoul talked about dividing the neck tissues. I never heard such dinner conversation in my life!"

Dru was even more upset a year later, when Ironwood mentioned assigning Monroe to supervise an execution. "Why in God's name would you do that?" she demanded.

"For the lad's future, Dru. I'd like to see him succeed me as warden someday. To do that, he has to be able to perform as a warden does. Besides, I'd like to have someone to relieve me of the chore now and again. I've presided at four of them. I'm weary of it."

"Isn't that what you've got a captain of the yard for?"

"Sam Colson won't do it. He says it's against his religion."

"My God! I've seen him flog men until they were a breath away from the grave."

"Flogging he'll do. Hanging, no." Ironwood put his arm around Dru and gently hugged her. He was in his middle fifties now and still loved Dru as much as the day he had met her. Whenever he felt something was going to hurt or disturb her, he tried to pave the way for it as easily as possible. "It'll be good experience for the lad, Dru. It can't hurt to have his name on the reports I send to Governor Lehman."

Dru sighed quietly. Jack was right and she knew it. It *would* be nice if Monroe could one day become warden. If he and Beth, and their children when they had them, could move into the mansion. Her expression softened. How good it would be to have growing children running through the place again. "When is the next execution scheduled?" she asked.

"In a week. The man's being brought in today. Killed his wife up in Lansing. Odd thing, they found out at his trial that he escaped from here more than twenty years ago. Man name of Theron Verne."

Dru managed to control herself on the surface. But inside she felt as if her heart had been sliced in half with a razor.

Dru watched through one of Ironwood's telescopes from her bedroom window as Theron, in chains, was delivered to Sam Colson at the prison gate. He did not appear to be markedly different from the way she remembered him. In his mid forties as she was, he nevertheless was still lean and rangy, his lips and nose thin, face unjowled. His hair was darker and he wore a moustache; otherwise, he seemed the same. He hopped down from the buckboard and waited while Colson signed the marshal's papers.

As Dru watched, Theron turned his head slightly and looked directly at her window. He smiled, almost as if he knew she were watching. Dru caught her breath and quickly stepped back. She felt a rush of warmth, in spite of herself. Moving to one side and using a curtain for a shield, she focused the scope again, just in time to see Sam Colson lead him behind the walls.

For two days Dru debated with herself whether to go see him. It would be relatively easy if she decided to do it. Condemned men were kept in a separate block of four cells on the original, smaller yard directly across from the women's section. Dru customarily went in to see Letitia Herraday once a week, so her presence on the Little Yard, as it was called, was not unusual. It was remote from the Big Yard, separated by the new wall, so there was no danger.

No *apparent* danger, Dru thought. But what of the effect Theron might have on her after all these years? Was not that also a kind of danger? Dru paced her bedroom in private, trying to decide in her own mind if she was afraid to see Theron. She knew she was no longer the girl he had seduced so long ago, and she was confident that she could now deal with him intelligently, maturely. After all, in the years that had passed she had given birth twice, buried two husbands and a son, and married a man who was perfect for her. Why then did she feel such apprehension about Theron's mere presence, particularly since it was to be of such short duration? Why did she even *consider* going to see him? Was it because she had borne his child and now he was going to die? Or did she simply want him to know how well she had done without him?

Whatever the reason, Dru was unable to put it out of her mind that she *had* to see Theron Verne, had to meet with him face to face, had to speak with him, communicate with him one last time before he died. It was insanity, she realized; but it was the kind of insanity that would give her no peace unless she yielded to it.

When Theron still had five days left to live, Dru took a letter from little Nell and a bolt of dress material in to give to Letitia

Herraday. Their visits were on the screened-in porch of the women prisoners' dormitory. Besides Letitia, there were only four other women there at the time. Dru usually tried to bring enough dress material for all of the women, so they could make gowns and shawls for sale in Prisontown. But aside from Letitia, she never became friendly with any of them. Letitia had been the first woman prisoner, and with Dru's help had given birth inside the walls. The women who came later were simply prisoners, no more.

The visit that day went as usual. The two women had tea on the porch. They examined and discussed the dress material, and the price a finished dress should bring. Dru let Letitia read the letter from Nell, and told her also of a letter from the girl's foster mother.

"She says Nell is learning to play piano and doing very well. And next fall they're entering her in Hattie Vinson's Academy. That's one of the finest finishing schools this side of Philadelphia. She's going to be a proper lady, Letitia."

"Thanks to you, Mrs. Niles. I'm sorry; you've been Mrs. Ironwood for five years and I still slip and call you your old name now and again."

"I've told you to call me Dru."

Letitia shook her head. "No, that wouldn't be proper. But I thank you anyway."

After visiting with Letitia for half an hour, Dru left the porch and walked toward the Little Yard's back gate, which was manned on the outside by a solitary guard. Halfway, she paused and looked over at the four death cells. Only one of them was occupied: the one that held Theron. He was lounging against the bars, his shirt off, watching her intently.

Bracing herself a little, Dru walked over to his cell. "Hello, Theron," she said, halting six feet away.

"Hello, 'Scilla." He smiled, his blue eyes twinkling. "You're as pretty as ever."

"Thank you." She studied him for a moment. "I remember asking you a long time ago how you ended up on Prison Hill. Maybe I should ask you now how you've ended up *back* here."

"Do you really care, 'Scilla?"

"Of course. I had feelings for you at one time." As he lounged against the bars, she saw the round, red birthmark just over the ridge of his left shoulder. How many times had her lips touched that place?

She looked at his face again. Theron frowned. Now he was studying her. "You seem different," he said. "Like you'd growed up."

"Neither of us is young anymore, Theron. A lot of years have passed." Her expression saddened. "How *did* you end up here again? They say you killed your wife."

Theron nodded. "I did. Strangled her. But she drove me to it, 'Scilla."

"*Drove* you to it?" Dru frowned. "How, Theron?"

"I wanted to marry somebody else. I was fixing to leave her. But she wouldn't let me go. Said if I run off, she'd tell the law I was an escapee an' get me sent back to prison. We had a bad fight over it—" His story trailed off to silence.

"So you killed her," Dru said quietly. She shook her head, both in pity and disgust.

"It wasn't my fault, 'Scilla." His voice took on a whine.

"No, I'm sure it wasn't, Theron. Nothing you've done wrong has ever been your fault."

Theron's eyes narrowed and hardened. There was a flash of unconcealed animosity. Just then, a tall man in a guard uniform approached.

"Mother?"

Dru quickly turned as Monroe walked up to her. From behind the bars, Theron stared at him.

"Mother, what are you doing here?" Monroe asked. "This man is a condemned murderer."

"Mr. Verne was a prisoner here before you were born, Monroe. He was your father's gardener back when the mansion was built. He planted the very first flowers around the house."

"Mother, you shouldn't be here."

"It's my fault, Mr. Van Hawn," Theron said, smiling. "I saw your mother and called her over. I wanted to tell her I was sorry to hear that your paw was dead. He was always real good to me when I was here before. I truly did admire him."

"Thank you," Monroe said stiffly. "Mother, please let me escort you home."

"Yes, Monroe. Mr. Verne, I'm truly sorry for your troubles. God bless you."

"Thank you, ma'am." Theron smiled. "Mighty fine-looking son you've got there. Sure does take after you. Except for the eyes. He must have his daddy's eyes. Goodbye, ma'am."

After they were out the gate, Monroe spoke sharply to her. "You shouldn't do things like that, Mother. Passing the time of day with a condemned man."

"I don't usually. It's just that he was one of the early prisoners here—"

"The man's a murderer, for God's sake. He's got nothing to lose. He might have grabbed you."

"You're absolutely right, Monroe. It won't happen again, I promise."

Dru walked up the knoll to her home, knowing that was not the last of it.

Two days later, Maggie Morrison visited her.

"I'm Theron's friend," she said. "He told me to come talk to you."

Dru took her into the parlor, silently thanking God that Ironwood was not at home. Although he left her pretty much alone as far as her own friends were concerned, he no doubt would have been curious enough to ask about Maggie Morrison. She had a generously developed body and a mop of soft red hair that most women would have envied. An otherwise not unattractive face was flawed somewhat by an unsightly wart on the left side of her upper lip. Dru guessed that she was not much older than Monroe.

"What do you want, Miss Morrison?" she asked, already dreading the answer.

"Well, ma'am, when I seen Theron yesterday, he said to come see you and tell you he wants to straighten out the matter of his son."

Dru felt ill. "His son?"

"The one who calls himself Monroe Van Hawn. Theron says he's the boy's father."

"That's—ridiculous."

Maggie shrugged. "Theron don't think so. He says he can

prove it. Says you and him done it a lot when he was here before. Says he can describe how your sewing room upstairs looks—"

"All right." Dru forced the words out and held up a hand to stop Maggie's voice. There was no point, she decided, in feigning ignorance or innocence. Theron obviously had armed his courier with an ample store of information. "Exactly what does Theron want?" she asked.

Maggie Morrison leaned forward conspiratorily. "He says he don't want to go to the grave without making peace with his own son. Says he'd be willing to let matters stay as they was if'n he weren't on his way to the gallows." She raised one eyebrow inquiringly.

Dru stiffened slightly. "What you're saying is that he wants me to help him escape. I can't. It's not possible."

"Theron says it is," the woman lowered her voice to a whisper. "He says you can do it and get away with it—nobody'd suspect the warden's own wife."

"No. I'm sorry. It can't be done."

Maggie sat back, her expression turning gray. "Then Theron's going to tell everybody that your son's a bastard. They'll believe him too; all's they have to do is look close at the two of them. I seen your son in town: he's got them light blue eyes of Theron's." She curled her warted lip. "Everybody's going to know what you done with Theron. In your sewing room, the pantry, outside by the well—"

"All right!" Dru said again, more sharply this time. Her throat and mouth felt very dry. "Tell him—that I'll try—to think of a way. You come back day after tomorrow."

"There ain't much time," Maggie reminded her. "Only four days."

"I know." Dru rose, nodding nervously. "Please leave now."

She showed Maggie Morrison to the door. After the woman was gone, she went out back to the privy and vomited.

After a day and night of agonizing soul-searching, Dru decided she had no choice but to do what Theron wanted. Or at least try. She was not afraid of what her husband would think if the story got out—Jack Ironwood was an understanding, forgiving man; he would probably laugh it off and pull the knot a little tighter around Theron's throat—but it was what it would do to Monroe that worried her. To find out that he not only was a bastard, but the son of a convicted murderer as well, Dru was certain would destroy him.

She had to save her son from that if she could. But she was certain she could not do it alone. She needed help, advice, support. There was only one person she dared confide in: Letitia Herraday. Because of all that Dru had done for Letitia over the years, and what she continued to do for little Nell, she was certain that she could trust Letitia implicitly. The first time she talked to her after Maggie Morrison's visit proved her to be right.

"I don't think you should help him," Letitia said after hearing the story. "If he gets loose, he'll never let go of you. Let him hang."

"I can't," Dru said miserably. "He'll tell everything. It would destroy Monroe." They were sitting on the screened porch of the women's dormitory. Across the Little Yard, Dru could see one end of the row of condemned cells.

"Suppose he wasn't able to talk?" Letitia asked.

"What do you mean?"

"I mean, suppose there was a way we could keep him from saying anything before they hanged him."

"I don't see how—"

Letitia looked around to make sure none of the other four women prisoners were near. She lowered her voice. "You're still friends with Dr. Robin, aren't you?"

"Yes, of course."

"Can you get at his medical supplies when he's not around?"

"I—I'm not sure. I suppose I could."

"Look for a bottle of clear liquid marked 'Colodone.' It's a drug used to treat infected tonsils. Doctors use small amounts of it to paint the throat. My husband used to order it for the doctors in our county. Before I poisoned him."

Dru nodded. "Yes, I remember: your husband was a chemist."

"Among other things," Letitia said bitterly.

"If I can get it, what do I do with it?"

"Bring it to me. I'll do the rest."

"I want to know what you'll do."

Letitia shook her head. "Best if you don't know. You just tell the Morrison woman that he'll be helped to escape at the very last minute, on his way to the gallows. After it's over, you'll have to attend to her yourself, you know."

"Yes, I know. Oh, Letitia, do you think whatever you're going to do will work?"

Letitia squeezed her hand. "Don't you worry. I'm not going to let my daughter's godmother be hurt by no son of a bitch of a man. You've done too much for little Nell and me. When it comes to men and how they try to walk all over you with shit on their boots, I know just how to handle them. Your Mr. Theron Verne is going to hang by his conniving neck—and he won't say a word before he does."

Dru stared at Letitia Herraday. The woman's eyes had narrowed to slits and her lips bore an almost evil little smile. For the first time since Dru had known her, Letitia truly looked like a murderess.

Dru stole the colodone from Doc Robin's house that very afternoon. It was quite easy. She simply parked her buggy in some nearby trees and waited until Doc left in his own rig to call on patients, and Cordelia walked uptown to do her daily marketing. Then she drove up to the house, entered through the always unlocked door, and went directly to the room Doc used for an office. The colodone was on a shelf with several dozen other medicines. Dru had brought a small bottle from home; she poured three-fourths of the colodone into her own bottle and left the rest. Then, in case a neighbor had seen her entering the house when no one was home, she wrote a note telling Cordelia she had stopped by, and asked her and Doc to supper that night.

Dru gave the colodone to Letitia the next morning. It was the third straight day that she had visited the Little Yard, and the gate guard gave her a peculiar look for it, but Dru ignored him. If he reported it to Sam Colson, and *if* Sam told Jack Ironwood, and *if* her husband happened to mention it to her, she would simply say Letitia was making a new dress for her, and the extra visits were for fittings. However, she doubted that anything would be said. She knew she was called the Mistress of Prison Hill by most guards and prisoners, and she knew that her person and presence carried almost as much authority as the figure of

Jack Ironwood. And, since she had been at the prison since the first brick was laid, her coming and going as she chose was an accepted fact. No one questioned the Mistress.

After giving the colodone to Letitia, Dru returned to the mansion to await Maggie Morrison's second visit. She had already worked out in her mind how she would deal with the woman.

"It's all arranged," she lied easily to her. "On the morning the hanging is scheduled, when Theron is supposed to be taken from the Little Yard to the Big Yard where the gallows is, he'll be freed and let out the Little Yard gate. The escort guards have been bribed, and the gate guard will be overpowered by a third man outside. There'll be a wagon waiting; I'll be driving it. I'll take Theron to the levee south of town. You meet us there. Then you and Theron can take the wagon and go. When the guards find me, I'll say I was abducted by a friend of Theron's."

"What about the bribed guards? What'll they say?"

"They will say they were forced to cooperate to save me from any harm. My husband will probably promote them."

Maggie Morrison's expression was troubled. "Theron ain't going to like waiting until the very morning he's to hang."

"There's no other way," Dru assured her. "The only time the key to his cell will be out of the yard captain's possession is when he sends the escort guards to bring Theron to the gallows." Dru suddenly realized that she loathed this voluptuous but wart-lipped woman. What earthly right did she and Theron have intruding into her life the way they had? Threatening to destroy her very existence, and her son's, over some ridiculous mistake she made when she was little more than a girl. What *right*?

"You're sure there ain't no other way?" Maggie Morrison asked. "To do it sooner?"

"No way at all," Dru replied coldly. "You tell Theron that when you visit him today. Tell him the choice is his. He can either do it this way, or he can tell everything he knows and then hang. Frankly, I don't care much either way anymore."

"Well, now ain't you getting uppity. For one who ruts with convicts, that is."

Dru wanted to hit her, to lash her face with a buggy whip, to tear her mop of red hair out by the roots. But she contained her anger. She knew the dangers. A woman like Maggie Morrison might easily sacrifice everything—Theron, the escape plan, her own future—to avenge a physical affront by Dru. Better to let it pass, thought Dru.

"You have what you came for," she told the woman. "Get out of my house."

With a smirk on her lips, Maggie Morrison left.

That evening, when the food was brought over for the women prisoners to cook their supper, Letitia waited outside the dormitory door for Elmer Widmer, the kitchen orderly, to leave. When he did, she spoke to him.

"Evening, Elmer."

"Evening, Miz Herraday," Elmer said. He was a gawking farmhand in his mid twenties, serving five years for stealing hogs from a slaughterhouse.

"How long have you been on the Hill now, Elmer?" she asked.

"Near 'bout two years, ma'am."

"Long time to be without a woman," Letitia observed. Elmer blushed.

"Yes, ma'am."

Letitia smiled knowingly. "Every time you come over here, I see you looking at Ilene."

"She's a right pretty girl," said Elmer.

"About the prettiest gal ever sent here," Letitia agreed. She winked at him. "Would you like her to be nice to you, Elmer?"

"What do you mean?"

"You know what I mean. Would you like to go back behind the sewing machines and get Ilene down on the floor with you? Suck her titties a little and then stick your cock in her? Would you like that, Elmer?" She knew he would by the bulge in his trousers.

"What would I have to do for it?" Elmer asked.

Letitia told him. Put the colodone in Theron Verne's breakfast on the morning of the hanging. "Do that and I'll let you rut Ilene once a week for as long as you're in here."

"I don't know," Elmer said hesitantly.

"What's the matter?"

"I heard tell she was—well, peculiar. They say she killed her own little baby."

"She did. But that's got nothing to do with how she ruts. She'll clean you out good, boy. Get all that poison out of your system. Once a week."

"Why do you want the stuff put in Verne's food?"

"I want to make sure he stays sober for his hanging. This stuff will keep him from getting drunk in case some guard smuggles him a jug. See, he did something to a lady friend of mine one time. Got her in trouble. Then he wouldn't help her out. This is just to pay him back for that. Will you help me?"

Just then, as if prearranged, Ilene came to the door to tell Letitia that supper was ready. Elmer looked once at her shapely figure and nodded his head. "Uh, when can I—you know, the first time?"

"Right after he hangs," Letitia said.

She went back inside and drew Ilene into a private corner for a moment. She told her what she wanted her to do.

"I don't know if I'll like doing that anymore after being with you," Ilene said with a half pout.

"You don't have to like it, precious," said Letitia. "Just do it. For me." She drew the younger woman close and kissed her on the mouth.

"All right, Letitia," said Ilene. "If you want me to."

On the morning he was to go to the gallows, Theron Verne was tense almost to the point of illness. This better work, he kept saying silently to himself, pacing the small cell. This goddamn well better work. If it doesn't, I'll scream the truth about that slut all the way to the trap.

A solitary guard, with orders not to talk to the prisoner, stood six feet away in front of his cell. The sun had come up minutes earlier; its glow could be seen above the far wall. Theron was to die one hour after sun-up. He still had plenty of time to worry. This better work, it better work—

A quarter hour after sun-up, Elmer Widmer entered the Little Yard from the Big Yard gate. He was carrying a large wooden tray laden with plates and bowls of food. When he reached the cell, he halted and let the guard lift the white cotton cover to inspect the tray. Passing inspection, he went up to Theron's cell door.

"Cook put some extra stuff on for you this morning," he said, a little self-consciously. He removed the cloth. "Got some plum preserves and fresh-churned butter, and a plate of fried eggs."

"I don't want food," Theron said. "Just give me the coffee."

"Yes, sir." It did not matter to Elmer. The coffee had as much colodone in it as the preserves and the butter and the grease around the eggs. He handed a mug of coffee through the food-pass. Theron took it and began to sip. Presently he made a sour face.

"Tastes like cow piss."

"Some preserves on a biscuit might make it better," Elmer suggested.

"Just give him all of it, you," the guard snapped. "You weren't sent out here to spoon-feed him."

"Yessir," Elmer said. He put the entire tray through the food-pass. Theron glared at the guard, wishing he could get close enough to throw the hot coffee in his face.

"Get on out of here now," the guard told Elmer.

"Yessir." Elmer paused a second before leaving, just long enough to see Theron sop a biscuit into the preserves and wolf it down, followed by a swig of coffee. He walked away, thinking about Ilene.

Theron knew something was wrong half an hour later when he saw Monroe Van Hawn crossing the yard with the gallows escort. If everything was arranged, as Dru had said it was, Monroe surely would not be the one coming to take him to hang. He watched apprehensively as the four-man escort approached. Quickly he decided that his choices were running out; he would have to speak directly to Monroe.

His cell door opened. Monroe stood in the doorway. He reminded Theron very much of his own dead father.

"All right, Verne, it's time to go," Monroe said.

Theron stepped forward to speak to him. "Ah—ah—aaaah—"

Theron frowned. Something seemed to be wrong with his voice.

"Come on, Verne," Monroe said.

Theron cleared his throat. "Ah—ah—aaaah—"

His eyes widened. He stared fearfully at Monroe. Good God! He couldn't speak!

One of the escort guards stepped up next to Monroe. He was Owen Landis, the rail-thin young man Monroe had met with his wife on the prison road the day of Monroe's twenty-first birthday. Owen had been looking for work as a guard. Sam Colson had hired him and he and Monroe had received their guard uniforms the same day. "What's the matter with him?" Owen asked, staring curiously at Theron.

"I don't know," Monroe said. "He acts like he's got something caught in his throat."

Theron swallowed, coughed, rolled his tongue around inside his mouth. "Ah—ah—aaaah—" *Almighty God, I can't talk!*

"We can't waste time," Monroe said quietly to Owen. "Everybody's waiting. Let's get him out."

The two young men stepped quickly in and grasped Theron by the arms. He did not resist them. Instead, he looked helplessly, pleadingly, at Monroe.

"Ah—ah—aaaah—" *Son. You're my son.*

Monroe and Owen walked him out of the cell. With the help of the other two escort guards, they cuffed his wrists behind his back. Then they hurried him toward the gate to the Big Yard. All the way there, Theron kept trying to force words out. *My son. Your mother. Me. My son!* But nothing came out except the gutteral utterings of a man whose vocal cords had been constricted by the colodone.

In the Big Yard, the inmate population, more than four hundred men, were assembled for the execution. The entire guard force was dispersed around the yard and on the main wall. Warden Ironwood, Captain of the Yard Colson, and three state witnesses were seated atop the gallows. Standing nearby was Reverend Kenney of the Baptist Church in Prisontown. Doc Robin waited below, under the trap, to make the official death pronouncement. At the top of the thirteen steps, rope in hand, stood Hubert Griffid.

Monroe and Owen maneuvered the condemned man up the steps. Doc, noticing him struggling to speak, guessed that the fear of death had caused him to lose his voice. Glancing up at the trap door, he shook his head. Barbaric, he thought. He turned his back to the crowd and sneaked a drink.

On the gallows deck, the preliminaries were moving rapidly. A hood had been placed over Theron's head. Griffid slipped the noose over that and knotted it in place. The other end of the rope was already clamped in place on the overhead beam. Standing close to Theron, Reverend Kenney mumbled words of comfort which no one really heard.

And from beneath the death hood: "Ah—ah—aaaah—"

It was over very quickly. The trap was sprung and Theron plunged downward. The rope caught and jerked him back up a few feet. His body heaved up and down several times, like a boat in choppy water. Then he hung squirming and twisting for a full three minutes.

Hubert Griffid had not done his job well. Theron Verne strangled to death.

While Theron was dying, Dru was driving her buggy out along the levee south of town. Maggie Morrison was waiting at the end of a grove of willows. She was wearing a traveling suit and had her red hair bound in a dust turban. When Dru reined up the buggy horse, Maggie came hurrying over.

"You said a wagon, not a buggy," she scolded. "I was expectin' a wagon."

"Do you always get what you expect?" Dru asked.

Maggie ignored the question. She peered into the buggy. "Where's Theron?" she wanted to know.

"Swinging by his neck, I hope," Dru said. She pulled an old percussion Derringer from the folds of her dress. It was a gun that had been issued by the state quartermaster more than a quarter century earlier; a gun that its owner refused to carry because he did not feel comfortable with it; a gun that had belonged to Aaron Van Hawn, whom Dru had betrayed for Theron Verne. She hoped now that the gun would end her youthful mistake once and for all.

Aiming the Derringer at the wart on Maggie Morrison's lip, Dru fired.

The ball tore through the woman's face and knocked her off the levee into the Mississippi.

Dru stood up in the buggy. She watched as the body was sucked in by the rapids and carried swiftly downstream.

God let it be over now, she silently prayed.

When the body was no longer in sight, Dru turned the buggy around and headed back toward Prison Hill, to her husband and her son.

CHAPTER 23

On a fall afternoon in 1860, Beth Colson Van Hawn was preparing to go down to Prisontown to shop. She was in the bedroom of their small frame house, pulling on her bloomers, when Monroe, in his underwear, came in carrying their naked son Nathan on his shoulders.

"Monroe, for lord's sake," Beth said, "will you take the child out of here. I'm not dressed."

"He's only three, honey," said Monroe. "Anyway, he's not dressed either." He tossed the boy onto the bed and fell to tickling him. Little Nathan shrieked with delight.

"Honestly," Beth complained. "I thought when we moved down here from the mansion, I'd have some privacy." She turned her back and continued dressing.

Monroe rolled and played on the bed with his son for a few minutes; then he noticed that Beth was still in her bloomers. She was bending forward at the chifforobe mirror, applying powder to her face. Her buttocks trembled slightly under the silk as she moved her arms. "Come on, partner," Monroe said to Nathan. "Time for you to take a nap."

Beth looked knowingly at her husband in the mirror. A hint of a smile played at her lips. While Monroe was out of the room, she took her bloomers back off, left her corset on, and lay down on the bed. She was waiting there when Monroe came back.

"Think you know me pretty well, don't you?" he said.

"Well enough to know when you've got something in your drawers that you want taken care of."

Monroe slipped out of his underwear. He started to climb on top of her.

"Kiss it first," Beth said. "Like you used to do on the levee."

"Shame on you. A respectable married woman wanting her husband to kiss her patch—"

Before he could say any more, she had pushed herself into his face and was writhing against him. In the next room, Nathan, in his sleeping pen, began to cry. Both mother and father ignored him until they were finished..

Later, with Monroe holding the child again, and Beth once more in her bloomers, she said, "When is Warden Jack going to let you work days again, instead of nights?"

"Why? Don't you like rutting in the daylight?"

"Monroe! Don't talk like that in front of the boy! And don't tell me he's only three." She slipped into a day dress. "You didn't answer my question."

"I won't be working night guard much longer. Andrew Veal is due to be stretched in three weeks. Black Jack will have me back on duty in time to take care of that."

"Do you realize that he has you in charge of *every* execution?"

Monroe shrugged. "Somebody has to hang them. Mother says that Jack is getting too old to do it. Your father won't have any part of it. Since I'm the guard lieutenant, that makes me next in line. Anyway, Jack says it's good for Governor Donnell to see my name on the execution certificate all the time. Jack's almost sixty-five, you know. As soon as I'm thirty, he's going to resign and have the governor appoint me in his place."

"Is he sure the governor will do it?"

"Of course. He and the governor are good friends. They fought in the Mexican War together."

"If you became warden, Monroe," she said thoughtfully, "will I be mistress of the mansion then?"

"Reckon so. Mother and Jack will probably build a house in town, down by Doc and Aunt Cordelia."

"I wish you wouldn't call her that. She's not your aunt."

"Closest to one I've ever had."

"I don't want Nathan calling her that when he gets older. It's a disgrace, you know; her living all those years with a man outside of wedlock."

"I thought they lived outside of Prisontown."

"It isn't funny, Monroe."

"Doesn't seem to bother anyone else."

"It would if this were a proper town instead of a prison town. Monroe, have you ever considered leaving here and doing some other kind of work?"

Monroe stretched out on the floor and put Nathan astraddle his chest. "Don't know any other kind of work, honey. Anyway, this is my home."

"Some home," she said sourly. "Right up next to a prison wall. Even in the mansion, the damned prison is practically all you can see. I just wish we could live someplace nicer. Someplace like Chicago or St. Louis. Someplace with theaters and opera houses and parks to walk in on Sunday afternoons."

Beth talked on about all they were missing by living on Prison Hill. They were, she decided, almost as much in prison as the convicts. Their lives were regulated by prison schedules, restricted by prison security, constantly under the threat of prison violence, and, in any other town but the one down the hill, stigmatized by the name attached to them by the convicts: that of being a keeper-man, or a keeper-man's wife or offspring.

Beth talked as she laced up her calf-high shoes, as she attached cotton cuffs and collar to her day dress, as she sashed her waist and tucked a hankie into one of the sash pleats. She talked without benefit of pause, and without confirmation of her audience's attention. When she finally stopped, she found she *had* no audience. Monroe had drifted and was snoring lightly. Nathan was fast asleep on his chest. Beth had been talking to herself.

As usual, she thought. She might as well address her remarks to a tree half the time when she talked to Monroe. If she wanted to discuss the prison or sex, she could count on his undivided attention. Otherwise, he was more interested in listening to little Nathan's gibberish.

Irritably, Beth left the house and, hitching up the buggy herself, drove down the hill toward town.

She was at the edge of town, almost to the point where Union Street began, when two men stepped into the road and stopped her horse. One of them grabbed the reins, the other came toward her on the other side. He had eyes so tiny and beady they were almost concealed by the shadow of his brows.

"Who are you? What do you want?" Beth asked indignantly. She was unused to such rudeness.

The beady-eyed one continued toward her. She jerked up the buggy whip and started to raise it. Leaping forward, the man grabbed it from her hand and climbed up beside her. She slapped his face.

"You bitch!" He slapped her back, hard, and shoved her to the bottom of the buggy. "Get aboard!" he yelled to his accomplice.

One held Beth down while the other drove the buggy off the road and into the woods. The one holding her down took the opportunity to squeeze her breasts. She started to scream but he raised a threatening hand. Then he went back to fondling her.

"Goddamn, she's got nice big titties, Roy," he said with a leer. "Maybe we can have us some fun while we got her."

Beth stared in horror at the second man. He was unshaven and had tobacco-stained teeth.

"We didn't take her to have fun with," the one called Roy replied. He glanced down from his driving. "If'n they goes ahead and hangs Andrew, we just might hack them titties off. Goddamn, I wish we could have got old Ironwood's wife. I guess this little bitch will have to do us, though. Watch her now, Milton."

"I'm watching her, Roy! Goddamn, she's got the best titties I ever *saw*!" He looked up and smiled. "Listen to me, will you! I ain't even seen 'em yet!"

The buggy went deeper and deeper into the woods, its wheels noisily striking rocks and fallen branches and chuckholes. Beth's shoulder blades began to ache from the jarring, but she nevertheless continued to press herself against the floor of the buggy; to do otherwise would have meant moving her body closer to the one called Milton, and it sickened her to even think of it. He already had one leg over her hips and one hand moving back and forth from breast to breast. Merciful Jesus, save me from these animals, she prayed.

When the buggy stopped, it was at a shanty cabin set in a small clearing. Roy Veal hopped down at once and pulled Beth out of the buggy, away from his brother. When her feet touched the ground, she stumbled to her knees.

"Take the rig around back and hide it," Roy said. "And unhitch that horse."

"What are you gone be doing?" Milton asked suspiciously.

"Tying this here bitch up, that's what." He glanced down at Beth. "Get off the ground and into that shack," he ordered.

As Beth was getting up, she looked past Roy Veal's legs and saw a man standing off in the nearby trees. At first she thought it was an Indian; his chest was bare and she glimpsed a feather attached to his head. But then she saw he was white. She started to call for help, but in an instant he had disappeared behind a tree. As she got unsteadily to her feet, she was not even sure she had not imagined him.

"I still aim to do some playing with her," Milton grumbled as he led the horse and buggy away.

Taking Beth inside, Roy shoved her roughly into a chair. He pulled her hands behind the chair back and began tying them with rawhide. Beth looked around the shack: it was filthy, stinking of unwashed bodies and rotting food and clothes. A wave of nausea flowed through her. When her hands were tied, Roy stepped around and stood in front of her. His beady little eyes looked like buckshot holes in his face.

"Now then, let's take us a look at them titties Milton was doing all the hollering about," he said, wetting his lips.

Beth swallowed dryly and closed her eyes. She felt Roy's big hands pulling down the front of her dress and clumsily opening her bodice. Sweet merciful Jesus—

Her breasts were out and his calloused fingers were rubbing her nipples. A moment later his wet mouth was slobbering on her—

Then there was a loud noise: the door being flung open. She opened her eyes, looking past Roy Veal's hair, to see the bare-chested man she had seen in the woods. He was standing in the doorway. She saw that the feather on his head was part of an odd-looking, narrow-brimmed hat that he wore.

Veal whirled around on his knees at the sound of the noise. He lumbered to his feet, reaching for a pistol in his belt. The man in the doorway quickly stepped over and knocked the gun to the floor. "Let's just use our fists, mate," he said easily.

"It'll be two on one," Veal threatened. "My brother—"

"Your brother's unconscious. Just as you're going to be in a minute." He bent his legs slightly at the knees and raised his arms, also bent, wrists up, fists closed. "Defend yourself, you dirty hog," he said, circling.

Making a fist, Veal threw an angry punch. The barechested man pulled his head back just enough for the blow to miss him by an inch; then he stepped in and drilled half a dozen perfectly timed, perfectly placed punches to Veal's face, breaking his nose, splitting his bottom lip, and knocking out two teeth. Veal dropped to the floor like a wet rope and lay still.

When he was sure that Veal was out, the barechested man hurried over to Beth. He pulled up her dress to cover her exposed breasts. Mortified, she turned a deep red.

"It's all right now, miss, I wasn't looking," he said gently. "Let me untie your hands—"

"Who—are you?" she asked dryly.

"My name's Gerald Lee, ma'am. They call me Boss Lee. I'm the peacekeeper in Lamp Kellerman's saloon."

He got her outside and sat her on a log. From a small pack, he offered her a drink of water from his canteen. "I haven't no cup. Sorry." Beth drank. Then Lee poured some water on a maple leaf. "Hold this against your cheeks; it'll cool you."

While she sat there, he dragged the Veal brothers out, tied them up, and threw them across the boot of the buggy. Then he took a shirt from his pack and put it on. Beth watched him curiously. He was about Monroe's age. His hair was black, shiny, slicked straight back. Under a flat, spread nose, he had a ready smile. "What were you doing out here in the woods without your shirt?" she asked.

"Training. Keeping my edge. I used to be a prizefighter, see. Back in the East. Bare-knuckle pugs they called us. But I got me hand busted up—"

He showed her his right hand. The top knuckles were gnarled and lumpy where they had been broken several times.

"I can hit a man a few times, like I just done to these two," he said, jerking a thumb at the Veals, "but I can't fight twenty or thirty rounds no more. If I do the old knucks just fall to pieces again. Too bad, too. Used to be pretty good, if I do say so myself. That's why they call me 'Boss'—'cause inside the ring I *was* the boss."

Lee drove Beth back to the prison. She had him take her to the mansion. Dru, stunned by what had happened, immediately put her daughter-in-law to bed. A trusty was sent to get Ironwood and Monroe. They hurried to the mansion, grim-faced.

"Brothers of Andrew Veal," Ironwood said when he saw the prisoners. "He's to be hanged shortly," he told Lee. "They probably hoped to bargain for his freedom by abducting Beth." Ironwood had them taken inside the walls and put in solitary confinement.

Later, after things had calmed down a bit, Monroe drove Boss Lee down the hill to Prisontown. "I'm deeply in your debt, Boss," he said. "And it's not the kind of debt that can ever be repaid. But I'd like to do something for you. Would you like my stepfather to give you a job at the prison?"

"Thanks, no," said Lee. "I like my job at Kellerman's. And there's no need to talk of any debts. I'm happy I was there."

Monroe let him off at the saloon. "I'll be warden up there someday, Boss," he said. "You'll always have a place there whenever you want it."

"Someday, maybe," the fighter said. "Someday."

Someday came sooner than Monroe or Boss Lee expected. It came in the form of a sudden, grotesque shock one afternoon the following spring when Jack Ironwood was conducting the daily discipline court. The convict population, now nearly six hundred men, was in formation on the Big Yard. Ironwood, Sam Colson, and Monroe stood before them; guards with clubs walked around them; guards with rifles paced the wall above them.

Ironwood referred to one of a handful of paper chits he held. "Loomis, step forward!" he ordered. A convict moved out of ranks. "Your officer says that you were malingering at your loom in the mill today. Five lashes."

A guard took Loomis over to a stake in the ground. There he stood, the beginning of the punishment line.

"Tatum!" Another came forward. "You failed to make your quota in the lint room today. One week in the pit. Lieutenant Van Hawn, assign a man to replace Tatum."

"Yessir, Warden."

Tatum fell in behind Loomis. After court, he would be moved into a cell in the rock quarry group.

"Bell!" He came forward. "Chewing tobacco inside the tannery. Three days in the hole."

As Bell was walking over to the punishment line, Ironwood

suddenly dropped the handful of papers and clutched his left armpit. He turned deathly white and his face contorted in pain. A low groan escaped his throat. "Uuuuuuhh—uhn—"

He started to fall. Monroe stepped quickly to his aid. Sam Colson also grabbed him. They lowered him to the ground. His head fell back stiffly; his legs straightened, locked, held. "Uuuu-uhh—"

Monroe called to the nearest guard. "Get Doc Robin, quick! Tell him the warden's had a stroke!"

At the word "stroke," a low, rolling cheer went up among the convicts. Monroe stared at them, horrified. Their faces turned happy, gleeful. They began to shout "Hooray! Hip, hip, hooray! Old Black Jack is going to his grave! He's dying, he's dying! Hooray!"

"Filthy bastards," Monroe said through gritted teeth. He turned to his father-in-law. "Help me carry him out of here."

With Sam Colson's help, he carried the big warden over to the gate and into the Little Yard.

The cheers of the prisoners were eventually heard all the way up to the mansion. Dru, sitting in the parlor sewing with Cordelia, grew chilled when she heard it.

"The war," Cordelia said. "I'll bet Mr. Lincoln has started the war."

"No," Dru said. "It's not the war." She put aside her sewing. "There's only one thing that would make the prisoners cheer like that."

They went out onto the north porch. Coming up the hill were two guards with a stretcher carrying Jack Ironwood. Following him were Monroe, Sam Colson, and Doc Robin. Monroe looked pale and angry. Each time a cheer rose from behind the walls, a vein throbbed at the side of his temple. "Dirty rotten scum," he kept saying half-aloud.

The stretcher-bearers stopped at the steps to the porch. Dru saw for the first time that Ironwood's face was covered. She came down the steps, dismissing offers of help from Monroe and Doc. Kneeling beside the stretcher, she started to lift the cloth from her dead husband's face.

"Mother, don't," Monroe said, touching her arm.

Dru ignored him. She took the cloth away. A gasp caught in her throat. Ironwood's face was grotesquely contorted. The left side of his mouth was drawn back nearly to his ear, exposing all his top teeth on that side. Trails of dry gray spittle streaked his cheek and chin. His left eye was bulged nearly out of its socket, the eyeball swollen, its blood vessels ruptured. Blood had dried beneath both nostrils.

"Oh my God!" Dru wailed. "Jack! Jack! My only Jack! Jesus, give him back to me!"

Monroe took her by both arms and led her inside. On the way, she began yelling other names.

"Aaron! Clement! Grover! Jack!"

The names of all those who had died before her.

Governor Donnell did not hesitate to appoint Monroe to the wardenship of Prison Hill. "You are carrying on a unique family position," the governor told him when he made the appointment at the state house. "Your natural father founded the prison, and your two stepfathers were both wardens there. There has been some comment about your age, some remarks to the effect that perhaps the responsibility of running a prison is too great for a young man of thirty. To those who so remark, I remind that you were born and grew up at Prison Hill, that you have lived all your life there, that you have been a guard for nine years and a lieutenant for four of those years. Not only that, but your predecessor, the late Warden Ironwood, personally recommended you in a letter to me more than a year ago. Therefore, it is with the utmost confidence and the greatest personal pleasure that I formally appoint you warden of the state penitentiary at Prison Hill. Congratulations, Warden Van Hawn."

Warden Van Hawn. How odd to hear that again, Dru thought. She was attending the appointment ceremony with Beth, little Nathan, and Beth's parents, the Colsons.

"Mother Dru," said Beth at the reception that followed, "You will be giving Monroe and me the master bedroom when we move into the mansion, won't you? I mean, since there are two of us and only one of you—"

"You may have whichever rooms you want," Dru replied.

"That's nonsense," said Monroe, who overheard. "We'll take one of the other rooms, Beth. Mother has had that room since the house was built."

Dru did not argue. She *wanted* to keep the big room; so much of her life had been lived in it. Beth, although she pouted, did not argue either. She had learned to let Monroe have his way when it came to Dru.

"Monroe, my boy," the governor said, taking him aside before the reception ended, "the tannery owners tell me they want to expand their operation on the hill. Do you think it would be possible to increase the working hours of the lease-labor convicts from ten to twelve hours a day?"

"Yes, sir, I think so," Monroe replied. He thought of the cheering at Ironwood's death. "Perhaps even to fourteen hours, Governor. After all, they *are* there to be punished."

"You're absolutely right, my boy," the governor said, patting him on the back. "Absolutely right."

"As a matter of fact, sir, I've been considering a number of new policies at the prison, practices I've picked up by studying European and eastern United States prisons. I wonder if I might outline some of them for you?"

"No need, Warden, no need at all. It's *your* prison; initiate whatever policies you feel necessary. All we ask is that security be maintained and the established work quotas met by each convict. Other than that, we leave everything entirely up to you. Confident, I might add, that you can handle it."

Monroe thanked the governor. He could handle it all right. And *would* handle it. The convicts at Prison Hill would rue the day they celebrated Jack Ironwood's death.

Beginning the day he returned.

Monroe had the population assembled on the Big Yard. He spoke to them from the deck of the gallows.

"There is a prison in New York State called Sing Sing," he said. "They have in that prison what is known as the 'silent system.' I'm going to read aloud the rules pertaining to that system." He unfolded one page of a lengthy letter he had received from the Sing Sing warden and began reading. " 'It is the duty of convicts to preserve an unbroken silence. They are not to exchange a word with each other under any pretense whatever. They are not to exchange looks, winks, or motions. They are not to communicate with each other in writing or by any form of signal. Further, they are not to sing, whistle, run, jump, dance, or do anything else which has a tendency in the least degree to dis-

turb the harmony or the rules and regulations of this prison.'"
Monroe folded the paper back up. His eyes swept the population. "There is another practice currently being used in some prisons to ensure orderly movement throughout the prison compound. That is called the 'lockstep.' Convict Whalen was a prisoner at Auburn Penitentiary and learned the lockstep there. He has taught it to Convicts Emon and Danzig. They will demonstrate it for you."

Three convicts came forward to the base of the gallows. They lined up in a row, left arms at their sides, right arms outstretched and resting on the shoulder of the man in front of them. Their heads were turned to the left, facing Monroe. At the shout of "One!" from Monroe, they all stepped forward with their right feet and brought their left feet up next to them. There was then a split-second pause, after which "One!" was shouted again. They repeated the step: right foot, left foot, lock. Pause. "One!" Right foot, left foot, lock.

"All right," said Monroe. "Return to ranks." He nodded to Owen Landis and another guard. "Bring it out."

They opened a tool shed and brought out a heavy wooden vise, shaped like a peach pit. It had hinges on one end, a cut-out hole in its center, and a hasp lock on the other end. With the hasp lock open, it spread out like the handles of a nutcracker.

"This is called a punishment yoke," Monroe said. "It opens on hinges, fits around a man's neck, then closes and locks. Once locked in place, it rests on the shoulders and is carried around all day while the man works. Sergeant Landis will now demonstrate."

Owen ordered forward the nearest convict. He and the other guard lifted the yoke and put it in place. They locked it on. The man was then made to walk back and forth in ranks so that all the prisoners could have a close look at it.

"The carpenter shed will start producing these yokes today," Monroe said. "By the end of this week, we'll have fifteen of them; by the end of next week, thirty; and so on. If necessary, I'll have one made for every prisoner in population. They will be used to enforce the silent system and the lockstep, which will begin in this institution at noon today."

A low rumble of discord rippled through the standing men. They shifted restlessly, muttering to themselves and each other, their expressions darkening, eyes growing cold as they looked at their new warden.

Monroe nodded curtly to his father-in-law. "Captain Colson, begin enforcing the new practices at the stroke of noon."

Monroe came down from the gallows deck. With Owen Landis at his side, he left the Big Yard.

Monroe and Owen, while not exactly friends, had, because of their ages and the fact that they entered the guard service on the same day, been more or less thrown together throughout much of their tenure in the prison. Owen had been hired by Sam Colson the same day Jack Ironwood had sworn in his stepson; the same day Monroe and Owen had met on the prison road. It was inevitable that much of their training be taken together, and natural that a sense of competition would develop between them.

During their first year on the job, it was quickly decided that Owen was the best shot, the best horseman, and the toughest, while Monroe clearly was the smartest, the quickest to learn, and the best administrator. In every category in which one of them was lacking, the other tried to best him by self-improvement. Monroe went deep into the woods to practice marksmanship and had Boss Lee give him secret boxing lessons in the storeroom of Kellerman's Saloon. Owen followed Jack Ironwood and Sam Colson around like a pup, pestering them with interminable questions and picking their brains for every scrap of knowledge he could get. At night, in the little one-room rented house in Prisontown, Owen laboriously wrote out prison rules and regulations and had Clara recite them with him until he knew them word for word.

The wives of the two men knew about their rivalry but never had the opportunity to discuss it.

Clara Landis and Beth Van Hawn knew each other slightly but never became friends, never socialized. They had little in common and, unlike their husbands, were not thrown together daily in their work. They moved in altogether different circles. Beth associated with her mother-in-law Dru, with her own mother, and with the limited number of other ladies in town who were considered to have social stature. Clara Landis had only two friends, both wives of lower-rank guards. Clara, unlike

Beth, did not require a great deal of social activity in her day-to-day life; she was quieter, more reserved, almost introverted.

"She's a country girl," Beth once said about her. "You can always tell a country girl. They never say *anything* worth listening to. And most of them have freckles from too much sun. Clara Landis has more freckles than any woman I ever did see. Why, they go clear down her *dress*. And that strawberry hair—why, that's the most awful color I ever saw in my life."

Monroe, who thought Clara was rather pretty, did not bother to contradict his wife. What the two women thought of each other meant absolutely nothing to him. Or to Owen, either. He and Owen never discussed their wives, or anything else personal. The one exception had been during their fourth year as guards, when Beth had finally given birth.

"It's a boy," Monroe told Owen the next morning. "We're naming him Nathan after Beth's grandfather."

Owen had congratulated him and shook hands.

"Do you and Clara plan to have a family?" Monroe asked.

"We've tried," Owen said quietly. "So far it ain't happened. Maybe someday, I hope."

Owen did want a child, just as he wanted many of the same things Monroe already had. Monroe was getting ahead in life; Owen felt himself standing still.

It was natural for Owen to resent it when Jack Ironwood started moving Monroe up through the guard ranks, first to sergeant of the guard, then lieutenant. Owen knew he was as good as Monroe. He had as much time in at it and he had worked as hard at it. He simply was not the warden's stepson.

Monroe realized how Owen felt. He tried to make it up to him whenever he could. When Monroe was given an assignment, such as the execution detail, and told to select his own men, Owen was always the first one he picked. Owen had been at his side when he supervised the hanging of Theron Verne and of eleven other men, including Andrew Veal. Owen had helped Monroe force Veal's brothers, Roy and Milton, to witness the hanging they tried to prevent; then he had chained the brothers to whipping posts so that Monroe, with Ironwood's permission, could cut their backs to ribbons with a cat-o'-nine for abducting Beth. "If either of you ever come back to Union County,"

Monroe told them when they were revived, "I'll hang you just like I did your brother."

Monroe's attitude toward prisoners changed after the Veal incident. He became less tolerant, more inflexible in his handling of the men. Before, he had always treated decently the convicts with whom he came into contact. After Beth's abduction, he seemed to grow harsher in his relationship with them. When he was promoted to sergeant, he grew worse.

By the time he was made lietenant, Monroe was known in population as a tough, unbending guard. He was no longer liked by any prisoner. The convicts called him "Cobra" because of the upright way he carried his head and the swiftness with which he would strike if a prisoner faulted. He eventually reached the point where he would not walk inside the walls alone. He always took another man to back him up. That other man was usually Owen Landis, whom Monroe finally had promoted to sergeant.

Owen was his bodyguard, his shadow: the watcher who protected his back from any convict who might decide to risk hanging by shoving a shank—a homemade knife—into the guard lieutenant's back.

Owen did not particularly like Monroe, just as Monroe did not feel close to Owen, but for a long time they had a need for each other's support: Monroe because he knew he could depend on Owen; and Owen because, after ten years, he still courted higher promotion. Owen had hoped to become lieutenant when Sam Colson retired and Monroe became captain of the yard. Then, when Ironwood suddenly died, Owen set his sights higher. Monroe would become warden, and *he* would become captain of the yard.

Monroe, however, had other plans.

"I want to quit, Monroe," Sam Colson told him one day after Monroe had been warden for a few months. "I don't like all this lockstep and silent system business. It's turned the prison into a graveyard full of walking corpses."

"Sorry you feel that way, Sam," Monroe said. It was a lie. He had wanted his father-in-law to retire since the day he became warden.

"I'm not sure these new practices of yours are good for the place, Monroe," Colson told him.

"They seem to be working, Sam. We've not had a guard assault, an escape attempt, or any other serious trouble since the day I took over."

Colson shook his head. "I still can't help thinking they're wrong. Those practices are really the only reason I'm thinking of leaving. If things was the way Jack had them, why, hell, I'd stay on and be your yard captain permanently."

"Where do you plan to go, Sam?" Monroe asked—and that was the end of Big Sam Colson's reign as captain of the yard.

The next day Monroe rode down to Kellerman's Saloon to see Boss Lee.

"I've been trying to get you to go to work as a guard since you rescued Beth from the Veal brothers," he told the ex-fighter. "Now I'm offering you something better. The number two job in the whole prison: captain of the yard. Will you take it?"

Lee smiled and shook his head. "Thanks for the offer, but I've no experience for such a job. Isn't there anyone you can promote?"

"I want my own man, somebody I can trust completely. There's too much conflict when you promote from within. It's best to bring in an outsider. When my first stepfather, Mr. Niles, was warden, he brought in Jack Ironwood. When Jack became warden, he brought in Sam Colson. Now I want to bring you in. As for experience, you'll get all you need the first month. The main thing is to be tough, and you're already that." Monroe looked around the saloon. Nearly empty, it had the stale, dull aura of all saloons in the daytime. "You don't want to work here the rest of your life, do you? Or worse, have to serve in the army when the war starts."

"You think there'll be a war, for sure?"

"No question about it. The South won't tolerate Lincoln six months without leaving the Union. But if you're working at the prison, you won't have to worry about it. Governor Donnell is signing a bill making prisonkeepers exempt from serving in state regiments. You can sit out the war just like I'm going to."

Boss Lee thought it over. He had no particular ambitions, and as far as work was concerned, he would as soon stay on at Kellerman's Saloon as do anything else. The job was easy, the drinks free, and the town's whores readily available. It wasn't as bad a life as the new warden seemed to think. On the other hand, service in the army was something to be avoided at all costs. Especially if the country was going to be in a war with itself. He didn't mind a good fight now and again, but not with bullets.

"All right, Warden," he said with a smile, "I'll be your yard captain."

On the day Boss Lee took over the yard, Owen Landis walked into Monroe's office and threw his ring of keys on the desk. "I'm through," he said coldly. "I won't work for no man who sticks a knife in my back."

"Nobody stuck a knife in your back, Owen," Monroe replied quietly.

"I should have had that captain of the yard job and you know it. I earned it. I'm as good a guard as you are."

"Being a good guard has nothing to do with it," said Monroe. "The yard captain job is special; it's above being a guard. Outside men have always been brought in for it." Monroe rose and walked to his window. He looked out on the Little Yard. "I'm going to be making a lot of changes in here, Owen. I need a captain who'll support new policies and practices. You've got too much of Sam Colson in you; I'm afraid you'd resist me."

"That's not what you're afraid of, Monroe," Owen Landis said evenly. "You don't want me up there as your second-in-command because you're afraid I might make you look bad. You know I'm as good a prison administrator as you are; you know if something goes wrong in the way you're running this place, the governor could always remove you and put me in your spot. But with Boss Lee as captain, they won't have anybody to fall back on—not for a few years anyway. They'll *have* to keep you, no matter what you do."

Monroe turned to face him. "You're deluding yourself, Owen. You've never been as good a guard as I was, and you're certainly not qualified to run this prison. No matter how good you *looked*, Owen, there's always been something lacking in you. I don't know what it is; breeding, maybe, or presence of mind—"

"Bullshit, Monroe. The only thing I *don't* have that you *do* have is a goddamned mean streak when it comes to convicts.

You treat them like animals—with this silent system and lock-step—"

"That's exactly my point, Owen," Monroe interrupted. "If you were yard captain, you'd want to run the place just like my father-in-law would have. You wouldn't *want* any changes, any improvements—"

"It's not an improvement when you do things to make prisoners worse instead of better."

"My job isn't to make them better *or* worse," Monroe said firmly. "My job is to *punish* them." He strode angrily back to his desk and snatched up the ring of keys Owen had thrown there. "There's no use arguing with you, Owen. This is how it would be every day if you were yard captain. That's why I picked somebody else." He jerked his head toward the door. "Go see the paymaster; he'll pay you what you've got coming."

"Sure," Owen Landis said. "I'll go see the paymaster. I'll get what I've got coming. And one of these days, Monroe, you'll get what you've got coming, too."

Owen Landis stalked from the room.

For a while after Owen left, Monroe sat at his desk drumming silent fingertips on its surface. Owen was weak, he told himself. Weak and not too smart. Just like Sam Colson had been. Both of them were satisfied to simply keep the convicts imprisoned, nothing more. Work them all day, keep them locked up all night. And when their sentences were up, turn them loose.

But there was more to it than that. Monroe knew it, just as Ironwood had known it. The prisoners were there to be *punished*, and mere labor and lockup were not enough. Ironwood had supplemented it with the daily discipline court: the lash and the hole for infractions of the rules or malingering. But even that was not enough, Monroe felt. Special punishment for a dozen or so men every day served as a good example to the rest, but it also let the rest of the men go comparatively *un*punished. Systematic, regimented punishment, such as Monroe was now initiating, was the best way. Punishment that affected *every* prisoner, *every* day. Such as the silent system, which made the convict's lonely world even lonelier; and the lockstep, which further reduced him from an individual to just another cipher. On the surface, the new practices were for the purpose of orderliness and discipline. But their real purpose, as Monroe well knew, was premeditated group punishment. Steady and relentless.

What Sam Colson and Owen Landis did not understand, Monroe decided, was that the warden of a prison was, in a sense, much like a deity, a god. He had absolute control over the lives and existence of the prisoners sent to him. And it was his duty to exercise that control. If he did not—if he merely *kept* the prisoners instead of constantly finding new ways to punish them—then he was not a warden, merely a keeper.

He, Monroe Van Hawn, was determined to be a *warden*. A proper warden.

No matter who had to suffer in the process.

CHAPTER 24

When the Civil War was in its fourth month, Governor Donnell telegraphed Monroe to come to the state capital for a conference.

"What in the world do you suppose he wants?" Beth asked at the supper table.

"Don't know," said Monroe. "Whatever it is must be important, though, for him to call me all the way up there."

"Maybe it is and maybe it isn't," Dru interjected. "Carter Lehman called your stepfather up there one time just to get his opinion of a new brace of pistols he'd received from Germany."

"Which one of Monroe's stepdaddies was that, Mother Dru?" Beth asked, feigning curiosity.

"Warden Ironwood," Dru said coolly. They all lived in the mansion together now, even though Dru and Beth could barely tolerate each other.

"My goodness, with all the husbands you've had," Beth said, "I declare I think it would simplify conversation if we just gave them numbers."

It would simplify conversation a lot more if we could gag you, Dru thought. She ignored the remark and leaned over to wipe her grandson Nathan's chin. "This child eats just like Grover used to," she said to herself, half complaining, half reminiscing.

"I'll bet the governor wants to talk to you about something to do with the war," Beth said.

"Possibly," Monroe allowed. "Boss Lee and I discussed that this afternoon. We wondered if maybe they'd devised an early release program of some kind to get men for military service. There's a rumor that Lincoln's asked the Congress to authorize an army of half a million men. Some states might have a hard time filling their quotas."

"Well, I don't care what he wants you for," Beth said. "It's enough for me just to get a trip to the capital. Anything to get away from this penitentiary for awhile."

"You aren't going," Monroe said.

"Just why not?" Beth demanded.

"Because it's not a pleasure trip, it's a business trip," Monroe said. "I'm going straight up and straight back. No time for dallying."

"I'll just bet!" Beth snapped. She threw down her napkin, rose, and left the table. At the dining room door, she turned and said, "I hope you enjoy yourself at Simmie Lou Holcom's Hotel for Gentlemen, which is where you'll no doubt spend the night. I also hope you get all you want while you're there, because you won't be getting any at home for a while!"

She stormed out, slamming the door behind her.

"What a pleasant, genteel girl," said Dru. "You're very fortunate, Monroe."

"All right, Mother."

"What won't you be getting at home for a while, Daddy?" asked little Nathan.

"Nothing," said Monroe.

"That's right," said Dru.

Monroe could not help laughing at that, and Dru laughed with him. Then Nathan, who was an extremely good-natured little boy and oddly reminded Dru a great deal of Aaron, joined in and they all laughed together.

Monroe went to Prisontown early the next morning to catch the first coach north. He took his mount to Polk's Livery for Kee to take care of. The old Sac was past sixty now. His squaw had died and he lived alone in a shack behind the stables. He drank a lot and kept mostly to himself. Once a week he put on his best store-bought shirt and climbed the hill to the mansion to visit Dru for an hour. She usually sent him back home with a tow sack full of preserves and salt pork and fresh greens from her garden.

"Mother's been asking for you, Kee," Monroe said as he led his horse inside. "She says you're overdue for a visit."

"Kee go up hill today," he said. "For last time."

"What do you mean?"

"Kee die soon."

"Rot," Monroe said with a grunt. "You'll live to be a hundred."

Kee shook his head. "No. Die soon."

"Are you sick?" Monroe asked, frowning now.

"Not sick. Just know. Dreams tell Kee. Die soon."

Monroe smiled. So that was it. Dreams. "Don't drink so much firewater before you go to bed, Kee. Then you won't have bad dreams."

Monroe started to leave. Kee followed him outside. With one arm, the Indian made a sweeping gesture that included all of Prisontown. "Many die soon," he said.

Monroe stared at him. Kee's expression had not changed at all. But there was something about the tone of his voice that struck Monroe as odd. Before he could question him further, Kee went back into the stable.

Monroe carried his grip next door to the coach station. Sitting inside, a day bag at her feet, was Clara Landis. Monroe removed his hat.

"Hello, Clara. How are you?"

"Hello, Monroe. I'm fine. And you?"

"Very well, thank you. Are you traveling?"

"Yes. Up to Corinth to visit an aunt who's been ill."

"Well, we'll be traveling companions for a few hours then. May I sit down?"

"Of course."

Monroe sat, slightly at an angle so that they could continue talking if Clara wanted to. This was the first time he had seen her since Owen had left the guards, and the first time they had had the opportunity to converse in probably a year or more. Monroe felt a little sorry for Clara, her being married to Owen, who he had decided would be a failure. He studied her for a moment, looking at the strawberry hair and the field of freckles that went down her dress, and remembering what Beth had said about her being a country girl. She was certainly not a beauty. Not nearly as pretty as Beth. As a matter of fact, she's really a touch homely, he decided. But there was a certain softness about her that made him feel pleasant sitting there next to her.

"How is Owen?" he asked, deciding to continue the conversation himself.

"He was well the last I heard," Clara said.

"The last you heard?"

"Yes. Owen is in the army. Hadn't you heard?"

"No, I hadn't."

"He volunteered a week after he left the prison."

"Which army?" Monroe asked.

"Union, of course. He was commissioned a lieutenant."

Didn't get to be a captain there either, Monroe thought. "Where is he?"

"Near Louisville, Kentucky. But they expect to be marching into Tennessee very soon."

Monroe nodded. "Well, I wish him good luck," he said. "Sincerely. Owen and I had our differences there at the end, but I hold no animosity for him at all. Nor for you, Clara."

"Thank you, Monroe," Clara said gravely, suppressing a smile. Saved from a fate worse than death, she thought: Monroe Van Hawn's animosity.

She was relieved to see the coach arrive and end the conversation.

At the capital, Governor Donnell introduced Monroe to Major General Grommand of the Quartermaster Corps, and a man named Edgar Sledd, who called himself a manufacturing engineer.

"Warden, an executive decision has been made to volunteer the labor services of our state prison to aid the war effort of the Union," the governor told him at the start of the meeting. "General Grommand here is in charge of procurement for the states of Iowa, Illinois, Missouri, and Indiana. His most pressing need in the near future is going to be barrels: plain old ordinary wooden barrels. According to the general, they are one of the most essential items necessary to the efficient operation of the army. Isn't that so, General?"

"Very definitely," said Grommand. He was a beefy man with a salt-and-pepper beard, out of which protruded a poorly rolled cheroot. "Without barrels, the goddamned infantry and cavalry would come to a dead stop," he told them. "Hell, everything from gunpowder to privy lye comes in barrels. Couldn't run a war without them."

"Well, we're here to see that you don't have to try," the governor said solemnly. Alfred Donnell was a small, sincere-looking man who reminded many people of a minister. He had a habit of holding his hands together prayer-fashion when he talked. "Mr. Sledd here is going to show us how to convert part of Prison Hill into a barrel factory. Monroe, do you have that diagram I asked you to bring?"

"Yes, sir." Monroe unfolded a large sheet of heavy-gauge map paper on the table. On it was a complete, top-view schematic of the Hill.

Edgar Sledd studied the drawing intently for several moments, then narrowed his attention to the Little Yard. "This area here seems to be outside the main prison enclosure. What is it used for?"

"That's the original yard enclosure," Monroe explained. "When the prison was first built, that's all there was to it. Now it's called the Little Yard. It's used for female prisoners—that's their dormitory here; and this small cell house over here is used to hold condemned men or extremely dangerous prisoners."

Of course, I'd have to actually see the place," Sledd said to the governor, "but from the diagram I'd say this Little Yard, as it's called, looks like a perfect location. If arrangements can be made to put the women prisoners and condemned men somplace else—"

"How many women do you have down there now, Monroe?" the governor asked.

"Twelve. And two condemned men."

Donnell put his hands together and tilted his head an inch. "A total of fourteen persons. Well, I think we can make other arrangements for them. We certainly can't let fourteen persons hold up an important war project like this, can we? What do you think, Monroe?"

"Sir, I wonder if I might speak to you in private for a moment?" Monroe said.

"I suppose so, yes," said Donnell. "Excuse us, gentlemen. A state matter."

They went out into the hall.

"Governor, I can put the men in the big cell house," Monroe

said, "but I'm not sure I can accommodate the women." He mustered his thoughts very quickly to see just how much he could get out of this situation. "If the legislature hadn't turned down my request to build that new block—"

"Some of the state representatives were reluctant to approve an appropriation to provide cells for women," Donnell said.

Monroe shrugged. "They're criminals too, Governor. They really should be in cells. In the dormitory arrangement we have now, there's very little control over them. I get reports about, ah, unusual practices they engage in. If such a thing ever became public—"

"What exactly did you ask for in that request?" the governor wanted to know.

"A budget to construct a single block of fifty cells. Twenty-five general confinement cells for women on one tier, backed up by twenty-five special cells for condemned men and discipline problems—"

"Money, Monroe," the governor said impatiently. "How much money?"

"Fifty thousand."

Donnell pursed his lips. "Suppose I can bully through a special appropriation for you, how long would it take for construction? Don't forget now that you've got a prison hospital ward to build; that's an appropriation you *did* get."

"The hospital can wait," Monroe said. "I think I can have the new block up in six months."

"Do it in four and I'll get you the money."

Monroe did some rapid calculating. Working the quarry fifteen hours a day instead of twelve, tightening up on layoffs for sickness, increasing all convict work quotas—he could make it. "Four months it'll be," he said.

They started back into the office.

"Monroe," the governor said, "wait around after the meeting, will you? I want you to tell me about the, ah—unusual practices in that women's dormitory—"

It was pouring rain the next morning when Monroe left Simmie Lou Holcom's Hotel for Gentlemen and hurried across the square to the coach station. He had spent the night with a charming quadroon from New Orleans, whose conversation he had enjoyed as much as her body, something he had not been able to say about his wife for some time.

The meeting with Governor Donnell and the other two men had gone well. Edgar Sledd would be visiting the Hill in a week to make sketches of the Little Yard and its buildings, preparatory to designing a barrel-making operation to fit the premises. General Grommand had been promised his first consignment of barrels, delivered to the army's St. Louis warehouse complex, in seven months.

Monroe wondered how much money would go into the governor's pocket as a result of this "war effort" to which he had pledged the state prison. The military would probably pay full price for the merchandise, just as if it had been manufactured by a private firm. From that price would be deducted the cost of the machinery and material, to keep the state treasury from showing a deficit for it. There would be no labor costs: convicts did not get paid. And no overhead: the prison was supported by general taxes. No transportation costs: the army had river barges to deliver the wood and pick up the finished barrels. About seventy percent of what the Quartermaster Corps paid for the product would be clean profit, Monroe estimated.

Someone is going to get rich off this arrangement, he thought as he waited to board the coach. Not that it mattered to him. He knew he could have a share of it merely by indicating that he was interested; but he was not. His mother was well off and so was he: the combined estates of Aaron, Clement Niles, and Jack Ironwood had seen to that. And being warden provided an almost expense-free existence: the mansion, food, domestic help, horses, buggies, firearms, ammunition—it was all provided by the state. All he really had to buy was his clothes.

What *did* interest Monroe was the prison. *His* prison. Doing to it the things he wanted to do; making of it what he wanted to make of it. He had been corresponding with other wardens for a year now, mostly in the eastern United States, England, France, and Germany. From them he had elicited suggestions for improving Prison Hill: ways to better security, discipline, punishment; ways to increase productivity, lower the cost of food, clothing, and medical treatment, reduce convict independence. From German wardens he learned new methods of rigid regulation, iron subjection, strict control. From the French he learned the philosophy of encouraging hostility and friction among the prisoners, for the purpose of keeping unity down. From the British he learned how to propagate a constant state of fear in the convict population: fear of punishment, loss of food, deprivation of the dubious sanctuary of one's cell, and the ultimate threat: extension of a man's sentence—something a warden had the power to do. All these things Monroe studied, and studied diligently.

Monroe's consuming desire was to make Prison Hill the most admired penitentiary in the country—from the point of view of other wardens, of lawmen, judges, prosecutors; and the most feared—from the point of view of the criminal. Someday, he thought in deepest secret, he would write a great book on the science of keeping men. It would be written as a tribute to what he had done on the Hill: how he had forged an ordinary prison into a classic penitentiary. Wardens, he told himself, would study it for a hundred years.

"Southbound coach! All aboard!" yelled a raspy-voiced driver, terminating Monroe's daydreaming. He turned his collar up against the pouring rain and climbed into the big Concord. There were only four other passengers besides himself in the nine-passenger coach. He took a window seat, lashed the leather curtain down tightly, and rested his head back to sleep. Although it was early in the day, his eyelids felt very heavy. The quadroon girl, he thought. He had stayed awake most of the night talking to her.

He was asleep before the coach was a mile out of town.

Monroe awoke in midafternoon when the Concord pulled into Corinth. He could barely believe he had slept so long and so deeply on a rolling, bouncing, lurching coach. But there out the window, barely visible in a now driving rain, was the Corinth depot.

And waiting there to board was Clara Landis.

Monroe jumped off to help her aboard. He put her day bag through the window, then took the shawl from her shoulders and held it over her tent-fashion while she climbed inside.

"Welcome to Noah's Ark," he said, wiping the water from his face.

"Isn't this terrible?" Clara said. "A man in the station said the

river was halfway to the top of the levee in Chester Village."
"It's a bad rain, all right," Monroe agreed. "Worst I've ever seen."
There were only three other passengers heading south from Corinth, so Monroe and Clara had the back of the coach to themselves. Monroe lashed the window curtains tightly again and they settled down for what was supposed to be the remaining four hours of the journey. The torrent outside continued to beat a relentless tattoo on the coach's top and Monroe noticed that they were not moving as fast as they had earlier in the day. At this speed, he thought, Prisontown was probably five or six hours away.
An hour out of Corinth, Clara asked Monroe if he was hungry.
"I'm starving," he said. "I slept through a meal stop sometime today."
Clara opened her bag. "I have a few things in here that my aunt gave me."
She had a brick of spiced yellow cheese, a loaf of dark moist bread wrapped in muslin, jars of peach and strawberry preserves, and a small, lidded basket of salt pork.
"My God," said Monroe, "this is a miracle. You've saved the life of a dying man. You're an angel, Clara Landis."
She blushed but smiled a pleased smile and arranged the food on the leather seat between them. They began to eat, she doing little more than nibbling, he wolfing down great slices of the bread and pork. Presently Clara stopped eating altogether and devoted herself to spreading preserves on bread and slicing cheese for him. He protested but she explained that she had eaten shortly before she boarded the coach. After that, Monroe did not argue further; he just ate. When he began to get full, he slowed down a bit and enjoyed it more. He leaned back against one side of the coach and smiled. "This is nice, Clara. Very nice."
"Yes," she said quietly.
Their hands touched once as he helped her put the remaining food, what little there was, back in order. "I feel like a hog," he said. "Did you see how much I ate?"
"You were hungry."
"Your poor aunt. Little did she suspect that most of her food wouldn't even make it to Chester Village."
When the coach arrived at Chester, the other three passengers

got off and rushed through the rain into the station. The driver swung down and stuck his head in the door. "If you folks was to stop the night here in Chester, we'd none of us have to fight this squall anymore today."

"Our tickets are for Prisontown," Monroe said. "It's only another hour down the road."

"The way this rain's coming down, I ain't sure there *is* a road no more."

"Let's find out, driver," Monroe said authoritatively.

They pulled out of Chester. As soon as they were well south of town, the rain seemed to increase. Monroe opened a forward curtain so they could see out but not get wet. Along the river side of the road, the water had flowed over the bank all the way up to their wheels.

"I wonder how the levee's holding in Prisontown," Monroe said.

"Do you think there's a chance it might wash out?" Clara asked.

"In this kind of deluge, anything's liable to wash out." He gave silent thanks that his prison was on high ground.

Halfway between Chester and Prisontown, they saw a sternwheeler caught in a whirlpool in the middle of the river. The powerful twist of water caught the boat by its bow and spun it around like so much driftwood. The boat held together during the first spin and no damage was done except for freight thrown overboard from the lower deck. But the second time around, the boat's hull split and two upper-deck supports snapped like twigs. When that happened, the whole boat began coming apart. Monroe and Clara watched in horror as it was crushed by the force of the water. From the passenger deck, scores of people were swept into the raging river.

"Oh my God," Clara said, white-faced.

Monroe stared mutely as the flood carried the boat away in a dozen directions.

"Those poor people," Clara said. Tears welled in her eyes. Monroe put his arm around her. Sadly, she leaned her cheek against his shoulder.

A little while later, the coach reined up and the driver swung down again. "We're 'bout a mile out of Prisontown!" he yelled above the pounding of the rain. "But we can't go no further—the bridge is out!"

Monroe turned up his collar again and pulled his hat down an inch. He left the coach and trudged forward a few yards with the driver. They stopped at the brink of a gap in the land where a wide creek coursed in from the river. Part of a bridge still hung over the gap on the side nearest them; but on the opposite bank the bridge pilings had washed away, dropping that end of the bridge timbers into the water.

Monroe hurried back to the coach. "The coach can't get through," he told Clara. "I'll have the driver take you back to Chester."

"Take me back? What about you?" Her eyes grew wide with apprehension.

"I'm going to try to get through. There's a footbridge over this creek about half a mile inland."

"Suppose you get lost?"

"I know the woods around here pretty well. I used to play in them every day." He saw that she was uneasy. He patted her clasped hands. "Don't worry. You'll be all right. The road is fine all the way back to Chester." He reached for his grip.

"Monroe, let me go with you," she said urgently. "Please."

He started to say no, but there was something in the way she spoke that stopped him. Her voice had a tremor to it, a catch, like that of a child asking for something that was very important. He looked out at the rain. "You'll get soaked to the skin," he told her.

"I don't care. I'd rather be soaking wet and be with you than dry and all alone in this coach on the road to Chester."

Monroe stared at her for a moment, studying the pleading in her eyes. Then he nodded brusquely. "All right." He put her day bag next to his grip.

Monroe told the driver what they were going to do and they got out on the side of the road. As the driver led his lead horse around to turn the coach, Monroe and Clara hurried into the woods. Monroe carried both bags and Clara followed a pace behind him, clutching to his coattail. As soon as they got into the trees, they had some protection from the rain. The treetops were heavily overgrown, many of their branches intertwined up high to form a natural roof. On the ground, much of the scrub, pine needles, and cones were still relatively dry.

"This isn't as bad as I thought it would be!" Clara shouted.

"Not so far," Monroe said. He glanced at the rapidly rising creek, fearing that if the rain kept up, the floor of the forest would soon be covered with water.

They pressed on along a fairly straight path that took them uphill on a grade so gradual that at first Clara did not notice that the stream was dropping below them. When she did, after they were forty feet up, she became frightened. "I—I'm afraid of high pla—places, Monroe—" she said, gripping his coattail more tightly.

"It's all right," he told her. "The path goes back down to the creek just ahead. That's where the bridge is."

He was right, and Clara began to feel much better as soon as they started down. Although they were still under the partial protection of the overgrowth, both were now wet to the skin. A wind had begun blowing, too, whipping through the woods in sudden, short gusts. They both knew that it was the evening wind. Nightfall was coming.

"There's the footbridge!" Monroe yelled.

It lay just ahead of them, a narrow strip of raw slats woven together with hemp lashings. It swayed precariously in the wind. In its middle, where it sagged the lowest, the rushing stream already covered its bottom.

"Is it safe?" Clara yelled.

"Come on, we've got to hurry!" Monroe said, not answering her.

When they got to the bridge, Monroe put the two bags in one hand and put his free arm around Clara's waist to steady her.

"Careful now—one step at a time!" he said.

Almost hesitantly, they stepped onto the slats and started across. Clara gripped the rope rail with both hands. Water lapped at their feet. Their bodies swayed with the bridge. A gust of wind swept over them from the direction of the river. They looked down at the threatening water, both terrified.

"M-M-Monroe—I don't think—we can make it—" Clara managed to say.

"I—don't—either—" Monroe answered. "Turn—back—"

They groped their way around to return to shore. As they did,

Monroe saw a large swell coming in from the river; an eight-foot wall of water, heading directly at them.

"Hurry!" he said, half pulling Clara off the bridge and back up the bank. He stumbled and fell to his knees, and she helped him back up. The wind preceding the swell engulfed them but they managed to stumble into the shelter of the trees. From there they watched as the big swell coursed into the footbridge and carried it away.

"Jesus!" Monroe said hoarsely. He slumped against a tree. Clara, limp with fatigue, slumped against him.

Monroe led her to a cave on a bluff twenty feet above the rising stream. He spread the clumped scrub from the entrance with a long stick and poked around inside for animal life. There was no response to the stick.

"It's empty, thank God." He tossed the bags inside, crawled in himself, and pulled Clara in after him.

It was very dark inside and smelled like dead wildflowers. But it was dry and free from the wind. Monroe and Clara huddled together against a side wall, sitting on a layer of pine needles that had blown in over the years.

"My brother Grover found this cave twenty years ago," Monroe said, shivering.

"I didn't know you had a brother."

"I don't anymore. He's dead." He felt Clara shivering also. "There used to be a fire pit back here somewhere."

Standing up, he felt along the wall to the back of the cave and explored with the toe of one boot until he located a hole in the ground lined with rocks. A brief, sad thought of Grover passed over him as he remembered his brother building the pit. Kneeling, he scooped the pit free of pine needles.

At the front of the cave, Monroe reached outside and pulled up some scrub that grew far enough inside to still be dry. He broke up enough to fill the fire pit and selected a smooth stone for a striker. In the very limited light he had, he hovered over the pit and began striking the top stone. On the fifth strike, the scrub caught a spark. Monroe blew gently on it until a tiny flame rose.

Clara sneezed twice as he went back to where she sat. He dropped to his knees in front of her. The fire spreading in the pit threw a half light on them.

"We have to get these wet clothes off," he said quietly.

"Yes, I know."

"Do you think anything's dry in your bag?"

She shook her head. "It's just a cloth day bag; I'm sure the water went directly through."

"My grip's leather; I'll get you some dry things out of it. Why don't you go back by the fire and, uh—"

"All right."

Monroe stripped to the waist and dried his upper body with the shirt he had worn on the trip up. Then he sat down and, with some difficulty, pulled off his wet boots and stockings. He dried his feet, trying not to look at Clara.

At the rear of the cave, her back to him, Clara removed her gown and petticoats. She hung them as neatly as possible on rock crags on the wall. Then, in pantalettes, corset, and high shoes, she crouched by the crackling fire. "Have you found anything dry for me yet?" she asked.

Monroe rummaged in the open grip and got out his extra trousers and a clean shirt. He took them to her.

"Do you have something for yourself?" she asked.

"A set of long flannels," he said. Standing over her, he saw that the field of freckles on her neck continued far down her bosom. She noticed him looking and blushed. Avoiding his eyes, she stood up.

"I'm sorry," Monroe said. "I'll get you something to dry on." He brought her the towel from his grip. As he handed it to her, his glance fell to her bosom again. And again she saw him.

"I wish you wouldn't stare," she said quietly.

"I can't help it. I've never seen a woman with so many freckles."

"They're ugly," she said.

"They are not. They're lovely. You're lovely, Clara."

They were standing close, between the fire pit and the cave wall. Clara looked down at the fire, then up at Monroe. Her eyes reflected the flames. She looked away, uncertainty in her face. Monroe took her hand. She did not pull away. He stepped closer. She did not move. He put a hand on her bare upper arm and stroked the wet skin.

"Look at me," he said.

She did. He bent his face to hers, covered her mouth, encircled her with his arms.

Clara dropped the clothes and towel he had given her. Her hands flattened on his naked back. She returned his kiss as fervently as he gave it.

The fire in the pit danced higher. Monroe drew back and opened the front laces of her corset. It fell away from her. He lowered her bodice and saw that the field of freckles spread over both breasts, surrounding her dark, lumpy nipples.

Monroe kissed her breasts, drew her gently to the bed of pine needles, and pulled the pantalettes off over her high shoes.

Outside, the water continued to rise.

CHAPTER 25

In January of 1864, Druscilla Foyle Van Hawn Niles Ironwood celebrated her fifty-fifth birthday. One of her oldest and dearest friends, Dr. Gilbert Robin, offered the initial toast to her.

"I propose that we raise our glasses," he said, "to one of the truly finest ladies this state and this community will ever have the pleasure and honor of calling a citizen. She has been a friend to all who ever needed her, whether that person was a free man or convict, white man, black man, or Indian, good man or bad, and—in my case—drunk man or sober."

The other guests at the big table laughed respectfully. Doc's penchant for whiskey was almost a legend in Prisontown now. Everyone still agreed that he was drinking himself to death, but after twenty-five years of clucking their tongues about it, they allowed that the funeral was probably not imminent.

"No more gallant lady has ever, nor *will* ever, trod the paths of our homes and our hearts as this one has," Doc continued. "We have rejoiced with her at births and mourned with her at deaths, and at each she has shown a humanity and a heart that was both admirable and enviable. We celebrate with her tonight the fifty-fifth anniversary of her birth, and in raising our glasses to honor her, let us wish her many more years of good health and happiness."

The guests drank, put down their glasses, and gave her a hearty round of applause. Dru smiled happily and raised her own glass in a silent toast to Doc.

The mansion dining room had never had more guests in it at

any time in the prison's history. As her eyes darted around the big table, she could not help being pleased at the number of friends she had. There was Grover, Aaron's friend from the old days of posting handbills to get Alton Monroe elected lieutenant governor. Lanky, stooped, his mane of red hair turned white, Grover was now sixty-seven. He was one of the wealthiest men in the state, with extensive real estate holdings, and had never married.

The Pullman brothers were also there, having come down from their headquarters in Chicago. They now had a string of thirty stores all the way out to California, as well as a thriving mail-order business.

With Doc, of course, was Cordelia Walls, still comely and vivacious, still Doc's mistress, housekeeper, nurse, and companion after two decades.

And on around the table, others who had settled in the town below the prison and, for one reason or another, had stayed on: Lettie Carmichael, who ran her mother's bakery and whose father had been a convict; young Peter Swann, a second-generation Prisontown butcher; the two Harrys—Fogel, the shoemaker, and Berg, the dry goods merchant—now proprietors of Berg and Fogel's Department Store; Elouise Starwell, who managed the ladies' section of the store for them, and whose highwayman husband Luke had died a convict; Nell Dohrman, the daughter of Letitia Herraday, now a twenty-three-year-old St. Louis beauty who still did not know who her real mother was, but who, Dru was determined, would at least meet her mother before this night was over; and Sid Polk, the livery stable owner who had, at Jack Ironwood's urging, given a job to Kee when the Indian finally completed his prison term.

Kee was dead now, drowned in the flood two years earlier that had destroyed half of Prisontown. He had visited Dru the day before the rains started and told her, as he had told Monroe, that he would die soon. Dru had dismissed his predictions of death as the mutterings of a senile old man who was still half savage. Nevertheless, she had finally allowed him to wring a promise from her that she would not leave the Hill until the sun shone again. It was cloudy when she promised—and the sun did not shine again for four days. By that time the flood was over, half the town was floating south in a mass of debris on the Big Muddy, and sixty-seven persons had drowned, including the Sac-and-Fox Indian Kee-te-ha, who had mysteriously known of the flood in advance.

Dru wisely did not tell people what Kee had said to her: she knew if they did not believe her, they would think she was crazy; and if they *did* believe her, they would be angry that she had not warned them. The only one she confided in was Boss Lee, with whom she had become fast friends since his arrival as Monroe's captain of the yard. Dru had taken to the young ex-prizefighter at once. His natural toughness, combined with an instinctive gentleness, reminded her so much of Ironwood. The flat nose and unattractive face, particularly when lighted up by his quick smile, endeared him to her all the more, and soon he had become her obvious favorite and confidant.

To Lee, Dru became an informally adopted mother of sorts, a replacement for the real mother he had lost in the famine in Ireland when he was a boy. Lee was fascinated by her long tenure on the Hill and by the stories she told of the prison's early days. Often, when she invited him for tea in the evenings, she would read to him selected passages from the diary she had kept for twenty-seven years. Before long, she had become a living legend to Boss Lee and he guarded her reputation and position with a fervent jealousy. There came a time when even Monroe learned not to criticize his mother in Lee's presence.

Fully aware of the yard captain's intense devotion and loyalty to her, Dru was not above using it for her own purposes. She planned to do so on the night of her birthday party. After dinner, she caught Lee alone at the punchbowl.

"Gerald, will you do something for me, please?" she asked. She insisted on calling him Gerald, just as she always called Doc Robin by his given name Gilbert. "I'd like you to go get Letitia Herraday out of lockup and bring her to the kitchen."

"What for?" he asked, eyeing her suspiciously. She had involved him in her schemes before.

"Oh, just as a birthday present for me," she said vaguely.

"I already gave you a present," he reminded her, nodding at a hammered silver necklace she wore. It had been made for him by the man in New York who made championship belts for the bare-knuckle fighters.

"Yes, and it's the nicest gift of my whole birthday," she

praised, fingering it lovingly. "Truly. I'm leaving instructions at once that I want to be buried in it. But this other little favor—well, I'm doing it for my godchild."

"Nell?" He glanced across the room at the beautiful young girl, who was the delight of the party. "What's she got to do with Letitia Herraday?"

Dru told him. Boss Lee was surprised but not stunned. Nothing that Dru was involved in was shocking to him anymore.

"Will you do it, Gerald?" she asked, those great round eyes of hers filled with instant pleading.

"You know I will," he said gruffly.

Twenty minutes later, Lee accompanied Letitia across the compound and into the mansion kitchen. Dru had her put on an apron and set her to work washing and slicing strawberries for the next morning's breakfast. "Now just act natural," she told Letitia, "as if you work here all the time. The rest of you," she said to the regular kitchen help, "go on about your business as usual."

Lee loitered in a corner drinking coffee. Several minutes later Dru returned with Nell Dohrman. "It's really a very modern kitchen," she was saying to the girl. "My first husband, Aaron, had the original room built, but since then it's been remodeled twice." She took Nell's arm and guided her toward the table where Letitia was working. "Hello, Letitia," she said casually. "This is my godchild, Nell. Dear, this is Mrs. Herraday."

"Hello, Mrs. Herraday," the girl said, smiling and holding out her hand.

"Hello, Miss," Letitia said. She quickly dried her own hands and accepted the hand Nell offered. Shyly, she turned her eyes to Dru. "She's lovely, Miss Dru."

"Yes, she is."

"Thank you, you're sweet," said Nell, squeezing Letitia's hand.

As they were talking, Monroe came in. "Mother, have you seen Boss Lee—" He stopped, his eyes sweeping over everyone. A scowl shadowed his expression.

"Here I am, Warden," said Boss Lee, crossing the kitchen.

Dru pretended to ignore her son and continued showing Nell the kitchen. Letitia, redfaced, kept her eyes on the work she was doing.

Monroe turned narrowed eyes on Lee. "You're going to bend a rule too far someday, Boss," he said quietly.

"No harm was done, Warden," said Lee, locking eyes with Monroe.

Monroe was the superior; he could discharge Boss Lee anytime, and they both knew it. They knew something else also: that in a matter involving Dru, it just might come to that, because the yard captain would never back down. Monroe did not want to lose Boss Lee, so he had no choice but to drop the matter. "Take her back to her cell," he said.

"Sure thing, Warden. Soon's the ladies leave."

Dru and Nell came around the other side of the big kitchen and Dru sent the girl back to the party. Boss Lee took a weeping Letitia out the back door.

"Someday," Monroe said to his mother, "you're going to get that man fired for doing things he shouldn't do."

Dru kissed his cheek. "We all do things we shouldn't do, darling," she replied easily. "Which reminds me, why didn't you invite Clara Landis tonight? I've always liked her."

Monroe's jaw clenched. His mother managed to get him every time. "Beth took care of the invitations. Ask her."

"It doesn't really matter," Dru shrugged. "I'm sure she had her reasons."

Beth did have her reasons. She had brought them up earlier that evening, as they were getting ready for the party. "Do you deny that you've been seeing Clara Landis?" she asked, tight-lipped.

"I don't *deny* anything," Monroe replied aloofly. "I don't have to. You've been listening to town gossip again."

"Town gossip, is that all it is? When every time you go to St. Louis, *she* goes to St. Louis!"

"I can't help what she does, Beth. And I have to go to St. Louis for production meetings with the army. There *is* a war going on, you know."

"Monroe, I give you fair warning," she said coldly. "If I ever catch you with that—that country whore!—or if I can ever prove that you've been sleeping with her, I'll leave you. I'll take Nathan and leave you!"

"*You* might leave me, Beth," Monroe replied evenly, "but

you'll never take my son away, and I wouldn't advise you to try."

"Oh, no?" she defied him. "Just what would you do about it?"

Monroe walked over to her, his brilliant blue eyes—Theron Verne's eyes—flat and hard, his lips so like Dru's drawn to a line. "I'll have you taken inside the walls and locked up, Beth. In a deep-lock cell in the women's section. With strict orders that no one but me is ever to enter it."

"You couldn't do that. The law wouldn't permit it—"

"*I'm* the law on Prison Hill," he snapped. "The *only* law. I can do any goddamned thing inside those walls that I want to. And I'll do that to you if you ever try to take Nathan away from here."

Beth stared at him in horror. He *could* do it, she knew. And he would.

She never again mentioned taking Nathan away.

But she mentioned Clara Landis as often as she got the chance.

In St. Louis, Monroe and Clara stayed at the Abernathy Hotel. Clara arrived on either the morning coach before Monroe got there, or the late evening coach after he had checked in. She always engaged a parlor suite, and Monroe took a small room on the same floor. The hotel, which was very busy due to the war, either did not notice their consistently coincidental arrivals, or was quietly discreet about it. Whichever the case, there was never any problem at the Abernathy, and the lovers spent many idyllic moments there.

Monroe used his room only to bathe and change. The rest of the time he was in the suite with Clara. They cavorted around in dressing gowns, lounged in foam-filled hot tubs together, had meals sent in so they could eat in bed, and in general made a temporary but total escape from their other lives.

"I love being alone with you," Clara told him each time they were together.

"And I with you," Monroe always replied.

They were very much in love, so much that it seemed impossible that either of them could ever have loved anyone else. When Monroe was with Clara, everything else completely disappeared from his mind: Beth, the prison, the war, all of it. And when Clara was with Monroe, the horrible guilt of what she was doing found itself smothered by her love for him.

With his head in her lap, she often studied his face while she played with his hair. Once he caught her at it. "Why are you staring at me?" he asked.

"Because I love you," she said. "And because I find it so hard to understand the things that are said about you."

"What things?" He did not really have to ask; he was well aware of his reputation.

"They say you're a cruel man. That you enjoy punishing the prisoners. That you've got a vicious streak—"

"Oh, I have that, all right," he replied bitterly. "Put there, I might add, by the same kind of men I'm accused of mistreating. Convicts! Convicts who kidnaped my wife, tied her to a chair, and fondled her tits like she was a common whore. Convicts who rejoiced when Jack Ironwood died and part of my mother died with him. Convicts who rape, rob, and kill on the outside, then plot and conspire against authority on the inside. Oh, I have a vicious streak, all right—and I mean to keep it."

Clara cradled his head to her bosom and gently rocked him. "Hush now," she cooed. "That's not the Monroe I know, or want to know." She stroked his hair. "*My* Monroe is gentle and kind and loves to tease. He picks wildflowers for me when we walk in the woods. He saves bread crumbs for the birds when we picnic. He sees to it that the families of his guards who are away at war never want for anything. He loves his son as much as any father ever has. And he loves me—as tenderly and softly as any man ever loved a woman. That's *my* Monroe."

Neither Monroe or Clara ever broached the subject of the future. Monroe knew that his deteriorating relationship with Beth would someday have to be resolved, just as Clara knew in her heart that someday Owen would come home from the war. But neither wanted to talk about it; both knew nothing could be done, so why bother? When the future arrived, they would deal with it as best they could. Meanwhile they enjoyed St. Louis whenever they could.

Monroe's business in the bustling wartime city was with Major General Grommand, who was still buying barrels and kegs that were turned out by the convicts on Prison Hill. The quartermaster officer met with all civilian contractors twice each month to check production figures and adjust the contractors' supplies to meet the army's demands. The war was going well for the Union: Grant had been made general-in-chief, Sheridan had defeated and killed Jeb Stuart, and Sherman was moving like slow death across Georgia. Another six months, everyone predicted.

"The goddamned Confederates are whipped already," Grommand told Monroe one day at their meeting. "Hell, their quartermaster must be completely out of *everything* by now. Supply depots are probably as empty as an old maid's brush. I'll bet they haven't *seen* any new barrels or kegs in a year. It's just like I told you before, Warden, it's us men in the Quartermaster's who win the goddamned wars, not the cavalry or the infantry." He laughed. "All they do is supply the casualties."

Monroe never stayed with Grommand any longer than necessary. He did not like the general, nor did he like being around an army headquarters; the officers reminded him too much of Owen Landis, and the fact that Owen's wife was waiting for him back at the hotel. He did not really feel guilty about her; after all, he loved Clara, and he could not be held responsible for having fallen in love; but he was acutely aware of how their relationship might *look* if it came to light. He had not purposely forced Owen to leave the guards—thereby causing him to join the army—in order to get at Owen's wife. But there were those who would believe he had. That was the thought that constantly plagued him: that he might be thought of as being worse than he actually was. After all, he still had his position to think of. The warden's reputation had to be protected.

Still, Monroe made no effort to hide Clara when they were in St Louis. They dined openly at Delmonico's, the Cotton Boll, and other popular restaurants; attended the theater on occasion; and went for long evening walks through Jefferson Park. Occasionally, although it was against regulations, a Union soldier, down on his luck, would approach them in the park and beg a dime or a quarter from them. It irritated Monroe to be approached like that, particularly since the enlisted men were often dirty and unkempt, but he always gave them money anyway. One night he almost thought he recognized a begging soldier.

"'Scuse me, sir, could you spare a soldier some change?"

The man wore a heavy beard and his hat was pulled low. Monroe gave him fifty cents.

"God bless you, sir."

He went on his way. Monroe looked back at him, frowning. Then he shrugged it off. Maybe the man had been a prisoner at one time.

The soldier walking away did not have to look back at Monroe. He had recognized him instantly. He carried the scars of Monroe's whip on his back.

Owen Landis was in the hospital in Memphis when Roy Veal found him. He had a broken elbow and two fractured ribs, suffered in a fall when his horse was shaken by cannon fire at Willow Creek, Georgia.

"Howdy, Cap'n Landis," Veal said, standing beside his bed in a crowded ward.

Owen squinted up at him. "Do I know you, Private?" he asked.

Veal pushed his hat back. His beady eyes looked like musket balls. "Name's Roy Veal, Cap'n. You helped hang my brother Andrew at Prison Hill a few years back. And tied me and my brother Milton's hands so's Monroe Van Hawn could whip us."

Owen nodded. "I remember now." He let his right hand rest casually on a holstered pistol next to his bed. Roy Veal smiled.

"No need for that, Cap'n. I didn't come here for no fight. I went to a lot of trouble to find you: run off from my comp'ny in St. Louie and came all the way down here by packet—"

"What do you want, Veal?" Owen asked flatly.

"I seen your friend Van Hawn in St. Louie last month. Him and a lady strolling through the park, only the lady weren't his wife. I remember his wife well enough; ought to. This here woman weren't nothing like her—"

"What are you getting at, Veal?" Owen's eyes were narrowed, dangerous.

"I followed 'em. They went to this big fancy hotel up on the plaza. I seen 'em go upstairs together. I axed one of the bellhops who the woman was. He said she was Mrs. Clara Landis from Prisontown—"

Owen pulled out the pistol and cocked it. Roy Veal's face drained of color. "Sentry!" Owen yelled. Two hospital guards came running. "Take this man to the provost marshal," Owen said. "His name is Roy Veal. He's a deserter from up around St. Louis."

"Yes, sir."

"Now hold on a minute—" Veal protested.

"Get him out of here!" Owen ordered.

The two guards dragged Veal out of the ward.

Owen put away the gun and laid his head back, closing his eyes. An image of Clara formed in his mind. Her face: smiling, then laughing, eyes wide with delight, the red hair he loved so much tumbling to her shoulders, the field of freckles flowing down to her naked breasts: she had no clothes on—and Monroe was moving into the image, striding toward yer, eyes fixed on her freckled breasts, lips parted hungrily—

Owen shook his head and blinked away the picture. Not Clara, he thought. Not his Clara. He wet his lips and closed his eyes again. The image of her returned: laughing, happy, naked, the way she had always been when they were in bed together. He pictured her whole body in his mind: mouth, breasts, spread legs, feet. He tried to project himself into the picture with her, but for some reason he could not. He frowned, almost in pain. Then he saw why.

Monroe was already there.

Clara Landis for a long time had resisted letting Monroe come into her little home, the house at the edge of Prisontown that she had shared with Owen. It was her first real home, the only place other than a tent or boarding house that she and Owen had ever lived. They had rented it from Pete Newagon, the town carpenter, who had built it in his spare time. Later, after Owen had been promoted to guard sergeant, they had taken a mortgage on it through Fogel and Berg, shopkeepers who also loaned money, and started buying it.

There were only two rooms, but over the years Clara had painted and trimmed and copied decorating ideas from the *Lantz Home Beautification Catalog*, which came all the way from Boston, and the result was that she and Owen had one of the nicest small homes in Prisontown. It was situated at the east end of Union Street, far enough in from the river to be away from the summer mosquitoes; and a half block back from the street front, so that it was removed from business traffic. It was convenient to everything: Owen's job when he worked up on the Hill, and all the local stores at which Clara traded; and whenever anything special came to town, such as a minstrel show or stockmen selling horses, the couple could usually view the activities from their front porch.

On the Fourth of July, 1864, Clara sat alone on the porch watching the festivities taking place up and down Union Street. It was just dusk and although she was waiting for Monroe, she could not help thinking about Owen. He had been injured and was in a hospital in Memphis, but his last letter had said he shortly expected to return to his regiment on the lines in Georgia.

Sitting in her swing, moving just enough to stir the humid evening air, Clara wondered with a depressed feeling how she would react when Owen returned to share the little house with her again. She had been letting Monroe clandestinely call on her there for so long now that it seemed more like his home than Owen's, a thought which struck her conscience like a hammer. She was deeply in love with Monroe, but she was sick at heart that she had to enjoy it at Owen's expense. Being a realist, she knew that there was no way that the relationship between her and Monroe could avoid eventually hurting Owen.

Clara had tried desperately to keep the two areas of her life apart. For a long time after their three days in the cave, she would not allow Monroe to come to her house. She met him in St. Louis whenever he asked her to; and they spent passionate hours at secret places in the forest; but her home, hers and Owen's, she kept sacred from what she was doing. There she cleaned and sewed and made shirts for Owen and wrote him long letters and slept alone. Determined to preserve the sanctity of Owen's house, she steadfastly refused Monroe's suggestions that she let him slip down from the Hill and visit her in the middle of the night. She said no firmly for a year. Then less firmly, for a half a year. And finally, after she had been seeing him for nearly two years, when being in bed with him seemed as natural as it ever had with Owen, she relented. Monroe came to her in the quiet darkness and she allowed him what she considered the ultimate trespass: the taking of her in her husband's bed.

Now Monroe visited her frequently; it was so natural and routine that it did not even bother her anymore. She sat in her swing often, waiting for him to speak to her from the shadowy trees at the foot of the hill where he left his horse. At the sound of his voice, she would go inside and open the bedroom window for him. Sometimes he would stay several hours, sometimes only long enough to fill her body with his love; but it made no difference to her. As long as he kept coming, for she was convinced she could not live without him.

As she watched the Fourth of July celebration, she saw Monroe's son, Nathan, run by now and again. He waved to her and she waved back. She was very fond of the boy; Monroe often stopped at her front gate with him to visit when father and son were on their way to town. He was a handsome lad, much like Monroe in looks, and his father was very proud of him. Clara had watched him compete earlier that day in the youngsters' footraces and jumping and wrestling contests. Just as she had seen Monroe himself in the horseracing and target-shooting competitions. Each had been observed from a distance, from the privacy of her front porch, because Beth Van Hawn naturally was up close—they were *her* husband and son—and Clara did not want to intrude or make anyone uncomfortable. The very last thing Clara would ever think of was creating an unpleasant scene.

It had been a long, loud holiday, Clara thought. She had a slight headache from all the noise. Since noon she had sat on the porch listening to speeches, watching grown men try to catch a greased pig, tapping her foot to Virginia reel music, covering her ears every hour when they set off a gunpowder charge, waving to people who happened to see her sitting there, sending a passing boy to bring her an ice cream, chatting with Nathan for a moment when he ran up to tell her he had come in fifth in the river-to-the-hill footrace, and in general seeing the afternoon slip away amidst the noise and milling about of the festive day.

Now it was nearly over, daylight was quickly fading, and tired, dusty people were beginning to straggle off Union Street toward home, or hitch up nearby buggies to drive back to the farm, or simply sit down where they stood to let the fatigue drain out of them. By the time darkness had settled, only a few diehard celebrants were still at it: some local bachelors with a jug, a few members of the town band, the usual tireless gang of young boys, and some visiting Indians from the Oswego camp across the river. The musicians were playing *My Bonnie Lies Over the Ocean* when Clara heard Monroe call to her.

"Hey, Clara Mae."

She rolled her eyes toward the sky. A year ago she had made the mistake of telling him her full given name was Clara Mae, and he had been calling her that ever since. She hated it, and told him so often. But the more she complained about it, the more he did it. He dearly loved to tease her, and she found it impossible to get mad at him for it.

"I know you hear me, Clara Mae," he said when she did not answer. "If you don't acknowledge me, I'll come out of these shadows naked and throw myself at your feet."

"You wouldn't dare," she said.

"Oh, no?" There was a pause, and then one of Monroe's boots landed in the dirt at the side of the porch.

"You're crazy," Clara hissed. She stepped quickly off the porch, retrieved his boot, and headed for the front door. "Come in the house," she said, "before somebody sees you."

She opened the bedroom window. From the deeper darkness at the side of the house, Monroe stepped into the room. He gathered Clara into his arms and began kissing her: short, quick, hungry kisses, which they both interspersed with words.

"I've been thinking about you all day," he said.

"Oh? It didn't seem to keep you from enjoying yourself."

"I was miserable without you."

"Yes. That's why you were laughing so much."

"It was an act."

His fingers worked the buttons at the back of her dress until it was open. He pulled his mouth away from hers and drew the bodice forward off her shoulders and down her sleeves. He let it hang from her hips as he removed each of her undergarments until she was bare to the waist. He kissed her nipples and played with them with his lips until they rose.

Straightening, he quickly stripped off his vest and shirt. He was bending to remove his other boot when the bedroom door crashed open and a figure with a lighted kerosene lantern stepped into the room.

"What the hell—" Monroe said. Beside him, he heard Clara's breath catch in a frightened gasp. Squinting his eyes, he tried to distinguish the figure's face in the blue-black glare of the lantern. He could not. Only the voice, when he heard it, was distinguishable.

"You've had your last look at my wife's naked body, you dirty bastard!"

Owen!

Then a single revolver shot tore into his throat and hurled him against Clara, a gush of blood spewing from the wound. As he was falling, he saw his blood lay a red trail across her breasts. Then he hit the floor and rolled over. He tried to rise but could not; his knees and elbows seemed to be fluid; they would not lock.

"Slut!" he heard Owen say. He let his head roll sideways and looked up. He saw Owen's hand lash out. Clara moaned and fell onto the bed. Again Monroe tried to get up, again he failed. He felt sick, dizzy. The blood from his throat was matting the hair under his arm. Seeming to come from far away, he heard Owen's voice again.

"If you want to be a slut, I'll help you!" Owen said. "I'll show you how we treat the white trash in rebel towns!"

"Owen, no—please—"

Monroe heard the sound of tearing cloth. Seconds later, leather slapped violently against flesh and Clara began to cry. Then—more clothing being ripped apart.

"Now you little bitch, I'll show you something new I've learned," Owen said coldly. "Bend your back! Bend it—"

Clara choked on her sobs. The leather slapped again.

"Bend, you slut—!"

On the floor, Monroe lost consciousness.

CHAPTER 26

Boss Lee personally led the posse that went after Owen Landis.

"I want eight men," he told the guard lieutenant on night duty. "Include Jessup and Strap in the group: they're the best shots; also Levy and Mackleman: they're the best horsemen. Have the stableman cut out his strongest eight mounts; not the fastest, mind you, the strongest. Rifle and sidearm for each man. And tell the belly-robber to put up two days' dry provisions in saddlebags. That's all—hop to it."

As the lieutenant hurried away, Lee strode out of his office and down to the telegrapher's post. There was no sign of the usual ready smile on his face now; his expression was grimmer than anyone had ever seen it. He had been the one who had to tell the Mistress that her son was shot, the duty guards thought. That would have made anyone grim.

"Telegraph the town marshal in Cape Girardeau, Chester, Paducah, Colvin City, and Forbesville," Lee instructed the telegrapher. "Tell them Warden Van Hawn has been shot and that his assailant may be headed their way. The man's name is Owen Landis. He's about thirty-five, wears a black moustache, may be wearing the uniform of a Union captain. Ask that they question all strangers passing through their areas."

Leaving the telegrapher, Boss Lee crossed the dimly lighted Little Yard and passed through the back gate. Rounding the corner of the old, original wall, he headed for his quarters. The house he lived in was a rock-and-frame structure of seven rooms, standing in front of the little cabin Aaron and Dru had occupied while the prison was being constructed. The house had been built to accommodate the Colson family when Big Sam came to work for Jack Ironwood. The little cabin was now used as a storage shed.

Boss Lee's face reflected the strain he was under as he entered the house and went to his arms cabinet for a pistol. It was not yet ten o'clock at night, barely two hours since the shooting, but it seemed as if an eternity had passed. Lee had been among the first ones summoned. One of the drinkers from Kellerman's Saloon had ridden up the hill to get him. The man and some friends had heard the shot from inside the saloon. Just more Fourth of July noise, they assumed at first. They learned differently several minutes later when they heard Clara Landis scream from the street.

"Help me! Somebody help me, for God's sake!"

When they ran outside and found her naked to the waist, her breasts and one cheek smeared with blood, they thought she had been attacked by a drunken Indian. Someone ran for Doc Robin and they tried to get her calmed down until he arrived. Only after several minutes of confusion did they finally understand that it was not she but Monroe Van Hawn who needed help. A few of the men ran to her house then, but there was nothing they could do for the wounded man except stay with him until Doc got there.

While Doc was doing what he could for Monroe, a rider had brought Boss Lee the news. Lee had ridden at once to Clara's house. He had found Doc laboring to stop the flow of blood from an unconscious Monroe's neck.

"Better get Dru down here," Doc had told him. "Beth too. I hate to bring them here, but I'm not sure he's going to pull through."

Riding back up the hill, Lee had taken the news to Dru and Beth.

"That woman!" Beth had snapped. "That goddamned whore! I knew it would come to this!"

"What happened to Daddy?" Nathan asked, coming from across the room where he had been playing.

"Gerald," said an ashen Dru, "will you have our buggy brought around, please."

"It's being done, ma'am."

"That dirty whore!" Beth said. "I knew it would happen—"

"What, Mommy, what?" Nathan persisted.

"Well, it serves him right for doing it—"

"Stop it, Beth!" Dru said sharply. "You're just upsetting the boy—"

"What's happened to my daddy?" Nathan said, beginning to cry.

Dru turned anguished eyes to Boss Lee. "Gerald, would you—"

"Right, ma'am." Lee scooped the boy into his arms. "Listen, lad, will you walk my horse down to the stable for me? While I take your mother and grandmother down to see about your dad. Then we'll come back up the hill and tell you about it. How's that now?"

Lee, who had a way with the boy as he did with nearly everyone, got him to do as he asked. Then he took the two women down the hill to the Landis house. At first, Beth refused to go in; but when she saw that no one was going to try to make her, she changed her mind. She joined Dru at the bedside, facing Clara Landis across the still unconscious form of Monroe.

"I'm so sorry, I'm so sorry," Clara said over and over, speaking only to Dru, looking only at Dru, seeming to be unable to meet the eyes of her lover's wife.

Outside, Boss Lee had been talking to Tom Vestman, the town constable, and learning who shot Monroe. Vestman, a carpenter who was only a volunteer lawman, had already learned from Clara that her husband was Monroe's assailant.

"Will you be taking a posse out after him?" Vestman asked Lee.

The captain of the yard nodded.

"Will you be wanting me to go along?"

"No," said Lee. "It's a prison matter." He saw the relief in Vestman's face. The carpenter was an older man; he had taken the job as honorary peacekeeper only because no one else wanted it.

Lee had gone back inside and stayed with the women for half an hour, then decided to get started. He whispered in Dru's ear to tell her he was leaving. "I'd best be getting after him," he said.

Dru turned to him, concern in her eyes. She touched his hand.

"Be careful, son," she said, as if she were speaking to one of her own.

"I will, ma'am."

After he had armed himself, Lee left his house and went back to the Little Yard, where the posse and its mounts had been assembled. Once inside the walls, he heard the sound of many voices coming through the double gate of the Big Yard. He stopped and listened. The voices made a buzzing, swarming noise: all the men in the near cell block were talking at once. Somehow, the news had already reached them. Warden Monroe Van Hawn, the Cobra, had been shot. And by a former guard sergeant. Interspersed in the convict voices were snatches of laughter.

Tight-lipped, Boss Lee continued over to the posse.

"Let's go," he said, swinging into the saddle.

They captured Owen Landis at daybreak the next morning, eighteen miles south, heading toward Memphis.

Owen heard the riders coming but did not have time to hide. Three members of the posse were men who had worked with him, so he was recognized at once. He ran and the group fired on him. He fired back. No one was hit in the exchange, and Owen quickly ran out of ammunition. After that, the men rode him to ground in the woods.

"Did I kill him?" he asked when Boss Lee and the men dismounted to shackle him. "Is he dead?"

"Wasn't when we left," Lee told him. The yard captain was surprised to discover that he felt no great hatred for Monroe's assailant. Animosity, yes, and some anger because Dru had been hurt, but no burning hatred.

"I demand to be turned over to the nearest provost marshal's office," Owen said. "I hold a commission in the United States Army. Under wartime regulations, the army retains jurisdiction over me for any crime except murder."

Ignoring him, Lee had handcuffs, a waist chain, and ankle snaps put on him. His wrists were then connected in front, held to his waist, and each one separately chained to its corresponding ankle.

"I told you I can't be held on a charge less than murder," Owen snapped. His dark eyes were angry, desperate.

"It'll probably be murder by the time we get back," Boss Lee said tonelessly.

He was right. The posse returned to Prisontown at noon. They learned that a mortician had already been summoned from Cape Girardeau.

Monroe had been dead since dawn.

Lee rode up to see Dru. She was in her day room, receiving no one, not even Beth. Lee understood. He went back out to his horse to leave. Before he could mount, Dru called to him from the window. He went back inside.

"I didn't mean for them to keep you out," she said. "Just the rest of the world." She drew him to the settee and had him sit close beside her, so that she could hold his hand. "Did you catch Owen?" she asked.

"Yes, ma'am. We've got him in an isolation cell."

"I want him hanged, Gerald." Her voice was ordinary, as if she were asking for tea.

"He probably will be," said Lee.

"I mean now, Gerald. You hang him."

"I can't do that, Miss Dru. Anyway, I don't think you mean it."

"I do!" Her nostrils flared slightly. "He killed my son. The last of the people who were mine—" Her calm voice quavered, almost broke, but she forced control of it. "He took away the last person on earth that I could say was mine," she continued. "Don't you see? Now I've outlived them all, outlived all the people I loved and who loved me. Outlived my Aaron, my Clement, my Jack, my baby Grover, and now my boy Monroe—"

Her voice did break then and a great, anguished sob burst from her. She buried her face in both hands, her shoulders shaking as sobs began to rack her body. Tears seeped through her fingers and ran down the back of her hands. Almost hysterically, she repeated the names. "Aaron—Clement—Jack—"

Lee put an arm around her, stroked her hair, cooed into her ear as if she were a child. "There, now, there now, cry all you want to."

Lee stayed with her for an hour. When from sheer exhaustion she could cry no more, he led her over to the bed and made her lie down. He removed her shoes and spread a light sheet over her. He adjusted the curtains so the light would not be in her eyes. And he sat at her side, holding her hand, for another hour. Finally she slept.

When Boss Lee left the mansion, he walked down to the compound to his office. A telegraph message was waiting for him. It read:

ASSUME DUTIES ACTING
WARDEN AT ONCE STOP REQUEST
YOUR PRESENCE STATEHOUSE
FOLLOWING FUNERAL STOP
SIGNED GOVERNOR ALFRED
DONNELL

He wants to make me warden, Lee thought. There's no other reason to be sending for me.

Sitting down at his desk, he studied the message. Warden, he thought again. That had to be it.

Warden.

Despite feeling bad about Monroe, Boss Lee could not contain a brief wave of elation. In the three years since Monroe hired him, he had taken to prison work as naturally as—well, as if he had been *born* to it, as Monroe had. He liked being captain of the yard, liked the authority and stature it gave him. In a way, it was a substitute for the prizefighting fame he never quite achieved. Now, he could not help smiling, it looked as if he had made it.

Warden.

The championship.

Owen Landis went on trial for murder five weeks later in the one-room schoolhouse that was closed for the summer. Circuit Judge Calvin Collins came down from the capital to preside, bringing with him a state prosecuting attorney. The army sent a major named Britman from St. Louis to defend.

"I plan to base our defense on mitigating circumstances," Britman told Owen at their first meeting. He was a tall, fair man, slim, almost delicate looking, with a precise manner.

"Do whatever you want," Owen told him. He was tired of everything: the war, responsibility, command, his rank, the pain in his poorly healed elbow—everything. His dark eyes, normally bright and alive, had gone dull and heavy-lidded, like his mind. His whole attitude was somber. If they had wanted to hang him that day, he would have tied the noose for them.

"It won't be an actual defense, of course," Britman explained. "As far as an actual defense, you don't have one. Your wife saw you do it. A neighbor saw you run from the house to the woods. And you asked the posse if you had killed your victim. Oh, you'll be convicted, all right. What I want to do is save you from the rope. Show you as a betrayed soldier, come home from the war wounded—"

"Injured," Owen corrected.

"—home from the war injured, to find betrayal and treachery by your wife and best friend—"

Owen fixed smoldering eyes on the major. "Don't say Monroe Van Hawn and I were friends," he said in a quiet, warning voice. "I hated him, and he probably hated me."

"So much the better," said Britman, undisturbed. "Your enemy. A man who managed to remain home from the war, safe and secure, free to seduce the women left behind, while you were suffering on the battlefield. Yes, I think that will wash very well."

The very thing that Monroe had dreaded during the final months of his life was made an issue at the trial: did he or did he not purposely force Owen Landis to resign his job, knowing that without an exempt prisonkeeper job Owen would have to go in the army and leave town?

"I say he *did* do it on purpose!" Britman pounded away at the trial. "I say that Monroe Van Hawn planned the seduction of the defendant's wife from the very beginning. Planned it and carried it out. Rather than keep the defendant around as captain of the yard, he hired a *saloon bouncer* for the job!"

From the front row of seats, Boss Lee glared at Britman. The slim attorney only smiled tolerantly. Dru, sitting next to Lee, patted his hand reassuringly. Beth, who was at the trial only at Dru's insistence, stared stonily ahead.

"If I could force the defendant's wife to take the witness stand," Britman proclaimed, "I could *prove* the truth of this sordid plot by Monroe Van Hawn! I could have her describe step by step just how he *lured* her from the role of a faithful respectable wife, and *transformed* her into a *lascivious* woman!"

None of the members of the jury knew exactly what lascivious meant, but it was obviously something terrible.

"Unfortunately," Britman continued, "Clara Landis has chosen *not* to testify. This is her privilege; since the man on trial is her lawfully wedded husband, we cannot force her to take the stand. But we can and will show by other testimony that the *real* criminal in this case was Monroe Van Hawn—and the real *victim* is Owen Landis!"

That was the way the trial went. At every opportunity, the reputation and motives of Monroe were impugned, and the unwritten right of Owen to defend the honor of his home was emphasized. After all, Britman reasoned to the jurors in a dozen ways, the defendant was a war-weary soldier who came back to his humble little home to find the woman he loved, the woman he *married*, half naked in the arms of the very man who had been responsible for his going off to war in the first place. It was such a shock to his already battle-strained nerves that he was able to do only one thing: fight it! So he shot the evil person who had soiled his wife and home. Wouldn't any man have done the same? It was unfortunate, of course, that Monroe Van Hawn had died as a result of the wound, but that was God's province, not Owen's, just as surely as it had been God's will to spare Owen with only a broken elbow when that cannonball had exploded so close to his horse. And just as it would now be the jury's will to spare him further punishment for an act that, while not exactly commendable, was certainly far from reprehensible.

The jury took the middle road, between the prosecution's demand that Owen hang and the defense's plea that he be set free. They found him guilty and sentenced him to life imprisonment.

That same afternoon, from his upstairs jail window, Owen watched Clara board the northbound coach out of town. He was never to see or hear of her again.

With her husband now dead, Beth Van Hawn was at last free to leave Prison Hill. That had been the first thought to come into her head the moment Doc told her Monroe had died, and it was a thought she carried with her like a plan for salvation all through the funeral, the trial, and the public display of mourning she had been forced into by her mother-in-law. But on the day that Monroe's estate was settled, when half of everything he had was signed over to her, and half the remainder to her in trust for Nathan—on that day she decided that the playacting was over. She went into Nathan's room, where Dru was reading him a story, and without a word began packing his clothes.

"What are you doing?" Dru asked.

"Leaving," she said simply. "Nathan and I are leaving."

Dru felt a pinch inside her chest. She had to exert control to keep her hands from trembling. Beth's decision was not unexpected; but it was no less difficult to accept.

"Where are you going?" she asked in a controlled voice.

"Ohio, to start. I'll visit my parents for awhile. After that—well, we'll see."

Nathan, sitting on the floor, tugged at Dru's dress. "Grandmother, finish the story."

"You don't have time to listen to a story right now," Beth said. "Go downstairs and tell whoever's in the kitchen to heat a tub of water for you to take a bath."

"But, Mother—"

"No buts. Do you want to go for a ride on a riverboat?"

Nathan's eyes lighted up. "Do I !"

"Then hurry to the kitchen. Come tell me when the water is ready."

The boy hurried from the room.

Dru watched Beth transfer her grandson's clothes from drawer to traveling bag. Her eyes filled with misery. "I don't suppose you'll be coming back."

Beth looked at her incredulously. "To *this* place? Hardly. Anyway, this isn't *our* home anymore; this is the warden's residence, remember? And this family seems to finally have run out of wardens. You can't stay here yourself very much longer." She did not bother to ask Dru where she would go.

Within two hours they were ready to leave. The buggy was at the door with a guard to drive it. The bags were loaded.

"Come kiss Grandmother goodbye," Dru said to the boy, holding back her tears by sheer force of will.

Nathan hugged and kissed her. "When will I see you again, Grandmother?" he asked.

"I don't know right now," she said. "But you'll be seeing your Grandmother Mildred and your Grandfather Sam very soon. You'll have a good time with them. Be a good boy now."

"Come along, Nathan," Beth called from the buggy. "You don't want us to miss the big boat."

The boy gave Dru a final great hug and ran to his mother. As the buggy drove away, he got up on his knees on the seat and waved to her for as long as they could see each other. Or at least for as long as he could see her.

She could only see him for a short distance, because the tears had finally come, blurring her vision.

As the buggy went down the hill toward town, a flatbed wagon slowly climbed up to the prison compound. Sitting in the back, his arms, waist, and ankles again chained, was Owen Landis, on his way to begin serving his life sentence. Boss Lee met him at the front gate.

"I'm not going to bother telling you the rules, Landis," he said. "Thay haven't changed much since you were a guard. Just the punishment has changed, but from what I've heard, I expect you'll be finding that out firsthand."

"Maybe I will and maybe I won't," Owen said sullenly.

A guard lieutenant kicked Owen in the heel of his shoe. "Say 'sir' when you address the yard captain," he ordered.

Owen turned his head and spit in the dust. The lieutenant drew his billy club. Lee stopped him from using it.

"Antagonizing officers isn't very smart for a man in your shoes, Landis," Lee said quietly. "You're not going to have many friends in the population in there. If the cons don't like you and the guards look the other way, it could get uncomfortable."

"Thanks for the advice. I'll let you know if I ever want any more."

Boss Lee smiled a tight smile. "Suit yourself, hard head." He nodded to the lieutenant. "Take him inside. Put him in general population and assign him to the rock quarry."

As Owen was being taken into the prison, Boss Lee walked up the knoll to the mansion. Dru was still standing on the portico. She had watched Owen Landis arrive. She hated him even more now that Nathan had been taken away from her.

"You should have hanged that man when I asked you to," she said to Lee. "He'll be nothing but trouble inside those walls."

They sat down together on the portico swing. Dru kept staring at the road.

"Are they gone for good?" Lee asked her.

"I expect so." Dru sighed a deep, silent sigh.

Lee removed an official-looking document from his pocket and handed it to her. "I went to the statehouse yesterday and saw the governor. He gave me the appointment. Warden."

Dru unfolded the appointment and read it. "Gerald *Arthur*?" she said, raising one eyebrow.

He shrugged. "They said my full name had to be on it. Gerald Arthur Lee."

Dru folded it up and offered it back to him.

"You, uh—you can have it if you want it," he said. "Put it with the others you've got." She had the appointments of Aaron, Clement Niles, Jack Ironwood, and Monroe. Framed, they hung in a neat row on the wall of her sewing room.

"Thank you, Gerald. Gerald Arthur."

He shook his head. "I knew it was a mistake to show it to you."

They sat in silence for a little while, swinging a few inches back, a few forward, watching the day turn to twilight.

"You know I don't have any family," he said finally.

"I know. Nor I now."

"This house, it's big enough for half a dozen people. What I'll probably do is move into the downstairs bedroom—"

The one Monroe took after his brother was killed, she thought with a tug in her breast.

"—and use the study for an office, like, uh—like the other wardens have done."

"The bedrooms upstairs are larger," she said.

"I'd like you to keep the upstairs," he told her. "All of it. I'd like you to stay here and, well, run the house just like you've always done. Will you do it?"

"If you want me to." Staring at the road, her eyes grew moist again.

"I want you to," Lee said. "I think it would be nice, you and me. Naturally I, uh—don't expect to take Monroe's place as a son or anything like that—"

"No, of course not."

"—but I could still take care of you, maybe like I was an adopted nephew or something. How, uh—how does that sound?"

Dru turned to him and smiled. "It sounds just fine, Gerald. Just fine indeed." She took his hand and gazed out across the compound. "This has been my home for so long. So very long. I really don't know where I would have gone."

Boss Lee patted the hand that held his. "That don't matter now," he said. After a pause, he added, "Aunt Dru."

CHAPTER 27

The day she returned home after completing her first year of college, Dru Hawn got off the train and looked around the platform for her father. He was not there, but a stocky young man in a guard's uniform came toward her. "Miss Hawn?" he said.

"Yes."

"I'm Clifford McKittrick. Your father asked me to meet you. He's escorting the governor and some dignitaries through the prison." He held out his hand. She started to take it, but he said, "Let me get your bags."

"Oh. All right." She gave him her baggage checks.

Clifford was driving Myles Hawn's new 1947 Nash. He put Dru's luggage in the trunk and walked around to the driver's side. "Hop in," he said, not bothering to open the door for her. Dru really did not care; she considered herself far too independent for that kind of mushy treatment. But it did irritate her the tiniest bit that he did not even offer. As they drove away from the depot, she studied him in several quick glances. Nice-looking, square chin, eyes that should be against the law, and just a hint of something else—arrogance, impudence, something.

"You're new, aren't you, Mr.—ah—"

"McKittrick. Yeah, I'm new."

"Do you like being a prison guard?"

He shrugged. "It's not a bad job. I don't much like being back in a uniform again."

"You a vet?"

"Yeah. Marine Corps."
"We have quite a few ex-Marines going to school at Midwestern State. They're studying on the G.I. Bill."
"That so."
He glanced at Dru, giving her a brief smile that she identified as tolerant. She tried to guess his age; twenty-six to twenty-eight, she decided. Probably thinks he's very worldly.
"I'm studying to be a teacher," she said.
"That's nice." Another glance, another passing smile.
Dru got the sudden impression that Clifford McKittrick was treating her like a child. The warden's brat, home from college for the summer. Had to pick her up at the station. Ho hum.
Dru searched her mind for an equalizing weakness. "Do you know many vets like yourself who are getting a college education on the G.I. Bill?"
"Some," he replied.
"I don't see why every vet doesn't take advantage of it," she commented, almost as if not talking to Clifford at all. "It's such a wonderful opportunity." She paused a beat. "For men with ambition, I mean."
Clifford did not respond. Instead he stepped down on the gas pedal a little.
Dru said nothing else until they had gone halfway through Union City. Then she looked out the window at the business section. "The town doesn't seem to have changed much," she remarked, in what she hoped was a travel-weary tone.
Clifford eyed her impatiently. "Things don't usually change much in two months," he said wryly. "Your father told me you were home at Easter."
Dru quickly looked out the window again so she would not have to face him. She felt herelf blush and immediately wondered if he could tell by the back of her neck. Damn! Why was she acting like such a ninny anyway?
They continued through town past the last stoplight where Union Street became the state highway that ran up the hill to the prison. The hill was now dotted with housing tracts: row upon row of prefab homes thrown up for the community's returning veterans. Only where the highway leveled off at the crest of the hill did the development of homes end; that was where prison

property began. It was cyclone-fenced now and posted with signs forbidding any loitering or picking up of hitchhikers in the area.

Clifford drove to a back gate in the fence, was passed through, and guided the car slowly along a narrow prison road that served the institution's huge farm complex. Prisoners in summer whites were at work on tractors and irrigators in the fields. Guards with rifles and megaphones patrolled in jeeps.

After they had passed through the farm and were drawing nearer to the big wall, Dru gazed out at a rise of land separated by a white picket fence.

"Would you please stop there for a minute?" she said. "I want to visit my mother."

"Sure," Clifford said quietly.

He parked the car at the gate to the prison cemetery. Dru got out. Clifford stayed in the car and watched her walk onto the grounds. She was not bad-looking, he thought.

She was also the warden's daughter, he reminded himself.

He shrugged. She was just a kid anyway. Nevertheless, he continued to watch her.

Dru stood silently at her mother's grave for several minutes, then returned to the car where Clifford McKittrick waited, and they resumed their drive to the prison. Clifford approached the big wall from the side and drove around to the front where Myles had a private parking space next to the main sally port. Just as they pulled up, Myles was bidding goodbye to the governor and his entourage. Dru remained in the car until they were all gone, then stepped out where her father could see her.

"Hey, there's my girl!" Myles beamed and started toward her. His limp was more pronounced now that he was in his middle fifties. But he still had the smile of a very young man.

Dru met him halfway and they embraced. Myles always held her extra tight for a moment when she returned after being away for a while. It was as if he wanted to reassure himself that she was real. She was all he had now. He had lost his mother twelve years earlier; Reba had been seventy when she died in Florida of a cerebral hemorrhage. Nathan, now ninety-one, was senile and living in a nursing home; he no longer knew who Myles was. But as long as Myles had Dru, he never felt alone or without a family. To Myles, his daughter was a delightful combination of the great-grandmother he worshiped as a child, and the wife he adored as a man. He was not a particularly religious person, but he selfishly prayed that he be allowed to die before Dru. The thought of living without her was agonizing to him. Which was why he always hugged her extra tight when she came home.

"How about this girl of mine, Cliff?" Myles said when McKittrick brought over her bags. "Didn't I tell you she was pretty as a picture?"

"You sure did, Warden," Cliff replied.

Dru noticed that he only acknowledged her father's words; he did not agree with them. Not that she cared. She knew that she was not the prettiest girl on campus—she was practically flat-chested—but she certainly did not need Officer Clifford McKittrick to verify it for her. He wasn't particularly good-looking himself. She flicked her eyes over him. Well, not *too* anyway.

"I'll have a trusty bring in the bags, Cliff," said Myles. "Thanks for meeting the train for me."

"You're welcome, sir."

Cliff walked away, leaving them alone.

"How long has *he* been here?" Dru asked after he was gone.

"About a month," said Myles. "Fine young man. He's part of a work-study program the state is sponsoring. He has a master's degree in penology; now he's working toward a doctorate. He'll be a brilliant penologist someday."

Dru stared after Cliff McKittrick, livid inside because he had not told her.

CHAPTER 28

On Sunday, while Myles was taking his afternoon nap, Dru went down to his office and checked the warden's copy of the guard roster. It showed Cliff McKittrick on day duty in the recreation yard. Dru walked down one more flight and was passed through the deadlock to the inside. She walked across a broad expanse of lawn to a ten-foot cyclone fence with a gate leading onto the rec yard. A softball diamond occupied one corner of the yard. A four-row stand of bleachers bordered the field. Several dozen convicts, some with their shirts off, were watching a softball game, which had already started. Dru looked around for Cliff McKittrick. She finally located him standing near the exercise track that encircled the rec yard. She started toward him.

McKittrick saw her coming but did not walk over to meet her. Dru felt herself already becoming irritated. She worked to keep it from showing.

"Hello, Mr. McKittrick." she said as she approached.

"Hello, Miss Hawn."

Dru tried to detect some animosity in his tone, something to justify her own feelings. All she could identify was indifference. Which made her all the more perturbed.

"I want to clear up something with you," she said. "In the car the other day, before I knew you were working toward a doctorate, I'm afraid I sounded a little derogatory talking about veterans who aren't taking advantage of the G.I. Bill to get an education. I want you to know that I wasn't being personal."

Cliff smiled a knowing smile. "Weren't you?"

"No, I wasn't." She felt herself stiffening a little.

Cliff nodded. It was a brief nod; Dru could not decide whether it was curt or brusque. "It doesn't really matter to me whether you were being personal or not," Cliff said. "But if it will make you feel better, you're forgiven."

"Forgiven! Now wait a minute, mister. I wasn't asking for your forgiveness—"

"Why'd you come over here then?"

"To clear up a possible misunderstanding between us."

"There's no misunderstanding between us, Miss Hawn," he said. "I think I understand you perfectly."

"Oh, you do, do you?" Cocky, arrogant—!

"Yes, I do." His voice, like his smile, was confident. "Excuse me," he said before she could retort, "I have to walk the yard."

He walked away from her. Half angry, half embarrassed, Dru stalked back the way she had come.

They met two days later in the commissary. Cliff was buying a carton of Luckies and Dru had stopped in to pick up some pipe tobacco for her father. At first it had been Dru's intent to ignore him, but he walked over and stood next to her.

"Hello, Miss Hawn," he said.

"Hello," she replied coolly. She moved down the counter a few steps to get away from him. He followed her.

"I'd like to apologize for Sunday," he said. "I haven't had much practice being a gentleman; I guess it showed."

"It most certainly did." She moved away from him again.

He followed her again.

"Look, I really am sorry I didn't accept your apology—"

She turned on him incredulously. "My *apology!* I wasn't trying to apologize! I just wanted to make sure you hadn't taken what I said personally." She shook her head in disgust. "Apology, my eye! You've got some nerve, mister." This time she walked all the way to the other end of the counter. Cliff still followed her. She turned on him angrily. "Will you please stop following me. I really don't want to talk to you."

Cliff shrugged and once again walked away from her.

"I can't understand it," Dru told her father over lunch. "Every time we try to talk to each other, sparks fly."

Myles sipped his iced tea and said nothing.

"Why is he so sure of himself?" Dru demanded. "Why is he so—*cocky*?"

"He's one of the new breed, honey," Myles said. "There are a lot of them around today: kids who grew up on the battlefield, and are now seasoned veterans back from the war. They've got a confidence that only survivors have. They're different."

"You can say that again," Dru asserted. "I think he's *too* different."

"I'm not so sure, honey," said Myles. "I'm not so sure the world isn't ready for young men like McKittrick. Especially my world, the prison world. He has some very interesting ideas about the field. He's a new kind of keeper who's only half penologist. The other half is sociologist. He believes in directing ninety percent of our rehabilitation effort toward the young first offender. As far as he's concerned, the old timers, the three-time losers, are already lost to society. Even if they get out when they're fifty-five or sixty years old, he doesn't think they'll be much good to the community. His theory is let the lifers die in prison while you're saving the ones doing five years so they won't come in again."

Dru frowned. "That's completely opposite to your own way of thinking, Daddy. Yet you sound almost pleased with the idea."

Myles sighed resignedly. "I'm smart enough to know that in a few years there's not going to be room in the practice of penology for wardens like myself, honey. My time is almost past. Since the war ended, the crime rate has started to climb again. Crimes of violence are changing from bank robberies and mail truck holdups to senseless multiple murders and slaughters of innocent people. Maybe the war did that to us, I don't know. I *do* know that the type of violent criminal we're going to be dealing with in the future isn't going to be the Depression-era outlaw that J. Edgar Hoover was so quick to label 'mad dog' and 'public enemy,' when in fact most of the time they were just farm boys who went bad. The *real* public enemies are the ones we're starting to get now: the psychopaths and schizos; the ones who have *got* to be helped while they're very young or they won't be able to be helped at all. And that job, my dear, isn't for the Myles Hawns; it's for the Cliff McKittricks."

"You seem to think a lot of his ability," Dru commented.

"I do. A hell of a lot. I think he has as much promise as I did at that age." Myles reached across the table and patted Dru's hand. "He's a good man, honey. Believe me. And he's come up the hard way. He's an orphan kid from the slums of Chicago; he earned his education fighting with the Marines in the Pacific. He graduated almost at the top of his class in college, was awarded high honors on the work he did for his master's, and now hopes to become the state's first doctor of penology. So try not to be too hard on him."

"I *have* tried," Dru protested. "It's just that every time we meet, we seem to butt heads."

"Do you like him?" Myles asked.

"I have a feeling that I could," Dru admitted. She felt a flush inside as she said it.

"Maybe you need to see him on a neutral ground, away from the prison," Myles said. He felt oddly like a mother instead of a father.

"I did see him on neutral ground," Dru said. "At the train depot."

"That was still prison business: him in uniform, driving my official car. No, I'm talking about someplace completely removed. Someplace like the Union City Public Library. He goes there on his night off, every Wednesday night."

Dru stared at her father with one eyebrow raised in curiosity. "This is a very peculiar conversation," she said. "I almost feel as if you're playing matchmaker."

"I don't think I'm going that far," her father said. "But I know you haven't made many friends at college; and I know you're very mature for your age. I just think Cliff might be a good friend once you get to know him."

"And suppose it goes beyond friendship? How are you going to feel then?"

Myles shrugged. "I don't know. But let's not worry about it until it happens."

The library was a neat, white, quasi-Colonial building a block off Union Street, not far from the corner where Monroe Van Hawn was shot by Owen Landis. On that lot now stood a two-story brick house resided in by a lawyer and his family.

On Wednesday night, an hour before closing time, Dru parked

halfway down the block and walked back to the front entrance. From outside, she looked through the door and around the big main room. Cliff was sitting at a table near the back stacks. A large, encyclopedia-like volume was open in front of him. He was studying it intently.

Dru started to go inside, then changed her mind. Her original idea had been to run into Cliff as if by chance; but at the last minute she found that she could not do it. It was too melodramatic, too devious. Instead, she went to a nearby bench on the library lawn and sat down to wait.

Cliff came out at five minutes to nine. He saw her at once. She had half expected him to ignore her and walk on past; she was pleasantly surprised when he did not. He came right toward her. She stood up to meet him.

"Hello," he said quietly.

"Hello."

"I'm sorry. Again."

"So am I. Again."

They stood looking at each other, not speaking. Between them, they seemed to instinctively know that their fighting was over. It was a strange moment. Each had been constantly on the mind of the other—and they knew it. Each had felt vaguely troubled by their quarrels—and they knew it. Each had been oddly drawn to the other—and they knew it. Their feelings were exactly the same. And they knew it.

"Want to go uptown and have a hamburger with me?" he asked.

"Yes."

He nodded down the street. "Bus stops at the corner."

"I have the car," she said. She handed him the keys.

As they walked to the car, their hands brushed and they glanced almost shyly at each other.

"What's happening to us?" Cliff asked.

"I think we're falling in love," Dru said.

Cliff grinned. "Us? Impossible."

"That's what I thought too. But it looks like we're wrong."

The tree-lined street was dark where she had parked. Cliff drew her into the shadows and took her in his arms. She felt his mouth coming and met it eagerly.

* * *

The kitchenette apartment he lived in was in the Union City Arms, a semi-transient hotel at the foot of the hill leading up to the prison. It was seedy and rundown, and he apologized for it.

"It's not the most romantic place in the world for a girl to lose her virginity," he said.

"It's not the place that matters," she told him from the cushion she had made of his naked shoulder. "It's the man that matters."

"That sounds pretty worldly."

"My mother told me that when I was seventeen. She'd been around. But in her whole life she only slept with one man—my father."

"How would you like to carry on that tradition? By marrying me?"

Dru sat up in bed, oblivious to the fact that the sheet dropped away from her breasts. "We're moving kind of fast, aren't we, Cliff?"

He shrugged. "Nothing wrong with moving fast if you know where you're going."

"Do we? Know where we're going?"

"I know where I'm going or at least where I want to go. I want us to get married, Dru. I love you. I want to go on loving you."

She went back into his arms and found her still-warm spot on his shoulder again. "I want to go on loving you too. Tonight was so wonderful. But we have to have more than love, Cliff. We have to have plans of some kind. You have the rest of your education to consider; so do I, for that matter—"

"Those are details that can be worked out later," he said confidently. "Tell me you'll marry me."

"Cliff, it's easy enough to say that details can be worked out later, but there are some things that should be discussed ahead of time—"

"Later," he insisted.

Dru felt his free hand exploring.

"Say you'll marry me," he told her again.

"Oh, Cliff—"

"Say you love me, then."

"I love you."

He shifted in the bed until they were on their sides facing each other. He maneuvered her left leg up enough to allow him to enter her again. "Still hurt?" he asked.

"A little. But I don't care. It hurts good."

He began ministering himself to her.

"Say you'll marry me," he prompted again.

Her head was back, her eyes closed. "All—right—"

"All right what?"

"I'll—marry you—Cliff—Oh, Jesus—"

Even as she said it, even as she went with him into the throes of climax, somewhere, deep inside her, was a tiny spark of doubt.

A spark of doubt that told her it was not to be.

CHAPTER 29

A month later, Dru told her father that she wanted to marry Cliff McKittrick.

When he thought about a possible future together for Dru and Cliff, Myles felt a tinge of guilt about Cassie. Her one great hope, aside from Dru going to college and becoming a teacher, was that she would not live her life in a prison environment. Cassie felt, as many penologists' wives did, that the keepers were as much prisoners as the kept. What Cassie failed to realize was that in some people there was an instinctive urge to be around a prison; a sense of refuge, of security. His Great-grandmother Dru had known that urge; so now did her namesake, the young Dru. Cassie could not be expected to understand such feelings; probably they came with the bloodline, and Cassie's bloodline had come from outlaws, not keepers. But Myles recognized it clearly in his daughter, and he was not prepared to force Dru to reject it. For Cassie's sake, he would insist that Dru finish college and earn her teaching certificate; but more than that he felt he could not justifiably do. Cassie had lived her life as she saw fit; Dru was entitled to do the same.

Myles had been studying his daughter since she began seeing Cliff regularly. From her soft, flushed glow when she came in at night, Myles guessed that she was no longer a virgin. He recognized the look, the *presence*, of a physically satisfied woman; it was something he remembered well from his early days with Cassie. His later days too, for that matter, he thought.

Myles was not overly concerned by the fact that Dru had given herself to a man before marriage. It was, he knew, a changing world. As everything rushed headlong toward the fifties, the values and morals of the forties and thirties were being left far behind. He was nevertheless relieved, in a way, that Cassie was not around when it happened. For all their private experiences, in both the far and near past, Cassie had been very straitlaced insofar as appearances were concerned. And downright old-fashioned when it came to their only child.

Cliff's profession aside, Myles was certain that Cassie would have liked the young man. He was honest and direct and levelheaded, traits she had always admired in a man. And he had come from nothing, to become something. Cassie would have respected that, because she would have understood what it had taken.

All in all, Myles felt good about the situation. On the morning after Dru had first mentioned marriage to him, he had an opportunity to discuss the matter with Cliff, when it was Cliff's turn to accompany him on his daily inspection tour.

"Well, young man," Myles said, "my daughter tells me that it's become pretty serious between you two."

"Yes, sir, it has, Warden," Cliff replied. They were walking toward the deadlock, Cliff carrying a clipboard on which to make notations during the inspection. "I wanted to come to you myself, Warden," he added, "but Dru felt she should talk to you first."

"She was probably right," Myles said. He smiled at Cliff to reduce the heaviness of the moment. "I don't suppose it's necessary to ask if you love Dru."

"I do love her, Warden. Very much." Cliff looked down at the highly polished floor as they walked. "You've got a file on me, Warden. You know my background. I never had a family to speak of. I came from people who were nothing, who were noncontributors, the dead weight of society. If it hadn't been for the Marine Corps and the war, I might never have made anything of myself. Hell, the only reason I even got into penology is because those and agriculture classes were the only ones not filled when I got to school. But I've come to really like the field and I think I can do very well in it—"

"There's no question in my mind that you will," Myles interjected.

The two men were passed through the deadlock and exited the admin building on the side within the walls. They proceeded toward the prison shops building.

"The point is," Cliff continued, "I'm determined to *be* somebody—myself, on my own. And I hope that you won't consider it a detriment that I don't have a family behind me. I know that your family, Dru's family, goes back a lot of years in this state and at this prison—"

"I'm sure you also know that my late wife's background was on the other side of the fence, so to speak. No, Cliff, I'd never judge you by your family or lack of it; I'll only judge you by what you do in life."

"That's all I ask, Warden."

At the shops building, they discontinued their conversation as they walked through the tag factory, where inmates operated metal presses to manufacture the state's license plates. The civilian shop foreman came over and accompanied them on their tour. The noise in the room was very loud and the men had to lean toward each other's ears and shout to be heard. Myles did not even try to relay any notations for Cliff's clipboard until they got back outside. Then he said, "Make a note to advise the Motor Vehicle Department that the next batch of plates will be shipped to them on August first."

"Yessir."

As they walked along an areaway to the shoe shop, they resumed their personal conversation. "What are you going to do about your education?" Myles asked. "Both of your educations, I should say."

"We haven't definitely decided yet," Cliff told him. "Dru wants to drop out of college and take a job while I finish work on my doctorate. Her theory is that when I'm finished with school, then she can go back."

"She won't, of course," said Myles. "People rarely do. The easiest thing in the world is to quit college; the hardest thing is to go back. Believe me, I know."

"That's what I told her, Warden. I don't see any reason why we both can't continue school. With the money I get from the G.I. Bill, I think we could manage. It would be tight but we could do it."

"Dru has some money coming from her grandmother's estate," Myles said. "My mother was a doctor, you know. She made a great deal more than my father did. Some of it was left to Dru."

"Dru didn't mention that," Cliff said.

"Dru doesn't know about it. I'm the executor. She gets it when she's twenty-one. Still a year away. But I could probably give her an advance against it, if everything else worked out."

"Everything else?"

"Yes. If she remained in school. Did she tell you that she made a deathbed promise to her mother to finish college and become a teacher?"

"No, she didn't."

"Perhaps I should remind her of it. At any rate, between you and me, are we in agreement that the best course is for both of you to continue your schooling, simultaneously?"

"Yessir, I think so."

"Good," said Myles. He patted Cliff lightly on the shoulder. "The finances are something we can work out later. Here's the shoe shop."

They entered a square room where inmates sat at a row of leather-trimming machines cutting out patterns for high-top shoes. In another area, the cut leather was fashioned into uppers and machine-stitched to soles. The shop foreman and a roving guard were talking at the foreman's desk when Myles and Cliff walked up.

"Morning, Warden."

"Morning, men. Everything running smoothly?"

"Moving right along, Warden." As the shop foreman spoke, he noticed an inmate leave his stitching machine and walk toward them. He frowned. That was not permitted. Inmates were required to raise their hands and obtain permission before leaving a machine.

"Get back to your place, McCoy," the shop foreman said, stepping toward the approaching man. As he was speaking, the convict drew a revolver from the back of his belt and viciously snapped its barrel across the shop foreman's temple. The assaulted man tumbled to the floor.

"Don't move, none of you!" the con shouted, leveling the gun at the other three men. The roving guard, armed only with a billy, raised the club and charged. The con moved the gun an inch and shot him in the side. The guard stumbled back and fell. "Next man gets it in the head!" the con warned.

Myles, his hands half raised, quickly evaluated the situation. The con with the gun was Barney McCoy, an armed robber from the southern part of the state, serving forty-five years. A small man with darkly circled eyes, he was cunning, clever, dangerous. "You'll never get out, Barney," Myles told him quietly.

"We'll see about that," McCoy snapped. He glanced at another inmate, Marv Hilliard, at a pattern machine. "Let's go."

Hilliard hurried to a corner and removed the lid of a shoe paste barrel. Plunging his hand into the paste, he pulled out a rubber inner tube that had been cut open to make a long, thin container. Both cut ends were tied tightly with picture wire. Quickly Hilliard took a cobbler's knife and slit open the tube. Out spilled three more guns and several boxes of cartridges. Hilliard tossed a gun and bullets to each of two other cons, Dutch Kretz and Buddy Thomas. They loaded the weapons and took up positions at the shop's two doors.

"Okay, Hawn," said McCoy, who was obviously the leader, "you're taking us out of here."

"You're a fool, Barney," said Myles. "You had fifteen years of good time—"

"Yeah, and what the fuck did it get me?" McCoy almost snarled. "A five-year set from the parole board. Which means I got to do at least twenty. They didn't even take into consideration what I done in that fucking infantile paralysis project. Those fucking bastards don't give a shit about nothing! Well, I do! I ain't going to stay in this zoo until I'm an old fucking man! I'm getting out the only way I know how! Now let's go!"

McCoy whirled Myles around, held him by the collar, and put the muzzle of the gun behind his ear. Hilliard did the same to Cliff McKittrick. With their two hostages as shields, the four convicts exited the shoe shop and started across the grounds toward the rear of admin.

"It won't work, Barney," Myles said en route. "My guards have strict orders not to open the deadlock."

"Then I hope you got lots of insurance, Warden, 'cause you're as good as dead."

When they were halfway to admin, the prison's big siren started. A tower guard had observed them and sounded the alarm.

Throughout the prison, guards from designated posts rushed to the armory to be issued weapons. The prison was sealed off from the road by highway patrol units and Union City police. Only off-duty guards, reporting to work in response to the siren, were let through. All of this was happening within minutes of the alarm being sounded, and just as the armed convicts and their hostages reached the inner side of admin.

"Get away from them doors!" McCoy shouted at the unarmed guard who checked admin passes. "Move away or I'll blast the warden!"

The guard backed off, as did two others on duty nearby. McCoy and his men cautiously moved with their hostages up the stairs to the second floor where the deadlock passage to the outside was located.

"McCoy," Cliff said when they were halfway up the stairs, "let the warden go and I'll show you a way to go around the deadlock."

McCoy's expression tightened. He removed the gun from Myles' head long enough to rake the barrel across Cliff's face, tearing open his upper lip. "You fucking creep! Think you're smarter'n me, huh? I been in this shithouse fifteen lousy years! There *ain't* no way around the deadlock!"

"Let me handle this, Cliff," Myles ordered, glancing back to see the young guard holding his bloody mouth with both hands.

"You tell him, Warden," McCoy sneered.

When the group reached the inside end of the deadlock, they found the barred double doors open and waiting. Since only one set of doors could be opened at a time, the ones at the other end—the end beyond the wall—were closed and locked.

McCoy guided Myles into the wide security corridor. "We're coming through!" he yelled. "Open them fucking doors or I'm gonna blow the warden's head off!"

Hilliard followed close on McCoy's heels with Cliff, whose entire coatfront was now dark with wet blood. Kretz and Thomas brought up the rear, covering them from behind.

In the middle of the deadlock, McCoy stopped. Ahead of them, beyond the barred doors, a dozen guards waited with shotguns and rifles. In a bulletproof-glass control room recessed into one wall, a corridor guard waited for his orders.

"Open up!" McCoy yelled again. He prodded Myles with the gun. "Give the order, Hawn!"

Myles looked at the corridor guard, safe and secure in the tight little bulletproof room. "Seal it off," he said evenly.

A button was pressed and at once the barred doors behind the men began to slide together. Buddy Thomas let out a choked cry and bolted for the doors. Dutch Kretz followed him. Both of them bounded out of the deadlock just before it was sealed.

"You stupid idiots!" McCoy yelled. "Now you're through, you're washed up!"

Terror in their eyes, Kretz and Thomas ran back down the inside stairs. Just as they reached the bottom, two shotgun blasts cut them down. They sprawled in the lower foyer like blood-soaked scarecrows, limp and still.

"Stupid idiots!" McCoy yelled again from inside the deadlock. He whirled and faced the corridor guard. "Come on, open up! This is your last chance!"

The corridor guard did not move. Infuriated, McCoy aimed his revolver at the glass and fired four times. The bullets grooved the glass and whined away.

"Son of a bitch!" McCoy yelled in frustration. He turned the gun on Cliff McKittrick and fired. Cliff's face seemed to explode in red.

Oh, no, Myles thought. No, please. No. A picture of Dru weeping flashed into his mind.

Marv Hilliard let Cliff slump to the floor. His own face was spotted with Cliff's blood and strings of his flesh. He stared wide-eyed at McCoy, and was still staring when a shotgun blast from the end of the corridor tore his chest out.

"Okay," McCoy said, so quietly that no one heard him but Myles. "Okay. But I'm still getting out."

McCoy put the gun back to the warden's head and fired.

CHAPTER 30

The hospital was a nightmare for Dru. She was shunted from place to place, put off in corners of waiting rooms, constantly handed containers of black, bitter coffee, and for hours on end told absolutely nothing. She resented the treatment, she revolted, she became angry, and she made vociferous demands of everyone who would listen to her. All to no avail. The only word she was given was that her father and Cliff had suffered very serious gunshot wounds in an attempted crashout, and both were in critical condition.

Personnel from the prison gathered protectively around Dru, especially when the press began to hover near her in the hope of getting a statement. The hovering increased when a rumor spread that the young woman's concern was compounded by the fact that she and the wounded guard had been about to become engaged. Despite the reporters' persistence, however, Dru said nothing for publication and managed physically to stay away from them by remaining behind a wall of guards and guards' wives.

Myles and Cliff were brought out of surgery late in the afternoon and put into an intensive care unit. Even then Dru was not permitted to see them. The chief of surgery was very firm about it. "I'm sorry," he told her, "but both your father and Officer McKittrick are clinging to life by a thread. I can't permit anyone to even go near them. Why don't you go home? Come back in twelve hours. Perhaps there'll have been a change by then."

Dru resisted leaving the hospital, but those around her insisted, and the hospital personnel encouraged it; they wanted to be rid of the reporters. So Dru was taken back to the prison. The doctor there gave her a sedative. It did not work. She paced the floor, wrung her hands, cried. The doctor gave her a sedative. Then she began to relax. Two of the guards' wives took her back to the prison and tried to put her to bed, but she refused to undress. Finally a compromise was reached: Dru took off her shoes, lay down, and permitted a comforter to be spread over her.

The wives departed the bedroom, hoping that Dru would sleep. She did not. The sedative seemed to work on her body but not on her mind. Her thoughts raced. Tears came. She shook her head, trying to clear it. She closed her eyes but found she had to open them again almost at once. In desperation, she reached to the bedtable for something to read. Her hand fell on a volume of her Great-great-grandmother Dru's journal. She drew it to her and tilted her head to rest a cheek on it. At once she seemed to feel better. Her head cleared and a rush of calm came over her.

Holding the journal like that, she fell fast asleep.

By midnight, Dru had awakened and returned to the hospital. For some reason she herself could not have explained, she held onto her great-great-grandmother's journal and took it with her. She had not even opened it since picking it up, in fact had never opened that particular volume at all, it being the next one in sequence that she was to read; but it gave her a strange kind of solace just to carry it, to have it with her. Almost as if her great-great-grandmother were there to comfort her.

Even in the middle of the night, the hospital was the same: impersonal, without warmth, uncommunicative. There was still nothing anyone could or would tell her. Myles and Cliff were still in intensive care, still critical. And Dru, if she wished to remain at the hospital, had to endure relegation to a tiny waiting room at the end of the corridor.

She sat alone in the room, smoking, sipping the ever-present black coffee, staring at the floor six feet in front of her. Occasionally a nurse would look in on her, but for the most part she was left alone. For several hours she barely moved; she was like a zombie.

Finally, in the very early hours of the morning, sometime around three o'clock, she noticed that activity in the hospital had all but stopped. She went to the door and looked down the dimly lit corridor. There was no one around except a single night-duty nurse, who was conscientiously making entries on patient charts.

Halfway between the waiting room and the nurses' station was the small red bulb over the door to Intensive Care. Dru had not even been allowed to go near the door on her way down the hall. But now there was no one around to stop her. If she could just get a split-second glance at her father and Cliff, she would be satisfied.

She took off her shoes. Biting her lip, she moved like a specter down the silent corridor. At the door under the red light, she paused and scrutinized the night-duty nurse again. The woman was totally absorbed in her work.

Dru held her breath and eased into the room. She stood just inside the door, in the soft yellow glow of a night light. She looked around, her throat suddenly going dry. Cliff was on the bed to her left, his entire face and head swathed in bandages, his head held several inches off the bed by a traction sling. Myles, his face as white as the sheet under him, was on the bed to Dru's right. His chest barely moved with breath; he lay as still as if already dead. Both men had intravenous needles feeding glucose into them.

Dru backed out of the room, tears streaking her face. Covering her mouth to stifle the sobs growing in her chest, she hurried back to the waiting room, snatched up her shoes, and curled up in a chair in the corner to cry.

"Oh God," she muttered through trembling lips, "please don't let them die."

Somehow as she cried and prayed, her great-great-grandmother's journal got back into her hands. She was sure she must have unconsciously reached over and picked it up. And even while she was crying, her hands were opening it, her watery eyes somehow managing to focus on the beautifully scripted words on the title page: THE JOURNALS OF DRUSCILLA FOYLE—1884.

Drying her eyes, desperate for escape from the dread of the present, Dru began to read.

* * *

On a warm spring day in 1884, a young man got off the Rock Island-Paducah local and stood next to the tracks for a while looking up the main street of Union City. A thin young man in his middle twenties, he wore glasses to compensate for his extreme nearsightedness. In each pocket of his coat he kept a handkerchief handy to use when he sneezed and his eyes watered from asthma and allergies. Despite it all, the thinness included, he was deceptively strong and easily handled the big Gladstone he carried.

After he had looked at the town for a while, he walked over to the stationmaster's window and leaned on the counter.

"Ticket?" said the stationmaster.

"No, I just got off the train," said the young man. "Isn't this the place that used to be called Prisontown."

"Used to," said the stationmaster. "Not no more. It's been Union City since the year eighteen-and-seventy."

"Is the prison still here?"

"Certainly. Right up on the hill where it's always been."

"Thanks," said the young man.

Carrying his bag, he left the platform and walked up Union Street. The trolley tracks, he noticed, went all the way to the end of the street and continued up the hill toward the prison. From where he stood, he could see part of the prison's wall: one corner and a gun tower. Past that, on a knoll off to one side, was the big mansion.

He glanced down the street; there was a trolley coming, its big dray horse pulling it along at a slow, easy pace. Changing his suitcase to the other hand, the young man crossed the street and waited for it. When he boarded, he paid his nickel fare and stood on the rear platform. As the trolley climbed the hill, he was able to look out over Union City to the big river beyond the railroad tracks. It was odd, he thought, that he remembered none of it.

He got off the trolley at the top of the hill and crossed the square to the prison's main gate.

He walked up to the outside guard post and put down his bag. "I'd like to see Mrs. Druscilla Ironwood, please."

The guard squinted. "Who? Oh, the Mistress." He looked the visitor up and down. "The mistress don't see many people. What's your name?"

"Nathan Hawn."

"Hawn, is it. We had a warden here once, name of *Van* Hawn."

"Two of them."

"Come to think of it, you're right." He took another quick look, decided the visitor was probably important, and reached for the prison phone. "Just a minute, sir, and I'll call up for you."

The gate guard phoned Boss Lee at the mansion. Lee took the call in his study, listened in surprise to the message, and told the guard to have the visitor wait there for him.

After he hung up, Lee sat thoughtfully at his desk and wondered whether he liked the idea of Nathan visiting. For twenty years it had been just Dru and himself. They had done very well together. Dru had received no news of Beth and the boy for years now, since Mildred Colson died. She had long ago resigned herself to the fact that her grandson had been taken from her permanently. Now, out of the blue, Nathan was there. Lee was apprehensive about the effect his visit might have on the old lady. He briefly considered sending Nathan away, refusing to let him inside the compound; but he knew he could not. It was not in him to deceive Dru.

Lee went onto the south portico where Dru sat shelling peas. "Post One just called," he said as casually as he could. "There's someone asking for you. Says his name is Nathan Hawn."

Dru stopped her work and sat absolutely still. She stared at Lee with an almost hurt expression. "After all this time," she said quietly, as if talking only to herself. She pondered for a moment, then set the bowl of peas aside and wiped her hands on her apron. "Is he on his way up?"

"No. I'll go down and fetch him for you."

"Thank you, Gerald."

Lee walked around to the north portico and crossed the broad, flower-lined lawn to the knoll that dropped down to the prison. At the base of the knoll was a natural corridor formed by the wall of the Little Yard on one side and the high cyclone fence of the outside compound on the other. Waiting there at the compound gate was Nathan. Boss Lee studied him as he approached. Skinny, he thought. Puny. Like most easterners. He was not surprised to see Nathan put on a pair of glasses as he walked up to him.

"I'm Boss Lee, the warden here. The guard said Nathan Hawn. Is that Nathan Van Hawn?"

"It was," Nathan replied. "I dropped the Van when I entered college. A lot of people are doing that nowadays. They call it Americanizing a name."

"Do they." He jerked his head toward the mansion. "Well, come along. The Mistress is waiting." He glanced at the big Gladstone. "Can you manage that up the hill?"

Nathan suppressed a smile. "I think so."

They started for the house.

"What brings you here after all these years?" Lee asked. "I mean, what brings you to this part of the country?"

"I'm just passing through. On my way to San Francisco to catch a boat for British Columbia. I'm going to work for the Canadian Pacific. They expect to have their transcontinental railroad completed in another year."

"Railroad, eh? What are you, an engineer?"

This time Nathan did smile. "As a matter of fact, I am. But not the kind you're probably thinking of. I'm a graduate mechanical and electrical engineer. Yale."

They reached the top of the knoll and started across the lawn. Dru came out onto the north portico and waited for them. Lee noticed at once that she had on a fresh dress. He glanced irritably at the visitor. The suitcase couldn't be very heavy, he decided.

At the steps, Nathan put down the bag and smiled up at the old lady who stood there. "Hello."

"Hello," Dru said. She felt a slight catch in her throat.

Nathan shifted self-consciously. "May I call you Grandmother?"

"If you want to."

Nathan stepped onto the porch and held out his hand. "I'm very happy to see you again, Grandmother."

"Thank you, Nathan." She did not know why she was being so reserved. Unless it was because she was afraid of being hurt again. "Come and sit down. I'm having lemonade sent out."

"Thank you."

Boss Lee took Dru's arm. "He says he's just passing through, Aunt Dru," he remarked, as if to reassure her. Dru glanced knowingly at him.

They sat in rockers placed strategically on the porch so that a stand of willows concealed the prison. The lemonade was brought out and Dru served. She decided to breach etiquette and give Gerald the first glass. She noticed his chin raise a bit smugly as he took it. Lord, I do spoil them, she thought.

"How is your mother, Nathan?" she asked.

"Mother passed away two years ago," he said. "She had a breast tumor. And my stepfather, Mr. Kennedy, died about five years ago. He was considerably older than Mother."

Of course, Dru thought. A well-to-do banker. Beth had married for position.

"With your Grandmother and Grandfather Colson both gone, you don't have any family at all then," Boss Lee said. His voice was polite but the meaning of his remark unmistakable. Dru threw him an irritated glance. That wasn't really necessary, it said.

"No, I don't suppose I do," Nathan answered. "No one close anyway."

"You're not married then," said Dru.

"No."

"Gerald said you were just passing through. Where to?"

Nathan told her about his two engineering degrees and the job waiting for him in British Columbia. "I'll be designing terminal and switching yards for them. Making sure everything mechanical and electrical works without getting in the way of each other."

"Sounds complicated," Dru said.

"It isn't, really. Not nearly so complicated as running this prison, I don't imagine."

"This place is a job-and-a-half sometimes, I'll grant you that," Lee said, at the same time sticking his chest out an inch.

"I admire a man who can oversee a complex like this," Nathan told him. "Someone who can keep everything running smoothly in so many quarters. That takes a special kind of ability. I'm sure I couldn't do it."

"Oh, you probably could," Lee said, somewhat grudgingly. "Once you got used to it, that is. Anyway, it's not all my doing, you know. I have a first-rate superintendent of prison industries to keep the factory shops going. And your grandmother here to look after the books and order supplies. About all I have to attend to meself is a little patch of tobacco we've got growing."

They talked away part of the afternoon and then Lee reminded Dru that it was time for her nap. She objected but he made her go along inside anyway. "I'll give Nathan a tour of the prison," he said. "We'll be back at suppertime."

"I'm afraid I can't stay for supper," Nathan said. "I'll be leaving on the five o'clock train. But I'll come back for my bag and to say goodbye."

"We'll make it a quick tour then so's you don't miss your train," Lee promised. He hustled Dru inside and led Nathan off the porch.

From inside the door, Dru watched them leave. For the first time in many long years, she was filled with conflicting feelings.

"You do ride?" said Lee as they approached the stables.

"Yes."

Lee had the trusty attendant saddle his horse and a mount for Nathan. "I'll show you the outside first; then I'll take you behind the walls."

They rode out to the tannery, now converted to a shoe factory. Lee introduced him to Andrew Myles, the superintendent.

"A pleasure, Mr. Hawn," said the Scotsman.

"Show him around, will you, Andrew," said Lee. "But not too long; he's a train to catch." Lee strolled over to talk with one of his guards.

Myles showed Nathan through the various rooms where the leather was cut, fitted, sewn, and trimmed into the finished shoe or boot. In the trimming room, a convict foreman came up to Myles. "The number two trimmer's down again, sir."

"Sparks?"

"Yessir."

"Damn," said Myles. "Every time we have to let that blasted engine cool off, we waste an hour's production time."

"What kind of engine is it?" asked Nathan.

"Some blasted German model. The only kind I could get without having one shipped over from England at a waste of two months—"

"Let me have a look at it," said Nathan. The convict foreman showed him where it was. "It's a Benz 1880," Nathan said. "Probably running on uneven brushes. Shall I repair it for you? Only take a minute."

"By all means," said Myles.

Lee came back while Nathan was working. He, Myles, the foreman, and several convicts watched with interest.

"See," said Nathan, showing the foreman, "when these brushes are out of alignment, the turbine throws sparks. To correct it, just open the face plate like I did, unscrew the clamp, and set both brushes back in place. Then tighten it up and you're back in business."

When they got outside, Myles said, "How would you like a job, young man?"

"Thanks," said Nathan, "but I have one."

"Could I interest you in committing a crime then, so's I could have you sentenced here?"

Nathan laughed. He had taken an immediate liking to the Scot.

On their horses again, Lee and Nathan rode past the abandoned knitting mill and on to the rock quarry. Nathan dismounted at the top of the huge pit and stood looking down at the sweating, grime-covered convicts swinging heavy sledges.

"When the train passed through the capital, I noticed a lot of empty gravel cars in the yards. Were they from here?"

"No," said Lee from his saddle. "The state brings gravel in from the pits in Indiana. They say it's cheaper than mining it down here. Something to do with power."

"That was probably true five years ago," Nathan said, "but not any longer. There's a portable steam-operated rock crusher available that could be set up right here in this quarry and run by a very small power plant. Doesn't your state have a qualified engineer?"

"Supposed to have," Lee said. He wanted to say something in defense of the state, but was afraid of sounding stupid.

From the quarry, they rode into the Little Yard and dismounted. Nathan noticed a number of faces in the windows of the women's dormitory. "Pay them no mind," said Lee. "They're always curious when they see a new man around." He took Nathan over to the single block of back-to-back cells where the old condemned row had once stood. "This is the cellblock your father built. The cells facing east are called Crazy Alley; they're for cons that aren't right in the head. The cells facing west are called Deep Lock. Those are for the tough ones, the ones who think they can't be broken." Lee paused a beat, then added, "The man who killed your father is in one of those cells."

"Owen Landis."

"You know his name?"

Nathan nodded. "I heard my mother speak it often enough." He studied the row of solid steel doors, their visors closed to the outside light. "How long has he been in there?"

"This last time—seven years."

Nathan's lips parted incredulously. Seven *years*! How could a man live that long in solitary confinement without losing his mind?

"I know what you're thinking," said Lee. "But there are men who've survived longer. Come on."

They went into the Big Yard.

"How much do you know of what happened?"

"Only my mother's side of it," Nathan said. "Maybe you can tell me what happened to Clara Landis. That's something my mother never spoke of."

"There wasn't much *to* speak of. She left Prisontown—that's what Union City was called back then. Nobody knows where she went."

"She never came back?"

"No."

"Never wrote to her husband?"

Lee shook his head. "Owen Landis hasn't had one visitor or got a single letter in the twenty years he's been here."

"Incredible," said Nathan. Had any man ever been so completely alone, he wondered. No mail, no visitors, a dark cell. Nathan hated to even think of it.

"Come along, I'll show you where your father is buried," said Lee.

He took Nathan up to Peckerwood Acres to Monroe's grave. Nathan stood by it in silence for a moment. I can't even remember his face, he thought. I should be sad standing here, but I'm not. Not for my dead father anyway. Perhaps for Owen Landis. And for my grandmother.

"I want to thank you for what you've done all these years," he said to Lee. "I know it's probably not my place to say it, but I want you to know that I'm grateful. You've been more of a family to my grandmother than any of her blood kin ever were. You're a good and generous man, Boss Lee. I'd be proud to shake your hand."

Lee stared at him, brow wrinkled in a frown. He's a lot like Aunt Dru herself, he thought, the realization suddenly coming to him. Rubbing an index finger along the bridge of his flattened nose, he tried to think of something to say. Finally he put out his gnarled right hand and shook hands with the young man.

"Listen, lad," he said, "what's the sense of rushing to catch that train when you could stay the night here in the mansion? It would please your grandmother no end for you to spend a little more time with her. What do you say?"

Nathan thought about it for a moment. He supposed he could spare one more day. "All right. If you're sure."

"I'm sure," said Boss Lee.

They started walking back up the hill. As they walked, Nathan looked back over his shoulder at the prison. He could not get Owen Landis out of his mind.

CHAPTER 31

Owen Landis was prepared to fight the first time he walked onto the Big Yard.

He had been in the prison as a convict for two days. During those two days he had been in the reception area: a small section of cells on the Little Yard. There he had been given a physical examination, had his face sketched by a convict artist, had his measurements taken and recorded, been given a number, issued two suits of stripes, and assigned to a cell. At the end of the second day, as the prisoners returned to the walls from work, Owen was let into general population.

He walked slowly out of his second-tier cell and down the concrete steps to the yard. Convicts who saw him coming fell quiet and watched him curiously. Others, from farther back on the yard, edged toward him. Owen began to walk the perimeter of the yard, taking care that he kept the big wall close to his side so that when the fighting started, he would have something to put his back against. As he moved among the men, his stomach quivered with spasms of fear and his sphincter muscle twitched.

This must be what it feels like to know you're going to die, he thought. Not even in the war had he been this afraid. But I'd do it all over again, he swore. I'd kill the son of a bitch all over again. Even if it meant dying right here on the yard—

"Hey, Sergeant!"

Owen glanced up at a dirt-covered convict from the rock pit. The man was blocking his way. Owen stopped and searched his memory for a name. After a moment it came to him. Twainer.

Doing thirty years for a killing. Owen had given him the lash four times.

"I was afraid they might hang you, Landis, and I wouldn't get a chance at you," Twainer said, almost leering.

Owen shook his head. "They didn't," he said flatly.

"I been waitin' for you to get here."

"Your waiting's over," Owen said.

Before Twainer could move, Owen was on him. He had learned long ago never to give an opponent the first blow. In a single leap he was at Twainer's throat with both hands, forcing him to the ground, kneeing him in the groin as he went down. There was a sudden burst of sound from the men milling around them.

"Fight! Fight!"

Owen straddled Twainer's chest and pummeled his face with blows, giving him no chance at all to defend himself. He heard a whistle sound, then another. Suddenly a shoe slammed into the side of his head and sent him pitching sideways. Another convict whom he vaguely recognized began lacing him with blows. He tried to raise his arms to ward off the punches but someone grabbed and held him from behind. Desperately, he kicked, felt his shoe make contact, saw the man hitting him go down. Then he pushed back as hard as he could, slamming the man holding him into the wall. In an instant he was free.

More whistles sounded. Footsteps ran across the yard. The milling convicts quickly spread out as a wedge of guards rushed in swinging billy clubs. Several men were hit and fell. A guard kicked Twainer, who was still on the ground. Two others ran up and clubbed Owen on the shoulder and forearm.

"It's you, is it, Landis," one of the guards growled. Owen recognized him. Staples. He had been a new guard when Owen left. "I figured we'd have trouble with you, you shit—" He punched Owen in the stomach with the end of his billy.

Owen saw red. He snatched the club from Staples and struck him solidly across the jaw with it. Staples dropped, his face a burst of red. Another guard rushed Owen. Owen swung at the man but missed. The guard knocked the club from Owen's hand and felled him with a single blow from his own club. As Owen went down, several shots were fired from the wall and the disturbance quickly ended.

For fighting with another convict on the yard, Owen would have been given fourteen days in lockup on short rations. But because he had struck down a guard, actually broken Staples's cheekbone, Boss Lee gave him thirty lashes with the cat and put him in deep lock for six months.

That was the beginning of it. Owen's path seemed to be clearly marked from then on. When his back was healed and his six months up, he was let out of deep lock. He went back to the yard and immediately sought out Twainer. "Ready to finish our business?" he asked.

"I'm willing to let it lay," Twainer said.

"I'm not," said Owen. "You got me six months in the hole. I aim to collect for it."

He attacked Twainer again and proceeded to beat him bloody. A yard guard rushed over to break them up. It happened to be Staples again. Owen, in the midst of knocking Twainer's teeth out, saw him coming. He whirled, surprising Staples, and for the second time took his club away from him. And for the second time broke his jaw with it.

Boss Lee was incensed. He gave Owen fifty lashes, literally whipping his back to pulp. Then he had him put in deep lock for two years. Staples became a tower guard after that; he was never assigned to yard duty again.

Late in 1866, Owen came out of isolation. He was put to work on the snow detail: sweeping freshly fallen snow from the Big Yard every morning. On the third day, he saw Twainer in line for breakfast. He broke the handle off his pushbroom and went over to him. "We've still got unfinished business," he said doggedly.

Twainer looked ill. "Get away from me, Landis. You're crazy!"

"You started it, Twainer," Owen said coldly. "You're the big tough con who waited for me to get here, remember? You're the man who stopped me in front of the whole population to show how mean you are—"

"That was two and a half years ago, for Christ's sake," Twainer said frantically.

"I don't care, you son of a bitch!" Owen snarled. "It's not over!" He lashed out with the broken-off handle and smashed Twainer's nose. Guards had heard the altercation and were already moving in on the line. Two other cons tried to help Twainer; Owen clubbed them both to the ground. Then the guards moved in, slowly, cautiously.

"Put down that piece of wood, Landis," one of them said.

"Don't be an asshole, Landis," another told him. "You hit a guard again and Boss Lee's liable to hang you."

"You think so?" Owen said. His eyes were wild, his breath labored. "Why don't you ask him: he's right there—"

The guards looked around, realizing too late that they had been duped. Before they could recover, Owen dropped them both with quick, perfectly placed blows, just like Big Sam Colson had taught him.

This time Boss Lee gave him sixty-five lashes, the greatest number given in the history of the prison. The cat-o'-nine cut bloody rivers in a back that was already crisscrossed with scars. And Lee would not let him escape the pain of it; each time he fainted, the punishment stopped until he could be revived with cold water. "He's going to feel every lash!" Lee swore. "I will not have my guards assaulted by this madman!"

It took two hours to complete the whipping. Owen had to be revived seven times.

When it was over and the guards started to take him down, Boss Lee stopped them. "Leave the son of a bitch there," he ordered.

Owen hung from the whipping post all night and all the next day, and all the second night. On the morning of the third day it was pouring rain, threatening to wash away the huge scab that had formed on Owen's back. When the cons were on their way to breakfast, Twainer stepped out of line.

"Cut him down!" he yelled through a thick bandage on his nose.

The yard sentries raised their clubs to the ready position. "Get back in line, you!"

"Cut him down!" Twainer yelled again.

"Yeah, cut him down!" another yelled, stepping out of line with him.

"Cut him down!" echoed several others.

It spread, until finally there was no line, just a ragged crowd of angry prisoners standing in the rain-swept yard, remembering how to be men.

Boss Lee was summoned. He rode into the yard on his great black mare. A shiny yellow slicker was buttoned up to his neck, courtesy of Dru.

"Cut him down!" the convicts chanted, rattling their tin cups and spoons. "Cut him down! Cut him down!"

At the post, trickles of fresh blood had begun to seep from the massive scab on Owen's back. Lee sat his mount, watching it.

From the crowd, a tin cup was thrown at the hooves of Lee's horse. It sounded loudly on the concrete. The mare skittered back nervously. Boss Lee glared at the men. Another cup flew. The mount reared up; it whinnied loudly. Lee reined her in firmly. Finally he nodded to a guard sergeant.

"Take him down. Put him in deep lock." His eyes swept the crowd of prisoners. "And close down the kitchen. There'll be no meals today."

The prisoners did not object; they had achieved what they wanted.

Owen spent the next five years in deep lock. When he got out, he never again fought with a prisoner. Instead, he became the most insolent, insubordinate convict in the entire population. He served five separate one-year lockups for starting work strikes, threatening officers, damaging or destroying prison property, and gross disrespect. At the end of thirteen years, he had spent all but eight months in deep lock.

One day in 1877, in an argument over a work assignment, Owen swung a large rock at a guard. The guard ducked, disarmed him. The incident was reported to the warden.

"I've reached the end of the line with you, Landis," Boss Lee said at the discipline hearing. "You might have killed that officer if he hadn't been alert. I've decided that you're too dangerous to be kept in population." He nodded to a sergeant. "Put him deep lock again."

"For how long, sir?"

"Permanently."

That had been seven years ago.

CHAPTER 32

Dru was not surprised when Boss Lee brought up the subject of asking Nathan to stay on with them. She had detected a softening of his attitude toward the young man almost as soon as it occurred. She did not let Lee know that, however.

"Stay on?" she said innocently. "I thought you didn't like the boy."

"I never said I didn't," he replied archly.

"You didn't have to *say* it, Gerald. You showed it well enough."

They were sitting on the back porch, their favorite place to talk. Lee stared off at nothing for a moment. "I didn't like him at first. But it was nothing personal. I just—well, I didn't want no one taking my place with you, is all."

Jealous, Dru thought. That pleased her. But she did not want to see Gerald hurt. She took one of his gnarled-knuckle hands in both of her own and squeezed it.

"You have been like a son to me, more than a son, for twenty years. There *is* no one who could take your place with me."

"You've got to admit, though, you'd like to see him stay. I can tell by the pleasure you take talking to him."

"Of course I'd like to see him stay. But if he did, it would be as my *grand*son. If he became a son to anyone, it would be to you."

"Me?" he said, just a hint irate. "How do you figure that?"

Dru shrugged. "You're the same age as his father would be, and if he stayed here you'd be the natural one for him to look up to."

Lee stared off into space again. His lips pursed as unresolved thoughts gathered in his head. It was funny, he thought, but being a father to the boy had never occurred to him. He had been adopting people most of his life: his fight trainer back east, old man Kellerman who owned the saloon, Dru; but always it had been someone older, someone *parental*. This was the first time he had ever considered *being* the older one. A father. He rather liked the idea.

"I'll put a proposition to him at supper tonight," he told Dru, almost gruffly. "We'll see how he takes to it."

"Fine," Dru agreed.

They rocked silently, each with personal thoughts: Lee contemplating his possible new role, and Dru thinking how delightful it was at her age to stir jealousy in someone.

"What I have in mind is a deputy wardenship," Lee said at the table that night. "Someone higher than the captain of the yard and the industries superintendent. Someone who could modernize the place, bring in new ideas—like that rock crusher you was talking about. I'd like to take that idea to the governor and see what he thinks of it. If I can get approval, and I think I can, then I'd like to have you do the buying and supervise the installation: be in charge of the whole project to get it running smoothly. How does it sound to you?"

"I, ah—I don't know," Nathan said, glancing at his grandmother. The offer was a complete surprise to him. If it had not been for Dru, he would simply have refused outright. But I must take care not to hurt her, he thought. She had suffered enough heartbreak without him giving her more. "The, ah—the Canadian Pacific people are expecting me—"

"Let them hire a Canadian," Lee said. "You don't want to be running off to a foreign country."

Nathan glanced at Dru again. She was watching him with those great round eyes of hers; eyes that made him cautious because he sensed that she could see so much more with them than was on the surface. Perhaps if he went at it another way—

"Your offer is very generous, Mr. Lee—"

"Boss," he corrected. "Call me Boss."

"All right, Boss. But you don't have to hire me in order to modernize the prison. I can spend a few days with Mr. Myles and outline a plan for him to follow."

"It wouldn't be the same," Lee said at once. He drummed his fingers soundlessly on the tablecloth. "Anyhow, that's not all there is to the offer. Aunt Dru and me—that is, your grandmother and me—were thinking we'd ask if you'd consider moving into the mansion with us. There's plenty of room, you could have all the privacy you wanted—"

"I couldn't do that, really. After all, this is your home."

"It was once your home also," Dru reminded him. "You were born in this house, Nathan."

He stared at her. "I didn't know that."

"It's true," Boss Lee confirmed. "When your mother's time came, your father sent me to fetch the doctor while he put her in the buggy and brought her up here for your grandmother to take care of. Your mother didn't like the idea, but your father was bound that you'd be born in the same house where he and his brother were born."

A thoughtful frown settled on Nathan's face. He suddenly felt very close to the big mansion. It was an unusual feeling, one he had never experienced: not in the home of his maternal grandparents, not in the home of his stepfather. Having a sense of the past, his *own* past, was unfamiliar to him; but here, with his grandmother, he discovered that he liked it. How odd, he thought. To find his sense of being with an old lady he barely knew, a tough ex-fighter who started out not liking him, and a half-century-old mansion on a prison compound. He looked at Dru. She was still watching him steadily.

"How do you feel about it, Grandmother?" he asked.

Dru did not answer. Instead, she rose and came around the table. She kissed him gently on the cheek. As she did, he felt a warm tear fall from her cheek to his. Then she left the room.

When they were alone, Nathan nodded to Boss Lee. "I'll stay on," he said.

CHAPTER 33

On a summer day in 1890, when Nathan Hawn had been deputy warden at Prison Hill for six years, Reba Myles, the daughter of Andrew Myles, came home from school in Scotland. Andrew and his wife Nancine drove their buggy down to the depot to get her. When they came back up the hill, they stopped at the gate to the Little Yard where Nathan and Owen Landis were checking in a load of medical supplies.

"Nathan!" Andrew Myles called. "Come greet my little girl!"

"Daddy, for goodness sakes," Reba said, as if embarrassed. But she did not blush. She was eager to see Nathan again. As he walked over, removing his glasses, she smiled.

"Hello, Reba," he said, holding out his hand. "How grown up you are."

"Hello, Nathan. It's nice to see you again." Reba was a thin, slightly stooped young woman with what some people called a very forward manner. Actually it was not that at all; she was simply more intelligent than most people, therefore seemed even more precocious than she really was. She had been in her teens when Nathan first came to the Hill. Now she was a mature young woman with an attractiveness and bearing he had never seen in her before.

"You look lovely, Reba," Nathan said. "All doctors should be as pretty as you."

"All doctors should be as *smart,* too," Andrew boasted. "She is the first woman to be graduated with high honors from the University of Glasgow medical school."

"Congratulations, Doctor," said Nathan.

"Why, thank you, sir," she replied. He's still holding my hand, she thought. She wondered if he was remembering that day in her parents' home, the summer she was eighteen. He had come to see her father, but her father had gone to town. And her mother was up at the mansion helping Dru Ironwood can peaches. Reba had just returned from school then too, after completing her final year at Illinois Preparatory for Young Women. She was waiting for word on her application to the University of Glasgow. Nathan had knocked once and walked into the Myles kitchen, as was his habit. He had caught her fixing herself a glass of iced tea in her underwear, as was her habit.

"I—I'm sorry, Reba," he had stammered. "I didn't even know you were home from school."

"I got home yesterday, Nathan," she said. She looked around for something of her mother's to put on: an apron, anything. There was nothing. Oh, well.

"I—I'll come back another time—"

Reba smiled a little half smile. Nathan had turned bright pink and it delighted her. "It's so hot out, Nathan," she said quickly. "Here, have some of my tea."

Before he could back out of the door, she had walked over to him, slightly stooped shoulders and long, too-thin legs bare. She forced the glass into his hand.

"Nathan, I've been thinking about something," she said almost conversationally. "I'll probably be going to Scotland soon to go to medical school. I don't think I should go over there a virgin, do you?"

Nathan nearly choked on the tea. "Reba, I have to go." He tried to hand the glass back to her but she would not take it.

"The way I look at it," she continued, "I'll be over there for six years, and I know I won't stay a virgin the whole time. Good lord, we'll be studying anatomy, intercourse, childbirth, breasts, male organs—"

"Reba, for God's sake," Nathan said. He set the glass on a shelf. When he tried to leave, she blocked the door.

"I'm a good American," she said. "The only reason I'm going

to school in Glasgow is because my grandfather's estate will pay my tuition only if I attend school in Scotland." She put one palm on his chest. "But I don't have to give my virginity to a foreigner—"

Reba sank back to the cool linoleum, drawing him down with her. Their garments came silently off. Then, for a few minutes, the afternoon quiet was disturbed only by Nathan's labored breathing and subsequent asthmatic wheezing.

Looking at him now, six years later, as he still held her hand in greeting, Reba knew he *had* to be remembering it.

"How is your asthma, Nathan?" she asked.

"About the same," he told her. "I still wheeze when I exert myself."

"Now don't start practicing on the man the minute you get home," Andrew scolded. "You'll have time for that tonight. The Mistress is having us all up to the mansion for supper."

The Myles family drove on toward their home, Reba turning once to wave, and to see if Nathan was still watching. He was, and waved back. Why do I feel so good all of a sudden? he wondered. He went back to the wagon of medical supplies.

"Feeling good all of a sudden?" Owen Landis asked.

Nathan grinned. "When did you become a mind reader?"

"Don't have to be a mind reader to notice how a man looks at a pretty woman like that," Owen drawled. "Held onto her hand for a right long time, too, I noticed."

"Since you're noticing so many things, Inmate Landis, maybe you could notice what we have left on the wagon to check in."

"Yessir, Mr. Deputy. Right away, Mr. Deputy." Owen pulled three boxes to the edge of the wagon for the convict work crew to unload. "Three cases of castor oil," he said.

"Three cases castor oil," Nathan repeated, checking it off on his invoice.

Owen Landis had been out of deep lock since Nathan's first day as deputy warden.

"Let's be clear on one point," Nathan said to Boss Lee when they went inside the walls that first morning. "I'm second in charge, answerable only to you, right? And only you can rescind an order of mine?"

"That's right, lad," said Lee. "And I'm not likely to rescind any order you give. I have complete confidence in your judgment."

"I'm glad to hear that, Boss." Nathan went over to the guard posted at the row of deep lock cells. "Give me the key to the end cell, please."

Lee frowned. "Owen Landis? Why?"

"Because I think he's been in there long enough."

"He's dangerous," Lee said.

"You mean he *was* dangerous. Six years ago."

"And if he still is?"

"Then you can put him back in."

"Yes, but while he's out, he could kill you."

"I won't give him the chance, Boss. I'll be very careful with him. But I want to try this. I want to try to put an end to something unfortunate that happened twenty years ago. It's gone on long enough."

"Your grandmother won't approve. She hates Owen Landis."

"I think she probably only hates what he did. Anyway, we don't have to tell her."

Boss Lee grunted softly. "The Mistress has more informants in this prison than *I* do. Every trusty in the compound wants to be in her good graces. Most of them think she *runs* the place. She'll know before supper that you let Landis out."

"I still want to do it," Nathan said.

Boss Lee sighed resignedly. "Give him the key," he told the guard.

Nathan went alone down to the last cell. He unlocked the solid steel door and stood in the doorway. At the back of the cell, a shaft of dim light fell on a bearded man sitting in the corner. A pair of narrowed eyes peered up at him.

"I'm the new deputy warden," Nathan said. "I've been hired to modernize the prison. I need an inmate aide: someone to help me keep things organized. I understand you were once an army officer, and before that a guard here. I thought you might like to have a try at the job."

For a long moment there was no reply from the dim corner. Only silence. Nathan waited patiently. When he felt that enough time had passed, he said, "Did you hear me, Landis?"

"I heard you," said Owen Landis. His voice was raspy,

strained, his vocal cords tight from long periods of inactivity. "Would you come a little closer, Deputy?" he said. "I want to spit in your face but you're too far away."

"Certainly," Nathan said. He stepped into the cell and over to the corner. Owen's expression turned to suspicion. But he did not hesitate in what he had said he would do. Raising to a half-crouch, he spat in Nathan's face.

Nathan took a handkerchief from his pocket and wiped the spittle from his cheek. "I hope that did you some good," he said quietly. "Now what about the job?"

Owen rose to his feet and stared incredulously at his visitor. "Who are you?" he asked. There was the slightest hint of fear in his voice.

"My name is Nathan Hawn. I'm the son of Monroe Van Hawn."

Owen leaned forward and studied his face. After a moment, his eyes widened a bit and he nodded to himself. "Yes," he whispered. "Yes, I can see it now. The nose, the chin. You're the Cobra's son, all right."

"The Cobra?"

"That was your father's nickname. The cons called him that because they hated him." He looked Nathan up and down. "What do you suppose they'll end up calling you?"

"I don't know" Nathan said. "Friend, perhaps, if things work out."

"Friend!" Owen scorned. "You'll never see the day! Cons and keepers are two different kinds. I know; I've been both. There's no place for friendship between them."

"Cons are men and keepers are men," Nathan reasoned. "Between men can always be found a place for friendship."

"You don't know what you're talking about. You're full of shit."

"And what are you full of, Landis? Fear? Afraid the world might not turn out exactly as you figured? Afraid to face that world and find out? You're a coward, Landis."

The bearded convict closed his fists. "Nobody calls me that—"

"I did," Nathan said coldly. "And I'd be careful of those hands, if I were you. I let you spit in my face and curse me so I could show you that I sincerely wanted to help you. But if you lay your hands on me, I'll beat your ass all over this cell. I'm a lot stronger and tougher than I look."

The two men locked eyes and held each other's stare. Owen's mouth tightened into a line that disappeared under his beard. His fists were poised, ready. But he did not strike.

Nathan held his ground, knowing his chin was a tempting target, knowing there was no way he could avoid one, possibly two, blows if Owen struck. Yet refusing to back down even an inch. This man doesn't have a friend in the world, he kept telling himself. If I don't help him, he'll die in this cell.

Finally, it was Owen who relented. "You're not worth hitting," he said in disgust and turned away.

A wave of relief rushed through Nathan. Swallowing dryly, he said, "I still need a convict aide."

Owen slumped down in the corner and stared moodily at the rock floor. "What does the great Warden Boss Lee think about your idea?"

"He doesn't approve. He thinks you might try to kill me."

"Smart man. Maybe you ought to listen to him."

"I would if I thought he was right. You killed my father, Landis, but you had a reason for doing it. You've got no reason to kill me." Nathan's shoulders sagged an inch. "Look, you don't have to work for me if you don't want to. Maybe it was a bad idea. It was just my way of letting you know that I'm willing to close the books on what happened twenty years ago. If you want to get out of this lockup cell and start trying to make a life for yourself here in prison, I'll see that you get all the help you need. You can send word to me anytime."

He turned to go. When he got to the door, Owen's voice stopped him.

"Just a minute, Deputy—"

Nathan turned back.

"I'll work for you," Owen said.

Nathan nodded. He walked out of the cell. As he locked the door behind him, he suddenly felt very, very good.

At the supper that Dru gave for Reba Myles when the young lady doctor returned to Prison Hill, Nathan discovered that he was in love with her. The realization came over him gradually as he and Reba were strolling the grounds later that evening.

"You've accomplished so much since you've been at the prison, Nathan," Reba said. "Everyone's so proud of you."

"There's still quite a lot to be done," he replied. "I've been talking to your father about reopening the old knitting mill and converting it to close-weave textiles. If we can get the right machinery and someone to train the men, we can weave bed linen, towels, maybe even work clothes. It would save the state a lot of money. And it would be good training for the men."

"You're the only one who calls them men, do you know that, Nathan? Everyone else calls them convicts or prisoners or inmates—never men."

"I hadn't realized that."

Reba took his arm. "Will you be warden someday, Nathan?"

"I don't know. I could be, I suppose. Boss has taken me to the capital twice now when he went to make his annual report to Governor Childress. I suspect it's part of a plan he and Grandmother have to show me off."

"Mother tells me you and the Mistress have been having your differences."

"Just one difference. Owen Landis."

"It's remarkable what you've done with that man. Father has written me about it over the years. He greatly admires you for it."

"Pity my grandmother doesn't share his feelings."

They came to a white stone bench backed by a high wall of hedge. Reba guided him to it and they sat down.

"Owen has been a model prisoner for six years now. He worked as my convict aide for four years: helped me modernize the rock quarry operation; helped me completely reorganize the lumber mill; helped me get the men interested in putting in tomato and bean gardens; came up with the idea for the apple orchard; and devised a new and cheaper way to irrigate the tobacco fields. For the past two years he's been in charge of the dispensary. Has full responsibility for all the medical supplies. Gets everything ready for Dr. Wilke's morning visit from Union City. Does an exemplary job. Yet last year, after he had served twenty-five years and was eligible for parole for the first time, Grandmother went all the way to the capital to formally oppose it."

"Was he turned down because of it?"

"Of course. She's the Mistress of Prison Hill. She's been here for more than sixty years, been the wife of three wardens and the mother of one. She was at Prison Hill before most of the parole board members were *born*. She's like a legend to them. They'd keep Owen Landis in here forever rather than take sides against her."

"How does Owen feel about it?" Reba asked.

"He's been very understanding. He doesn't have any particular place to go when he gets out; and he's sure he'll outlive Grandmother. He's fifty-nine, she's eighty-one. I'm afraid he might have to do it, too. She swears he'll never be paroled as long as she's alive. And she usually gets things her way."

Reba nodded knowingly. "Yes, she does. She asked me tonight why I didn't consider staying here, starting my practice in Union City, and marrying you."

Nathan's eyes searched her face in the moonlight. Her tone gave no hint of how she felt about Dru's suggestion; her expression was equally inscrutable. Nathan had to ask. "What was your reply to that?"

"I told her I didn't think the people of Union City were quite ready for a lady doctor. Can't you just see old Lamp Kellerman's face if I told him to drop his pants so I could press his testicles for a rupture? Or proper Mr. Lon Kern if I told him to lie on his stomach and spread his legs so I could put my finger up his anus to feel his prostate gland. God, Nathan, I don't even know if Union City's *women* would come to me."

"What about the marriage part?" Nathan said. "What did you tell her about that?"

She shrugged. "I told her you didn't love me."

"That's not true. I do love you."

"Oh? When did you decide that?"

"About an hour ago."

Reba tilted her head curiously. "When you were holding my hand today when I first got here, were you remembering that time in Mother's kitchen?"

"Yes. Were you?"

"Yes."

Nathan took her by the shoulders and gently pulled her to him. He tried to kiss her but his glasses got in the way. Taking them off and carefully putting them in his pocket, he tried the kiss again. It worked this time—deliciously.

"I thought about you so many times while I was gone," she told him.

"I thought about you a lot too," Nathan lied. I wish I *had*, he thought guiltily.

They kissed some more, experimentally, trying each other's lips from this angle and that, trying them softly, lightly, firmly, closed, open—

"Let's go behind the hedge," Nathan said.

"All right—"

They undressed and looked at each other's bodies in the moonlight. Reba was still thin, still stoop-shouldered, but to Nathan she was beautiful. They lay down on the grass together. It was already wet with evening dew.

"Let's hurry," she said. "It's cold."

They hurried, and it was not a really memorable experience for either of them.

While he was drying off her back and bottom with his handkerchief, Nathan asked, "Did you do this with a lot of men in Scotland?"

"Not a lot," she said. "Most of the time I was too busy or too tired. Usually I just borrowed a dildo from Li-Tang, a Chinese girl in the next room. She had an *assortment* of them."

"But you did have men?" he persisted.

I'd better pull this thorn out of his side right now, she thought. She turned to him, naked, and put her arms around his neck. "A few," she said. "None that mattered. And always remember that you were the very first. And if you want, you can be the last."

He kissed her, long and lovingly.

"I want."

CHAPTER 34

After their marriage, Reba moved into the mansion. She and Nathan occupied half of the second floor, sharing it with Dru, who still had the original bedroom and sitting room that she and Aaron had designed for themselves so many years ago. She offered to give those rooms to the newlyweds—in fact, almost insisted on it, something she had not done for Nathan's parents—but they refused to take them, and instead remodeled two other rooms for their needs.

Dru and Reba got on famously; probably, Nathan decided, because Reba left the running of the mansion entirely to Dru. Reba herself was kept busy setting up her medical practice: finding office space in Union City; ordering furniture, supplies, and equipment from Merck and Herrick in Philadelphia; having shelves built to accommodate all her medical books which had been shipped over from Glasgow; traveling to the capital to go before the board for her license to practice; writing personal notes to nearly every woman in town—"Dr. Reba Myles Hawn announces the opening of her General Medical Practice at Number 402 Union Street, Suite 3,"—and in general doing the hundred-and-one things none of her professors had prepared her for.

In addition to everything else, she discovered almost immediately that she was pregnant. Oh, no! she thought. Not so soon. Not when she had so much to do. She simply had no time to be burdened with a baby right then.

She aborted her pregnancy two nights later, timing it so that everyone would be asleep when it happened. She told no one.

Nathan was very proud of his wife and what she was doing. He devoted all of his free time to helping her however he could: painting, moving furniture in, unpacking books. He even asked Owen Landis to help her, and gave him permission for the first time in twenty-five years to leave the compound. Some of the Union City townspeople were a bit taken aback to see the community's infamous murderer on their streets again, but they soon became accustomed to it, some of them even to the point of speaking to him in passing.

With his experience in the dispensary, Owen was a valuable temporary assistant to the new doctor. Because she had never had her own stock of medicines before, Owen set up her supply closet for her, on the order of his own dispensary. Reba was extremely pleased and praised the convict highly to everyone except Dru.

"The man's an absolute marvel," she told Nathan. "It's awful that Grandmother Dru is so determined to keep him in prison."

"That's one controversy I'd advise you not to get involved in," Nathan said. "It's bad enough that *I* have to do battle with her about it; there's no sense in you fighting her too."

Reba did not argue with Nathan about it, but she made up her mind that the next time Owen's parole was on the docket, she herself would appear in his behalf—even if it meant alienating her grandmother-in-law. Fair, after all, was fair.

In the fall, when she had her medical office almost ready to open, Owen did something that made her all the more determined to help him win his release.

"You know that desk you described to me that you wanted for your office?" he said one morning. "Well, there's a lawyer named Pandeal over in Bloomington who has one for sale. Sounds like just the kind you want."

"How did you find out about it?" Reba asked.

"Pandeal has a client doing time up on the Hill. He mentioned it to him and his client told another con, and eventually I heard about it."

"How far is Bloomington?" Reba asked.

"Only about two hours. It's a nice buggy ride."

"I'd planned to hang my office shades this afternoon."

"I can do that for you. If you postpone going, the desk might get sold."

"I suppose you're right. I'll call Nathan now."

That afternoon Nathan drove her to Bloomington. There was indeed a lawyer named Pandeal in town, but he did not have a desk for sale, and had never had one for sale.

"How odd," Reba said, perplexed.

"It was a nice drive anyway," Nathan said to soothe her disappointment. "And I'm sure you'll find the desk you want somewhere else."

They drove back to Union City. A guard was waiting at Reba's office for Nathan.

"There's been trouble at the prison, Mr. Hawn," he said urgently. "You'd better come right away."

Nathan dropped Reba off and raced up the hill in the buggy. Reba nervously went inside. Owen was there with a cup of tea for her.

"Drink this, Miss Reba, it'll calm you down."

"Owen, what's happened up at the prison?"

"A break," he told her. "Four lifers managed to get guns smuggled in to them. They got to the warden's office in the Little Yard and took him hostage."

"My God! Nathan's office is right next to his—"

"It happened a few minutes after the noon meal. You two were already on the road to Bloomington by then."

Reba stared at the old convict. A slight frown pinched two wrinkles between her eyes. "Owen, we saw Mr. Pandeal. He doesn't have a desk for sale. He never has had."

Owen shrugged. "Must have been a misunderstanding, Miss Reba. Sorry."

Reba continued to stare at him for a long moment. Then she nodded thoughtfully. She never mentioned the desk again.

The four pistols had been smuggled into the prison securely wrapped in sealskin and submerged in a barrel of lard. The barrel was delivered to the storeroom, where the weapons were retrieved by John Curtain, the leader of the break gang. He passed out the weapons and each man concealed one on his person. At midday all the men were marched inside for the noon meal. Curtain and his three partners filed into the dining hall and ate along with everyone else. When the meal was over, they marched out to the Big Yard for the rest of the meal hour.

In the Big Yard, the men ambled casually up to the gate to the Little Yard. Once in position, Curtain drew down on the solitary gate guard on duty on the other side.

"Open it up, hack," he said, "or I'll open you up."

The guard opened the gate. Curtain had him lead them in formation across the Little Yard to Deputy Warden Hawn's office. The deputy warden was not there, the first time in weeks that he had not been. Curtain had planned the break very carefully. Both the warden and his deputy always remained inside the walls until the noon meal was over and the men returned to work. They almost never deviated from that routine. But that day, the deputy had.

Curtain took his men to the next office. He kicked the door in and leveled his gun at Boss Lee.

"On your feet, Warden," he ordered. "We're going for a little ride."

The gang took Lee out of the Little Yard and across the compound to the stables. They had five horses saddled. With the warden as hostage, they rode off.

Six miles south of town, they reined up.

"End of the line, Warden," said John Curtain.

He shot Boss Lee once in the chest. The warden pitched backward off his horse. The four convicts rode off.

Boss Lee lay where he had fallen and bled to death.

Dru mourned the death of Gerald Lee more than she had ever mourned anyone except Jack Ironwood.

"He was as true a son to me as my own flesh-and-blood kin," she told all who came to the wake. "And he loved me like a mother; he told me so many times." That was not true: they had never spoken of their affection for each other; but they had felt it, and each had silently acknowledged it. So Dru did not feel that it was really a lie. And even if it had been, no one would have mentioned it because it was so obvious that she was heartbroken over her loss.

Governor Childress came down from the capital to attend the funeral. While he was there he took the opportunity to speak to Nathan about the wardenship.

"I'd like you to take the job, of course," he said. "You're the natural candidate for it, by blood as well as position. How do you feel about it?"

"I'm not sure, sir. I'm not yet over the shock of Boss Lee's death enough to say. At any rate, I'd have to consult my wife before I made a decision like that."

"You will assume temporary charge in the meantime, won't you?"

"Of course."

Boss Lee was buried in the administration section of Peckerwood Acres, in a grave directly next to Monroe Van Hawn. He was the fifth warden to be laid to rest in that little section of the cemetery.

Only after the graveside service was over and Nathan and Reba were escorting Dru back to the mansion did the Mistress finally give way to her emotions. "This goddamned prison," she said in an anguished voice. "It takes and takes and takes! It's like a great sore on the land, full of germs in striped suits. The keepers are supposed to prevent the germs from getting out of the sore, supposed to contain them and control them, but the germs are too vicious: they won't *be* controlled."

She stopped at the top of the knoll and looked down at the prison. Her eyes were awash with hurt, her lips trembling with anger.

"Bastards!" she yelled. "Bastards! You took Aaron and you laughed when my Jack died! One of your kind took Monroe, and now you've taken Gerald Arthur! I hope God brings down a horrible, terrible pox on all of you! I hope you all burn in hell!"

As she cursed the prisoners, a black cloud opened above and a slant of cold rain began falling.

"Come on, Grandmother," Nathan urged. "Come on, Grandmother, please."

With Reba's help, he finally got her to start through the rain toward the mansion.

CHAPTER 35

The three of them—Nathan, Reba, and Dru—had breakfast together every morning in a pleasant, sunny alcove which Reba had suggested, Dru had designed, and Nathan had ordered built on the east side of the mansion. They sat in the morning sun at a large, round table, each reading a different newspaper: Reba the St. Louis *Dispatch*, Dru the Chicago *Tribune*, and Nathan the Quincy *Herald*. The two women frequently shared their metropolitan dailies, but both were scornful of Nathan's country newspaper and never touched it.

"I can't imagine what you find interesting in that little paper," Reba often said. "My God, *nothing* ever happens in Quincy."

"Maybe that's why I like it," Nathan replied. It was August and he was wheezing more than usual.

"I suppose we'll be getting this mad slasher down here pretty soon," said Dru, studying the front page. "Lord, I don't know what this world's coming to. The man killed twelve innocent women and the jury gave him life. Have they forgotten we hang people anymore?"

"He's a sick man, Grandmother," said Nathan.

"He's not sick, he's a madman. Slashing all those women like that. It's not safe to walk the streets anymore."

"The women he killed were prostitutes, Grandmother. All of them. The man obviously has some kind of deranged hatred for women like that. The jury probably realized that it would serve no useful purpose to execute him."

Dru grunted loudly at such radical thinking. People got away with anything nowadays. What those juries needed were a few Aaron Van Hawns and Jack Ironwoods. *Then* they'd see some quick justice.

"Anyway, I thought I told you," Nathan said, "we won't be hanging condemned men anymore. There's a new way of doing it now: something called an electric chair. Supposed to be painless."

"Yes, I read a medical journal article about that," Reba said. "It's based on the theory that electricity travels faster than pain."

"What does the medical profession say about it?"

"From the tone of the article, doctors seemed to be about equally divided on it."

"As usual," Dru interjected.

Reba patted her arm fondly. Nothing Dru said or did ever upset Reba. Since the death of her parents, she and her grandmother-in-law had grown very close. They almost never disagreed on anything important, were never cross with each other, and regularly sided against Nathan in matters in which they had a voice, and often in matters in which they did not.

"If all doctors agreed with each other," Reba said, "it would put an end to research. Then we'd never have any improvements."

"I suppose you're right, dear," Dru said, patting her hand back.

If I had made that comment, Nathan thought wryly, my loving wife would have taken me apart, while sweet old Grandmaw cheered her on. Not that he really minded. It was wonderful that they got on so well.

From upstairs came the sound of the baby crying. Reba started to get up but Dru stopped her. "I'll go. You finish your breakfast."

Dru climbed the stairs with a sprightliness that belied her eighty-three years, and followed the sound of crying down the hall. The nursery occupied the middle bedroom, which had once been Grover's room. Dru entered and bent over the crib to comfort the squalling, kicking baby.

"There, there," she cooed. "Everything's all right. Great-grandmother's here to take care of you."

She felt the diaper, found it wet, and set about changing it.

Under her practiced hands the baby stopped crying almost at once. When Dru was finished she picked up the baby in her arms.

"That's Great-grandmother's good boy," she said. The baby touched her face, smiled and drooled. His name was Myles Hawn, after Reba's family name. He had been born late one night in the same room in which Monroe, Grover, and Nathan had been born. Dru, who had so wanted a girl, had at the first sight of him completely forgotten her preference. He was the most beautiful, perfect infant she had ever seen, and she took immediate possession of him. Reba and Nathan permitted it; they both loved Dru very much, and if their son could bring her last years an extra measure of happiness, that was what they wanted. Neither of them ever interfered with Dru's love for the child or her prerogatives regarding his care.

Leaving the nursery, Dru took the baby downstairs and into the kitchen for Lemuel, the big black cook, to fix his bottle.

"Hey there, little fella," Lem said with a smile when he saw Myles. "Is you hongry this mornin'?" Lem was a murderer doing life. He had killed a white man who had seduced his sister into a house of prostitution.

"Mix some of that wheat germ in his milk, Lem," said Dru. "Just a spoonful."

"Yes, Mistress. That be good for him. Reckon we should put a taste of honey in it too?"

"Yes, that's a good idea. We'll see if he likes it."

Unknown to his parents, the infant Myles consumed many foods that were not commonly given to babies in that day. At various times he had milk formulas containing beef gravy, bacon drippings, crushed peaches, berries, watermelon, crushed peanuts, tiny bits of calves' liver, raw eggs, and all manner of grains, from wheat and barley to oats and even hops.

When Dru took him into the breakfast room with his bottle, she let Nathan hold him while he ate. "I can't get over how he's growing," Nathan said. "Look at the size of his legs."

"I've noticed that myself," said Reba. "He didn't weigh that much at birth either. Is he still on the same formula, Grandmother?"

"Of course," Dru lied. "Milk and sugar, mixed just as you said."

Reba shook her head. "At the rate he's going, we'll have to put him on solid foods sooner than I planned."

"Whenever you think," said Dru. She and Lem were already feeding him strawberries, mashed potatoes, and soggy biscuits dipped in maple syrup.

After breakfast, Nathan was off to the prison to begin his daily routine, and Reba went down to Union City to tend to her medical practice. For the rest of the day then, except for a brief period at lunchtime, Dru had Myles all to herself. Just as she liked it.

The boy began to grow, always in the shadow of the Mistress.

Prison Hill became the ninth penitentiary in the country to install an electric chair. The apparatus itself was manufactured in Philadelphia, and a scholarly-looking man named Rhodes traveled west with it to supervise the installation. It was uncrated and set in place in a small room specially constructed for it in the Little Yard. Nathan and his guard officers came in and studied it curiously.

"Beautifully crafted, isn't it?" Rhodes said proudly. He adjusted it just so on a cement slab where it was to be bolted down.

"I didn't expect it to be wooden," Nathan said. "Won't it burn?"

"No, sir," said Rhodes. "The electricity never touches the chair itself. You see, it's direct current: it goes into the condemned man's head, paralyzes his brain and heart, and comes out through his right calf. Actually you don't need a chair at all; you could use a post or plank, anything to keep him still while that jolt goes through him. The reason the inventors decided to use a chair is that it looks so goddamned ominous. They figure to send one around the country on display, in the hopes it'll scare hell out of kids and make them grow up law-abiding."

"I hope the kids that see it don't take it as a challenge," Nathan said.

Nathan did not believe in capital punishment; he could not see where it did anyone any good. He did not publicly speak against it because it was the law of the state and the land; but privately, to Reba, he expressed his doubts that it accomplished anything in the way of crime prevention or deterrent to youngsters. Reba, whose life was devoted to healing, agreed with him, though for different reasons. She did not feel that a human body should be deliberately destroyed, no matter what its deficiency. To her way of thinking, there were but two courses of life: treatment and natural death. Dru, of course, disagreed with both of them. People who committed certain crimes were simply not fit to continue living in civilized society. They should be done away with as quickly and cheaply as possible, by bullet or rope.

Nathan dreaded the day when they would have to use the new electric chair for the first time. Rhodes had tested it for him several times after its installation and assured him that it was in perfect working order. To prove it, he even electrocuted a large sow that was bound for the slaughterhouse anyway. A small spot was shaved on the sow's skull, and electrodes were placed there and on its right front hoof. Strapped into the chair so that it could not escape, the animal squealed and twisted frantically until Rhodes threw the chair's control switch. Then it stiffened as if struck by a bolt of lightning and died instantly.

"I personally guarantee that pig felt no pain whatever," Rhodes said solemnly. "Believe me, this is the quickest, most humane method of execution ever devised."

Nathan and his officers were impressed, but Nathan's dread remained. It was only a matter of time, he knew, until he would have to put a man in the chair instead of a sow.

The inevitable happened one morning when Reba showed him the front page of her newspaper. A headline in the center of the page read:

BILLY DEAN
TO DIE IN
DEATH CHAIR

Dean, a young outlaw from the northern part of the state, had shot down two members of a posse that had pursued him after a bank robbery. He had escaped that day but was captured a month later at the home of a girlfriend in another town. Returned to the scene of the robbery, he was promptly tried, convicted, and sentenced to death.

When Dean arrived at Prison Hill, everyone was surprised to see that he was not the sneering, cold-eyed young killer that they expected. Instead, he was a freckle-faced, towheaded lad with an easy smile and immediately likeable ways. From the first day nearly everyone on the Hill called him Billy. He was very philosophical about his situation.

"I got it coming, I know that, and I aim to take my medicine like a man," he told one and all. "I didn't start out to kill nobody; all's I wanted to be was a bank robber so's I could have lots of money. But them fellers in the posse was bound they was going to kill me. Believe me, it was them or me. So I just naturally defended myself. I'm sure sorry for them two I killed, and I'm sorry for their families too. If I could bring them back, I would. But I can't. So I reckon the only thing left is for me to join them—in the cemetery, anyway. I guess I won't be going where they went."

During his stay on Death Row, Billy became the best-treated condemned man anyone could remember. Guards and convicts alike were forever giving or sending him little things to make his wait more pleasant. He received homemade cakes and pies, regular copies of the *Police Gazette,* a pint of whiskey now and again, a comfortable pair of slippers, and numerous other items that most men awaiting execution had to do without. Nathan did not object to this preferential treatment—he rather liked the young man himself—even though he knew that it was going to make Dean's execution that much harder to carry out. And he was right.

The time set for the execution was ten o'clock in the morning, when there was less load on the prison generator than any other time of day. The chair was tested twice that morning to make sure enough voltage was coming through for a quick death. When all was in readiness, Nathan went to Dean's cell with a convict barber.

"We're ready for you now, Billy," he said.

"Sure thing, Warden Hawn," the youth said with a smile.

"The barber has to shave your head and one leg."

"Sure thing."

A minister and a state doctor sent down from the capital were in the cell with Dean and they watched quietly while the young man's mass of unruly hair was quickly clipped away and his skull shaved.

"I bet I look like a plucked chicken," Billy grinned while his right calf was being shaved.

There were four guards to take him to the execution chamber in the Little Yard, but they really were not necessary. Billy strolled along, chatting with Nathan and the minister as if they were merely out for a morning walk. When they got inside the chamber, he stepped up to the chair, studied it for a moment, and slid his hand over its polished wooden arm.

"Mahogany, ain't it, Warden?" he asked curiously.

"Yes, it is," Nathan replied quietly. This is barbaric, he thought. A senseless ritual. It will accomplish absolutely nothing.

But it's the law, he reminded himself.

Nathan nodded to the guards and they guided Billy into the chair. The restraining straps were fastened around his chest, wrists, thighs, and ankles. The guards had difficulty buckling the straps.

"It's 'cause they're new," Billy said helpfully. "The leather's stiff. Next time, rub some linseed oil in them first."

One of the guards nodded but none of them spoke; their throats were too dry.

The electrodes were fixed to Billy's head and calf. He was all ready. Nathan stepped up with a black cloth. "This is to go around your face, Billy." His voice was so low it could barely be heard.

Billy swallowed tightly. "Sure thing, Warden."

Nathan covered his face with the cloth and stepped back. A guard, selected by lot, was at the switch. Nathan glanced around; everything seemed to be ready. He drew in a deep, silent breath and nodded. The guard threw the switch.

Billy's body strained forward against the straps. The mask over his face slid down an inch, exposing his eyebrows. The electrode on his calf slipped off and a live current jumped between it and Billy's leg. A thin wisp of black smoke rose from his scalp. He screamed.

Nathan's expression turned from revulsion to horror. "Jesus—"

The guards and witnesses stood petrified, eyes wide in disbelief, stunned.

Billy screamed again. "I'm cooking!"

The smell of burned flesh spread throughout the room with a wrath. Several men began to blanch. Everyone, including Nathan, looked around helplessly. No one knew what to do.

In the chair, Billy was twisting and squirming much as the sow had done. His fingers clenched and unclenched. The mask slid down a little farther.

Nathan strode over to the switch and raised it back to its neutral position. Billy's body immediately went limp. When it did, his head fell sideways and the mask came all the way off. His face was horrible: eyes wide but clearly not dead; a trickle of blood from each nostril; a gray, foamy substance bubbling from his mouth.

Sickened, Nathan threw the switch again. Another jolt hit the bound man. More smoke rose from the electrode on his head. The body shivered and trembled. The odor of evacuated bowels mixed with the smell of burned flesh. Several witnesses hurried from the room. Billy looked up with tortured eyes. "G-g-god—" he blubbered.

Nathan, staring at him with a bloodless expression, shook his head slowly.

"God isn't in this room, Billy," he said, more to himself than to the condemned man.

It took Billy Dean twelve minutes to cook to death inside. By the time he was dead, Nathan had made up his mind to resign as warden.

CHAPTER 36

Dru was aghast when Nathan told her.

"I don't believe it. No member of my family has *ever* resigned the wardenship."

"No member of your family ever had to fry a human being to death either. I'm sick of it, Grandmother, sick of the whole place: the walls, the bars, the smell of the men on the yard, the sound of the cell doors opening and closing, everything. I'm sick of being a prisoner."

"A *prisoner?* You?"

"Yes, a prisoner. And I *am* one. I'm just as much a prisoner as any con in population right now. You of all people must realize that, Grandmother."

"Oh?" said Dru, raising her eyebrows. "And just *why* must I realize it?"

"Because you're one too. You've been a prisoner here most of your life."

The old woman stopped rocking and stared hard at her grandson. "I resent that remark," she said quietly. "And I resent your thinking that about me." She shifted her eyes and looked past him, off the portico and across the sweeping lawn that sloped down to the wall. "I was a prisoner *before* I came to this place," she told him. "Little more than a bond servant for an uncle who stole my dowry. I had to cook, clean, garden, mend, tote, carry, and do every other manner of physical labor, and all for nothing. Never a dime did I get, never a thanks, never a scrap of material for anything new; just bed and board, like a common nigger slave. That's the kind of prisoner *I* was, until your grandfather came along and took me away from it. He brought me here, to this piece of land, and together we saw to it that this prison got *built.* We may not have had to fry a human being, as you put it, but we had to survive blizzards and riots and escapes and floods and deaths, a lot of things you *haven't* had to survive. And never once did I ever feel like I was a prisoner. This place *freed* me, Nathan Hawn—Nathan *Van* Hawn. I found more freedom here than I could ever have found anyplace else."

"All right, Grandmother, I'm sorry," said Nathan. "Maybe you *did* find freedom here, but *I* haven't. All I've found is a trap. I run this place, and yet I don't. I'm as much bound by the rules that govern the convicts as the convicts themselves are. Except that with me, the rules extend farther: I have to murder when the state says murder."

"Execute, Nathan, not murder," Dru said with an edge. "I won't have you insinuate that your father and grandfather were murderers."

"I didn't mean that, Grandmother." He paced the porch for a moment, then sat in the rocker next to her. "Did it ever occur to you that I simply might not be suited for this job?" he asked wearily.

"Who in the world is?" Dru demanded. "Is anyone ever *suited* to keep other men penned up like cattle, however much they may deserve it? Was Aaron Van Hawn suited for it? A born builder? Or Clement Niles, an accountant? Or Jack Ironwood, a frontiersman, a soldier? Or Gerald Lee, a *prizefighter,* for God's sake? None of them were *suited* for the job, Nathan. But they took it. And they did it. Because it was there to be done."

Dru laboriously got out of her chair and walked to the balustrade. Nathan's eyes followed her. His expression was a combination of personal agonies. He hated to hurt his grandmother in any way, but he still had the stench of burning flesh in his nostrils.

"You talk about being bound by rules," Dru said, turning to face him. "Don't you think there are rules out there too? There are even *more* rules to follow on the outside. At least in here the rules are written down. Out there, people make them up to suit themselves. Besides, there *have* to be rules. Any of the men who've ever run this prison would tell you that. They knew the importance of rules."

"Maybe they were better men than I, Grandmother,"

Dru came over and stood in front of him. Looking at him, her eyes suddenly filled with love. "Nathan," she said with a quiet, simple sincerity, "you are probably the best warden this prison ever had."

"You can't mean that, Grandmother."

"I do mean it. You've got a combination of common sense and formal education and engineering ability and compassion—"

"Compassion? Surely you don't think *that's* an asset," he said in mock surprise. "Not my cold-hearted, unforgiving grandmother who thinks hangings should be weekly events."

"Kindly do not exaggerate my views," Dru replied aloofly. "There will always be *some* people for whom execution is the only intelligent solution. Just as there will always be some for whom compassion and tolerance is the answer." She thought briefly of Kee as she spoke. "If you had to deal with more murderers than thieves and robbers, I would probably say you *weren't* a good warden, that you had too *much* compassion in you. But since it's the other way around, since the prisoners who don't deserve to be executed will always, God willing, far outnumber the ones who do, then your compassion and tolerance will serve you well. In case you're interested, you are the first warden who has shown a genuine forbearance for the prisoners as a body. None of the others did. Aaron Van Hawn was a strict disciplinarian who never bent a rule under any circumstance. Clement Niles was an indifferent warden; he didn't care how the men were treated as long as the work quotas were filled. Jack Ironwood: I loved him with all my heart, but he was a cruel and intolerant keeper who thought nothing of crippling a man for a minor infraction. And your father, my son Monroe, was a narrow, self-righteous man who deluded himself that his job was not merely to contain and work the prisoners, but also to punish them in any way he could. He regarded them as so much human waste, and the prison as their cesspool."

"What about Boss Lee?" Nathan asked.

"He didn't have the disposition for it," Dru replied. "Which is ironic because he was warden for longer than anyone. Gerald liked *being* warden; he didn't care much for working at it. I did most of his thinking for him and Andrew Myles kept the prison running properly." She fixed her eyes on him, steadily, unblinking. "You're the best that's come along, Nathan. Whether you like it or not. Whether you stay or not."

Nathan rose and stood at the end of the portico, looking down at the prison. Whether I stay or not, he thought. If he did not stay, what then? Go to work for some railroad designing terminal yards? Work on factories or bridges or boats? Would he be able to do that after working on *men*?

He smiled wryly to himself. Whom was he kidding?

He turned around and reached over to take his grandmother's hand.

"You know, Grandmother, I've been thinking that I'd like to design a completely new type of prison. Something like no one has ever seen before. A prison that would be like a small, self-contained city. A place where there would be no cruelty, no corporal punishment, where a man could be rehabilitated and learn an honest trade. I'd like to create a prison that I'd be *proud* to say was mine. Does that sound foolish to you?"

"No," Dru said, her eyes shining proudly. "It sounds like a fine idea, Nathan. Just fine indeed." She patted the hand that held hers. "You do it," she said almost fiercely.

Nathan never again spoke of leaving the prison. He threw himself into the improvement of the institution with all the fervor and determination that Aaron had put into builiding it. With the dedication and persistence of a man inspired, he began slowly to change not the face but the spirit of the prison. The body would come later, he told himself, when the old walls and old cell houses needed to be refurbished and he could legitimately press for a complete new prison. In the meantime, he would work on the mind, the personality, that would go into the new body. He would have it all ready when the time came. Like his father before him, he determined to build a monument. Not to punishment, as Monroe had planned, but to the reconstruction of men.

As Nathan began work, Dru watched him with pride. God, how she wished Aaron could have seen him! His grandfather—for that was how she thought of Aaron; the Theron Verne mistake had been purged from her mind; only the Van Hawn bloodline remained—his grandfather would have been as proud of him as she was; perhaps prouder. How Aaron would have jutted out that chin of his to see what Nathan was planning and doing to the prison that *he* had loved so much.

And how, too, he would have enjoyed young Myles. For while Nathan was devoting most of his time to the prison project, and Reba was occupied with her practice, Myles was left to his great-grandmother. At six, he could easily pass for nine. And by the time he was ten, he was the size of a teenager.

"Dat boy is gon' be a strappin' big man, Mistress," Lemuel said. "He gon' be big as I is." Lemuel was six-four and weighed two-forty.

"I don't think so, Lem, not quite," Dru said. "He's not as big-boned as you are. But he'll be a good size, nevertheless."

As the boy grew up and Dru grew older, she began to devote herself less and less to routine duties and more and more to Myles. Besides Lem, she had several other household trusties who both worshiped and feared her, and to them she gradually left first this responsibility, then that one, until eventually the mansion was being routinely run without her. Nathan and Reba did not know it for a long time. They assumed if they had lamb chops for dinner that Dru had selected them and overseen their preparation, as she always had. It did not occur to them that Lemuel had taken over that duty most of the time. They were so used to having Dru around that they did not notice that she had slowed down to a marked degree. Even Lemuel was not aware of it. The only person who knew was Myles, because he was the one whom she summoned when she required help putting her shoes on, or climbing the stairs for her nap, or moving her rocker into the shade.

Myles adored his great-grandmother. From infancy, she was the person he was most familiar with. His mother and father were people who came and went, and he loved them when they were around and not busy doing something else; but Great-grandmother was the one he depended upon to be there when he was lonesome or bored or had a scraped knee or a guilty conscience or was afraid of something. It was Dru whom he saw first thing in the morning and last thing at night; Dru who had helped him take his first steps, say his first words (which were "gweat-gwandmamma" and "I wuv you"); Dru who had taken him to kindergarten the first day, who had raved over his early scribblings; Dru who had decided when he should have haircuts, when he was too big for short pants; Dru who did everything for him, who raised him well into boyhood.

Old woman and boy, together they saw the century change as they sat bundled in blankets on the west portico at midnight on December 31, 1899, and watched a multitude of fireworks shoot into the air as Union City welcomed the year 1900. Then three years later they marveled together at something called an automobile, and were the very first ones in the county to go for a demonstration ride in one.

The times were good, very good. Dru was completely at peace: with the past, the present, the future. She was content with the peace she felt, even though the mirror constantly reminded her that she was extraordinarily old now and could not possibly live much longer. It distressed her sometimes to look at her face: there was not an unwrinkled inch of it, and her neck seemed to hang from her chin in streamers of ancient flesh. She became frighteningly thin and fragile-looking as she entered her nineties, and for the first time Nathan and Reba became concerned about her health. There was even some talk about Reba closing down her practice for a while so she could stay home with Dru during the day.

"You'll do no such thing!" Dru snapped at that. "If you closed down your practice, half the puny people in the county would be dead in a month. Anyway, there's nothing for you to do at home. The boy and I keep our own company; you'd only distract us from our pleasures."

Reba maintained her practice.

Myles was asked several times by his parents what he and his great-grandmother did for their "pleasures." His answers were usually vague. "We just go for walks," or "We just sit and talk."

The walks they went for were through the prison cemetery, Peckerwood Acres. And the talks they had were about the dead.

"Those two graves there," she would point out, "belong to a murderer named Lewt and a holdup man named Jingo. They were killed in 1831 after they escaped.

"And those ten graves there all in a line: those are the men who were hanged after the riot in 1837. That was when your great-grandfather was killed. Aaron Van Hawn was his name, and he was a fine, fine man. His grave is over this way."

Sometimes, if Myles was off playing with his friends, she visited the cemetery alone and wandered without design to whichever graves attracted her. Her thoughts wandered as she did.

By the spring of 1904, Dru had taken to spending most of her days on the portico, sitting, rocking, remembering, dozing. Lemuel ran the mansion now and everyone knew it. He had learned well enough to step directly into Dru's shoes.

"Ah wants you to come directly home from school today, young man," he would say to Myles, and Myles would answer, "Yes, Lem." Or to Nathan, "Ah don't thinks Miz Reba ought to go to her office today. She look peaked to me." Reba usually went anyway, then had to find some way to make it up to Lem for ignoring his advice.

One person Lem did have absolute control over was Dru. He cared for her as if she were a baby. Never did she get a chill for lack of a shawl around her frail shoulders. Never did she miss her nap, and woe be to anyone who made a noise to disturb her. Never did she miss any of the gossip from behind the walls or down in the town. And never was she allowed to get lonely.

Myles spent each weekday afternoon on the west portico with her, sitting at her feet, holding one frail hand while she balanced one of her ledgers on her lap and leafed through its aging pages, her spectacles resting on the tip of her nose as she shared the more exciting entries with him. With each telling of a particular tale, the story often grew in danger and adventure. In the blizzard of 1827, for instance, the snow drifts were first eight feet high, then ten, then twenty. Or when Ironwood returned from the Mexican War in 1846, he had been wounded twice, three times, six times. During the Civil War, in 1862, the men at Prison Hill had manufactured a thousand barrels a week, then three thousand, finally all the barrels the army used throughout the entire war.

Myles was a smart lad and recognized each embellishment as Dru added it to the story, but it in no way reduced in his esteem either the event or his great-grandmother. He idolized the old woman and was enthralled by the things she told him. Much as Boss Lee had once been, and as big Lemuel now was, Myles considered himself a protector of his great-grandmother. She could do no wrong, and he would not tolerate even an insinuation that she could.

The boy and the old woman had their secrets, even from Lem. In the afternoons when Lem would go to the meathouse to select cuts for supper, Dru would send Myles to her room to fetch Aaron's old pipe. Myles filled it for her with tobacco he stole from his father's bowl, and Dru puffed contentedly away while the boy stood watch lest she be caught. Myles also sneaked her an occasional sip or two of brandy when she wanted it.

Myles became her eyes and ears, seeing to it that she missed nothing that was going on. He became her legs, running to fetch whatever she wanted, whether she was permitted to have it or not. He became her chief witness, testifying that she had napped when she had not; that she had not taken the exerting walk to the cemetery, when she had; that she had eaten all her lunch, when he had put half of it under the porch for the dogs. He would lie to anyone for her; she had only to ask.

Dru loved the boy more than anyone she had ever loved, or so she thought. She loved him because he was there and the others, most of them, were gone; because he was the future, and they were the past; because he was more completely *hers* than anyone had ever been. But most of all, she loved him because he was so truly devoted to her, so totally faithful, so utterly dependable. Sitting on the portico in the afternoon, she knew that if she dozed, he would still be there when she awoke. He never abandoned her, not for play or food or even other duties. If her frail old hand was in his strong young hand when her eyelids slipped closed, it would still be there when they opened. With Myles, she never had to face what so many very old people fear: aloneness. Myles was always there, sitting next to her rocker, holding her hand, listening.

Sometimes when Dru looked closely at the boy, she was certain that she could see in him some of the things that she remembered in her first love, her Aaron. It was a strange sensation that reminded her there was nothing of Aaron in the bloodline; the convict Theron Verne produced Monroe; Monroe produced Nathan; Nathan produced Myles.

Yet more often than not when Dru looked at Myles, Aaron was there. And it was not her imagination, not wishful thinking or senility. He was *there*. Myles was taller than Aaron, of course, but he had the same thickness, the same solidity to him. The piercing, direct eyes that rarely blinked were definitely Aaron's. But most of all it was that jutting chin that stuck out with such natural pride and defiance; a chin that could *only* have come from the genes of Aaron Van Hawn.

Could it be, the old lady wondered, that she had been mistaken for *seventy-three years* about who had fathered her first son? Was such a thing possible?

Dru rested her head back against the rocker. A slight smile played at her lips. Of course it was possible. With all the powerful lovemaking being done to her by Theron Verne, short little inexperienced Aaron Van Hawn might just have been the one to put the seed in her. And damn the fact that Monroe had those light blue eyes—Theron's eyes, she had thought at the time. Maybe that was just a quirk of nature.

Yes, she preferred to think that it was Aaron's seed. Aaron's bloodline. Aaron's legacy. "What are you smiling about, Great-grandmother?" asked Myles.

Dru patted his hand and reached into her vast store of memories for an answer. "I remember once when your Grandfather Monroe and your Great-uncle Grover ran away," she told him one day. "In 1844 it was. Monroe was just your age; Grove was a year younger. They were adventurous boys, always off in the woods in some cave, or sneaking aboard the side-wheelers when they docked down in Prisontown. Especially Grove: he was the worst of the two. It was his idea to run away. To California they said they were heading. Though they didn't get much past St. Louis. Captain Ironwood rode and fetched them home for me. I was married to Mr. Niles at the time, but Captain Ironwood fancied me, you see—"

She closed her eyes then.

Myles held her hand for a very long time before he realized that she would not be opening them again.

Druscilla Foyle Van Hawn Niles Ironwood died at the age of ninety-five years, four months, and twenty-one days.

Her funeral was the largest most people had ever seen. Burial had to be postponed for two days because mourners traveled as far as five hundred miles to attend. More than a thousand people passed by her bier in the main dining room of the mansion.

The governor of the state, two former governors, and a United States senator were among her pall bearers. Her gravesite was on a slight rise in Peckerwood Acres, just above the neat row of three graves belonging to Aaron, Clement Niles, and Ironwood, and not too far from those of Monroe, Grover, and Boss Lee.

Her coffin was solid mahogany, handcrafted in the prison carpenter shop by five convicts who worked forty-two straight hours to have it ready for the day of her funeral. Her headstone was made the same way, chiseled from a solid piece of quartz found some years earlier in the prison rock pit.

Because she had, a dozen years earlier, cut up the blue dress she had worn when she married Jack Ironwood—cut it up to make a christening gown for the little girl Reba never had—she had changed her funeral instructions with respect to her burial dress. She was now laid out in the simple, bleached frontier dress in which she had married Aaron. With her pure white hair and the many colorful flowers arranged around and over the casket, the old dress had an antique dignity to it that Dru would have thought was just the right touch.

At her services, which were held in the mansion, seven eulogies were delivered, by speakers as diverse as the governor, a state supreme court justice, a descendant of the original Pullman brothers, a granddaughter of Carrie Carmichael the first bakeshop owner, a town marshal from Oklahoma who had corresponded with her for years, the mayor of Union City at whose birth she had been midwife, and a woman ex-convict, who spoke proudly of how much Dru had done for women prisoners over the years.

On the way from the mansion to the cemetery, the prison band, dressed in freshly starched stripes, followed the casket playing a mournful version of "Rock of Ages."

Myles was so devastated by his great-grandmother's death that not even Reba and Nathan could console him. They had to put him entirely in the care of Lemuel, who somehow managed to subdue the boy's grief.

It was a bright, sunny afternoon when they buried her, with a gentle breeze and the fragrance of willows coming up from the Big Muddy. Birds were singing. From somewhere far down the river, a steamboat's whistle blew.

It was oddly quiet inside the walls that day. Many of the prisoners who had come there during the previous decade had never even seen the Mistress, but all had heard of her. They knew who she was, and much of what she had done. They realized that a legend was passing and they were silent in the face of it.

When the band played the funeral retreat march and its sound reached inside the walls, an old-time con nodded his head and said quietly, "She was a real lifer, the Mistress was."

She had been at Prison Hill for seventy-seven years.

CHAPTER 37

At the hospital in Union City, an exhausted Dru Hawn had fallen asleep reading the last of her great-great-grandmother's journals. As she slept, dawn arrived, and through a crooked venetian blind slat in the waiting room window a thin shaft of sunlight fell on her cheek and warmed it. She awoke slowly, aware of daylight in the room, aware that her body felt terribly stiff, aware that one leg, curled under her on the chair, was numb from lack of circulation. She opened her eyes and blinked several times, and then she saw that several people were sitting around her. People from the prison. Guard officers. Their wives. The doctor.

"What is it?" she asked urgently, sitting bolt upright. She did not notice that her numb leg sent a painful charge through her when she moved. "What is it?" she repeated. "What's happened?"

Glances were exchanged; then one of the women leaned over and put an arm around her shoulders. "They're gone, honey," she said.

Dru frowned. "Gone?"

Another woman knelt and gripped Dru's hands. "They went peacefully, Dru. During the night."

Dru's frown deepened, became incredulous. "Both?" she said. It was barely a question. "Both of them?"

"Both of them." The terrible truth was affirmed.

Dru felt blood rush to her head. She suddenly became very warm. I'm dying too, she thought.

Then she felt strong hands helping her to her feet and guiding her as she walked.

Dru was devastated by her loss. She attended the double funeral almost in a stupor. Half the time she was not even aware of what was going on; her mind shut it out, dwelling instead on pleasant memories of the two men she loved; twenty years of memories of one, a scant six weeks of the other.

Myles was buried at the foot of the big oak tree, next to Cassie. Cliff was put in a plot in the guards' section. The ceremony was attended by the governor, two U.S. senators, the entire state supreme court bench, dozens of other lesser dignitaries, scores of former guards who had worked under Myles over the years, and a dozen ex-inmates who had benefited from his enlightened administration. Attending for Cliff, who had no family and whose funeral Dru had insisted be joined with her father's, were a few Marine Corps friends with whom he had kept in touch, and several professors under whom he had studied.

The news media had a field day with the funeral. Morgue clippings going as far back as Ma Baker's days were dredged up and built into new stories of the prison warden who had married the daughter of a mad dog public enemy. The story of the four Baker brothers was retold; so were stories of the ambush that took the life of Lannie Baker; the manhunt for Doc and his daughter Cassie; Doc's final shootout and all the rest, recounted again in the vivid prose and colorful tradition of America's desperado days.

Dru did not read any of the new recaps. She had known the stories all her life, known the *truth* of them, as told to her by her parents. She had read the inaccurate, embellished versions printed at the time of her mother's death, so the current press held no appeal at all for her.

One of Myles's deputies had been made acting warden as soon as the news of the tragedy reached the capital. He closed Myles's office and began running the prison from his own. The first thing he did was order a general lockup: all imnates except kitchen help were kept in their cells. Word was sent to Dru that she could remain in the warden's living quarters as long as she desired. Two of the officers' wives planned to move in with her for a few days. But they were surprised to find her packing almost immediately.

"I can't stand it here," she said simply. "There's just too much around here of both of them."

"What in the world will you do then?" one of them asked with a pained expression. "You don't *have* anybody."

"I'll probably go to Chicago. Cliff and I planned to move there this fall anyway. I'll go back to school. That's what Mother wanted."

The women wept and tried to make Dru change her mind, but in the end she left. Her father's personal belongings, what was left of her mother's things, and the few possessions of Cliff's were all put into storage in Union City. Her own personal things she put in the trunk of her father's car, along with a small footlocker of family valuables, which she did not trust to the storage firm.

She said her goodbyes to the people at the prison on a rainy August morning. As she drove away from the front of the place where she had been born, she did not even look back. Her young face was set. In her mind was a determination never to return.

She managed to maintain her grim composure almost all the way to the highway. Only when she drove past the gate to the Peckerwood Acres cemetery did the tears finally come.

Then she cried all the way to Chicago.

CHAPTER 38

A soft but persistent knocking forced Dru's eyes open and made her sit up on the side of the bed. She had no idea how long the knocking had been going on or, for that matter, even how long she had been asleep; she had lost all concept of time weeks before and, except for one of her infrequent trips outside the apartment, rarely noticed whether it was day or night. Daylight or dark, it was all the same as far as she was concerned. Her world was the one-room kitchenette in which she lived. Outside of that, there was nothing. Everything else was buried.

The knocking continued. It was joined by a worried voice. "Miss Hawn? Miss Hawn, dear, are you all right?"

It was Mrs. O'Connor, the landlady. Dru brushed her hair back with both hands and went to the door. She did not open it.

"I'm all right, Mrs. O'Connor. I was just resting. Did you want something?"

"I thought you might like to come downstairs for a cup of egg-nog and some fruitcake. Several of the other tenants are already there—"

"Thank you, Mrs. O'Connor, but I think I'll stay in. I'm rather tired."

"But it's Christmas Eve, child. You don't want to stay all by yourself." Mrs. O'Connor's voice was quiet, sad.

"I'm fine, Mrs. O'Connor," Dru said. "And I'm really too tired to join you. But thank you for asking. Goodnight now."

Dru listened until Mrs. O'Connor went off down the hall, then she returned to the bed and sat down heavily. It was a Pullman bed that lifted into the wall, although Dru had not put it away in over a month. What for? she had asked herself. She spent half her time in it or on it, so what was the point?

Next to the bed, on a small round table, was a half bottle of bourbon whiskey and a glass tumbler. Brushing her hair straight back again and sighing deeply, Dru poured herself a double shot and drank it neat.

A month ago I wouldn't have been able to do that, she thought. I would have choked. And two months ago it would have made me sick to my stomach. But not now, friends. Not anymore. She poured herself another and downed it.

Carrying the empty glass, she rose and went to the window. It was a double bay window that looked down from the second floor onto Division Street. The apartment was on the near North Side. The neighborhood was nothing special, but it was reasonably clean, not too expensive, and had both a grocery and a liquor store that delivered, which was why Dru rarely had to go out. She could have lived in a better place; money was no problem: she had all of Myles's insurance and when she was twenty-one she was due to receive her Grandmother Reba's legacy. Continuing her present standard of living—providing her liquor bill did not increase much more—she could live without working for a good twenty years.

Dru saw out the window that it was snowing again. Rather heavily now. She wondered if the neighborhood delivery boys were going to have trouble getting around when the stores opened again after Christmas. Feeling suddenly apprehensive, she went into the little Pullman kitchen and quickly checked her cabinet. There was still one unopened bottle there. She calmed down at once.

Dru had been drinking steadily for most of the four months that had passed since Myles's and Cliff's deaths. When she first arrived in Chicago, it had not even occurred to her to try liquor as an escape from the constant, painful thoughts that plagued her every waking hour. The grief, she thought, was something she would simply have to bear. And she might have managed too, if it had not been for the terrible sleeplessness.

She first realized that her insomnia was permanent about a week after she arrived in Chicago. She had not been able to sleep before that, but she attributed it to the trauma of the tragedy, the subsequent funeral, the move north, finding a place to live—all the things that generated the nervous energy that kept her going, kept her from collapsing. Without really giving it any thought, she simply assumed that when all the pressure of activity was finished, she would begin to unwind and get some decent rest.

After settling in her kitchenette, the night finally came when it was all over: the moving, the running around, the things that *had* to be done. Nothing lay ahead of her, except a day in which she had nothing to do—*nothing*. She took a long hot bath that night and crawled under the covers like a war-weary infantryman. Blessed relief, she thought, and closed her eyes.

That was the first night she could not sleep. New bed, she thought. She tossed and turned most of the night, finally falling into a fitful doze just before dawn.

The next night was the same. And the next. She tried warm milk at bedtime. She tried going for a long walk to tire herself. She turned the mattress, bought a new pillow. She put the radio next to the bed and played soft music. She even tried counting sheep. Nothing worked. As soon as she felt as if she might doze off, she would suddenly think about her father or Cliff. The memory of one of them would penetrate her mind with relentless authority, *demanding* conscious thought, conscious attention. And Dru would immediately come wide awake.

When the images of Myles and Cliff began, Dru did not try to fight them. She felt too much love for the two men to resist any thought of them, any memory or picture. When they came into her mind, she immediately surrendered to them. It was a bittersweet pleasure at first because the memories were all good; only later every night, when exhaustion began to grip her, when the good memories evolved into funeral and burial images, did it become depressing and emotionally grim. At those times she would curl her thin body into its embryo position and huddle under the covers like a frightened child.

The bad memories usually passed very quickly, the culmination of her sleepless thoughts for that evening. She would stretch out in bed then, aggressively finding a comfortable position, and wait for sleep. An hour. Two. Six. It did not come. All night, every night. Her body literally ached for sleep, begged for it, but her mind would not permit it. It was a maddening cycle: close the eyes, force relaxation, breathe regularly, begin to doze, blissful sleep coming, coming, coming—then *snap!* Wide awake. Thinking, incredibly, about *sleep.* Coming wide awake actually *thinking* about sleep.

Dru got out of bed. She paced, she cursed, she smoked—then she tried again, *certain* this time that she would finally go to sleep. But she never did, not until just before dawn every morning, when she would finally fall into the hour or two of surface sleep that the evil spirits of insomnia had to allow to keep her from totally collapsing. Then she would wake up to the early morning bleakness feeling as if she had crawled out of a vacuum cleaner.

After ten days of it, Dru had deep circles under her eyes and was too nervous to do any but the simplest things; she did not even prepare hot meals anymore for fear of burning herself or accidentally turning on the oven and forgetting to light it. Finally, in desperation, she went to a nearby pharmacy to see if she could get some sleeping tablets. She could not. They required a prescription. The druggist advised her to see a doctor. Dru thanked him and said she would, knowing as she left the store that she would not. The last thing in the world she cared to do was go to a stranger and have to recite the story of how in the space of a double gunshot she had lost father, home, lover, and, as far as she was concerned, future. She did not care to talk to *anyone* about *anything.* All she wanted was to be left to herself, totally and completely.

But she *had* to get some sleep.

Walking, almost dragging, back to her apartment, she had passed Star Liquors and noticed it for the first time. She stopped and went back to its window. The bottles on display looked colorful, inviting—harmless. Dru went inside. She looked at the long rows of bottles, shelf after shelf of them. She had never had a drink, except a toddy on Christmas, champagne on New Year's, and an occasional sip of ale from her father's glass on a hot summer night. But whiskey, she presumed, was whiskey. She picked up the nearest bottle and took it to the register. It was bourbon.

Dru woke up again on Christmas Eve, not from knocking this time but from hunger. She had eaten nothing since breakfast that morning and her stomach was now revolting against the bourbon she had consumed during the day. Nevertheless, as soon as she woke up, she drank a shot to steady herself for the chore of preparing something to eat.

She went to the refrigerator first. It was practically empty. Part of a bottle of milk that smelled sour. She poured it out. Some cheese, improperly wrapped and hard. A jar of peaches with green mold beginning at the edge. Part of a leftover apple pie, its crust whitening with age. Dru shook her head and threw it all out. She could not remember when she had last ordered food.

She opened the pantry cabinet. A box of stale oyster crackers, a package of spaghetti but no sauce, one tin of sardines, some canned beets, and part of a carton of sandwich cookies. Dru grunted softly. Earlier when she had been awake she had panicked at the thought that she might run out of liquor. But it had not occurred to her to check on the food supply. You're finally a real drunk, she told herself.

She went to the phone and called the market, quickly thinking of half a dozen things to order. She kept repeating them to herself as the number rang. And kept ringing. She waited a full two minutes, then hung up. Damn. It must be after ten o'clock. Or else the market closed early because it was Christmas Eve. She looked at the clock on the dresser; it was stopped. She found her watch on the bathroom sink, also stopped. Damn, damn.

She had to have food. Without food, she could not drink, and unless she drank she could not sleep or even rest. She would have to go out. There was another market a few blocks away; they did not deliver but might still be open. She looked out the window; the snow had stopped. Good. She put on her coat and got her purse.

Dru very quietly let herself out of the apartment and slipped down the stairs. She heard voices and Christmas music coming from Mrs. O'Connor's flat on the first floor. She moved slowly in order to make less noise. God forbid that anyone should hear her and come out and drag her in there with the merrymakers.

Once outside, she found that it was much milder than she expected. With all the snow, she had thought it would be freezing cold. It turned out to be crisp but not at all unpleasant. Still, she hurried along, knowing that she had several blocks to go.

It took her fifteen minutes to reach the market. Thankfully, the lights were still on. But not by much. "You barely made it, miss," the clerk said. "We're getting ready to close."

"I'll just be a minute," Dru said.

She picked up a basket and started filling it. Soup, chili, bread, crackers, a pound of bologna, some cheese. Not too much now, she warned herself. You have to carry it back. She got some cookies and cocoa, and asked for a bottle of milk at the counter.

While the clerk was totaling her order, Dru dabbed at her watery eyes with a handkerchief. She thought about the bottle next to her bed. It was going to taste very good after her walk back. Very good indeed.

Back on the street, with the bag of groceries in her arms, Dru suddenly felt very tired. The bag was heavier than she thought it would be, and now it seemed colder out than it had before. Her eyes were watering continuously and her breathing became labored from the thinness of the cold night air. Her chest began to hurt.

Twice on the way home, she had to stop to rest and get her breath. Once, while she was leaning against a doorway, she heard a siren. It became louder and louder, very near to the block she was on. Suddenly the sound swung around the corner and headed toward her. It was accompanied by a bright red light that blinked on and off. Dru cringed back in the doorway and watched it pass. It was a police ambulance.

When she stepped onto the sidewalk and resumed her walk home, Dru saw that the blinking red light had stopped in the middle of the next block. The siren was no longer sounding. In the light of a street lamp, Dru could see people gathering around the parked ambulance. As she drew nearer, she stepped off the sidewalk to go around the people, but just then a policeman ordered everyone to back up.

"Clear the way now," he snapped. "Come on, back up! Move back!"

The people reluctantly obeyed, and when they moved back Dru could see the body of an old woman lying in the snow on the sidewalk. The headlights of the ambulance, which was angled in to the curb, shone starkly white on her face. Dru, who had not moved back with the others, stared at her.

"That's Millie, ain't it?" someone nearby said.

"Yeah," another voice answered. "Looks like she finally had one too many."

"That old gal sure could drink."

"Sure could. She wasn't so old either. I remember when she first moved in the neighborhood, back around 'thirty-eight or 'thirty-nine. She was only about thirty then. Couldn't be no more than forty now."

"She sure could drink."

"Sure could."

Dru stared incredulously at the dead woman. Forty—she looked *sixty.* Doughy face, bulging eyes, red heavy-veined nose, a trickle of spittle running out of one corner of her mouth.

Dru's eyes were wide. *Someday I'll look like that,* she thought.

"Come on, lady, let's move back," the policeman said. "Clear the sidewalk."

Dru lowered her head and hurried across the street.

In the apartment, she stared at herself in the bathroom mirror. She still had her coat on; her purse and the groceries were on the kitchen table. She had been home for ten minutes. And for ten minutes she had been staring at herself.

That's how you'll end up, she told herself. *Lying on a sidewalk with somebody remembering how much you could drink.*

She could see it coming already. She had all the signs. Watery, bloodshot eyes with dark circles under them. A red, angry nose that was constantly running. Trembling hands. Nervous, jerky motions.

Dru frowned and thought of the bottle of bourbon next to the bed. Did she really look that bad? she wondered. Or was she exaggerating?

She went to the bedtable and looked at the bottle. Reaching down, she pulled open the drawer of the bedtable. There were several photo albums in the drawer. She took out the one containing the most recent pictures. Flipping the pages, she found a photo of herself taken by Myles during her Easter vacation. The picture was held in place by four small triangular corners pasted onto the page. Dru slipped it out and took it into the bathroom.

At the mirror again, she held the photo up so that she could see both it and her face at the same time.

My God—!

She stared at the reflection in disbelief. It was like looking at two different generations. A young, smiling Dru and an old, deteriorating Dru.

What would Cliff say if he could see me now? she suddenly thought. She began to cry.

Pressing the picture to her breast, she ran sobbing back to the bedtable. She snatched up the bottle and hurried to the kitchen sink. Pouring, she watched the whiskey swirl down the drain. When the bottle was empty, she stopped sobbing almost at once and stared at it.

Now the other one, her conscience told her. The full one in the cupboard.

Dru turned and looked at the cupboard, frowning. I could leave it there, she thought, as a kind of test. A hint of desperation was growing inside her.

Pour it out, her good sense told her.

I might need just one drink to help me over the hard part, she argued. Quitting is going to make me sick, and just one drink would make it so much easier.

Pour it out!

No! That is foolish, that is weakness, I am strong enough to quit without doing that.

Then an image of Cliff came into her mind. Not the aloof Cliff she had first met, or the infuriatingly tolerant Cliff at whom she had become so angry; but—she could tell from the softness in his eyes—the gentle, patient Cliff she had come to know in his bed.

Pour it out, honey, the image said quietly.

Yes, Dru thought. From that single word she seemed to draw strength, determination. She took the new bottle from the cupboard and grimly poured it down the drain.

Now what? she wondered.

Dru sat on the side of her bed and looked around the little apartment. The bourbon was gone. It was past midnight on Christmas Eve and she had no way of getting any more. She had eaten, bathed, put fresh linen on her bed for the first time in a month, and now—what? Just sit there and wait to get sick?

She had turned on her radio and found an all-night music station which, for a while, had distracted her. But listening to music had soon become monotonous without anything else to do. She looked through the photo albums again, sadly reminiscing over pictures of her parents and grandparents. She sniffed back a few tears as she thought of Cliff and realized again that she did not even have a photograph of him. She had hoped there might be one among his things, from his Marine Corps days, but there had not been. The only picture she had of him was in her own mind.

She finished looking at the pictures and put the album away. From the bed, she looked around again. What now? She did not even have anything to read—

Or did she? She looked over at the footlocker she had brought with her in the trunk of the car when she left the prison. Two months after coming to Chicago, when she had been drinking for a while and seldom went out, she decided to sell the car rather than let it grow old at the curb. Before she did, she paid two neighborhood boys to carry the trunk up to her apartment. There it sat, in the corner where it was hardly noticed.

Dru went over and opened it. There was a wealth of heirlooms in the top tray: a newspaper with a headline about the St. Louis dock fire in 1849; a faded photograph of Nathan Hawn and Reba Myles on their wedding day in 1890; a flintlock pistol with an ink-printed tag on it which read "Last fired on June 1, 1853, by Druscilla Ironwood"; a beaded-and-feathered necklace, very intricate and mysterious-looking, also tagged "A gift from Kee-te-ha, a Sac-and-Fox warrior, 1861"; and other articles, numerous others.

Dru, beginning to feel nauseous, put the tray aside and looked in the well for the journals. They were stacked neatly along the bottom, just as she had put them when she finished reading them the first time. Dru took out the nearest one, which had a number one carefully inked onto the buckram cover.

Dru took the book and went to bed. She began to read: *I, Druscilla Van Hawn Niles, begin this diary of my life at the age of twenty-eight, on August 29th in the year 1837. . . .*

One hundred and eleven years ago, Dru thought. She rubbed her fingertips over the book with a new sense of awe. She continued to read: *I am widowed once, of Aaron Van Hawn, who was killed by convicts in a prison riot at the age of fifty. Aaron was a gentle, kind man, quick and direct to act once his course had been set for him. He was a good husband and an exceptional father to his two sons, Monroe and Grover. . . .*

Through a long, agonizing night, Dru reread the diaries. She was halfway through the first one when she became sick to her stomach the first time. She went into the bathroom, threw up, drank a glass of water, and returned to bed. She resumed reading.

. . . at that time in 1831 consisted of sixty-six convicts. Forty-five worked in the knitting mill, seven lay in the Idle Box, and the other fourteen were assigned to domestic and cleanup chores. One of our house workers, a gardener named Theron Verne, ran off with two other men and made Aaron very angry. He sent for a man named Cleon who bred bloodhounds for slave owners to use to catch their runaways. . . .

By three o'clock in the morning, Dru was trembling so much that she could barely hold the book steady enough to distinguish the words. Still she read on.

. . . with the help of Captain Ironwood and me, delivered of Letitia Herraday a healthy baby girl whom the mother named Nell. The poor innocent thing, born of a murderess, fathered by the victim, seeing the first light of day in a penitentiary room. I have promised myself this day in 1841 that I will do everything in my power to help this poor child through life—

During the early hours just before dawn, Dru's cramps started. They mushroomed in her stomach and tied her in knots. She moved to a chair, crossing her arms over her midsection and doubling over to try to relieve the pain. She rocked back and forth like an Indian woman in mourning, keeping the volume she was reading balanced on her knees.

. . . and so I am widowed a second time. My kind and generous Clement will no more be torn by the wracking cough that so plagued him. . . .

Dru, torn by her own misery, managed to get from the chair to the footlocker. As carefully as her trembling hands would prmit, she replaced one volume and took another. She was bathed in cold sweat from the effort, so she returned to bed and wrapped herself in a blanket. She left one hand free to hold the book so that she could continue reading.

. . . on this day in 1853, my son Monroe turned twenty-one and was formally sworn in as a member of the guard force by Warden Ironwood. I have given Monroe my blessing—or rather my permission—to take Beth Colson for his wife. Monroe claims he wants to marry her in order to have a son. He says he misses his brother Grover dearly and thinks a baby son will replace him.

I believe Monroe is lying. He is a scheming deceitful person. But if he wants the Colson girl so badly that he will lie about his poor dead brother to get her, then so be it. I think they will not be happy for long.

Dru suffered cold chills until after daybreak. When her trembling tapered off to the point where she could do so, she made a pot of black coffee. She sat at the tiny table and tried to drink it. Seconds after the first swallows reached her stomach, she was in the bathroom, sick again. Wearily she finally went back to bed. And to the diaries.

. . . the blackest day of my life. Owen Landis, the murderer of my son, has been sent to Prison Hill to serve a life sentence, when he should have been hanged. Beth has taken little Nathan, my joy, away to Ohio, and I know in my heart that I shall never see him again. The one ray of sunshine in my life is Gerald. He has asked—no, insisted—that I stay on here and run the mansion for him. . . .

By 9 A.M., Dru was vomited out, retching dryly with nothing to come up. She tried again to put something digestible into her stomach—soda crackers this time, just a few bites. To her relief, they stayed down. Now, in her twelfth hour without a drink, blood vessels in her arms and legs began to feel as if they were crawling inside her. She could not sit or lie still; her only relief was in movement. She began to pace the apartment holding a volume of the diary in front of her.

At noon, Dru collapsed. She fell across the bed in a deep but fitful sleep, unaware that she was jerking, jumping, and talking out loud. She dreamed: of Myles and Cliff in their graves, of scores of empty whiskey bottles falling from the sky and breaking all around her, and of her Great-great-grandmother Dru sitting in a huge prison yard, surrounded by hundreds of convicts while she wrote her memoirs on a long, never-ending sheet of ledger paper. Fortunately, Dru's sleep was so deep that she did not remember the dreams when she woke up. All she remembered was the horror of the previous night, broken only by moments of intense admiration for her namesake and the journal she had written.

Dru awoke at six that evening. She felt as if she had been beaten all over with rubber hoses. She was pale, weak, terribly unsure of herself, and still badly in need of a drink. She tried again to get down some black coffee, cold this time. Thankfully, it worked. She went a step further and tried a piece of bread. It was delicious—and it stayed down. But she still needed a drink. Got to get past that stage, she told herself. Got to beat back that urge. Shakily, she returned to bed. The last volume of the diary was there where she left it. She propped up the pillows and resumed reading.

. . . even though it is 1884 and I am in my seventy-fifth year, I feel like a girl again. My grandson Nathan has returned to me! He is a grown man, twenty-seven, and a well-educated engineer. Gerald has talked him into staying on for awhile. . . .

Dru read on into the night. She read of Gerald's death, Nathan's marriage to Reba, the birth of her father, the installation of the electric chair, the first automobile in the county, and much more. All of it was told in glowing, colorful prose, with the spirit and zest of the great woman coming through in every word.

Finally Dru again read the last entry, dated May 27, 1904, the day before her great-great-grandmother died. *I am very old and very tired, and I think I shall soon die. I could have died already, several times, if I had wanted to give up and do it. But I as a woman had the love of three good husbands, of two natural sons and one adopted son, of a grandson and a great-grandson. For me to ever give up would be to dishonor who I am and what I am. I think I shall die soon—but only because it is time, not because I ever gave up.*

Dru closed the last volume. There were tears in her eyes. But there was also a new strength in her spirit. She knew she would never need liquor again. She had something far better.

Her great-great-grandmother's blood.

CHAPTER 39

Dru reported to the civil service testing room at 8 A.M. She was assigned a chair at one end of a short table and given some forms to complete prior to testing. Rummaging through her purse, she discovered that she had failed to bring a pencil. Oh, no, she thought with sagging shoulders. She looked around in panic.

"I've got an extra one you can use," a quiet voice said.

Dru looked across the testing table at a young man with straight black hair and an easy smile. He was holding a pencil over to her. "Thanks," she said, taking it. She shook her head. "I don't know where my mind was when I left the house."

"It's probably the test," he said, "I'm a little nervous too."

Dru smiled. You don't know what nervous is, she thought.

Dru had been off liquor for four weeks. During that time she had been going to physical fitness classes at the YWCA, had bought a sun lamp to help get some of her color back, and in preparation for this day had read everything she could find on what to expect in a civil service test and how to prepare for one. And after all that, she had forgotten to bring a goddamned pencil.

The first half of the test began at eight thirty and lasted ninety minutes. When it was over, the applicants were allowed to go into the courthouse hall for a half-hour break. Dru got a cup of coffee from a crippled man with a cart and went to a corner by herself to drink it and smoke a cigarette. The man who had given her the pencil saw her and came over.

"How are you doing on the test?" he asked, smiling.

Dru shrugged. "I'm not sure. How are you doing?"

"Pretty well, I think. I hope, anyway. What job are you applying for?"

"None in particular. They said they'd classify my test results and application, and tell me which areas of government I was most suited for."

"Same here. I was kind of hoping to get into the forestry service but I don't know if I'm qualified for that or not. I only have a year of college, and no special background."

"Maybe they'll find something you like better," Dru said.

"Maybe. What do you want to get into?"

Before Dru could answer, the test monitor summoned them back inside for the other half of the test.

The second part of the test was also scheduled for ninety minutes, but Dru finished it in an hour and was allowed to turn in her answer sheet and leave early. On her way out, she smiled at the young man who had let her borrow the pencil, and returned it to him. He looked at her as if there was something else he wanted to say, but Dru pretended she did not notice; she merely waved as she went out the door. There was no sense in trying to make new friends, she thought, not in her present state. The young man seemed nice, and he was certainly handsome enough, though in a less mature way than Cliff had been, but she felt she should keep to herself for a while longer.

At least until the desire for a drink went away.

If it ever *did* go away.

Two weeks later, Dru reported to the office of a Miss Holmes, a federal service placement counselor. She was a pleasant, efficient woman in her fifties, and she had Dru's file on her desk.

"You scored very high on the entrance examination, Miss Hawn," she said. "On the basis of that and your background application, the government would like to offer you a job in the federal service."

Dru only smiled cordially, but inside she felt elated. Getting a job was, for her, the first big step forward since the night she quit drinking. "What kind of job is it?" she asked.

"Female custodian," said Miss Holmes. "At the new federal prison at Dannacan, Colorado."

"A prison?" Dru said incredulously. She sat back in the chair, her elation evaporating.

"Not just a prison," Miss Holmes said. "A brand new federal institution not even open yet. A very modern, progressive prison, probably the most advanced in the world. It would be a perfect place for you."

Dru fixed her in a level gaze. "Why, exactly?"

"A number of reasons. Your family background, for one. You've literally grown up around prisons and prison people. You won't feel the least bit alien in the environment. You've had one year of college and indicated on your application that you might resume your education in night school. We want people who are ambitious, who are interested in self-improvement. Unfortunately, too many of our present-day prison custodians let themselves fall into an institutional rut; all they look toward in the future is the next federal pay raise. Incidentally, there's a branch campus of the University of Colorado only twelve miles from Dannacan—"

"Miss Holmes," Dru interrupted, "I don't really think I'd be interested in prison work."

"May I ask why?"

"Personal reasons."

"Your father's death? And the death of the young man you were about to become engaged to?" Miss Holmes noticed a look of surprise cross Dru's face. She smiled at the younger woman. "We *do* have a very able investigation section," she said.

"Apparently. Since you know all that, why are you bothering to offer me the job?"

"Because you're qualified. No. You're more than qualified; you're *suited*."

Dru shook her head. "I'd like to know how."

"Let me ask you a question," said Miss Holmes. "Do you hate the convicts who killed your father?"

"How can I? They're dead."

"Would you hate them if they were alive?"

"Yes, I would."

"How about the convicts who *weren't* in on that break? Do you hate them?"

"Certainly not. Why should I?"

"You shouldn't. But many people would. Many people would hate *all* convicts, as a class, just as many people hate all Jews as a class, or all Negroes, or all Catholics. But you're too intelligent for that, and your background check proved it." Miss Holmes leaned forward and folded her hands on the desk. "This new prison is going to be a unique experiment in penology," she said. "Dannacan is actually going to be *two* prisons. One, inside the walls, will be a maximum security facility for persons who have committed serious crimes involving violence or bodily harm to someone. The other prison will be a minimum security facility *outside* the walls. To this one will be sent first offenders who have not used a gun or physically harmed anyone. There they will be given the opportunity to go in one of two directions: inside the walls to serve their full sentences, or back out into society after a token period of punishment. Believe me, it's a very new and positive approach to our problem of recidivism."

Positive perhaps, thought Dru, but certainly not new, not in concept anyway. Her father had tried for years to promote a variation of such a plan at the state level. Even Cliff McKittrick, as new as he was to the field, had been a proponent of directing a maximum effort toward the first offender, even at the expense of the second and third offender.

"What kind of people do you have at the administrative level in this new prison?" Dru asked.

"The best," Miss Holmes said with a touch of pride. "The brightest, most liberal, most progressive people we've been able to find. Believe me, Miss Hawn, we are totally committed to this project. If we weren't, you'd have received a form letter instead of a sales pitch."

Dru rose and walked to the window of the office. She stared down at the cold Chicago street, its automobiles steaming, its pedestrians hurrying. Everybody seemed to have someplace to go. Except her, she thought wryly. But now she was being offered a place. Prison.

She sighed and turned back to Miss Holmes. "You'll have to forgive me if I'm not overly enthusiastic about your project, Miss Holmes. I saw my father disappointed so many times when he tried to make changes and failed because of some shallow legislative committee or narrow-minded state senator—"

"I know exactly what you mean. We have the same obstacles

in the federal service. We've been *years* getting Dannacan off the ground. Now it's finally funded for three years. We've got that long to make it work. That long to prove a new system."

"A new system," Dru said, almost to herself. She nodded slowly. "I hope you're successful. The old system certainly hasn't worked. It's had over a *hundred* years, and all it's done is repeat the same mistakes over and over."

"We know that. And the fact that you know it too is why we want you. Will you take the job? Join the fight?"

Again Dru looked down at the street. Everyone going somewhere. Everyone except her.

"I don't know," she said, turning back to Miss Holmes. "I'd like to think about it. May I phone you?"

"Of course."

Miss Holmes handed her a business card.

Dru left the federal building and walked into the Loop. The day was clear and cold; shoppers and store clerks and businessmen hurried from place to place, their cheeks and noses red, breaths frosty. Dru moved with the flow of traffic up State Street, so engrossed in her own thoughts that she was not even aware of how far she was walking. Before she knew it, she had gone the length of the Loop and was at Lake Street, under the elevated station. She felt half frozen. Across the street was a Rexall drugstore with its big plate-glass windows covered with steam. Dru hurried toward it.

Inside, in a tiny wooden booth, she loosened her coat and scarf and ordered tomato soup and tea. When the order came, she cupped her hands around the soup bowl and felt the heat bite at them.

Prison, she thought. My God, what would Mamma say?

She began to eat, slowly, savoring the soup for its warmth as much as for its taste.

Do I dare even consider it? she asked herself. She tried to weigh what her decision might mean in terms of emotion. First of all, to accept the job at Dannacan would mean breaking a deathbed promise to her mother. Unless, of course, she continued her education at some time in the future and eventually earned her degree. But for now—one broken promise.

It would also mean returning to a lifestyle and environment that would constantly remind her of her father and Cliff. How would she be able to handle that? she wondered. Like she did the first time: with liquor?

No, she vowed. Not like that. Never again. The price of being a drunk was too much to pay. In self-respect.

How then? How would she deal with sleepless nights that might be generated by a new prison? How would she justify what she was doing with what she had told her dying mother she would do?

Dru paused with a spoonful of soup halfway to her mouth. A frown pinched the space between her eyes. Justify? Was that what she had silently asked herself? How would she *justify* her decision?

She returned the spoon to the bowl and turned her head to stare at her own image in a Coca-Cola mirror that formed the wall of the booth. "You *don't* justify it," she said aloud.

No, of course not. Cassie was dead. The promise she had extracted had been from a girl who had never loved a man, never had a man inside her, never lost a man, never lost a father, never been a drunk. That girl, Dru suddenly realized, was no more alive than Cassie was.

Justify? There was nothing *to* justify. If Cassie were there with her at that moment, Dru knew in her heart that the promise would not be asked.

As for the other—the memories, the insomnia, the liquor—she would simply fight it, that's all. She would fight and she would win. Her name was Dru and she came by subsequent generations from the womb of another woman named Dru. And that woman's blood flowed in her veins just as certain as if no century separated them.

Justify? Never. Fight? Always.

Dru rooted in her purse until she found a nickel. Then she left the booth to find a pay phone to call Miss Holmes.

She was going to Dannacan.